THE SLEEPWALKER

L C GEORGE

INKUBATOR
BOOKS

Return

Published by Inkubator Books
www.inkubatorbooks.com

Copyright © 2023 by L C George

L C George has asserted her right to be identified as the
author of this work.

ISBN (eBook): 978-1-83756-103-2
ISBN (Paperback): 978-1-83756-104-9
ISBN (Hardback): 978-1-83756-105-6

PROLOGUE

SAM

My eyes shot open with that panicked sensation of falling as my body propelled itself forward, my hands flat against the bed sheets. Dread weighed heavy on my chest, but I didn't know why. My heart hammered as I searched my foggy brain, attempting to untangle my mind from my dreams and identify the cause for such panic.

Had I been having one of my nightmares? I gripped the bedding tighter, reassuring myself that I was, at least, still in my own bed this time.

Daylight was starting to seep through the curtains, and I noticed with a jolt that my wife was still sleeping beside me. The room was oddly quiet, still. A deeper unease wound itself around me.

I squinted through the semidarkness, past my wife's sleeping form, in the direction of my daughter's crib nestled against Tessa's side of the bed. But I couldn't make out Cora's tiny form in the dim light.

Her crib was empty.

The three-month-old Cora couldn't have gotten out of the

crib by herself. Tessa was a light sleeper. Cora must have woken her during the night, and Tessa would have taken her somewhere else in the house.

But my wife was still in our bed.

My mind raced. Could Tessa have fallen asleep with Cora in our bed? She was usually so cautious, almost paranoid, about these things.

"Tessa?" I half whispered. There was no response.

No longer feeling in the slightest bit drowsy, I pulled the duvet back from her face, now desperate to wake her.

"Tessa?"

I recoiled, crying out.

Her lips were tinged blue. Her cheeks colourless – so pale they were barely distinguishable from the egg-white bed sheets. Her eyes open, staring.

She was, unmistakeably, dead.

1

TESSA

SIX MONTHS PREVIOUS

I smiled at my friend across from me, my heart clenching and a heat rising to my cheeks as she rolled her eyes for the millionth time that morning.

I knew it was probably getting tedious, but I just couldn't help steering the conversation back to that subject – my impending arrival. I stroked my ever-expanding stomach in the hope that he or she might give a little poke or wiggle in response. I'd waited so long for this moment. At least that was how it felt. I couldn't help that it was the only subject that seemed to hold my interest. I stretched my legs out under the table, trying to offer some relief to my throbbing back.

"Let's just hope it's all worth it when it arrives," Bella remarked, rolling her eyes again. I wondered if she was aware she was doing it. "I mean, you might be excited, but you look like total crap!"

I blinked in an attempt to mask my reflexive flinch at her harsh words.

A smile pulled at the corners of her mouth as her eyes softened.

"Well, thanks for the vote of confidence," I retorted, struggling to maintain an impassive half smirk.

Such remarks were just Bella's way, but knowing that didn't take the slight sting out of the dig.

It was undeniable: I did look bloody awful. Besides the severe lack of sleep, I looked like an elephant, my swollen stomach so round it was as though I had swallowed a beach ball. And it didn't help my self-esteem to have this reality confirmed by my extremely glamorous friend. With her shiny swish of near jet-black hair, her piercing blue eyes and flawless skin, Bella was everything I could never hope to be.

She waved her hand in front of her face as though to swipe the comment away, and leaned back in her chair.

I lifted my mug to my lips, discreetly studying my beautiful friend as she perched across from me in my warm, sun-drenched kitchen. I pushed away the stab of envy for her natural perfection, filling my mind instead with the idea of the tiny heart beating away inside me. The thought brought some comfort, softening the remaining sting of Bella's remark and my sadness at her news.

Bella had been living in the house opposite for a while already before the two of us actually got to know one another. It had taken a few awkward moments, bumping into each other on the street – neither one of us seeming to know if we should greet one another or pretend not to notice the other was there – before I had finally plucked up some courage and seized an opportunity to start a conversation. Since Sam and I had moved, I hadn't managed to form anything more than acquaintances and was craving the closeness of a true friendship. I'd never appreciated the ease with which I'd forged friendships during my younger years – the confident student I'd once been, fearlessly approaching my peers, feeling nothing but excitement for the uncertainty of what my future held.

The fact I'd allowed those friendships – formed through drunken nights out and an easy familiarity – to fizzle out filled me with regret. Once Sam and I met, I became so consumed by my feelings for him that everything else seemed to fade into the background. Sam had gently encouraged me to respond when my friends reached out, but I let them slip away, the friendships fading into the past. It seemed to happen so quickly, but in those early months, any time away from Sam seemed only wasted. To be apart from him was almost physically painful.

I had tried to resurrect some of those old friendships, attempting to arrange nights out or lunch dates – but for the few of us who did meet, it felt forced and awkward, like we were trying to relive the past. Eventually, they stopped answering my increasingly desperate texts, the tables having turned, and I was once again cast out. The outsider of every group. The closest I seemed to get to friendship was shamelessly watching other women with envy as they chatted comfortably over a coffee. They made it seem effortless, making me wonder what I was doing so wrong for it to always remain so far out of my grasp.

I just hadn't seemed to be able to find my place anywhere. Until I met Bella.

After an awkward initial meeting where I was certain I had blown any chance of friendship, something clicked into place, and Bella and I gelled, forming a solid friendship, talking every day. I would still fizz with nerves every time we were due to meet. On this occasion, I'd spent the morning trying to find an outfit that I could still fit into, one she might approve of. I'd scrubbed the kitchen and mopped the floors, attempting to view my home through her eyes. It left me exhausted but satisfied. I was so caught up in making the place appear like a show home, I even popped out and bought flowers to sit in the window. I froze when Bella asked me where they'd come from, then heard myself announce that Sam had bought them for me. I had no idea why I'd lied – the lie slipped out so easily before heat rose to my cheeks.

Not long after Bella arrived, she reached into her handbag and produced a small paper bag, waving away my gushes of gratitude as she handed it to me.

I carefully peeled back the tape to reveal a beautiful silk maternity shirt folded inside.

"I thought I'd get you something nice to wear that'd fit your ... new shape." Bella made a circular motion with her hands, her eyes narrowing before her lips formed a wide smile.

I was so touched by the gesture, stroking the fabric and beaming – that is until I saw the size on the label. Two sizes larger than I would wear – even in my very pregnant state. Did I really look that huge? Too embarrassed to say anything, and desperate not to appear ungrateful, I'd thanked her profusely, reminding myself how lucky I was to have such a good friend – especially one who would do something so lovely. She'd probably been worried she'd get something too small and upset me that way.

"I'm certain it'll be worth it," I said now, running my hands across my bulging stomach once again. "I already love this little one so much, I just can't wait to meet him or her." A rush of emotion caused my eyes to fill. Humiliated, I averted my eyes, avoiding Bella's gaze.

She wrinkled her nose, lip curling. "Rather you than me. Ruin this body for years of sleepless nights, screaming, shitty nappies and puke? I don't think so!" She chuckled, running her hands over the shape of her perfect hourglass figure and raising her eyebrows to emphasize her point.

"Anyway." She sighed, glancing at her watch, eyes widening. "I need to get back." She stood, her chair scraping back, and checked her phone.

"You could always hang on and say hi to Sam?" I suggested eagerly. "I'm sure he would love to meet you properly and put a face to the name I mention so regularly. Especially now, what with your plans and all ..." I trailed off, avoiding meeting her eye.

"Oh, I can't tonight, unfortunately," Bella replied breezily. She shook out her mane of dark hair, the ripples shining, reflecting the sunlight. "Stuff I need to get done. Another time though for sure." She flashed her perfect smile, briefly placing her hand on top of mine.

I forced a smile in return and waddled after my friend towards the front door. I nodded back. "Another time," I agreed, wondering if it might actually be for the best that my husband didn't meet the beautiful Bella.

As I pushed the door closed, Bella's scent lingering the air around me, I sucked in a deep breath. I had managed to hold it together, actually forgetting everything for a while during my afternoon with Bella. But now it all came back to me, and I felt suddenly cold.

2

SAM

PRESENT DAY

My fingers trembled as I punched in the number for the emergency services, hesitating as my frantic brain resisted the decision. It felt so alien to call the forbidden number.

I had retrieved the phone without casting a glance in Tessa's direction, but the frightful image of my wife's blue-tinged lips and waxy skin was already etched in my mind, unshakable.

I clutched the phone to my ear, waiting for the call to connect, and crossed the landing in a few long strides, shoving open the door to Cora's nursery. The phone clicked, and a woman's nasal voice shattered the thick silence around me.

"Nine nine nine, which service do you require?"

"Erm. Police?" I croaked. The words felt as though they had broken the delicate surface of the morning's odd stillness, a stone sabotaging the deceiving serenity of some deep, treacherous pool. Somehow, hearing another voice made it all the more real. Guilt bubbled inside me, and I ran my free hand over my face as the emotion threatened to overwhelm my senses. I was making this horrific phone call from within my baby daughter's bedroom. Decorated in white and pale yellows, it was the epitome of innocence. We'd wanted the gender of the baby to be a surprise reserved for the day of the birth, so all preparations had been made avoiding overtly gendered blues or pinks.

A vice-like grip constricted my heart at the thought of my wife. I gasped for air, gripping the wall for support and wondering if I might be sick.

"Please hold whilst I connect you." The monotone voice broke into my thoughts again, snapping me back into action. I needed to move.

I took the stairs two at a time, stumbling and landing awkwardly on my ankle as I reached the ground floor.

"What's the address of the emergency, please?" the authoritative voice questioned as I tore from room to room, continuing my fruitless search for our daughter. Every room conjured vivid images of her: swinging in her rocker in the kitchen, kicking out at toys on her play mat in the living room. As I turned around, a vision so clear of Tessa cradling Cora, cooing at her, hit me with such force I was stopped dead in my tracks, gasping for breath as I blinked away the woman I loved and our beautiful child.

My brain raced through images of my family, replaying the moment I'd discovered Tessa on a torturous loop. I battled the thoughts to rattle off our address.

The operator continued, "And what is the nature of the emergency?" I gripped the door frame for support, unable to voice the events of the morning. How could I explain when I had no idea myself?

I caught sight of the torn wedding photograph left on the mantel. My stomach clenched. Why would anyone ...?

"Sir? Are you still with me?"

"Yes ... I'm ... I'm here." I panted as I crossed the room and snatched up the shreds of photograph. I stared down at the pieces between my fingers, fear bubbling up from my guts. I couldn't believe Tessa would do such a thing, but who else would have a reason to destroy something so personal? It certainly seemed to have been done to inflict pain. Anyone else would surely conclude the same. I stuffed the frame into the back of the cupboard, tucked the scraps in amongst a pile of photographs, and slammed the door. My voice trembled with effort, as if by saying the words, I was making this real. "It's my wife ... a-and my child. Erm, my, my w-wife ... she ... I think she might be dead."

"Okay. Try to keep calm. I'm going to be with you here until help arrives. You mentioned your child. Are you and the child safe?"

"I don't know ... I have no idea where Cora is!" My voice cracked. As I came face to face with a framed photograph of her in the hallway, the weight of the horror sank in. "She was gone when I woke up. I ... I've searched the house, but ... sh-she isn't here! I don't know where she could've gone. She's only three months old." I gripped the newel post, afraid I might sink to the ground without its support. I stared at the front door, willing Tessa to walk through, Cora in her arms, for it all to be some hideous, unexplainable hallucination. I'd take being crazy over this reality.

"Okay. So, your daughter is missing. Your wife – is she breathing? Did you manage to check for a pulse?"

I froze again, chest heaving as my mind flooded with unwelcome images. I bent double, phone still pressed against my ear whilst my other gripped my thigh too tightly. I fought for breath, swallowed down the waves of nausea.

"Sir? Can you check for a pulse?"

"No. I ... I can't ... she's gone. It's too late." I struggled to force out the words, hoping that they were audible enough to be heard and that I wouldn't have to repeat them. My emotions were spinning into a tornado inside me. Before long they would rip me apart. "Oh god, oh god." I dropped my head forward, my free hand gripping the back of my neck, fighting another swell of nausea as I tried to remember how to breathe.

"We already have units on the way to you. Take some nice deep breaths. Can you tell me your name?"

"Sam, it's Sam." I was gasping, chest heaving with the effort.

"Okay, Sam. If you're able to check on your wife, I can talk you through CPR. I'll stay right here with you on the line. We'll do everything together."

A shiver ran through me, goose pimples rising. "I ... I can't go back into that room. I can't see her like that again." My hand flew to my mouth, stifling a gasp. I had paced the ground floor of our home – as if Cora might suddenly appear in one of the rooms since I'd last checked. I'd even pulled back the lid of her toy chest in desperation, as if my three-month-old daughter might have shut herself inside, hoping by some miracle that Cora might be peering up at me from somewhere through her perfect round eyes, safe and well. Having run out of places to search, I lingered in the hall. A chill chattered my teeth. I was still only wearing my underwear.

The first wail of sirens screamed out in the distance.

"I hear them coming." My voice was shrill as the hysteria finally swallowed me. "You have to find my daughter!"

"We'll do everything we can for your wife and daughter, Sam. If you just stay on the line with me until help arrives with you ..."

The operator continued to speak, but I had tuned out, staggering to the window at the front of the house. My breath came in short bursts, panic rising as I craned my neck to search for the first glimpse of help. The pain was almost physical now, and I felt desperate to pass the responsibility of this on to the professionals, not wanting it to be mine alone to carry for another second. After what seemed to be an eternity, the car screeched into the road, a smudge of fluorescent yellow, closely followed by two more emergency vehicles.

I stumbled to the door, pulling it open.

"Please," I sobbed. "Please help me!"

3

TESSA

THREE MONTHS PREVIOUS

The beautiful baby slept peacefully in my lap. I gazed down at her, still unable to fully comprehend that she belonged to me, then let my head fall back against the cushions of the sofa. I'd spent more time there than in my bed over the past few weeks. Exhaustion was taking over, yet I felt too wired to rest. What if something happened to my baby while I was sleeping? It would make me the worst mother in the world.

I thought back to that first night in the hospital, my body physically drained from the labour but so full of adrenalin I couldn't imagine sleeping ever again. I'd spent the entire night staring at my baby in complete awe, determined to commit every tiny piece of her to memory whilst simultaneously monitoring her, ensuring that her little chest continued to rise and fall in its quick rhythm.

Three weeks had passed since, yet sleep remained elusive. Cora only ever seemed to settle whilst she was attached to me, leaving me so afraid of rolling onto her – or her falling – that I was almost afraid to move, let alone close my eyes. The couple of times that I'd managed to get her to sleep in her own cot, I'd found myself unable to switch off for fear of a blanket covering Cora's face, or sudden infant death syndrome snatching her away from me. I was quickly discovering that being a mother could be both a beautiful and cruel gift. The insomnia coupled with my baby's erratic schedule was slowly eroding my sanity. I was surviving on the adrenalin of my fears, and I was cursed with more of those than the average new mother.

I adored my daughter but was beginning to wonder how much longer I'd be able to continue to function, running on empty. I wished my mother were around to call on. I'd moved to London for university ten years previous, leaving my parents behind in Wales. Although we still spoke regularly, it didn't compare to having them close. My mother had become too unwell to travel recently. I'd never thought of them as old, but my parents were in their early forties when I was born, so age was catching up with them already. My anxieties prevented me taking Cora to visit them, so ours remained a virtual relationship conducted with deceitful cheerfulness, on both sides. Sam helped where he could. He was pretty clueless as a new father, I admit, but he was eager to do his part. Our days together as a family went by in a happy blur. The nights, however, were a different story. After his two weeks of leave, he'd made the return to work, leaving us – mother and baby – home alone.

I found myself sitting in the dim light of the early morning whilst my husband slept upstairs, undisturbed, lucky enough to be able to snooze away the hours and await the sound of his alarm. My eyes stung, and my head throbbed. I wondered if Bella would call in today. With the thought of Bella came a wave of disappointment so strong I sucked in air, fighting the tears.

She was leaving. I thought back to the conversation in my kitchen a few months ago, when she had broken the news.

Her words had slammed into me, piercing my happy facade. Bella, my best friend, my only true friend, was leaving for Australia. I wanted to be the friend that I should be – that she deserved – and share in her joy but felt only selfish devastation at the idea of being abandoned – this time not alone. This time it was worse. I was immersed in fears and dilemmas. I assured myself it was the hormones making me feel so low, so pathetic.

The move wasn't necessarily permanent, but Bella had no plans to return in the near future. She was a free spirit. It occurred to me now that perhaps she'd never intended on settling here for long. Suburbia didn't seem the right fit for someone like her. I'd always sensed that my friend looked at me with some kind of misguided pity, viewed me as being "stuck in a place like this", now saddled with a baby. As if this life had been thrust upon me without a choice. She couldn't have been more off the mark; Cora was a longed-for child. I'd been the happiest woman alive when I'd finally discovered I was pregnant, imagining the perfect foetus forming inside my body at last.

But for Bella, children were nothing more than a chore. A tie and an inconvenience. We'd formed such an instant bond, but I'd felt a shift in our previously easy relationship since Cora's arrival. It cast a shadow, her inability to share in my joy.

I was so *very* grateful for my little girl, but at times – and I was ashamed to admit it – I did mourn my old life. I couldn't confide in Bella this time, unable to abide the "I told you so" looks. How did other mothers do it? The continuous crying. Piles of soiled nappies, dirty clothes. The boiling frustration when the need to simply "pop out" for some milk became a half-hour process. The one time I had tried to leave the house, by the time I'd battled to get Cora dressed and into her pram, my energy was finished – only to find she needed changing again. I couldn't even remember the last time I'd looked in a mirror.

It had been so easy before. I hadn't appreciated being so carefree. The ability to drop everything and go out, or laze on the sofa all day in front of the TV if that's what I wanted to do. I hadn't valued that time. Now I would give anything for just a few hours of undisturbed sleep. I stared down into my daughter's perfect sleeping face and felt the now familiar prickling in my eyes. How could I love something so much, yet feel so resentful?

Life with a baby was so different to how I'd imagined it being. I'd dreamed of nights snuggled up together, waking in the morning and cuddling in front of daytime TV. Afternoons filled with visits from new friends, bringing their babies along to play together with mine whilst I brandished my latest home-baked delights for us mothers to enjoy, basking in their admiration.

Instead, I found my days long and empty, exhaustion and loneliness my only companions. The exhaustion made a dreaded chore even of simply getting dressed. I showered on the rare occasions that Cora would settle in the Moses basket, bringing her into the bathroom with me so that I could still keep a watchful eye. Most of the time, though, I smelled of baby puke and probably shitty nappies. The monumental effort to bother with my own hygiene felt pointless, knowing I'd only be sprayed with milky sick again, or have another nappy explosion to deal with.

But worse than all of that, worse than all of the other emotions lumped together, was the gut-wrenching guilt. I felt so very, horrendously guilty that I wasn't loving every second of my new life as a mother. Hadn't this been what I had wished for? Pleaded for? I should have been enjoying every second, delighting in watching my baby grow and change, swelling with pride. Instead, I wished the days away, counting down hours and minutes until Sam came home and I could hand her over.

To add to the anguish, my mind seemed to punish me for my ungrateful thoughts. I would find my brain wandering, envisaging something dreadful happening to Cora. I dreamed up all sorts of scenarios – tripping down the stairs with her in my arms, even somehow managing to drop her out of a window. I feared I might be losing my mind. Another reason I avoided leaving the house – not even daring to pop to the shop for essentials – was my fear I would somehow forget I had a baby and leave her home alone. Or worse, leave her behind at the shop, too caught up in gathering my shopping. Everyone would see me for the failure I was.

I would *never* hurt Cora intentionally; that I could be sure of. But I couldn't stop these fears from eclipsing rational thoughts. What if, in my sleep-deprived state, I was to do something terrible by mistake?

After all, taunted my tortured brain, *just look at Sam*. I had only just begun to see what he was capable of.

4

SAM

PRESENT DAY

The endless questions had left me completely exhausted, even the tears having dried up. My body ached with the urge to lie down, close my burning eyes, and just give up. To be back with Tessa. I had assisted the police in every way I could, yet I'd been useless, I knew. My nerves jangled at the thought of how little information I'd provided. In the midst of the panic swirling around my mind, flashes of memory kept rushing back at me, winding me over and over like physical blows. Tessa's pale skin. Cora's empty crib. It would take my breath away, leaving me gasping and vacant. I'd lost count of the number of times I had spaced out, suddenly becoming aware of the officer staring at me, waiting for an answer to another question that I hadn't heard. Their expressions were inscrutable. Was that sympathy in their eyes – or suspicion?

The officer in charge questioned me about Tessa's wedding and engagement rings – where they were, if she usually wore them – and I'd stared at him blankly, aware that she'd never taken them off. Had she taken them off because she was thinking of leaving me? That our marriage was ending? Between her missing rings and the torn wedding photograph, it was starting to appear that way. That would give me a motive for murdering her, make me look immediately guilty ... The lie just slipped from my lips – she removed them to clean or wash up – as though it were someone else speaking the words. I instantly wished I'd told the truth.

A torrent of emotions ravaged me. Desperation. The need for answers. The senseless fervid hope that Tessa would burst in, Cora snuggled in her arms, and announce that there had been some huge misunderstanding.

Pain. Physical pain that twisted itself around me, invading every part of my body, rooting in tissues like a cancer.

And the anger. Pure, undiluted fury at everyone and everything. At the police, for wasting time sitting there in a room with me instead of being out looking for my missing child, my wife's killer. At Tessa, for not being here when Cora and I needed her the most. How could she have just *left* me? At the rest of the world, for carrying on like it was a normal day, giving no acknowledgement that *my* world had come to an end. But the majority of my rage was reserved for myself. What kind of husband – father – slept peacefully whilst the worst possible scenario played out right beside him?

Why had some sort of instinct not woken me up to rush to the aid of my wife and child? Had they cried out for me, pleaded for me to help them? A tiny seed of doubt began to take root in my mind – my wife crying out in the darkness whilst I ...

No, I scolded myself, pushing the thought aside. I simply could not allow my mind to speculate.

I walked out of the police station into the bustle of the day, the bright sunshine a stark contrast to my mood. I wished it would bloody well cloud over. An officer had collected some clothes for me whilst a paramedic wrapped me in a foil blanket. They requested that I place my worn underwear in an evidence bag, leaving me red faced. I was thankful I didn't have to go back inside. The smell of my freshly washed clothing brought with it an agonising ache. The familiar reminder of home offered no comfort. I barely remembered retrieving the clothes, or even leaving home, but I didn't seem to have a jumper. Goose pimples rose on my skin in the morning breeze.

The police were finished with their questions for now, they told me, but I couldn't return to my house while forensics were still working there. They had swept through my home within minutes of arriving, ushering me out and suggesting that we go to the station so I could "assist" them, all while more and more vehicles arrived and officers swarmed the house ant-like, working in orderly unison. I was left feeling oddly detached from the situation, like an extra on a movie set, the shock having left me numb. They ushered me into a squad car – to my shame – and I was relieved to realise I wouldn't be there when they moved Tessa. But the relief was shortly drowned by a swell of guilt – I'd left her there alone.

Asphyxiation. The word ricocheted around my mind like a pinball. Had she known what was happening? Been afraid? Felt pain?

I left the interview room in a daze and realised that my car was still at home on our driveway. They likely hadn't thought me fit to get myself there in one piece. They were right, no doubt. I couldn't recall arriving at the station. I couldn't recall the journey at all.

One of the officers asked if there was anyone they could call for me, his eyes soft with sympathy. I quickly declined, cheeks burning – he thought me incapable of making a phone call. I couldn't bear the thought of a stranger telling anyone what had happened. I called Mike, myself, from within the station, offering no explanation, simply pleading with him to come and get me. Our friendship, spanning back over the last fifteen years, meant enough that he agreed without demanding an explanation for why I was there first thing on a Saturday morning. I sent thanks to a God I no longer believed in that it was the weekend, so my best friend was home. I didn't exactly have a list of people I could call, and I couldn't imagine facing the normality of getting on public transport.

I managed to get my rubbery legs moving, one foot in front of the other, until I made it out to the car park, our arranged meeting spot. I perched on a low stone wall and gulped in some of the dewy morning air, refreshing in comparison to the thick, stale air inside the station. My mind was in overdrive, trying to work out what the hell I was going to say to Mike when he arrived, fighting the rush of emotions as I imagined having to answer his questions. I rubbed the tiny scars on my face as I closed my eyes and tilted my head back, lifting my face to the sun.

I could feel the stench of the place clinging to my clothes and skin, making me feel dirty. Guilty.

Being sat on the cold hard plastic of the chairs inside that stark, stifling room had been the stuff of nightmares, and I had plenty of experience with those. I'd attempted to lose myself in the cold instant coffee and in reading the *inventive* messages carved into the table by the room's previous occupants. *Dave woz ere* didn't do much to hold my attention, though. I had been so desperate to get out of that place, but now that I was, I felt lost. Listening to the noises of the city beginning its day, I would have traded everything I possessed for the chance to rewind time.

A sharp toot of a car horn snapped me back to the moment with a start. I could make out movement from within the car, but whatever signals Mike was giving me were impossible to decipher through the reflection of the sun on the windscreen. Not wanting to spend a single second more at that place, I was at the passenger door in a couple of long strides, wrenching it open and dropping into the cool leather seat. Taking a moment of respite in the safety of the familiar car, I let my head drop back and blew out a breath, puffing my cheeks. Mike gawped at me, open mouthed, from the driver's side. He shook his head and gave a low chuckle.

"Jesus, mate, you look like total shit. Quite the bender last night, was it?"

When I didn't reply, instead massaging my throbbing temples with my fingertips, Mike continued as he put the car into gear and pulled away.

"Cheers for the invite. Although by the state of you, I'm glad I didn't come. Trouble with the missus? Drunk and disorderly?" He wobbled his head on his shoulders in jest. "Glad I'm not in your shoes today, mate. Mine would hit the friggin' roof ... Rather you than me."

He glanced in my direction before returning his eyes to the road. "Am I taking you straight back via the lion's den on your way to the doghouse?" He sniggered at his own joke, then fell suddenly silent when he realised I hadn't uttered a word since entering the car.

"Is everything alright?" His eyes darted sideways, taking in the atmosphere hanging around me, along with my starkly grim mood, for the first time.

"My god, Mike, no. Nothing is alright. At all ... I don't ..." I gasped as my breath caught. "I don't think anything can ever be alright again."

5

TESSA

THREE MONTHS PREVIOUS

I t had been an awful night. Cora had barely slept for more than twenty minutes straight without waking, and had been sick, twice, all over us both. It left me with such horrible anxiety – something could be terribly wrong with her. Was it normal for babies to cry quite this much? Was the vomiting a sign of something serious? The weight of worry and my sense of failure crushed me. Every other mother seemed to have it so together – even those with multiple children to care for – yet I seemed to be spiralling further and further out of control. Once again, I longed for my own mother, for the unmarred relationship we should have shared, and would have – but early onset dementia was slowly robbing us of her.

On more than one occasion during the night, listening to Sam snoring away peacefully in our bed, a swell of frustration and anger had shaken me. I knew Sam had to be up for work, and this *had* been our agreement – me taking on the lion's share of the nights with Cora during the week – but I'd had no idea what I was signing up for. My desperation for sleep, to just be able to close my eyes for a few short hours, was overpowering. I craved it like an addict in withdrawal. My awareness of Sam's peacefully sleeping away the hours while I moved from room to room, shushing our baby and pleading with her to give it up, was taking its toll on me. Tears streamed down my face within the veil of darkness that engulfed me.

I paced at the window, watching the steady rain made visible by the glow of the streetlamp. I risked a fleeting glance down at Cora nestled in my arms, praying that she had dropped off. Her little eyes fixed on mine overwhelmed me. Desperate, exhausted disappointment crashed against a forceful wave of love for my perfect child.

By the time the first light of day began to stretch across the room, and the vibration of Sam's alarm calling him from his slumber shattered the peaceful dawn, my fury was simmering.

"Oh, here you are." He appeared in the doorway to Cora's nursery, sleepy eyes smiling at us as he stretched his arms above his head. "My two favourite girls." He stepped into the room and planted a soft kiss on Cora's head. Her little eyelids fluttered with the light sleep she had finally surrendered to.

"Nice of you to notice we were gone," I hissed through gritted teeth, pulling my head back and turning to avoid his kiss. He drew back, shock and hurt clouding his expression.

"Oh. Have you been up long?"

My blood seared my skin at his apprehensive tone. "I didn't even get to go to fucking bed! Someone had to be up, clearing up the sick, trying to stop her crying. To get her to sleep for more than ten *bloody* minutes. Not that you noticed of course, while you were happily snoring away in there! I *do* hope we didn't disturb you."

Venomous sarcasm dripped from my words, the outburst doing nothing to extinguish the fiery ball of anger. Sam stared at my face, his features slackening as his jaw dropped.

His usually calm, easy-going wife was nowhere to be seen in that moment, replaced by some demonic wraith.

"Tessa, I'm really sorry. I had no idea. You should've woken me. I would've come and taken a shift for you."

"For me?" I hissed, whipping my head around with such force that I felt my neck twinge, my fury shifting up a gear. Had Cora not been in my arms, the temptation to throttle him might have overtaken my self-control. Only my fear of waking her held me back. "She's your goddamned child too, or do you get to *conveniently* forget that when you fancy yourself a good night's sleep?"

I knew I was being unreasonable, sure that if I *had* woken Sam, he would've come and taken over for a while. His response was well meaning and sincere. But he wasn't saying the right things, somehow. The frustration of his failure drove me on.

"I didn't mean it like that." He sighed, a weary look crossing his face. "I'm so sorry that you had such a rough night – and I can take over as soon as I get home so you can have a break." He looked defeated. "Why don't I order in a takeaway too, save you … us worrying about cooking?"

A pang of guilt deflated me. I was behaving like such a spoilt child. Sam couldn't grasp what he had done wrong, and yet he was still trying to put it right.

I closed my eyes, taking a deep, shuddering breath, and nodded.

He sighed again, shoulders sagging, shaking his head and moving towards the doorway. I watched from the corner of my eye as my husband made his way to the shower, despairing in the dim hope that I'd manage to get one.

The looming thought of the lonely day ahead darkened my mood. The dread of the desperate empty hours stretching ahead swirled like a whirlpool, dragging me in. My phone pinged with a text; I froze as Cora stirred in my arms. She snuffled and snuggled herself back into me, remaining asleep. Thank god. I reached for my phone and opened the message.

> Hey Tess, how are you and the sprog? I have a little time to spare today if you fancy a visitor? Let me know. B. xx

Relief washed over me. I really needed this to lift my mood and pass the day. I quickly typed out a reply.

> We are good, would be lovely to see you, pop over whenever suits. Xxx

I hoped I hadn't come over too keen. I meant to sound easy-going, saying she could come any time. But did that sound pathetic? Should I have waited a while before I replied?

"She's your friend, Tessa, get a grip!" I muttered to myself just as the first whinges from Cora began to shatter the silence.

"Wonderful!" I groaned, now certain I wasn't going to even manage a shower before the beautiful Bella breezed in.

———

BELLA HAD REPLIED that she would be with me at ten. Had it slipped her mind that "me" was now an "us". I sometimes found myself wondering if she left out Cora on purpose. She certainly made no secret of her feelings towards my baby. By just gone eleven, there was still no sign of her. I couldn't settle. Every time I started at something, I was sure I heard someone outside and would move to peer out of the window, expecting her to come waltzing in.

Cora, who'd been surprisingly chirpy all morning, was due a change. I gave her a fresh nappy, and she began to grizzle. Aware she was probably getting hungry, I settled down and lifted my top to offer her a feed. She rooted around for a few seconds before latching and guzzling down milk. I enjoyed those moments. It was as if we were the only two people on the earth, and nothing mattered but supplying my baby with what she needed until content.

The one thing I seemed to be doing right.

We were only a few minutes in when the doorbell chimed, a loud intrusion into our little bubble. I cursed under my breath and debated what to do. I could attempt a shuffle to the door whilst Cora continued her feed, but my cheeks burned and my stomach clenched just picturing the horror on Bella's face. I slipped my little finger between my breast and Cora's pursed lips, breaking her latch. Squeals of protest reverberated off the walls, and she squirmed in my arms. On the way to the front door, I struggled to keep a grip on my angry daughter with one arm whilst covering my modesty with the other, attempting to compose myself, not wanting to seem flustered. With a final yank at my top, I pulled open the door and took in Bella's appearance, her scent swirling around us. She looked perfect, of course. Not a single hair out of place, her makeup perfectly applied. Her outfit looked as though it was tailored to fit the curves of her body. Cora momentarily calmed, seemingly stunned into silence by Bella's presence. Even my infant daughter was mesmerized by her perfection. I felt oddly betrayed.

To her credit, Bella quickly hid the immediate look on her face. But it was too late. I'd caught it. Horror, sympathy, disgust. It was all there, impossible to miss as our eyes met. Sadness washed over me. I fought the impulse to glance down at the frumpy, stained clothing that had somehow seemed good enough that morning. This was me now – a woman once young, attractive, and carefree, no longer.

My daughter is worth it, I scolded myself. But my shoulders slumped.

"Hi." Her wide smile was firmly pasted back in place. "Sorry I'm running late. Work stuff, you know?" She gave a little shrug. I smiled back, nodding and standing to one side to let her pass. I didn't know, though. I'd never had a high-flying career that demanded my time like that. Once again, I felt painfully inadequate in the company of my perfect friend.

She slipped past me, edging in sideways so as not to get too close. A *click clack* echoed through the house as she swept down my hallway on her heels. We never wore our shoes inside the house, but asking her to remove them seemed petty and awkward, so I never mentioned it. As I pushed the door closed, annoyance sparked at my own pathetic cowardice. I scurried after her, my bare feet slapping the laminate floor, whilst Cora, no longer spellbound, resumed her roaring complaint.

I entered my kitchen, almost bumping straight into the back of Bella, who had stopped just inside the doorway.

"Gosh," she gasped. "What happened in here?"

I cast a glance around, suddenly seeing it through an outsider's eyes. The dirty dishes stacked up beside the sink. The grubby work surfaces, in desperate need of a scrub. The bin, overflowing with the rubbish thrown in its direction, tainting the air with a stale smell. Heat crept over my face.

"Erm, I haven't really managed to get around to the housework for a day or two," I replied, waving my hand casually, voice raised in competition with my screeching daughter. I attempted to inject some cheer into my words, to come over as indifferent to her scathing remark. "Other priorities now." I forced a smile, gesturing to the still squirming child whom I was desperately trying to keep hold of.

"Umm, I guess so." She nodded, raising her eyebrows as

she took in the scene before her. She attempted a smile, but her lips were pursed, a slight wrinkle of her nose breaking through.

For the first time since she'd arrived, her eyes dropped to take in Cora. A look passed over her face that I couldn't quite put my finger on. I rocked my daughter, shushing her and holding her close.

"Err, Tessa, you have a bit of ..." She broke off mid-sentence, gesturing with her hand around the area of her breast. I glanced down, realising with horror that a wet patch was spreading rapidly across my T-shirt.

"Oh shit." The burning sensation in my face returned full force, then spread down the length of my body. In my rush to get to the door, I hadn't had the chance to clip my nursing bra. The milk had been freely soaking through my shirt, the flow made worse by Cora, who was still howling about her feed having been cut short. I considered claiming I'd spilled something, but the lie would have been obvious, what with the patch spreading like that.

"I'll just pop up and change my shirt." I attempted a good-humoured smile, unsure which of us I was trying to convince. "Would you mind?" I nodded down at Cora, hoping she would scoop her out of my arms, allowing me a few precious moments to pull myself together, regain some form of composure. A flicker of hope sparked that they might even bond a little.

Bella, fixated on her phone, didn't even glance in my direction. "No, of course." She gave a wave of her hand, dismissing me. "You carry on."

"Oh ... erm ... I meant ... would you mind holding on to Cora for me – just for a minute – while I change?" I squirmed.

Her wild eyes flew up from her phone screen, locking on to mine.

"Better not." She shrugged with a cool smile and ran her

free hand through her glossy hair, giving a tinkle of a laugh. "Don't want to risk messing up my clothes, too. I have more meetings this afternoon. Plus, I have no idea how to even *hold* a baby. I'll pop the kettle on though?" She cocked her head, her smile brightening.

"Right. Course." I nodded, shifting Cora in my arms. "I won't be long, then."

"Uh-huh." She waved her hand once again, her eyes fixed firmly back on the screen. I spun to leave in one swift but inelegant motion. I was desperate not to have Bella witness me falling apart completely.

Despair sank its claws into me, and I plunged to a new low. How much worse could things possibly get?

6

SAM

PRESENT DAY

The rest of the drive to Mike's house passed in a blur. Upon our entrance to their house, Lauren recoiled. She took in my red-rimmed eyes and tear-stained cheeks. A look of panic settled over her face. Her eyes flicked between us, questions brimming, but Mike cut her a warning glance, followed by a brisk shake of his head. She held her tongue, to her credit, despite clearly wishing to know what on earth was going on, concern piercing her expression. She snapped her jaw shut and led us through to the kitchen.

I found myself crumpled, head in hands, on a dining chair at Mike and Lauren's kitchen table. Whilst I sipped a mug of very sugary tea, they – on the pretence of "sorting out the children" – spoke in hushed tones just outside the door.

Once the children had been banished, delighted to be granted free rein of the living room in front of the TV, I did my best to fill Mike and Lauren in on the events of the past twenty-four hours. The heat of shame crept over me as I realised how painfully little I actually knew. Mike couldn't hold my gaze. He tossed me the occasional look while mainly studying the tabletop, a mixture of shock and sympathy etched onto his face. Lauren, who had turned deathly pale, stared, her mouth slightly open. A vision of Tessa's wax-like skin shoved into the forefront of my mind. Lauren's eyes – fixed on me until that point – suddenly darted sideways at her husband.

"Fuck!" Mike breathed, shaking his head slowly. "I'm so sorry, Sam. What happens now?"

Lauren cleared her throat before opening her mouth to say something, but only a squeak passed her lips. She and Tessa had become more friendly recently; they seemed to have bonded since Cora's arrival. And so the shock was hitting her hard, as well.

She tried again. "H-how can you be sure that someone ..." She swallowed hard. "Well, that someone ... actually ... hurt Tessa, and that it wasn't just a tragic ... natural thing?"

I replied, struggling as well to find the right words, "Because if no one else was ... involved ... then we have no explanation for where Cora could be." I blinked back the tears that were once again threatening to fall, trying to keep myself detached from the horrific reality.

"Of course." Her cheeks flamed, the colour of beetroot, and her hands flew to her face. "Sorry, I think it's the shock." She swallowed hard. "I can't think straight."

"Don't apologise." I attempted a half-hearted smile, focused on keeping my voice steady. "The same thought occurred to me, too. I've just had more time to process it all. The police need to confirm, but believe it was asphyxiation." I numbly reeled off the information.

"Who would've wanted to do something like that? To *Tessa*?" Lauren's words, heavy with dismay, echoed those of the police earlier that day. Fat tears formed in her eyes. I had been through this question until my head ached, and the word "enemy" spun behind my eyes. I released my clenched jaw again. For the second time in less than twelve hours, a face intruded into my mind: Lindy. But as I had done earlier, at the police station, I pushed it away, dismissing the thought and chastising myself for it. It had been so many years; I didn't even know where she was. Besides, ex-girlfriends didn't just show up to murder your wife. I shook my head and answered her in much the same way as I had the police officers.

"No one that I know of. Tessa was an open book. If she'd had a problem, I think I'd have known about it. I don't believe she would've been able to keep something like that hidden from me or wanted to." I thought of her missing wedding bands. Shock and disbelief riled me, that this conversation could be real. "It's mad; this is *Tessa* we're talking about!"

They both nodded their agreement, words failing us all.

Mike's hand moved up to rub his neck. "So what do we do?"

His question softened my heart; my shoulders relaxed a little. He had used the word "we". I'd never felt so alone sat with my best friend in his kitchen.

"I have no bloody idea." I puffed out my cheeks, shaking my head as despair and frustration swelled. "It's not like Cora's a teenager. I can't just go searching the streets or her favourite hangout spots. I don't even know where to start. She's just a baby! What kind of person *takes* a baby? And would ... do what they did? From all we know, and from what the police seem to think, all I can guess is that some psycho has her. God, what would Tessa say if she ..."

My stomach clenched with anguish. The sugar from the tea had left me nauseous, and my head suddenly felt too heavy for my neck. I dropped it forward onto my crossed arms resting on the table.

The silence was broken by a squeal from the living room, then an angry shout of, "IT'S MINE," booming through the walls, breaking the tension.

"I'd better ..." Lauren stood, gesturing towards the living room and throwing me an apologetic look before scuttling away from the table to referee her fighting children. I hoped she and Mike realised how lucky they were – having each other and their children safe within the four walls of their home.

"Mate, I don't even know what to say." Mike regarded me with such concern etched onto his face, it almost broke me down. My best friend, who made crass jokes at every opportunity, seeming to be incapable of being serious, looked at me with such gravity. It was odd, but I found myself filled with sympathy for him. I'd landed all of this on him with no warning, and he clearly felt useless – unable to offer anything that could help. I knew that feeling all too well.

I raised my eyes to meet his. "There isn't a lot *to* say. But I'm bloody grateful to you for being here for me," I added with sincerity.

"Absolutely. For whatever you need." He nodded enthusiastically but struggled to maintain eye contact. In all the years of our friendship, we had never had to expose such raw emotion to one another. We'd always shared such easy banter, feeling most comfortable taking the piss out of one another in the typical way blokes do. We'd known each other since secondary school, having been the only ones to join from each of our separate schools. Out mutual status as outsiders had forced us together at first, but in time we'd formed an especially tight bond because of it. The other groups came to intermingle, reconfiguring as friendships evolved, but Mike and I, having come to rely on no one else as we did one another, were inseparable.

There was no place for our usual banter today. This was new territory for us both, and I found myself mourning that easy relationship with my best friend along with so much else.

I let out another sigh and raked my hands through my hair. "Well, I'm no use sitting here." I made to stand from the table, needing to relieve the tension and break us out of our shared discomfort. My vision swam, and I felt oddly separated from the reality playing out around me. Through the haze in my brain, my motions on autopilot, I searched once again for evidence I was dreaming.

"I'm going to call the station, ask them if I can at least pick up my car, maybe pick up some bits from the house, too, if I can go in. I need to find out what I can do to find Cora. I can't just sit around on my hands, hoping whoever has her will come to their senses and deliver her back to me." I rubbed my scars.

Mike's head snapped up. "Do you think they'll ask for a ransom?" His forehead creased.

I hadn't thought of that, imagining much darker things planned for my beautiful little girl. A wave of nausea hit, and I swallowed hard, pushing away the unbearable idea.

"I can't imagine this is about money," I replied, somehow conveying a deceptive calmness, shrugging. "It doesn't make a lot of sense for anyone to target us. It's not like we're sitting on a fortune. We have the house, but it's mortgaged. It wouldn't be a case of just going to the bank and drawing out a wad of cash. And why ... hurt Tessa? There must be bigger, easier targets than us, if it's money they're after."

I realised then that whoever had Cora had become a "they" to me. A faceless group of thugs who'd stolen my world out from underneath me as I slept.

"Yeah, I guess so." Mike visibly deflated. "Can I do anything? I could drop you back to your place if you want?"

"Thanks, mate, but you enjoy some time with your family. God knows it's precious." Somehow my mind had managed to block out the hell going on around me, just for those few seconds of conversation. But as I thought of my broken family, the pain hit again with the force of a sledgehammer, taking my breath away and forcing me to lean on the table for support, leaving me terrified that the physical ache in my chest would never leave.

IT WAS ONLY a short walk from Mike's house to my own. I hoped the time alone in the fresh air might help me to gather my thoughts and come to an idea of what I should do next.

I dialled the number for the station and waited for the call to connect. Unsurprisingly, they didn't yet have any updates for me. The officer's detached tone was a stark reminder of the morning I'd spent there. A shudder passed through me. As if the situation weren't horrific enough, I found myself having to ask the complete stranger on the other end of the phone if I had permission to enter my own home. I was glad no one was around to see my face burn with indignation while he informed me that the forensics team were still working there, adding gently that me being there could hinder their investigation.

Brushing the stinging sensation aside, I questioned him on what I could do. As expected, he advised me to allow the police to do their job and that, basically, I could do nothing. The heat returned to my face once again as I was strongly advised not to go far – just in case they needed "further assistance" from me. I jabbed the screen to end the call and kicked out at a crushed can on the pavement. I hadn't thought it possible, but after my call to the police, I found myself feeling even worse. I'd been useless for my wife and child, and now I felt like some kind of criminal.

My home had become an episode of *CSI*. Crime scene tape fluttered in the breeze across my driveway, and people in white suits swarmed. I couldn't bring myself to look at the neighbours hanging out of windows or huddled in groups outside the surrounding houses, as I imagined what they would be saying. An image of me and Tessa at our front window, watching the scene unfold in one of the other houses on the street, agonisingly clear, jolted me to a stop. I could almost see her face in the front window, scolding me with a sly smile as I made a distasteful joke about the effect all this would have on the value of the house. I gulped back some air and leaned my hands on my knees. I needed to keep it together.

I had to check in with an officer before I could take my car. I uttered a silent prayer of thanks that my car and house keys were on the same ring, meaning I already had them with me.

On the journey back to Mike's, I made a quick stop at a supermarket to buy myself some clean clothes, needing to be out of the stale ones I'd been wearing all day. I imagined the smell of the police station woven into the fabric. I pulled into the car park and slammed on my brakes as I came to the parent and child spaces. My heart plummeted and my stomach clenched as I watched a father lift his child from the rear of the car, his wife watching on. She noticed me staring and threw me an odd look. A loud beep from behind me snapped me back into action, and I revved the engine and drove right back out of the car park.

I STOOD on Mike's front step, bouncing on the balls of my feet, filled with nervous energy. The sound of the doorbell echoed through the hall before Mike's shape appeared in the glass.

He slowly pulled back the door, looking utterly wretched. "Any news?" His eyes flickered to meet mine before dropping away. His hand rubbed the back of his neck.

I shook my head with a deep sigh. "Nothing."

"Erm, Sam, mate, there's something I need to talk to you about." He moved out onto the step, forcing me to take a step backwards myself as he pulled the door closed behind him. My heart beat so hard, like it would break through my sternum, I thought surely he could hear it. What the hell could he be about to say? As he opened his mouth to speak, a look of pure anguish twisting his face, my phone buzzed in my pocket. I held up my hand to silence Mike, gesturing towards the phone as the police station's number flashed across my screen.

7

TESSA

THREE MONTHS PREVIOUS

I kept going over the morning's events in my head. It couldn't have gone as badly as I thought. But no matter which way I tried to look at it, it really had.

I'd left Bella in the kitchen and climbed the stairs, muscles throbbing in my arms from holding onto my combative infant. Placing Cora in the middle of our bed, I turned to the wardrobe to retrieve something milk- and vomit-free. My clothes pile was getting low, a reminder that there was also a ton of washing mounting up that I really should have gotten to by now. I fought the urge to scream along with my daughter and lash out at everything around me. I snatched the shirt on the top of the pile and turned back to Cora. I started to pull the T-shirt over my head, then decided to instead try to finish off her feed, hoping that would stop her waling for a while. I offered my engorged breast, attempting to latch her, but she was having none of it, having worked herself into such a temper that she was now seemingly making a point, putting herself on hunger strike. Frustration simmered – I couldn't even manage at something as basic as feeding my own child.

After a few more attempts, with her thrashing her head side to side, she pushed her body away from mine, a final rejection.

"Fine," I huffed petulantly, plonking her back on to the bed. "Suit yourself."

Her wails continued to increase in volume, her little face screwing up, turning red with anger. I pictured Bella downstairs, embarrassed by the commotion. I wondered if she wished she hadn't come.

Ensuring that my bra clips were in place – a last-ditch attempt to save what dignity I could still muster – I pulled my clean shirt over my head, wriggling it down into place and risking a glance in the mirror.

I stared in horror, revolted by my reflection. My swollen breasts and stomach made it appear as though I had life rings wedged under my shirt; there was a big gap where my T-shirt ended and my jeans began. I could focus on nothing but the area of excess skin.

Rushing back to the wardrobe, I grabbed at the other shirts in the pile. They were all fitted, pre-pregnancy clothes that would never cover my awful new shape. I dissolved into tears, flopping down onto the bed next to my hysterical daughter and wishing I never had to leave the safety of the bedroom.

I'D EVENTUALLY PULLED myself together enough to pick out a bulky jumper from the back of my wardrobe, swamping myself in it. I knew I looked awful – especially in comparison to Bella – but at least it hid the shame that the shirt seemed so determined to display. I rubbed some concealer under my red, puffy eyes and added some bronzer in an attempt to appear unfazed by my chaos. It was the first time I'd even looked at my makeup bag for weeks, but I needed to get through the rest of the morning and hoped that, by some miracle, my concealer would disguise more than just my tears.

By the time we returned to my kitchen, Cora had almost exhausted herself with her continuous screams and had toned it down to a low, steady moan. I paused before turning into the kitchen, taking a deep, shaking breath, and pasted on my best "you know how it is" smile. Bella's perfectly manicured nails tapped out a slow rhythm on the table in front of her. I glanced at them, a spark of jealousy flaring, causing my stomach to tighten – best-case scenario for me was that mine didn't have baby shit under them.

My kitchen smelled of cleaning products, and I wondered if I'd imagined how bad it had been earlier. I glanced up to see that the dishes were in soak, and the worktops had been wiped.

"You cleaned?" I gulped, unsure if the emotions rising this time were gratitude or mortification.

"Just ran a cloth around and opened a window." She studied her nails.

I was touched by the gesture but couldn't ignore the awkwardness hanging thick in the atmosphere, both of us clearly humiliated. I rushed to change the subject.

"Sorry about all of that." I forced a smile, coming across as breezily as I could manage after my episode upstairs. "The joys of mum life. Almost as crazy as a high-flying career, I guess?" I tried to giggle but only managed to splutter something forced. Bella had been eyeing me since I'd spoken. I was silently begging, pleading with her not to have noticed me falling apart. Or did I wish she *would* ask? Would comfort me, make me feel as though someone cared? I chastised myself, glancing once again at the kitchen she'd just tidied.

"You can't really compare *motherhood* to a *career* though?"

Bella's reply seemed curt, but I was likely being oversensitive again.

"Working for a living – closing on million-pound deals, compared to getting to sit at home all day, cuddling a baby!" she continued. "The worst thing that can happen in your day is a leaky nappy." She offered a tight smile, rolling her eyes. "I would *love* a few days of lazing around on the sofa, catching up on the latest trashy TV." She let out a little laugh. "Maybe you can fill me in on it all. I've made us coffee."

I couldn't stop my face dropping, the last of the wind taken from my sails. I bit my lip, willing myself not to lose it again.

"Yeah ... well ... obviously I didn't mean ..." I stuttered, trying to explain away my stupidity, but found myself lost for words. The feeling of hurt and offence, knowing that she viewed me as lazy and boring, was stifling, but I was too ashamed to admit it. Though I was unsure if it were even possible, I was afraid that she might think even less of me if she knew I was finding something that should be so easy – so natural – almost impossible to manage.

I turned in on myself, wondering how I had become such a pathetic excuse for a human being and how I was failing so spectacularly at everything. Even my friendship that had seemed so unshakable before I'd fallen pregnant seemed to be wobbling under the strain of my act.

Cora, having finally burned herself out with the relentless screaming, had fallen asleep, nestled in my arms. I gazed down at her beautiful face, blotchy from all of the crying, and guilt wrenched at my heart. I eased her into the pristine Moses basket, and – unbelievably – she barely stirred before resuming her gentle snores.

Bella's eyes were fixed on me, watching as I turned around, finally victorious in something. There was an unreadable expression on her face that I just couldn't fathom.

I busied myself searching for biscuits, wishing harshly, now that she was finally here, that Bella hadn't come. All I wanted was to actually take this one rare opportunity to curl up on the sofa and zone out in front of the TV. *Like you would be able to do every day if you were a half-decent mother,* the mocking voice in my head taunted.

Bella must've been telepathic, or I was giving off signals unknowingly. She swallowed her coffee back so quickly I couldn't believe she wasn't scalding her mouth. We made small talk between gulps, avoiding any touchy subjects. An uncomfortable heaviness hung between us, and I got the feeling that she couldn't wait to leave, escape from the chaos that had become my new norm.

The conversation ground to an awkward silence. "Well, I should get going." She stood, draining the last of her coffee in one swig. "*So* much to do!" She shrugged, slamming her empty mug back onto the kitchen table. I shot a glance towards Cora's basket. She slept peacefully on, undisturbed.

Bella, having picked up her phone and bag, moved out towards the hallway. Once again, the *click clack* of her heels echoed, and I trailed along behind her to the front door, watching as her shoes collided with my floors.

She turned suddenly to face me, stopping me in my tracks. "Should you be leaving her alone in another room like that?" She gave a nod back in the direction of the kitchen, arching a perfect eyebrow.

"She's safe in her basket." I willed myself not to turn back towards the kitchen as the self-doubt crept in. "I wouldn't go far anyway." I shrugged, hiding the feelings of inadequacy.

She pursed her lips, mirroring my shrug. "You know best. I'll call you soon – treat you to lunch out." She placed her hand briefly on the top of my arm. "See you soon, Tessa."

She waved as she stepped out the front door, pulling it closed behind her. It slammed so hard I was certain it shook the house. I froze as the first sounds of Cora's cries began to fill the silence around me.

A buzz from my pocket – I reached for my phone. Seeing my husband's name on the screen, I opened the text.

> Tessa, so sorry but I'm going to be late home. I'll get back as soon as I can but if you are hungry, go ahead and order in. I can warm it up when I get back. Love you both. Give Cora a kiss from Daddy. Xx

Cora's wails increased in volume by the second. I sank down onto the bottom step; letting out a scream to rival my daughter's, I hurled my phone at the wall.

8

SAM

PRESENT DAY

The officer's words ran on a loop inside my head as I raced to the station.

Make your way here as soon as you can ... Something we need to discuss with you ...

Myriad scenarios rocketed through my brain. If they had found Cora, wouldn't they have just told me that over the phone? Surely they wouldn't be so cruel as to keep something like that from me.

So that means they must have found her, but she ... she's dead, isn't she?

Sucking in deep breaths, I tried not to lose my head, aware that if I didn't calm down, I was going to give myself a heart attack before I made it. Then I'd never know.

My tyres screeched as I pulled into the car park that Mike had picked me up from only hours before, struggling to comprehend how it could still be the same day. How could it be possible that time always moved at the same speed? I abandoned my car in the first space that I came to and yanked my keys from the ignition before the tyres had even stopped rolling. My mind, now back in overdrive, was reeling with questions. Could my daughter possibly be inside that hulking building? If not, what *was* waiting for me inside?

Once I was out of the car, the burning need to get there that had consumed me suddenly vanished. What reality would I come face to face with in there? If I lost my daughter, too, what was left for me? Would I be able to find the strength to carry on? Was there even any point trying? My head spun, and I struggled to focus my eyes. I reminded myself to breathe, to stop my thoughts from running away with themselves. "Man up, Sam!" I chided myself under my breath. "This isn't about you."

I was up the stone steps and pulling at the door to the station before there was time to change my mind. At the desk, I gave my name and was told to take a seat on one of the cold plastic chairs. I discreetly glanced around at the people I was sharing the small space with. A woman with a cut lip and a black eye forming was accompanied by a man old enough to be her father but bearing no resemblance. An older lady sat a few chairs away from them, fiddling with a tissue in her hand. She twisted and untwisted the corner of it, avoiding looking up. A sadness engulfed me as I studied the tissue, aware that it could never be the same again.

A young guy wearing a baseball cap, probably in his early twenties, paced up and down, occasionally throwing questions at the uniformed officer manning the desk on the whereabouts of his mate. I wondered what had happened in their lives to bring them all to this dank, dreary place. My heart constricted with the overwhelming feeling that I didn't belong here.

"Mr Fulford?"

I snapped my head up to face the officer with the dark hair whom I had spoken to earlier that day. From first glance, he looked like he had suffered a tough life. I realised I'd barely taken in his appearance before and wondered now how old he was. I'd have guessed in his sixties, but I could imagine this job aging a person quickly. He eyed me from the doorway.

"Do you want to come through?" It wasn't really a question. I dragged myself from the uncomfortable chair and followed him along the hall. Behind me, I could hear loud shouts from the guy in the cap.

"How come that guy gets to skip the queue? He only just got here! I've been here for fucking hours ..."

His shouts faded out as I stepped back into an interview room for the second time that day, where a second officer was waiting. With his tightly cropped hair, olive skin, and designer stubble, he looked much younger than his colleague, and like he'd fit better as a catalogue model than a police officer. He invited me to sit and offered me refreshments. There was nothing refreshing about anything there, so I politely declined. I hadn't eaten anything since the previous day. The last thing I'd had to drink was the sweet tea at Mike's that morning, and the buzz from the sugar had long worn off. I just wanted to know what this was about and get it over with.

"Do you mind?" the officer who had led me through asked, nodding towards the tape recorder. He went ahead, pressing the buttons without waiting for an answer. A long beep signalled that it was recording.

I nodded anyway, aware now from our earlier meetings this was procedure. The younger of the two officers cleared his throat.

"For the sake of the tape, I'm DI Garcia, and with me I have DS Sanders. Interview commencing at sixteen thirty-eight with Mr Samuel Fulford."

"Could someone please just tell me what is going on? Why am I here?" I gasped, unnerved by his tone and feeling as though the air had been sucked from the room. I tucked my trembling hands under the desk.

"Of course." It was DI Garcia who responded to me. For a brief moment I studied him, wondering if he was new to the job. Was he experienced enough to deal with something so crucial as my family's case?

"Actually, we were hoping that you could help us," he continued. I didn't like his tone. "Was there any information that you may have forgotten to mention when we were chatting this morning?"

I prickled at his casual use of the word. *Chatting?* Was that how he described being interviewed about your wife's murder and child's abduction? I shook it off and instead focused on processing his question. His choice of words was the least of my problems.

"I'm not sure I know what you mean?" My brow creased as I shook my head, trying to decipher what he was getting at.

"As we mentioned this morning, every bit of information is critical at this time. Especially in a case as serious as this." His tone seemed flippant considering the magnitude of his words.

"I couldn't agree more." I glanced between the two men, their brows dipped so low they formed a V shape. DS Sanders leaned back in his chair, arms folded across his chest. "So if you could tell me what the hell's going on instead of playing these games, we can all get back to what's important here." My words were sharp.

Garcia tilted his head to one side and studied me for a few seconds. I held his gaze, reminding myself that I had nothing to hide, the pounding in my ears notwithstanding.

"We were wondering, did you just *forget* to mention your ... problem, Mr Fulford?" He waved his hand around in a breezy gesture. "Or did you feel that we didn't need to know?" His expression turned serious. Both officers now had their eyes locked on mine. Heat rose to my cheeks, flushing my face. My breathing picked up speed again, and I struggled to hold my nerve. "What problem?" I scoffed, echoing his tone to keep up my bravado.

"We know all about it, Mr Fulford, so we would appreciate it if you could start being honest. Tell us the truth. What might you be capable of doing during one of your *episodes?*" He waved his hand around, and the emphasis on the last word caused my stomach to flip.

This is it, Sam, the little voice in my head piped up. *They know. They are no longer on your side ...*

9

TESSA

TWO MONTHS PREVIOUS

Sam had invited Mike and Lauren over that evening, and I was consumed by panic. I'd managed to avoid seeing anyone in the weeks since that awful spectacle I'd made of myself with Bella. I just wasn't ready to have people in the house again, witnessing my shortcomings. I did everything I could to talk Sam out of it, but everyone else thought that it was a great idea. I found myself outnumbered and overruled.

"But the house is a mess!" I threw back at Sam when he'd put the suggestion to me. I knew I sounded pathetic as I searched for an excuse, exasperated that he could even suggest the idea.

"We can give it a bit of a spruce-up. Won't take long between the two of us." Sam appeared at the living room door and shrugged, steaming mugs in hand and that lopsided smile on his handsome face. Sam seemed genuinely unaware of how attractive he was, which only served to make him even more so. I'd never seen pictures of him when he was younger, and I couldn't imagine his face without the tiny scars that speckled it. He'd always shrugged and brushed it off when I'd asked if his mother had any family photos. Sam hated the scars. To him they were a disfigurement, but I'd always thought they only added to his looks, making him ruggedly handsome.

"The house really isn't that bad. It won't take long. And anyway they won't care what the house looks like. They're our friends, and they want to see us and Cora, not inspect the house!" His grin widened. He knew that he was wearing me down. My eyes travelled over his shoulders to his biceps. His looking so good did nothing to help my self-esteem. I struggled to remember when I'd last washed my hair as I pushed a strand back from my face.

"What if Cora's difficult?" I cringed, hearing the whine in my own voice. "It won't exactly be a pleasant evening if she cries the entire time, will it?"

"Tessa, they have kids; they *know* what babies are like!" he replied gently.

"I'm bloody knackered, and I can't face cooking and playing host to your friends, Sam," I snapped. My panic was rising as I quickly ran out of valid excuses. I felt awkward, aware I'd never made much of an effort with Lauren despite our husbands' unshakable bond. Although craving true friendship, I'd pushed her away out of jealousy – her ability to provide Mike with a family made me feel even more inadequate.

"They're our friends," he soothed. "And that's fine; we already agreed we'll grab a takeaway. We were going to take you out, but I didn't think you'd relax and enjoy it, having Cora with us. And before you say it, I know you're not ready to leave her. That's why they're coming here. I'll host; you can relax."

I prickled, annoyed that he had me pegged. "Well, I'm sure you wouldn't be too keen on going out, either, if it meant getting your boobs out in front of everyone."

"If it will make you feel better, my love, I will sit with my boobs out all evening," he smoothly replied, a mock-serious expression on his face. All of the fight drained out of me, and hard as I fought it, my lips cracked into a smile despite myself.

So that was it. The decision was out of my hands. To be fair to Sam, whilst I was busy feeding and comforting Cora, I could hear him vigorously working away in the kitchen. Guilt prickled – here I was being lazy, sitting around again and leaving Sam to do the housework – but fatigue soon suffocated it. Cora was sleeping in my lap when Sam's face appeared around the door frame of the living room again.

"Hey," he whispered, smiling down at our sleeping beauty. "Why don't you take her up, have a lie-down with her? Get a bit of rest while I finish up down here. I can take her in a bit so you can get yourself ready for this evening."

"Are you sure?" Guilt snaked its way through me again. Sam was doing too much while I lazed around – my usual habit as of late.

"I could finish the tidying while you sit with her if you like?" I offered, half-hearted, eyes already heavy.

"No. Enjoy the peace while you can – we both know it doesn't last long." He rolled his eyes, but his smile gave him away, his adoration for Cora radiating. A surge of love for him knocked me sideways. I edged gradually off the sofa, cradling Cora softly in my arms, and crept towards the door. Sam, who had been gazing at his sleeping daughter, stepped to one side to let us pass, but I shuffled closer to him, planting a soft kiss on his lips. As I pulled back, I locked my eyes onto his and whispered my thanks.

I slinked around our room like a cat burglar, then eased Cora onto our bed ... slowly ... slowly. I used Sam's pillows to form a makeshift safety barrier along the outside edge before

I climbed in alongside her. I wouldn't sleep, I'd just get a little rest.

MY EYES FLEW open at the sounds of Cora's gentle murmurs. I sat bolt upright to see her gurgling away next to me. My heart raced with lingering panic. Where was Sam? Was he somewhere else in the house in the midst of another nightmare? How could I have fallen asleep? Anything could have happened to Cora. A rustle from the doorway drew my attention, and I remembered it was still mid-afternoon.

"Hey, you two. I thought I could hear your little voice, missus!" Sam pulled a silly face at Cora, whose arms and legs kicked wildly in response. He scooped her off the bed, smothering her with kisses. She wiggled with delight.

He noticed my silence. "You okay?"

"I fell asleep, Sam." My voice came out in a gasp. "What if something had happened to her?"

His face folded, brows dipping deep in question. I couldn't bear telling him the true fears that had wrenched me from my slumber, and watching him crumple. The reason for my relentless insomnia.

"What if I had rolled on her?" Distressing thoughts invaded my mind, seeming to catapult their way in.

"Hey, hey, calm down!" Sam dropped onto the bed next to me. "She's totally fine!" He gestured to her cooing in his arms as if proving his point. "You deserve to rest, too, Tessa. Give yourself a break. She's tougher than you give her credit for."

He nuzzled his face into hers and blew raspberries on the bare flesh of her neck, her little eyes lighting up with joy. I rubbed my own gritty eyes and sucked in a breath, wondering if he was right. Maybe I was just being paranoid.

"Right, you have a relax. Take a shower, whatever you like.

I'll take this beautiful princess out of your way." His eyes didn't leave his daughter, his smile fixed in place. "Mike and Lauren are due to arrive in an hour and a half."

The long, hot shower was just the tonic I needed. For the first time in longer than I would have cared to admit, I lathered my hair with fresh floral shampoo and ran the razor over my fuzzy legs. By the time I'd finished, I felt like a new woman. Searching my wardrobe, I found the loose-fitting shirt that Bella had gifted me and some fitted jeans. I left the shirt open at the bust over my vest top and added a belt. I had to fasten the jeans up over my belly using a hair band, but it was just about hidden under the oversized shirt, so no one would know. I risked a look in the mirror – ally turned enemy. I turned side to side, regarding myself with a critical eye. Actually, I looked okay. No – better than okay, I looked good. The silky fabric hugged my chest, thanks to the belt, and it flowed over my stomach without clinging, somehow giving the illusion of it being flat. The rich autumnal colours complemented my complexion, and the material's softness stroked my skin. I thought warmly of my friend and made a mental note to thank her again.

Twisting my hair up out of my face, I clipped it in place and grabbed my make-up bag. Going to work on my face felt like meeting an old friend – or at least how I imagined it would – as we slipped back into comfortable habits. I kept it as natural as I could whilst hiding the many flaws – the betrayal of my own face. I finished off with a generous spritz of perfume and felt ready for anything the evening had to throw at me. I felt good! I could hear Sam in the hallway, singing away to Cora in some tuneless melody. I couldn't help but smile.

"Tess, are you alright if I jump in the shower really quick? I just don't want to stink when we're having ..." Sam looked up at me and stopped mid flow. "Jesus, Tessa." His eyes widened, almost popping out of his head. "You look amazing! Look at that butt!"

I stifled a giggle, realising that, since becoming a mother, I hadn't bothered to put a lot of effort into being a wife. Baggy clothes and lack of showers had become the norm for me. Between that and continually comparing myself to an invariably flawless Bella, my fragile self-esteem had all but shattered.

"It's such a shame that no one is going to notice how hot you look tonight." He shrugged.

I turned to look at him, brow creased in question.

"Well, everyone's going to be too busy looking at my boobs." He grinned.

REACHING the bottom of the stairs, I froze as if I had stepped into the wrong house. Sam had worked so hard. Every surface gleamed, the dirty dishes nowhere to be seen. Even the floors had been hoovered and mopped. I was overwhelmed by the effort he'd put in. I had forty-five minutes before Mike and Lauren were due to arrive, so I settled down with Cora to feed her. As usual, she gulped down the milk, and by the time Sam reappeared at the bottom of the stairs, I had her changed into a clean nappy and a beautiful lacy dress.

"Wow, look at you two!" He reached for Cora, and she snuggled into him. I caught his scent, drinking it in with thirst and letting it wash over me with the comfort of blissful memories. I watched my husband cradling our daughter, and my stomach swooped.

"Sam, the place looks amazing. Thank you so much for all your hard work," I gushed, placing my hand against his chest.

Before he had time to respond, a gentle tapping came at

the front door. I tousled Cora's hair as I passed, planting a kiss on her head and padding into the hallway. Flicking on the light, I cracked the door and peered around it.

Lauren, standing in the drizzle outside, beamed a giddy grin at me and waved an enthusiastic hand. Mike nodded in greeting.

"Didn't want to ring the bell in case Cora was sleeping," she whispered quietly. I pulled back the door, stepping to one side to let them pass.

"Ah, thanks. That's so thoughtful." I pushed the door closed behind them. At the soft click of the door, I remembered Bella's slamming of it and was struck by a sharp jab of annoyance. A swell of guilt immediately drowned it. Bella didn't have children and wouldn't have thought about it. Of course it was an accident. She had been good enough to come to my bombsite of a home in her few hours free from work and spend time with me when I was barely able to function – let alone engage in an interesting conversation. She'd even taken the time to clean my kitchen. I fondled the fabric of my beautiful shirt. Lack of sleep was making me irrational. I pushed my spiteful thought aside and made another mental note to send a warm text to my friend to make up for it.

"But as you can see, she's raring to join us." I gestured at Cora and Sam, rolling my eyes in mock annoyance, but unable to hide my smile.

"Oh, even better," Lauren squealed excitedly, slipping out of her jacket and hopping from foot to foot as she pulled off her boots. "I get my fix of baby snuggles in that case – gimme, gimme!" She abandoned her boots in a heap and held out her arms towards Cora, fingers wiggling. Sam delivered her into Lauren's gentle grasp as Mike unlaced his own trainers and heaved a dramatic sigh.

"Can't you even wait until we've gotten through the front

door, woman?" He shook his head, eyes glinting in amusement.

"Nuh-uh!" she answered, shaking her own head, eyes never leaving Cora. "I've been looking forward to getting my hands on this gorgeous one for hours! You're not spoiling my fun."

A smile spread across my face as I found myself caught up in their light, easy banter. I privately chided myself for not reaching out to Lauren sooner. The coolness between us had been my doing. My jealousy of the perfect family she had provided for Mike, so easily – whilst I was failing to do the same – had caused me to avoid her. I hoped it wasn't too late to do better.

She turned to face me. "Tessa, you look *amazing*, by the way! How do you do it? I'm so jealous!"

She looked me up and down while bouncing Cora gently in her arms. My baby gurgled away happily at her admirer.

"You really do look great," agreed Mike with a mischievous grin. "Please – do tell her how you do it!" He sniggered, but his eyes were full of warmth. Lauren – with no arm free to swing – kicked out at him, and we all shared a chuckle. My cheeks glowed with pride.

This evening might actually be fun, I dared to think.

10

SAM

PRESENT DAY

The officers' eyes hadn't strayed from my face. A queasy feeling had come over me, my attempt to appear impassive now beyond hope. My mind tumbled down a rabbit hole of memories. The voice in my head was now at full volume, taunting me. *Just what* are *you capable of, though, Sam? Are they on to something?*

What if they believed *I* was guilty? Would they still do everything possible to help find my baby and discover just what had happened to my wife? My desperation to project my actual innocence made it feel like I was putting on an act. Panic rose. What if the officers were picking up on something I didn't even know I was hiding?

I remembered seeing it in a documentary once, that trained officers could tell if someone was lying just by the direction that their eyes moved in when questioned. The suspect would lift their eyes, shifting to the left or right, recalling or inventing. I focused on keeping my eyes fixed straight ahead, then thought better of that, too. Would that seem more forced? Would that mean something else to them?

Maybe they know something you don't.

"Well?" DI Garcia was clearly losing patience. I attempted to speak, unsure of what I was going to say, but my tongue had become so dry it felt too big for my mouth.

"Could I have some water, please?" I choked out.

DS Sanders glanced at his colleague, annoyance tightening Garcia's features. He nodded once, waiting as the older man got up from his chair and left the room. I could feel the detective's eyes boring into me, so I fixed my focus on the table for the second time that day, sucking in air. I tried to arrange my thoughts before I let anything get as far as my mouth.

DS Sanders returned with my tepid water, crushing the plastic cup slightly in his grip, and placed it in front of me. A splash of water pooled on the surface of the table. Snatching up the flimsy cup, I gulped back the liquid with urgency. Even with its stale taste, it was nectar to my parched mouth, but it failed to quench my thirst. As I worked to clear my throat and figure out where to begin, my fingertips automatically searched out my scars. I tumbled back in time – that little boy in the doctor's office all over again – trying to find words to explain something I had no understanding of. As if reading my thoughts, DS Sanders broke into my memories.

"Perhaps you want to begin by telling us a little about your condition ... what the symptoms are?" he pushed.

I took a deep breath and cleared my throat again ...

"They're called parasomnias," I began, attempting to keep the quiver from my voice. "They started shortly after my father passed away when I was a child." I rubbed harder at the scars, nerves tingling. The detectives watched me closely, showing no sign of sympathy. Not that I was expecting any, but still ... a shard of sadness pricked my heart.

"The doctors believe that's what triggered them. Why they started, anyway. They worsen if I'm particularly stressed or overtired, ironic as it is." I continued, "Sometimes it's as simple as talking or shouting in my sleep; other times, it can go a bit ... further." I swallowed past the lump forming in my throat and gave a shrug, hoping that explanation might satisfy their inquiry into my dark secret. Of course, it didn't.

"And when you say a bit further?" DS Sanders prodded for more.

"Erm ..." I raised my eyebrows as if trying to think back, hoping to play the situation down. "On the odd occasion I've been found sleepwalking, talking to people who aren't there, that kind of stuff. It's usually during a nightmare, so I can wake up pretty freaked out, especially as it can be a bit of a shock when I wake up somewhere other than my bed, to say the least." I gave a half smile, hoping they would show some empathy, view me as the victim – the poor guy who suffered night terrors.

They didn't. Garcia didn't miss a beat, going straight for the jugular. "When you have these ... para ... your episodes, have they ever caused you to be violent?" He cocked his head.

If my cheeks were beetroot before, they were now molten lava. I wondered if they had any information or if they were just fishing, hoping I would bite. I was trapped – a wounded animal backed into a corner. I didn't want them to waste time focusing on me, so decided to tell them what they wanted to hear.

"Erm ... unfortunately, I don't know what I'm doing whilst they're happening. And so ..." I swallowed hard. "If someone tries to help, well, that can mean ... I can end up ... accidentally hurting them."

"How many times has this happened? Do you *accidentally* hurt people regularly?" DI Garcia spat the words at me.

I glared at him, my chest rising and falling too rapidly. "No. It's only happened once or twice. Like I said, I have no control of what I'm doing while I'm sleeping, Detective. Do you have control over what you dream?"

"It was just a question." He lifted his hands, showing his palms. "Seems you struggle with a temper that you can't control, too." He tilted his head, wide eyed.

The desire to wipe the satisfied look off his face was staggering.

"Not really." I tried to keep my retort light, devoid of any anger. "Just not seeing how any of this is relevant."

"Because, Mr Fulford, your wife has been murdered, and your child is missing. We then come across a piece of information that tells us you have a history of violence. Which you *conveniently* forgot to mention."

I froze, stunned. "A history of violence?" I gasped back at him. "That's hardly the case. I'm not some common criminal. I suffer from a condition! You can ask my GP!" My voice was rising against my efforts to stop it.

"No, you're right there, nothing common about this." His taunting was not subtle. "And we absolutely will be calling on your GP, don't you worry about that." His tone, openly patronising, made his point. To him, I was nothing but a violent scumbag with a condition I used as an excuse – and a prime suspect.

"I would *never* have hurt them." I felt winded in my desperation to be believed. The person they saw me as ... that was not me.

"But you *have* hurt women in the past?" The challenge came from Sanders this time. His tone came gentler, but his eyes held sharp accusation. I wondered whether he'd mastered his emotions with his years of experience or just genuinely gave less of a shit.

I screwed up my face, scrunching my eyes closed and pushing the tips of my fingers into them.

"Yes," I conceded, trying to keep my composure. "But not

in the way that you're making out." A hot poker drilled through my brain. The ridiculous game of cat and mouse was infuriating. I knew that as exhaustion overwhelmed me, I could only evade their trap for so long.

I snapped my head up, a stunningly obvious question suddenly slapping me in the face. One I should have asked right from the start. "How did you find out about my condition?"

"It isn't really relevant where we got the information, Mr Fulford, just that we will need to be made aware of anything that could potentially be important to the case."

"Of course it's bloody relevant," I ranted, exasperated by his attempt to brush it off. "Whoever told you about it clearly wants you to think of me as some sort of violent bully! It means you're wasting time with me while my daughter is out there with god knows who!" I threw my hands in the air, the fury overtaking me, shaking with frustration.

"Can *you* think of anyone who may see you like that, Mr Fulford?" he asked, his tone mocking. "Maybe they've taken your daughter for what they believe to be her safety?"

"Her safety?" I snapped back. I narrowed my eyes. "No. Absolutely not!" But my brain was processing the idea.

Lindy.

I dismissed the thought once again. She wouldn't. We hadn't been in contact for years. Why would she suddenly decide to reappear now? My brain whirred, but my thoughts were jumbled. So few people even knew about my condition. Who could have passed such intimate knowledge of me to the wrong person, someone who would use it against me?

"Well, if you do think of anyone – or anything else – perhaps you could be the first to tell us." Open contempt dripped from Garcia's voice.

"And maybe you could do some actual work on finding

my wife's killer and my missing daughter," I retorted with a snarl, slamming my fists onto the flimsy tabletop.

"Exactly what we are doing, Mr Fulford." His eyes flashed as they lifted from my clenched fists and bored into me. His accusation was clear. I despised the man and his know-it-all attitude. *You know fuck all!* I silently seethed.

"Is there anything else I can help with, or is that it?" I growled, throwing the sarcasm back at him. "Am I free to go?" I scraped my chair back from the table, not waiting for an answer.

"Oh, you can go, Mr Fulford. Just nowhere too far." He narrowed his eyes and cocked his head. "I've a feeling we may have a few more questions for you in the near future. It would be in your interest if you're easy for us to track down." His smile was predatory, and I felt every inch his prey.

I MADE my way from the station, a headache brewing within the dense fog of confusion. How on earth had I ended up in this situation? *Of course I would never have hurt Tessa*, I reassured myself. As the cool evening air crept over my skin, so did a prickle of doubt.

No! I stamped the seed of thought down before it had time to germinate.

I unlocked my car and slid behind the wheel. For a fraction of a second, my mind forgot the nightmare I was trapped in as I planned my route home. When reality slammed into me once again, I felt the urge to lash out. But I refused to play into Garcia's hands, so I shoved the keys into the ignition and reversed out of the space, ready to make my way back to Mike's.

As I pulled out of the car park, I remembered Mike's

strange behaviour earlier. In my haste to get to the station, I'd never asked him what was going on.

Maybe he knew the police were looking for me and was worried about why. I shook off my concerns once again, refusing to believe the day could possibly have any more shit in store for me.

11

TESSA

TWO MONTHS PREVIOUS

The first strains of Cora's squalling broke my slumber. I squinted at the daylight creeping around the curtains and chased after the memory of my dream, but it danced away, just out of reach.

I stretched to retrieve my phone and tapped the screen to wake it. I blinked, trying to clear my bleary eyes, and took in the time displayed on the small screen.

7:43 a.m.

Memories of the previous night surfaced, a warm glow within me. Cora had loved every second of the attention, gurgling and cooing her way into everyone's affections. She'd finally burned herself out and crashed in Lauren's arms at around eight thirty – much to Lauren's delight. Thrilled to have my arms free for a couple of hours, I had relaxed into their company.

Sam opened the second bottle of wine after we finished dinner. Out of habit, he started to pour me a glass along with the others.

"Oh, I totally forgot." He laughed and then handed Mike and Lauren full glasses, leaving mine half-empty.

I sighed a dramatic sigh. "The price you pay for being a mother, hey?" I smiled at Lauren.

"One won't hurt," Lauren replied seriously.

"I'd love one, but I'm still breastfeeding." I shrugged.

"Ah, I used to have a small glass occasionally while I was feeding mine." She gazed down at Cora snoring softly in her arms. "Might even help her to sleep a little longer." She raised her eyebrows in a conspiratorial smile. "Don't be so hard on yourself, Tessa. You deserve a break, too. You won't get any judgement from us."

Sam and Mike nodded in agreement.

"If you fancy a glass, Tessa, have it," Sam encouraged. "I can always add some lemonade for you if you'd feel better about it?"

I looked around at their warm, smiling faces, caught up in the joy of the moment.

"Oh, bugger it, why not!" I threw my arms up in defeat, face splitting into a huge grin. "Just a *small* drop of wine with lots of lemonade, though, Sam." I wagged my finger at him.

"Yes, ma'am!" he called over his shoulder, saluting me as he left the room with my glass.

My neglected body received the one small glass of wine with gratitude, the tiny dose of alcohol enough to give me that glorious floaty sensation after so many months teetotal. I felt better than I had in longer than I could remember and slid with ease into the buzz of conversation, laughter, and wine. Cora awoke shortly after I'd finished my drink, delighted to find her adoring fans still present.

"I'd better get her into her PJs." I pushed myself up from the sofa, feeling slightly light-headed, and drifted over to where Lauren snuggled with her.

"Do you want a hand?" Lauren beamed up at me.

"Sure." I nodded eagerly. The confidence the small amount of wine had provoked, and a desire to make amends for always having been so closed off, made me feel unusually open. I desperately wanted her friendship now. A comrade – someone else familiar with the mad journey of motherhood. I loved Bella, but things had shifted since I'd fallen pregnant. The easy flow of conversation had dried up, and we were no longer able to understand each other. Anyway, she was moving away. Time to adjust to life without her.

Sam and Mike were so close. I'd always been envious of their easy friendship. I'd never have admitted it to anyone, but I'd recently played out daydreams of Lauren and I becoming equally close. Forming an unshakable foursome. I'd always held her at arm's length whilst she had the family I had so desperately desired. But now that Sam and I had our own family, the idea of having Lauren around more became more appealing. Sam had always wanted us to spend more time together. With my jealousy out of the way, I was keen on the possibility of a real friendship.

We chatted easily on the way up to Cora's room together. Lauren wound up cooing over the contents of Cora's wardrobe, reminiscing about her own children being small enough to fit into the miniature clothes, whilst I changed my baby.

Lauren's shrieks of delight at each of the tiny pieces of clothing were infectious, and I found myself giggling along at her reaction to each item she held up. Even Cora seemed to be amused at the display and would watch closely as her clothing was inspected, awaiting Lauren's screeches, her little arms and legs going crazy in response to the game.

"Oh, I'm so jealous!" she whined, taking another sip of her drink. "It's amazing when they're so small, isn't it? The love is just overwhelming." She gazed across at Cora, eyes glazed.

"It really is," I agreed, feeling a swell of love rise within me. "You think you're prepared, but you have no idea until you meet them, do you?" I lifted Cora into my arms and cradled her close, breathing her in.

"Oh, god, no." Lauren flicked off the light as we left the room, heading towards the stairs. The sound of the men laughing and chatting loudly echoed in the kitchen, but we returned to the cosy warmth of the living room. I laid Cora on her play mat and watched her stretch out, kicking her chubby legs and enjoying her freedom.

"Fucking hard, too, though, right?" She rolled her eyes and flopped back onto the sofa, words slightly slurred. For a second or two, I was completely taken aback. I'd never breathed a word to anyone about how tough I had found motherhood to be, wary even of opening up to Sam about the full extent of my struggles, assuming that it was just me, that I was just a spectacular failure.

Lauren shifted around, uncomfortable at my lack of response, and spluttered, "I mean ... not for *everyone*, I guess ... You probably have it all completely under control ... just look at your spotless house ... I just ..."

"*So* fucking hard!" I cut her off, making the decision that I could trust and confide in this woman. "I spend so much of the time feeling like a *complete* failure at this. I'm sure I'm the worst mother in the world," I admitted, embarrassed as I realised my eyes were filling.

Lauren let out a snort. "Join the club!" she squawked. "It's only the hardest job in the world, comes with no experience, no training, and no bloody pay cheque. Oh, and you're on shift twenty-four seven. I still feel like I'm failing on a regular basis." She threw up her hands. "But if this gorgeous little one is anything to go by, you must be doing something right." She lowered herself onto the floor next to Cora and tickled her tummy, and Cora wiggled with joy. I breathed out a long sigh, my shoulders loosening slightly.

"She just cries so much. I'm afraid to leave the house with her most of the time. And I'm *so* tired. I often can't even remember what I've actually done and what I've dreamt. I struggle to function some days, and the house is always a bloody state! I feel lazy and incapable of taking care of one tiny baby. I'm so bloody useless."

As if someone had pulled a stopper, the truth spilled out of me. I snapped my jaw shut, aghast at how much I'd just blurted out. Lauren plopped down next to me on the sofa in one swift movement.

"Oh, Tessa! It's totally normal to feel like that," she soothed, placing her hand over mine. Her face was the definition of concern and empathy. "We all lose control when a baby arrives. It's totally life changing and turns everything upside down. If anyone tells you they didn't struggle, they're lying to you!" She gave my hand a tight squeeze and moved her head to fix her earnest gaze onto mine.

"You're doing great, and that little girl is living, breathing proof of that." Her smile was full of warmth, and I could smell the alcohol on the heat of her breath.

"Let's meet up. Go out somewhere, have lunch. I'll help with Cora, and you'll see you're doing great."

I swiped at my watery eyes and let my shoulders sag. Lauren's words had just lifted a tonne weight from my back. Maybe I wasn't as alone in it all as I'd thought I was.

Cora's whines became more urgent, her frustration rising at my lack of response, as I basked in the memories of the previous evening.

"Good morning, beautiful!" I cooed at her, lifting her

small body from her crib and bringing her into our bed. "That was a super sleep, just what Mummy needed." I nuzzled her cheek, laughing as she tried to latch to my nose.

"Maybe you enjoy a drop of wine as much as Mummy does." I stroked her hair as she began her feed.

I snuggled back against my pillows, cradling our baby, the sound of my husband's soft snores floating around us. Contentment washed over me. I could finally see a pinprick of light in the never-ending darkness.

"I think everything might just be okay," I whispered to Cora, pressing my nose into her hair and breathing in her scent.

12

SAM

PRESENT DAY

Pulling up in front of Mike and Lauren's house, I wrenched the handbrake, glad to have once again put space between myself and the wretched police station. I hauled myself from the car, stretching out my back and playing out Mike's reaction to my latest conversation with the police in my mind. I imagined his face – full of outrage on my behalf. Once they had been brought up to speed, I was going to allow myself the time to have a hot shower and regroup, I decided. Wash the stench of that mire from my skin and decide my next move.

I was halfway up the front path when I flinched at the front door springing open. Mike stepped outside, pulling the door closed behind him.

"Any news?" He looked at me expectantly, eyes searching my face.

"Only that the people in charge of the case are arseholes," I growled, outrage simmering once again.

"Nothing on Cora, then?" he questioned, rubbing the back of his neck.

Sharp guilt ripped through me – that should have been the first thing I reported.

"No. Nothing," I replied. I was completely drained and desperate to be under the hot jets of water.

"Sam, there isn't an easy way to say this, so I'm just going to come right out with it."

My brows dipped, almost meeting as I waited for him to look at me, but his eyes darted around. Anguish was etched onto his face. He seemed to have aged in the few hours I'd been gone.

"Erm, Lauren feels that it may be better if you ... erm, had somewhere ... quieter to stay." He shifted his weight from one foot to the other, bereft of his usual confidence. He looked more uncomfortable than I had ever seen him.

"Quieter?" I questioned, screwing my face up.

"Yeah. You know, without the kids under your feet and the constant queue for the bathroom." He attempted a smile, but it didn't reach his eyes.

"I really don't mind," I replied too quickly. An uncomfortable sensation crept over my body. "In fact, I could use the company – even the noise – as a distraction, to be honest. I don't think I could handle silence." I gave a half smile. My heart pounded as I watched him visibly squirm in front of me, picking non-existent bits of fluff from his jumper.

"Mike, how about you cut the crap and tell me what's really going on here?" I shook my head against the weary exhaustion of the day clenching me in its grip. "You're my best mate; just tell me."

"Fuck!" Mike kicked at the ground, causing me to start. His face was the definition of wretched, and he covered it with both hands before running them back through his hair.

"Lauren has asked that you find somewhere else to stay," he blurted. His cheeks glowed with heat in the cold evening air, and his eyes held conflict. I stepped back in confusion, brow creased.

"What? Why?" I thought back to that morning, trying to work out what I could have done wrong.

"She just thinks we would all be more ... comfortable." The irony was not lost on me. I had never seen my best friend look *less* comfortable. A dense fog of confusion clung to my senses.

"Why would you turn your backs on me right now? When I need you more than ev—"

As I looked up at Mike, the realisation slammed into my chest like a physical blow. The air was too thick to breathe.

"She thinks that *I* hurt them?" The words came out barely more than a whisper. Pins and needles crept up my legs; they wobbled beneath me. "Is that what you think, too, Mike?" I forced the question out past breathless shock.

"No, no. Of course not, mate!" He rubbed his hands over his miserable face again. "Neither does Lauren really. She's just concerned about your sleep thing – worried that this might flare it up, I guess. We've paid for a room for you at the ..."

My breath caught in my throat, and I had the sudden feeling that I might throw up, right there on Mike's front path. His words were drowned out by the whooshing of blood in my ears. I leaned forwards, resting my hands on my thighs.

"Was it her?" My face screwed up in pain as I asked the question – I wasn't sure I wanted the answer.

Confusion gripped his expression. A flame of doubt ignited in me for a split second, but it was instantly extinguished by the obvious question: *Who else could it have been?*

"She told the fucking police!" I snarled. "How could you let her do that to me?" The blood had drained from my body; molten fury ran through my veins in its place. Mike was studying my face, his was a mask of confusion – my furnace of rage flared.

"Because of *you* two, the police are wasting their time on *me*, insinuating all sorts ... all sorts ... when what they should be doing is anything else. Anything to find the people who actually did this, to find my daughter." I spat the words at him, despising him in that moment. "She could be with *anyone*. But you run back to your little wife, cosy up together, and shut your door in my face now you've fucked me over." The words erupted from me in a roiling fury beyond my control.

"But know this, Mike, if they do anything to hurt my baby whilst the police are screwing around with questioning me, it's on you! You and your ... your *bitch* of a wife! And I will not be responsible for my actions. How fucking dare you!"

A dark cloud, matching my own fury, drifted over his confused expression.

"I don't know who you think told the police what, but I can tell you, nothing came from us." His voice was low and even, laced with rage. "Lauren just wants to keep the kids out of all of it. It's just weird that you're so ... calm. You know I wanted to help. Of course. But you think you can stand on *my* doorstep? And threaten *my family*" – he hissed the words at me – "and then still expect my support ... well, you can shove it, Sam. I'd get the hell off my property if I were you, before I really do contact the police." He stood simmering for a breath before turning on his heel, striding the few steps to his front door, and slamming it behind him.

Sadness trickled through me as my anger slowly deflated. It must have been them who had betrayed me, I thought. But they were still my best friends. Without them, and with my baby still missing, I was alone in this nightmare. I let out a yelp of frustration and kicked out at the closest thing to me. It happened to be a tree with a pretty sturdy trunk, which didn't so much as quiver at my attack.

"FUCK!" I screamed. I heard a snicking sound; my toes instantly beginning to throb. I hobbled back in the direction of my car, feeling as wretched as Mike had looked just moments before. Did I appear calm? That certainly wasn't my experience. My skin stung from their betrayal. That house, the family inside it, that earlier the same day had been my sanctuary, now felt tainted, somehow yet another perpetrator of this horror. A neighbour's curtains twitched. I glared at the window but saw nothing but the reflection of the street. I fought the urge to hurl abuse likely unwarranted.

I slid behind the wheel of my car and fired up the engine, which ticked, not yet having had the chance to cool. I revved the engine hard and pulled away in a screech of tyres, leaving a cloud in my wake.

As I neared the end of the street, a realisation hit me – I had no idea where I was headed. Usually when I needed to get away, I'd make a stop at Dad's spot. But that placed harboured enough pain and trauma already; it felt wrong to heap this on. The gravity of the situation dawned on me. My wife was dead. My child, missing. I was the primary, the only, suspect. Even my best friend was regarding me with suspicion. I had no one. Feeling unable to remain in control, I pulled over and allowed the emotions to overwhelm me.

My phone vibrated in my pocket. My heart skipped as hope swelled. It had to be Mike, calling to apologise, begging me to come back and share a beer with him.

The name Keith flashed across the screen. My brow creased as I stared down at the ringing phone in my hand, trying to place this name that somehow wasn't *Mike*. Then my heart hammered. I knew who it was. Heat crept over me as I imagined he knew I was ignoring his call – could sense my desperation to avoid the conversation. The phone stopped ringing, and I let out my breath, then flinched as it instantly started up again. I couldn't take this call; what could I say? He would want answers I couldn't offer. His daughter was dead, his grandchild missing, all while I walked around unscathed.

A jolt of realisation left me reeling – the reason I couldn't speak to my father-in-law was the same reason I was so furious with the police and with Mike. Somehow, a terrible seed *had* sprouted. I had to ask myself the very question that I had been running from all day.

Did I do this?

13

TESSA

TWO MONTHS PREVIOUS

The blissful night's sleep that Cora had treated me to turned out to be a one-off. She'd lulled me into a false sense of hope. Perhaps we'd turned a corner with her sleep pattern. Alas, my eyes once again met the clock faithfully at every hour of the night. As I sat curled on the sofa, rocking her in the darkness, thinking of the empty day ahead, the cold, familiar dread snaked itself around my body. My day had begun two hours earlier, and Sam would be leaving for his job as a successful company accountant shortly. The hours of loneliness before he returned stretched before me. He would arrive home – probably late, it was that time of year, he'd say – and attempt to relate the details of his day. I would nod along, nowhere near intelligent enough to understand even the basics of what he was sharing.

As the accustomed feeling of sadness washed over me, hot tears pricked at my eyes. I didn't want to go back to this place. I blinked them away and, before I could change my mind, felt around blindly for my phone with my free hand. The phone lit up on command, and the light from the tiny screen seemed blinding to my unadjusted eyes. I squinted at it, turning the screen away from Cora, who slept peacefully in my arms, desperate not to disturb her. She didn't stir. A couple of quick swipes of the screen and the blank space for the message stared back at me, Lauren's name and number displayed at the top.

Morning, I don't suppose you fancy ...

I cringed at my own words and deleted the message, my mind clouding with doubt.

Maybe I shouldn't bother her. Why would she want to see me? She probably has loads of friends of her own.

I chewed my lip and reminded myself of the day ahead. The evening we'd spent together. Sucking in a deep breath, I quickly tapped out a message without giving myself time to overthink.

> Hey, I'm at a bit of a loose end today and just wondered if you fancied meeting for a coffee or lunch? Would be lovely to catch up with you. I know Cora would love it too! =0)
> T. xx

I pressed send before I had even read it back, knowing otherwise I'd only pore over it and change it at least a dozen more times before I sent it. I opened up my social media, scrolling to distract myself from waiting for her reply. Nothing new had been posted from when I had been scrolling only half an hour before, most of the world still sleeping. Dropping the phone onto the sofa, I rested my head back, closing my eyes.

Five minutes passed with no reply. Was it too early to text someone? I checked the time on my phone with a rising unease that I hadn't looked before sending the message. 7:36 a.m. It was fine; Lauren would be up. I unlocked the screen once again and opened the message that I had sent. The two blue ticks confirmed that she'd read it. I dropped my phone and laid my head back once again.

The buzz of my phone woke me from the light sleep that I must have slipped into. I checked on Cora. She lay fast asleep in my arms, lips parted slightly where her dummy had dropped from her mouth. I reached over and grabbed for my phone, the screen still lit with the new message notification. I tapped to open it, my nerves tingling with hope.

> Hey Tessa, I would have absolutely loved to but unfortunately, we are all being taken down one by one with an awful bug! E is off school today so stuck at home obeying her every command! Hopefully sort something soon though. Big (non-contagious) kisses to Cora. xx

I reread her message a couple of times and wondered if they really did have a bug or if it was just an excuse not to have to meet with me.

"Oh, stop feeling so bloody sorry for yourself, Tessa!" I muttered, rolling my eyes at my own dramatics. Still, my stomach sank with the disappointment. The first light of the day was filtering into the room as if on a dimmer switch. My arm was cold and numb, and my body ached from sitting still for too long. My phone buzzed once again, notifying me of a new message. Bella's name filled the top of the screen. A funny feeling welled at the sight of her name, but I couldn't put my finger on what it was. Brushing it off, I opened the message.

> Hi Tessa, I have a bit of time to kill today between meetings, thought we should do something as I'll soon be jetting off. Shall we say 11ish? Xx

I searched for an excuse not to go, unsure why I was so

reluctant. I felt a stab of annoyance. She assumed that I would be free, which of course I was, but I wished I could tell her I was busy – meeting Lauren. Another stab, now of guilt. My friend was trying to arrange to see me before she left. Nothing more to it. And wasn't this what I wanted? To make plans, not sit at home alone all day? *It's just tiredness making me sensitive over nothing*, I consoled myself, shaking off the guilt and typing out my reply to Bella.

> Sounds good, we could do with getting some fresh air so shall we meet at the coffee shop on the corner? T. xx

The thought of going out made me nervous, but it was only a couple of streets away. I couldn't bear seeing the judgement on Bella's face again, her feeling the need to clean my house. Her perfection set my shortcomings in stark relief. I was in awe of her confident independence, often slyly watching her comings and goings from my windows as I paced with an unsettled Cora. I sometimes wondered about her past, what had shaped her to be the driven, self-sufficient woman I had come to know. I envied her assertive nature, along with most things about her. But I had been doing so much better; this was just the next step. Cora was almost seven weeks now. High time I embraced my new life instead of obsessing over Bella's. Cora wiggled in my arms, unsticking her sweaty face from my arm and throwing her arms above her head in a stretch. I gazed at her, the way her eyes fluttered open. She blinked a couple of times before fixing her eyes on me.

"Morning, sleeping beauty. Fancy a little trip out today?" I asked her warmly. "We can come straight home if it gets too much, can't we?" I nuzzled into her cheek. She wiggled. The corners of her mouth twitched, and her eyes lit up with her first dazzling smile. I gasped, scooping her up and swinging her around. "Oh, my clever little angel!" I gushed at her. "You smiled at Mummy!"

She stared back at me, face blank, wondering what all the fuss was about.

A COUPLE OF HOURS LATER, having managed a successful if super quick shower whilst distracting Cora – now resting in her Moses basket on the bathroom floor – with every nursery rhyme I could think of, we were ready to leave the house.

Cora, bundled up in her pram as if we were about to face a blizzard, gurgled happily as we set off. Her changing bag weighed with such bulk on my back I felt I might topple backwards with the slightest gust.

The aroma of fresh coffee and pastries hit me as I rounded the corner, and my mouth watered. Such liberation, having escaped the walls of our house, my safe haven, that I had unwittingly become a prisoner in. I felt a sense of pride that we had made it this far. I struggled to hold open the heavy door to the coffee shop and push Cora's wide pram through the opening, but the wheels caught, jamming it to a stop. A few people glanced up. Heat crept over me; my skin flushed. A middle-aged man who was in the queue at the counter dashed over and pushed the door back out of the way.

"Oh, thank you so much." I flashed him an awkward smile as I pushed the pram through.

"No problem." He nodded with a warm smile, standing back out of the way. "My wife and I have twins. We gave up trying to get in anywhere with a double pushchair." He rolled his eyes.

I gave him a sympathetic look and made my way inside, the sudden warmth enveloping me. A layer of sweat formed

on my skin. I cast my eyes around the bustle of busy tables
and spotted Bella tucked away at the back. I navigated the
pram as best I could, disturbing as few of the other customers
as possible. I found myself continually having to mutter
"sorry" and "excuse me, please", leaving a seeming Mexican
wave in my wake as I reached Bella's table. I looked up,
sweaty and flustered, to find Bella's eyes were firmly fixed on
me. Coffee cup in hand, she was a picture of calm serenity.
But her face read as if I were something nasty that she had
stepped in.

In a blink, the expression vanished, replaced by a wide
grin. I questioned myself, certain I must have imagined the
way she had been looking at me before, dismissing my para-
noia. As we exchanged greetings and I shrugged off my
unnecessary winter coat, Cora let out a loud whine. A knot
formed in my stomach. Bella's smile slipped slightly at the
noise. As I lifted Cora from the pram, I realised the reason for
her moans. Both her outfit and pram sheets had a wet yellow
sludge smudged into the fabric. The smell of baby poo filled
my nostrils at the same time that I noticed I'd managed to get
it on my hand too. As I held my squirming child away from
my body to stop the sludge contaminating anything else, she
began to squeal.

I muttered my apologies to Bella and grabbed the
changing bag, trying to avoid meeting her eye. Disgusted
horror radiated from her. Squeezing back through the gaps
between tables towards the loos as quickly as I could, I
disrupted everyone again, narrowly avoiding bashing one
person over the head with my huge bag. One thought was
doing a loop in my brain, over and over.

I wish I had stayed at home.

14

SAM

PRESENT DAY

I'd driven the few streets over to the hotel as if drunk, weaving all over the road. My loss of composure, ricocheting between furious outrage and bitter, gutwrenching sobs, had left me woefully inept at manoeuvring a vehicle. Only after a near miss with a cyclist did I snap to my senses, trembling as I apologised profusely through his string of curses.

The receptionist eyed me through her bright, welcoming smile. In her boredom, my exhausted, red-rimmed eyes and deflated demeanour presented an intriguing distraction. I offered up my bank card, unaware of which hotel Mike and Lauren had paid for and unwilling to accept their gesture of guilt. My jaw clenched; nostrils flared at the thought of them.

I found my room and stumbled through the door, legs barely able to support me. My phone buzzed again. I yanked it from my pocket, cutting the call and putting it on silent before thrusting it onto the bed. I needed to shower, knew I should eat. But my head pounded, and I was desperate to close my eyes, just for a minute. I was certain I wouldn't sleep; I'd just lie down until my head cleared a little.

I WOKE WITH A JOLT, a shout resounding through my brain. I couldn't bring anything into focus, to decipher where I was. I blinked repeatedly, trying to clear my vision and pinpoint something. My breathing was rapid, and my heart pounded painfully. A fuzzy realisation swam into focus: I was being attacked. I lifted my head, my bleary eyes making out the shape of a person holding something out in front of their body. A gun?

My thoughts were coming too fast for me to process. This was it, I thought. Whoever killed Tessa had tracked me down and was coming after me now, too. At least that meant I was innocent. My thoughts raced in overdrive through a brief moment of relief. Now I had to fight. Cora needed me; otherwise, this person, whoever they were, had won. No one else would hunt for her relentlessly like I would. How long would it take for the police to just write her off? Another missing child. I owed it to Tessa.

I was more afraid than I'd ever been in my life, but I knew what I had to do. I threw myself forward, charging at the intruder, launching my entire body weight at him in the hope that I could at least knock him off balance and get the gun away from him somehow. Before my body made contact with his, something slammed into my shoulder and knocked me backwards, off my feet. As the pain took over every nerve in my body, I tried to scream, but no sound escaped.

He shot me; I've been shot.

It was a strange sensation, not at all what I'd imagine. A feeling of cramps over my entire body – in every muscle at the same time, agony radiating from my shoulder. I felt my bladder release its hold; a warm sensation passed over my crotch. For a second, I wondered who would find my urine-soaked body. Who would clear it up?

The pain seemed to ease, so I guessed I must be losing consciousness. My head swam, and I felt no sense of peace. My last thoughts were of Cora, now so completely alone in the world.

"I'm so sorry, baby!" I wasn't sure if the words made it out of my mouth, or if it was just a thought.

Everything went black.

15

TESSA

TWO MONTHS PREVIOUS

For once, I was thankful for my overcautious nature. I had Cora cleaned up – as best I could manage with a packet of wipes – and in a clean outfit. Not as cute as the one I'd had her in, but at least she was no longer covered in poo. I wrapped up her soiled clothes in a nappy sack and put them back into the changing bag, thankful that I still had another change of clothes, plus a clean pram sheet, tucked inside. *It's worth looking like a tortoise*, I told myself, rolling my eyes.

To my saviour, I gave my reflection a once-over in the grime-smeared bathroom mirror as I washed my hands. A small fleck of yellow poo dotted my cheek like a freckle. I swiped at it, smudging it across my face, and thanked god that I'd noticed before I left the bathroom. *How had she even managed to get it on my face?* I wondered, aghast.

I unlocked the door to the pungent baby-changing cubicle and stepped back out into the hot, crowded cafe, threading back through the tables. The morning coffee run was slowly transforming into the lunchtime rush, the crowd never really having dwindled.

The queue was longer than when I'd arrived, and the thought of having to stand in it, waiting for my order, suddenly seemed overwhelming. I got back to our table, certain I was giving off an odour of sweat and baby poo. I pulled the clean pram sheet out of the changing bag. Swapping it over with my one free hand whilst keeping a tight hold on Cora in my other arm was a painful challenge. Had I not already sunk so low, I probably would have dissolved into tears. I wished Bella would offer to help but couldn't bring myself to ask. *Can't risk blemishing her pristine clothing, so I already know her answer*, I thought bitchily as sweat beaded on my lip.

Finally, after I'd battled both sheets, the soiled one was off and replaced, if not brilliantly, with the clean.

I flopped into the empty chair with Cora still balanced in my aching arm and rested her weight on my legs. A sense of pride that I had managed the disastrous situation lifted me a little. We'd come out of it fairly unscathed. I imagined giggling with Lauren about the scene next time I saw her. We would both find it hilarious, going on to share tales of horror caused by our bundles of joy.

"Something funny?" Bella questioned, studying my face. I prayed that I really had wiped the poo off properly. I realised I was grinning and that Bella was still awaiting an answer. I rearranged my face into a neutral expression and shook my head.

"No, nothing." I sighed. "Just the joys of parenthood. You're so lucky you can enjoy a hot coffee without a poonami to contend with mid drink!" I widened my eyes dramatically and forced a little laugh, waiting for her to agree, allowing her the chance to drop in some sarcasm as usual to break the tension.

A thunderous look crossed her face. She regarded me for a second or so before she replied.

"Your choice, Tessa, no one *forces* you to have them." Her lip curled, and her words seemed curt. I was stung by her misinterpretation of my comment, as well as taken aback.

"Oh, I know. I *absolutely* wouldn't be without her," I began to justify myself. "I just meant I don't think you're ever prepared for how much life changes with a child around." I smiled guiltily down at Cora, hoping to make it clear that I felt no regret.

"I guess not." Bella shrugged, pursing her lips. "No sleep, no alcohol, no adult time, no fun!" She widened her eyes in mock horror. "Why you would make that choice is beyond me." She shook her head, her perfect tumble of dark hair shimmering under the artificial lighting.

Bella's bluntness around childbearing often shocked me. She'd never made an attempt to cover her feelings of contempt, or consider that I might not feel the same way. Her derogatory comments had shocked me at first, along with her behaviour towards children. I'd even hesitated at the thought of pursuing our friendship, debating whether I could form a true bond with someone so different to me. But we *had* seemed to bond, and somehow, despite our differences, we just seemed to gel, regardless of her not being a natural at forming friendship, either.

I'd scolded myself. Of course she was entitled to her own feelings and life choices, too. I myself hated the assumption that all women wanted children, along with the pressure of other people's nosey questions when it came to marriage and children. Questions were somehow deemed socially accept-able. Bella and I seemed to occupy opposite poles, yet she was the one person I could trust and rely on.

Plus – and this I hated to admit – her lack of desire for a child meant one less thing for me to be jealous of. It was refreshing, whilst I was battling infertility, to be certain she wasn't going to pop up with some surprise pregnancy, leaving me reeling at the joyful announcement. Such had happened too many times before with colleagues and acquaintances. Nor was she going to be questioning me, pushing to find out when I planned to finally start a family of my own. Being around Bella had felt safe; the lack of that safety was why I'd never been able to allow Lauren too close.

Grateful for her understanding, and wanting to move to a safer subject – having made clear I did not regret my daughter – my face split into a goofy grin. "She smiled at me for the first time this morning." I beamed as I gazed at Cora, recalling the precious moment.

Cora was beginning to make her specific whine, the one I had learned meant she required milk. I unbuttoned my shirt and unclipped my feeding bra, latching my baby before the tenor of her request escalated.

"Is it okay to do that in here?" Bella's eyes darted from side to side, a wild look in them. She scanned the café; it took me a moment to realise what she was referring to.

"Of course it is," I scoffed, filled with indignation. "I'm feeding my baby. It's the most natural thing in the world." But heat rose to my cheeks, and I shifted Cora and tugged at my top to ensure I was covered.

Bella still looked uncomfortable. I reminded myself that she wasn't maternal, that situations such as this were the reason that she didn't want children. I glanced around us before changing the subject again, hoping to put us both at ease. Regardless of her feelings towards my baby, I missed the closeness I had felt to her before my pregnancy, the way we had been drawn together. The pregnancy had shaken things up between us – that had been down to changes I had brought to our relationship. I wanted to fix things.

I asked Bella about her job and the plans for her move. She visibly lit up as she filled me in on the details, eyes firmly fixed on my face. Once again, I was sunk in the swamp of information around her job role. I knew she was high up in a pharmaceutical company – and that she was paid a generous salary – but that was about as far as my understanding went. I pasted on a bright smile, nodding and gushing in all the right places, but my mind drifted. A tiny part of me was glad that she'd never met Sam, that she probably never would now. She was so much more than I could ever be. Striking in both intelligence and beauty. Sam would have to be crazy not to be attracted to her, someone who could match him, be on his level whilst always looking pristine. I would hardly blame him.

I had no wish to compete with my best friend. I squirmed with shame at my spiteful jealousy. Bella had done nothing to justify my thinking of her like that.

She had stopped talking. I wondered how long we'd been in silence. Desperate to fill it once again, I spluttered the first thing that came to mind.

"It all sounds great." I paused. "We'll have to do you a little leaving party. You should meet Mike and Lauren too before you go. We had a great time with them on Saturday evening." I bumbled on, attempting to clear the unease hanging between us. "Sam invited them over. He cleaned the entire house before they arrived. I felt totally spoilt. I binged on far too much Chinese food and even treated myself to a small glass of wine." I felt lighter at the memory.

Her eyes locked onto mine. An expression of shock engulfed her face.

"But you're breastfeeding!" she exclaimed.

"Yeah." My face reddened. I instantly regretted the admission. "But like Lauren said, one small one won't do any harm."

"And Lauren is a healthcare professional, is she?" Bella's perfectly shaped eyebrows rose in question.

"Well, no." I gave a little tinkle of a laugh, attempting to cover the discomfort – knowing she was right and hating myself for my selfish actions. "It was only a tiny bit. Mostly lemonade, really – and just a one-off," I assured her.

I felt like a foolish teenager, like I had been trying to impress her, forge a tighter bond, but instead had been reprimanded. Suddenly guilt ridden, I cringed at the realisation that Bella did work in the healthcare industry. I glanced around, making sure no one else was listening, ready to dial social services on the unfit mother.

"Hmm, well, I guess it's up to you if you think it's worth the risk," Bella muttered, gesturing down at Cora, who'd fallen asleep at my breast and unlatched, leaving my nipple on show. I scrambled to cover myself, feeling exposed in every way, and lowered Cora into her pram.

"Can I get you another coffee? I'm starving," I offered as brightly as I could manage. My cheeks still burned, and I was brimming with guilt. I felt somehow as though I needed to make it up to her.

"I would love a juice, actually, and I'll have a sandwich too if you're having one. It *is* practically lunchtime now." She glanced down at her watch. My guilt flared, and my cheeks burned hotter.

"No problem, I'll grab them!" I spluttered, scraping back my chair so quickly that I almost pushed it right into Cora's pram. She didn't stir. Grabbing my purse, I made my way towards the counter and the ever-growing queue, praying for Cora to remain asleep while I was waiting.

I glanced back towards Bella, who was peering into the pram, checking on Cora. Her eyes snapped up, meeting mine, and a surge of warmth thawed something within me. I smiled warmly at her, but she looked away quickly, obviously embarrassed at her show of affection. I felt guilty that I made such harsh judgements of her at times, didn't always view her in the best light. We were both adjusting to the changes that Cora had brought to our friendship, and she did try to be supportive, even if she didn't always get it right. Hadn't I made my share of mistakes, too, as a new mum?

I resolved to be a better friend as well as mother.

16

SAM

PRESENT DAY

M y eyelids fluttered, my eyes dry and scratchy. A familiar darkness enveloped my mind. Like I'd been having a nightmare. The memory smacked me between the eyes; pain seared through my head. Was I in hospital? Or was he still there? Did he know I wasn't dead? Would he kill me if he realised? The questions bombarding my brain did nothing to ease my throbbing head. My shoulder ached, but not as much as I'd have expected after being shot. I slowly cracked my eyes, hoping that he wouldn't notice if he was still there.

"Can you open your eyes for me? Nice and slowly, no sudden movements." The voice was unfamiliar but full of authority. Relief flooded me. I must be in hospital, on something to relieve my shoulder, which explained the lack of pain.

Cora. I needed to find out if she was okay. I had no idea how long I had been there. My eyes snapped open, expecting to see a white sterile room around me, a doctor ready to run tests on me now that I had awoken.

Instead, I was greeted by the face of a young woman

wearing a police uniform. I was still in the hotel room. My gaze travelled the room, slivers of pain shooting through my eyes, and took in the scene. The mirror was smashed, shards of glass littering the small dressing table in front of it. The bed sheets were strewn around the room, and there were blood smears on the walls. The wall-mounted TV had a crack across the screen. One of my trainers lay abandoned on its side at the foot of the bed.

I lay flat on my back on the floor, my damp trousers sending a chill through my body. For the second time in two days, a stranger asked the simple question.

"Can you tell me your name?"

"Cora?" Her name came out as a croak through my cracked, dry lips as the stranger's brow furrowed. I attempted to shake my head, but pain seared, blurring my vision. "Sam, it's Sam. Do you have Cora? My daughter?" I felt as though I hadn't had a drop of water in days. My desperate question scratched at my throat. I sensed the desperation in my pleading eyes as they studied the officer's face.

Something dawned on the young officer. "No. Not yet, Sam," she replied solemnly. Disappointment threatened to swallow me, but I clung to a tiny strand of hope. "Did he get away?" I rasped.

Confusion slid over her features. "Did who get away?"

"The man who broke into my room." I gestured around at the state of the room. "I think he shot me." I gingerly lifted my opposite hand to my injured shoulder. "I was trying to stop him. Disarm him."

I no longer felt much pain in my shoulder, more like muscle strain or a bruise than a bullet wound. My toes throbbed more from the previous night's altercation with the tree.

The confusion cleared from her face, replaced by a sheepish expression. "Erm, you weren't shot at, sir." The officer didn't meet my eye. "The hotel staff called to report a disturbance. They gave us the key to your room when no one could get an answer, and we found you in here ... trashing the place and thrashing out. I tried to stop you, calm you down, but you ran at me, so I'm afraid I had to use the taser on you."

Her words slowly sank in, but I couldn't summon a response. It couldn't be right. Her eyes finally fixed on mine as she continued on, filling the silence.

"Normally we would've cuffed you, but you seemed to be having some sort of attack, and we weren't sure if you'd require treatment." She spoke quietly and gently, still regarding me as if trying to decide if I did, indeed, require some form of treatment.

"B ... but then, who trashed the room?" I questioned dumbly, still utterly bewildered by her version of events.

"Erm ... we believe you did." The officer cleared her throat, clearly unsure of what to make of the situation. "Were you under the influence of alcohol or drugs last night?"

A cold trickle crept over my body. "What? No, no, I haven't had anything like that," I insisted, trawling back through my memories of the previous night. The fight with Mike, pulling over in the car, the unrelenting calls from Keith, checking in to the cheap hotel, and falling into bed partially dressed. Then nothing. Until I awoke to discover the intruder.

There was a rapping noise and the sound of a door opening. In my daze, I hadn't yet moved from my position on the floor. I raised my head slightly, hearing a mumbled exchange. A second police officer, whose presence, up until this point, I hadn't even been aware of, was stepping aside to allow someone entry into my room. A paramedic who looked like he should have been retired appeared, nodding in response to whatever the officer was informing him of in hushed tones.

"Good morning, chap." The paramedic was over to where I lay on the ground in a few long strides. Avoiding the shards of glass, he crouched next to me. His eyes darted downwards to the wet patch on my trousers. My face burned. "How are you feeling? Can you tell me your name?"

"Thirsty," I wheezed. "And my name's Sam, Sam Fulford." The officers exchanged glances. The paramedic hovering over me looked up.

"Could one of you do me a favour and grab our guy here some water, please?"

They frowned at taking such menial orders, but the female officer shuffled into the bathroom in search of it regardless. The other officer's radio crackled into life. He stepped from the room and into the corridor to listen. I could just make out his low voice – feeding back information – but not what he was saying. The female officer returned and handed a small glass of water to the paramedic. He thanked her and turned back to me.

"Right, Sam, let's sit you up slowly, see if we can get some fluid into you." He slotted a hand under my good shoulder and gently assisted me. "No rush, let me know if you feel unwell at all," he chirped.

Once I'd made it into a sitting position, leaning against the wall for support, he handed me the glass of water. I lifted it to my lips in desperation, but he placed a firm hand on my arm.

"I know you want to gulp it down in one, but it's best you sip it. It's likely to just come right back up otherwise." He removed his hand and watched me closely.

Nothing had ever seemed as refreshing as that first sip. Although desperate to swallow back the entire glass, I heeded the advice of the paramedic with greedy sips.

Once I was better hydrated, the paramedic gave me the once-over, ruling out anything serious. He took some time removing shards of glass from my hands and forearms – the explanation for the blood smears – and cleaned up the cuts. I wondered if I'd add more scars, remembering with a sharp twist of my stomach the last time I'd had the same treatment. All of my wounds were superficial, but I still gritted my teeth against the sting as he applied the antiseptic.

"Okay, we're done here. Drink plenty of water today and take it steady. You should feel fine a bit later on." He threw a glance in the direction of the officers, who loitered awkwardly. He stood and collected his few bits of equipment. My tongue still felt like a dry sponge, too big for my mouth.

"Thank you," I muttered, cheeks burning once again. "Sorry to have wasted your time."

"Not at all." He looked back at me, his expression soft. "It's the best outcome for us when it turns out we're not needed." He smiled and winked at me before he slung his bag over his shoulder, turned, and left the room.

The male officer pushed the door to behind him, but it didn't latch. He crossed the room towards me and unhooked the handcuffs from his belt, staring down at me with a hard look.

"Sam Fulford, I am arresting you ..."

My panicked brain turned to mush, and my body to jelly. The officer continued to read me my rights, but I didn't hear anything more, the ringing in my ears becoming too loud, drowning him out.

17

TESSA

TWO MONTHS PREVIOUS

As had become our routine, I had been up with Cora
from 4:37 a.m.
As usual, I slouched on our sofa in the dark,
waiting for the rest of the world to join us. The previous night
had been a particularly bad one. Cora had whined in her
sleep and cried out for her lost dummy more times than I
could count. For the sliver of time that Cora hadn't been
awake, Sam had snored and thrashed around in his sleep,
leaving me too on edge to risk getting any rest myself, just in
case his nightmares escalated.

Countless times before, when I had tried to comfort him –
or nudged him to stop his relentless snoring – I had taken a
clout of some sort, his sleep-borne retaliation. This had been
such a night, as I'd gingerly nudged him in the hope of
rousing him from whatever nightmare held him in its grip.
The sound of his almost animalistic growl as he'd lashed out,
catching me perfectly on the side of my face, still reverberated through my mind. Although my cheek had just about
stopped throbbing, I was wary of checking it out in the
mirror. Not for the first time would I be leaving the house

bearing an injury inflicted by my husband. I knew he couldn't help it, and I didn't blame him, most of the time. But since Cora's arrival, I felt terrified that some well-meaning observer would take me for a battered wife, bruises hidden under thick layers of concealer. I was petrified of social services getting involved and flagging up what a terrible job I was doing as a mother. There was something else I had never mentioned to Sam – afraid that if I did, he would doubt my feelings for him, my trust in him and his ability to be a father.

If social services were to call, were to check in on the woman with the perennial suspicious bruising, would they be able to sense that actually, sometimes, I was a little afraid of him?

What if they saw through me instantly, took our baby away, certain in their estimation that I was unfit to manage alone – and that Sam couldn't be trusted.

He adores our baby girl. He would do anything in his power to protect her and would never hurt her.

I repeated the mantra to myself every evening as we were going to bed. But another voice always replied: *Maybe not intentionally.*

I pretended not to hear it, but it was impossible. Why else would I jolt awake at every movement Sam made? Struggle so badly to sleep, even though I was completely exhausted? Sam's assumption was that my lack of sleep was all down to Cora – both her restlessness and my fear that something might happen whilst I slept. I allowed him to believe it, even attempted to convince myself, finding it easier to go along with the half-truth. But Cora wasn't the one responsible for my insomnia. My fears weren't just that of the average new mother. No, my worst fears were of my own husband.

Awful visions flickered. Sam lashing out at our baby or lifting her tiny sleeping form from her cot and carrying her away into the darkness. My beautiful girl, stirring in his arms, opening her eyes and looking up to see her daddy's face. She would feel safe with him; she wouldn't even cry out to alert me. The thoughts were always at their worst during the night, submerged in the darkness.

My body shuddered at images playing as if on a screen before my eyes. I shook my head vigorously, attempting to dislodge them from my overactive brain. A single tear slid down my cheek, and I swiped at it, angry at myself for being so worked up over tricks of my frazzled mind.

"Ouch," I hissed, wincing as my knuckles brushed against my cheek. I'd have to put off the next video call with my parents until I could cover the bruising. I knew – as always – Sam would be mortified to see what he'd done during the night. I tried to console myself, forcing a false confidence into the words that came to mind.

He wouldn't hurt her. Some sort of parental instinct would kick in, and he would stop before ...

Before what, Tessa? Instinct has never stopped him taking a swing in your direction.

Sam was a great husband and a wonderful father; my heart physically hurt at the thought of life without him. Besides, I was failing badly enough with a second parent involved. I simply wouldn't cope alone – even without having to care for Cora. I had no family to turn to. I couldn't put this on my parents, not with Mum like she was. Dad was barely coping. I imagined reaching out to Lauren, sharing the burden that weighed so heavy, but she'd tell Mike. Of course, they knew of Sam's condition, but the person they knew was *my* Sam. Mike would never believe Sam would hurt us. He loved him as much as I did and, to my knowledge, had never seen Sam's parasomnias at their worst.

Images of Sam rocking Cora in his arms, singing to her softly – totally out of tune – and kissing her nose so gently, as if he thought she might shatter, filled the imaginary screen before my eyes. Guilt joined the squadron of emotions battling to seize their host.

I couldn't believe I was even considering the idea of leaving Sam ... I'd taken my wedding vows seriously, meant every word. Memories of our wedding day swept in upon a fresh wave of anguish. It had been a tiny but perfect affair. I'd worn a vintage dress and felt, for the first time in my life, truly beautiful. Sam had looked more handsome than I'd ever seen him, and I'd spent the day mentally pinching myself. Sam's mother and stepfather lived abroad, so it was the first and only time that I'd met them. His mother, Carol, was a timid woman, painfully polite. His stepfather, Frank, was a hulk of a man who seemed to be clockwatching, itching for the day to be over. Sam had a sister; he never spoke of her. He had shut me down the few times I'd pried for information on her. I wasn't even certain where she lived, or if Sam knew himself.

To my shame, I barely noticed Sam's family, so enjoying a rare day spent with my own parents. Mum had mostly remembered who I was. She might not have really understood what was happening, but she had enjoyed the gathering – getting to socialise, a few glasses of champagne. The one damper on my day was my critical lack of friends, the crippling humiliation at having no one to be my bridesmaid. I had wanted to die when Sam – aware of my grievous lack of options – offered to ask Lauren. I'd brushed it off, muttering something about not needing the extra expense. It was at that point I'd insisted on an intimate affair – with only family, and Mike and Lauren, to attend – any childhood dreams of the big white wedding pushed aside. It would have been so different had I known Bella then. Before Cora had arrived, there was never an awkward moment, the things we had in common outweighing our differences. She'd have dismissed such notions of mine, helped me past them, and taken the reins to organise every detail. We'd have spent the morning of my big day together, her insisting we do something with my ratty hair and dull skin while I pretended to resist. I could never match her flawlessness. But we'd have laughed over bottomless glasses of champagne as she despaired, sorting me out to be finally "presentable".

I loved Sam so much – I still did. But my priorities had shifted when I'd brought our tiny, defenceless daughter into the world. When it had been just him and me, it was my choice. I'd resigned myself to the sleepless nights with him. The thrashing around. The getting out of bed to follow him, ensuring that he didn't get too far, do anything too dangerous. Plus, of course, the cuts and bruises that I was subjected to when he lashed out. Through his eyes, behind the veil of his nightmares, I was the enemy, the one to be feared. His lashing out at me hadn't been his fault, and most of the time, the good outweighed the bad. But then there was Cora.

If he harmed her, could I forgive him? More than that, could I ever forgive myself? I was her mother; was it not my *one* job to protect my child, even from her own father?

I stared down at my daughter quietly playing on her mat on the floor. As her arms and legs hit out at the small pieces of plastic that dangled, a soft music sounded, and tiny lights twinkled in response to her movements. They illuminated her face like miniature stars, and she gurgled back at them.

I hauled myself from the sofa and lowered my aching body down to the floor beside her. Her face lit up at the sight of me appearing from behind the lights to lie down close to her. I brushed my lips against her warm cheek and breathed the words in a whisper against her skin.

"Mummy would die before I let anything happen to you, baby."

18

SAM

PRESENT DAY

C riminal damage and attempted assault.
I was back, but this time in a different interview room and feeling every bit the criminal. The duty solicitor whom I had been assigned looked as rough as I felt in his dishevelled suit, like he hadn't yet been to bed. He continuously ran his hands through his unruly hair, which stood on end in greasy tufts, whilst chomping his way through a tube of mints. I'd taken an instant disliking to him. Garcia entered the room once again, his composure a stark contrast to that of me and my jittery solicitor. His shirt was crisp and fresh, the air around him a blend of aftershave and confidence. Perfectly put together as he was, he looked thoroughly pissed off.

"Well, trouble certainly seems to find you, doesn't it, Mr Fulford?" His lip curled as he spoke my name. "The good news for you is that on finding out who you are, the hotel owner has taken pity on you and doesn't want to press charges. That is, on the understanding that you pay for the damage you caused." He regarded me with revulsion. This time, I couldn't actually blame him.

"We will have to agree on a fair settlement," the solicitor rasped. "Have the damages you speak of been assessed by someone impartial?"

"What do you mean? Finding out who I am?" I asked, ignoring the solicitor, confused as to why my identity would make a difference.

"I take it you haven't seen the news, then?" Garcia cocked his head as I shook my own, my forehead creased.

"Well, you're *it*. The local news teams never take long picking up on something like this. Often they're tipped off by a neighbour. But I'm afraid the nationals have picked it up now, too. Of course, nothing has come from us – your name hasn't been released – but that doesn't mean much when it comes to the bloodhounds. Fortunately for you, they, so far, haven't drawn any aspersions on you." He glared at me then. "Hence the hotel taking pity on you." He spat the last words, unable to hide his opinion that he thought it was more than I deserved. "Must be something in the air, as it seems DC Smithe feels the same way." His words rang with irritation.

"DC Smithe?" My blank face remained slack with my attempt to process it all.

"The officer you attempted to attack." He screwed up his nose, and his lip curled again. "Seems *she* feels bad for hurting *you*."

"Oh." The feeble response was all I could manage. Shame pulsed through me at the memory – the officer leaving the room, lending me some dignity whilst her colleague watched me change out of my damp jeans. His eyes had remained bored into me, hard and vacant of sympathy. My face burned as I recalled the morning's entire sorry performance. I could hardly lift my eyes to meet Garcia's.

"I will be discussing with my client how he feels about the severity of your officer's actions. Using a taser against an unarmed civilian. It could be seen as police brutality." The solicitor spoke around the mint that he moved around his mouth. I gawped at him, aware of the type of clients he must usually represent. He was not doing me any favours by making me more of an enemy.

Garcia threw him a look but continued, aiming his words directly while fixing his cool glare on the man beside me.

"You'll be receiving a hefty fine, but you're getting off incredibly lightly." A muscle flexed in his jaw as he spoke.

I squirmed in the hard plastic chair. "Thank you," I mumbled pitifully.

"Trust me, it isn't down to me, Mr Fulford."

I nodded but kept quiet, as anything I said seemed to piss him off further – and this time the evidence was unmistakable. I most certainly was guilty.

"So I suggest you leave. Try to keep your violent side at bay for a while. I'm sure we'll be seeing you here again very soon." The emphasis on his last words made his point perfectly clear.

"And if you could ensure your officers do the same." My teeth clenched at the crunch of the mint in my ear. "My client is dealing with enough without being brutally attacked by police during the night. We'd appreciate it if we aren't brought back here until you find a good reason."

He turned to me, seemingly unaware of what his use of the word "until" insinuated. I stared at him, aghast, wondering how he had possibly ever gained his qualification – that is if he even had one. I wondered if there was a reason he was the duty solicitor I'd been assigned. He extended his grubby hand to me, ready to shake, and his lips split into a smarmy smile. My eyes were drawn to his crooked, yellowing teeth.

"Great, good to see we got the right outcome," he enthused. My stomach rolled at the smell of stale alcohol and mint mixed with his body odour. "We'll discuss the other issues privately." His piggy eyes shot towards Garcia, who had reached the door. He yanked it open, throwing the solicitor a thunderous look before turning to leave.

I turned away from the outstretched hand of the grimy solicitor and craned my neck towards Garcia's retreating back. "Detective?" I called after him, unsure of how to address him but trying not to give myself time to change my mind.

He turned, glaring at me, making no attempt to hide his annoyance that someone he detested would dare take up more of his day. I continued, undeterred. "I know what you think of me. If the roles were reversed, I'd probably think the same." I swallowed hard and closed my eyes, trying to find my composure and decide how best to continue.

"I would *never* want to harm my wife or child. I love them both with everything I have and would lay down my life for either one of them without question." He visibly fought the urge to roll his eyes. I was losing him. I needed to get to the point.

"If I knew what had happened to them, I swear to you, I wouldn't be hiding it. If I *had* done something to hurt Tessa, then I'd deserve everything that was coming to me, and wouldn't try to make excuses. The truth is, my wife is dead, and my baby is missing, and before last night, I didn't believe that it could be possible that I might be responsible for any part of it." My breath caught, but I resolved to hold it together. Garcia studied me intently, his interest piqued.

"I genuinely don't care what happens to me; right now the only thing that I care about is getting Cora back safe. I don't know how to help because I have no memory of what happened, but I *want* to help, I really do. Please tell me what I can do! I need to help my baby. I have nothing left to lose. I need to find her, even if that sends me to prison for the rest of my life. I just need her to be safe, with someone who'll take care of her."

My body deflated with each word, begging this man with everything that I had left. I had no fight left.

The solicitor's hand had dropped along with his face, and discomfort oozed from him, almost palpable. The skin seemed to hang from his face, slack with shock, my outburst stopping him mid chew. He'd clearly been prepared to enjoy the rest of his day searching for the bottom of a bottle.

His bloodshot eyes darted between me and Garcia, his mouth hanging slightly open, and he shifted his weight from one foot to the other, unsure how to react to the scene playing out in front of him.

Garcia fixed me with a hard stare. Something had shifted in his eyes, and I prayed to God that he had the experience to know when someone spoke the truth. Only the previous day, I'd hated the man as much as he did me. In that moment, I had nothing left but desperation. I didn't have the energy to hate him.

"Mr Fulford, don't allow these people to pressure you into an admission of something that you haven't done. Shall we have that private consultation before continuing this conversation?"

The solicitor looked pale and startled – unsure on his feet with this change of footing. He snapped his jaw shut as if the speech had tumbled from him accidentally, shocking him as much as anyone. His anxious glance darted between me and Garcia.

I whipped my head back around to focus on the detective, but the spell had been broken. His eyes had become dark and hard, the shutters firmly back in place.

"Rest assured, Mr Fulford, I won't stop until I have found the person responsible. They deserve to rot in hell, and I intend to personally make sure they get there."

19

TESSA

FOUR YEARS PREVIOUS

I hadn't been looking for a relationship when I met Sam. I didn't feel anywhere near ready to settle down. I'd been walking home alone early one evening. It was the time of year where it was dark by 6 p.m. It had just begun to drizzle, and I had found myself confronted with an unruly group of men. I guessed it was a stag do or something, but they were clearly intoxicated. They didn't say anything bad and were clearly just having some fun with me, but I froze, intimidated by the large group and feeling incredibly alone. Sam had appeared, telling them in a jokey fashion that they didn't have a hope, and to move it on. They took his easy banter and laughed along before staggering off, holding one another up as they swayed, raucous laughter echoing after them.

I'd offered to buy him a drink as a way of thanks. He'd seemed reluctant at first, but, both freezing cold and soaked through, we made our way to a crowded bar on the edge of the city. It was filled with damp punters seeking shelter, creating a warm atmosphere. We chatted until last orders, both reluctant to part ways, agreeing on waiting for what had become endless rain to stop – silently aware that it wasn't going to. I was completely engrossed by him, barely noticing the crowds moving around us, becoming more and more intoxicated before thinning out. I was afraid that if we parted ways, I'd never have seen his crooked smile again, or find out where his perfect spattering of scars had come from. After that, our relationship had moved fast. We became a couple without either of us ever actually stating it, spending every free moment together. Being with Sam always brought back the same spread of warmth, leaving me wondering if the magical atmosphere that first evening actually had anything to do with the bar at all. But it didn't take long for me to begin to wonder why he would never stay over, or invite me to stay round at his. He seemed to be so enjoying our time together, I couldn't fathom why he would cut it short come the end of every evening, ending it each time with *I must be getting back* or *Early start tomorrow. When can I see you again?*

After a few weeks, his mixed signals were playing games with my mind, filling me with doubt as to whether he actually liked me as much as I'd thought. He'd seem so keen, but then would go cold, shutting himself off from me at the end of each evening. Maybe it wouldn't have felt so bad if I had someone to confide in or turn to for advice – but I'd recently watched most of my friendships fizzle. Being all consumed by my relationship with Sam, I'd closed myself off to the friendships I'd had. But then again, most of my friends had moved out of London by then, or on to nicer areas with their partners. Those who were still clinging on were full of false promises – "It's been too long; we must catch up" – neither party having any intention of following through with those plans. I stopped replying to the odd messages I did get, the thought of seeing any of them a dull prospect in comparison to time with Sam. I couldn't bear the thought of the relationship slipping away, desperate to make him as happy as he made me.

He'd always seem so desperate to fix our next date, bombarding me with text messages to confirm that I was still coming. When we were together, everything else would melt away, and I would find myself caught up in the whirlwind of how perfect he was – always seeming to know just the right things to say, the best places for our dates, places that he knew I'd love. He was one of the most attractive men I'd ever met, but somehow still made me feel like he was the lucky one, seemingly unaware of his looks. But each time, as he kissed me goodnight and walked away, I'd be left brimming with insecurity, returning to my empty little flat wondering where I was going wrong.

I conjured up images of him going off to meet another girlfriend, his lips having only just left my own, now pressing in greeting against those of some faceless girl.

But I couldn't believe Sam to be like that. It had only been weeks since we'd met, but I felt I knew him.

My mind tortured me with the myriad scenarios, but none of it felt right. I just couldn't accept that I could've got it so wrong.

Maybe I was the one giving the mixed signals. Maybe I just needed to be clearer with him.

Soon after I came to this conclusion, we shared a perfect night. We enjoyed a quiet dinner together at a cosy little Italian place. We had shared a bottle of wine and basked in the hazy drunken glow that hit when we stepped outside.

As we left the restaurant, giggling together like teenagers, Sam had offered to call us a taxi.

"No, let's walk." I breathed in the fresh, cool air of the summer twilight. "It's such a beautiful evening."

We'd fallen into step, hands intertwined and our bodies

pressed together. He walked me to the door of my flat, where
he stopped, spinning me to face him.

"Can I see you tomorrow?" He brushed a loose wave of
my hair back.

The wine had given me some Dutch courage, so with
false bravado I attempted a husky tone.

"Why don't you just stay with me? Then we'll already be
together tomorrow?" My cheeks burned with the forwardness
of my question.

Sam's eyes fell away from my gaze, looking anywhere but
at me.

"I, erm ... I don't have anything with me ..." He trailed off,
rubbing the back of his neck.

"So?" I was beginning to feel desperate. "You don't really
need anything. And we can make a stop at yours first thing in
the morning."

Humiliation flared at the awkward silence that followed
while Sam rubbed his scars, still refusing to meet my eye.
What was wrong with *me*? Palpable discomfort radiated
from him.

Resentment followed quickly on the heels of shame, a
feistiness fuelled by the wine.

"Sam, I don't know what is going on here, but I think you
just need to be honest with us both." My simmering anger
had fizzled into a tone that was almost pleading. "I don't
know why it is that I'm just not quite good enough for you,
but I think it's best that we have some space. I can't keep
dealing with you being so hot and cold."

I spun unsteadily on my heel and aimed the key at the
lock. Unsure if it was the effect of the alcohol, the blur of the
threatening tears, or the adrenalin that coursed through me,
but I found myself incapable of making it fit, jabbing at it in
annoyance.

"Tessa, please ..." Sam started, desperation saturating his voice. I didn't even offer him a glance. "Just go home, Sam," I bit back defiantly, finally managing to slot the key into the lock. "Okay, you're right. Please, I owe you an explanation. If you'll let me come in, I'll tell you the truth. Then you can decide if you want to see me again."

Panic engulfed me, and I froze, suddenly sober but unable to turn the key. I had been sure there was something that he was keeping from me, but on some level had hoped that I was being paranoid and would be proved wrong. My heart skipped at his admission. I turned slowly to face him, my breaths coming in short bursts. He was pale, his jaw clenched. My anxiety rose. I swallowed hard and lifted my head, stealing myself, prepared to finally hear about the other woman.

"Well, you'd better come in, then," I replied, cold and curt. I held my head up with as much fake confidence as I could muster. Inside, I was falling apart.

We perched on my sofa while he began his explanation. I sat as far from him as I could get, squashed up against the arm, the pain of it digging into my back a welcome distraction. I kept my arms folded tightly across my chest and fought to keep my breathing even.

He didn't look at me as he spoke. The words jumbled in my head. *Parasomnias. Sleep disorder. Afraid of scaring me, of hurting me.*

Relief that he didn't plan to leave me – or have another girlfriend waiting – washed through me, making me feel tipsy again. I couldn't have cared less about some sleep problem. Everyone had their faults. If his worst was suffering from a few nightmares, it was hardly a deal breaker.

He'd stopped talking and was watching my face for a reaction. I unfolded my arms and leaned towards him, pressing my lips hard against his and pulling back to look at him. His face was set, hard.

"This is serious, Tessa; it's not just some ..."

"Is it too soon to tell you I love you?" I whispered, cutting him off. His eyes widened; then his features softened.

The corners of his mouth twitched, and his face glowed. "Only because I wanted to tell you first."

He stayed that night, and the next, and the one after that.

Those nights were wonderful. We lay together in the darkness, bodies intertwined, talking until the sunlight stretched its way across the room.

Everything seemed perfect.

20

SAM

PRESENT DAY

I pushed through the front doors of the police station for what felt like the hundredth time in a couple of days. The cool air hit my face, and I filled my lungs.

As I reached the bottom of the stone steps, I let out a groan. My car was still parked at the hotel. I could walk to get it, I decided. It wasn't like I had anywhere else to go, and with the walk, I might reach some clarity as to where I could start to look for Cora. I'd already wasted too much time. The police were due to put out an appeal for her safe return later that day, but it'd been strongly recommended that I not make an appearance in it, with all that was going on. I was furious with myself, having sabotaged the one thing I could've helped with, sick to my stomach to think of how Tessa would have reacted. The image of her face made me light-headed, unable to accept I'd never see her smile again.

The world around me was continuing on. I was supposed to be at work the following morning. Would they be expecting me, or would they know? I couldn't bear to see the looks of sympathy on the faces of my colleagues. Or worse, accusation.

As I stepped out of the grounds of the station, a crowd of people rushed towards me. At first, I flinched, wondering what could be happening to cause the group to run, trying to determine if I too should be moving in the opposite direction. But as flashes from every angle blinded me and the clamouring started, a bolt of shock struck me – I knew exactly what was happening.

Cameras flashed like rocket flares, blinding me. Shouting voices merged; it was impossible to distinguish where one ended and another began.

I dropped my head, focusing on getting one foot to move in front of the other.

The shouts continued, increasing in volume. I managed to make out some of the words.

"... *tell us what the police had you in for this time?*"

"... *doing to find your missing daughter?*"

"... *idea why your family may have been targeted?*"

"... *one-off attack? The public have a right to be warned.*"

"... *explain what happened to your arms?*"

My head pounded. I crossed my arms tightly over my chest, attempting to hide my bandages.

The flashes disorientated me. I felt the urge to curl up into a tiny ball right there on the pavement until it all just went away. A burning sensation throbbed in my eyes, and a hard knot formed in my throat. I couldn't let them get to me, allow them to witness my weakness. I had to keep it together.

I directed my focus to how I could dislodge myself from the throng; they had no intention of letting me free. If I continued to walk, they were just going to follow me. How strange it was, I thought, that rivals would work together like that to bring someone down. Hyenas circling their prey, preparing to attack.

Aware that I needed to clear my mind, I reached for my phone in my pocket. Whom could I call? I considered a taxi, but what would I do while I was waiting? I couldn't stay out there circled by these predators.

I stole a glance back at the police station. Would the press be allowed in there? The memory of DI Garcia's face appeared in my head. I couldn't imagine him rushing to my aid, ushering them out the door. Besides, I'd be made to subject myself to that odious building while I still had a choice. I'd rather take my chances with the hyenas.

Panic had all but consumed me when the blare of a car horn added to the din.

I glimpsed a look at the car with a momentary hope of seeing Mike, our bitter words forgotten – but it wasn't his car. Perhaps it was a police officer trying to disperse the crowd.

A further, more urgent series of horn blasts followed, and a woman's voice called out from the car.

"Sam, get in – *now!*"

The voice was familiar, but my overwrought brain couldn't place it. I couldn't waste time thinking about it, seeing as I was so low on options. In three strides I was staring at my gaunt reflection in the tinted glass, then yanking the passenger door handle and diving inside the unfamiliar car.

More flashes illuminated the inside of the vehicle, accompanied by further shouting.

"*Who are you?*"

"*Is this a mistress, Sam?*"

"*Is this why you ...*"

I slammed the door behind me with no concern for any reporters who might get caught by it. As I attempted to regain my composure, I glanced at the driver. My mouth dropped open in a gawp, the calm that I had just found evaporating.

"What the ... how ... what the fuck are you doing here?" I gasped.

21

TESSA

FOUR YEARS PREVIOUS

Sam and I had been together for around six months when I came down with the worst bug of my life. I had been off sick from my admin job for three days straight. I was wiped out, and I still didn't feel up to going back, but I'd started to worry about the security of my position.

Exhaustion from the continuous vomiting overwhelmed me. On day four I had to peel my dry eyes open at the sound of the alarm clock. I lay squinting in the dreary daylight, struggling to prevent them from sealing closed again.

Nausea hit. I sprang from my bed and made a dash for the bathroom, stubbing my toe on the door frame in my haste. Stumbling into the bathroom, I reached the sink, which was closer than the toilet, suddenly thankful for my tiny flat. I retched until my stomach was empty. My wrung-out body seemed unable to make it back to my bed. I lay down on the bathroom floor, finding relief in the cool surface against my clammy skin.

I awoke freezing cold. My teeth chattered, and one of my arms was numb.

It took me a second or two to get my bearings, to make out where I was. My stomach lurched at the memory of the vomiting. I peeled my face from the tile.

"Shit!" I yelped. My alarm had awoken me earlier. I should've been getting ready for work. How long had I been passed out on the bathroom floor?

I hopped to my feet too quickly, then willed myself not to faint, gripping the sink for support.

As soon as my vision cleared, I staggered back through to my bedroom as quickly as I dared, grabbing my phone and flopping back onto the bed. I checked the time, relieved to find that I wasn't late yet. Finding the number in my contacts, I dialled to let them know that I wouldn't be in again. My nerves pulsed as the phone rang.

My boss was sympathetic when I explained that I couldn't phone before, as my head had been down the loo. She also insisted that I should visit the GP with a bug that was dragging on for so long, gently adding her requirement for a sick note. Guilt prickled my skin. I assured her that I would phone for an appointment as soon as we'd hung up. I ended the call and noticed that I had a new message.

> Morning beautiful, how are you feeling today? Love you. Xx

I tapped out a quick reply to let Sam know that I was still sick and not able to go into work again. Within seconds, my phone rang in my hand, his name flashing across the screen.

"Hey you," I croaked, my voice hoarse from throwing up.

"Hey." His voice was soft with concern. Tears sprang to my eyes, I had no idea why, and I flushed. At least he wasn't there to witness my pitiful reaction.

"I can't believe you're still sick. You're calling your doctor today, right?" It wasn't a question. From anyone else, being told what to do would have irritated me. Instead, a warm feeling came over me. With my parents so far away, I was grateful for someone who cared.

"I just had the same conversation with my boss, actually." I sighed, fatigue creeping over me again. "I doubt there's much they can do, though."

"I still want you to go." Sam's voice was insistent. "You might be dehydrated, and it isn't normal for a bug to go on this long."

I was too tired to argue and had already promised my boss that I would go, so I agreed to arrange an appointment right away. If nothing else, I needed a sick note.

The receptionist booked me in. I had just enough time to shower and throw on some clothes.

I tapped out a message to Sam, letting him know the time of my appointment, as I'd promised that I would, and dragged my stale body to the shower.

HALF AN HOUR LATER, I was weak from the effort of getting ready to go. Normally I would have walked, but I doubted my body could make it that far. I daren't drive, either – a dizzy spell could come over me at any time.

I considered calling a taxi, but doubted my money would stretch that far with all the unpaid sick days. And I definitely didn't want to worry my parents by asking for money. The thought of getting onto a bus filled me with dread – what if I needed to throw up again? My stomach gave a warning gurgle, and I sucked back a few deep breaths.

I'd have to risk it and walk, I decided, and reached for my coat. I'd have just enough time if I left right away. My phone buzzed with a text just when I'd pulled the door to my flat closed. My heart skipped when I saw Sam's name on my screen.

I'm outside when you're ready. Xx

I stared at my phone in confusion. Maybe he'd sent it in error. I eased myself down the stairs and out the front door of my building, trying not to be hopeful – Sam was at work, so his text must have been a mistake – but my eyes scanned the cars parked close by anyway.

I heard the toot of a horn. A smile sprang to my lips when I spotted Sam's car. He hopped out and jogged towards me.

Heat rose to my cheeks – I hadn't even glanced at a mirror. I smoothed my hair as best I could, aware I must look awful.

"What are you doing here? Shouldn't you be at work?" I smiled, so glad to have him close, even if I felt like death.

"I, erm ... I told them I had an urgent appointment," he admitted, his own cheeks filling with colour. "I was worried about you."

Warmth spread over me, and I struggled to believe my luck. I placed my hand on his face and offered a weak smile.

"Come on, we don't want you to be late." He placed his own hand on the small of my back, guiding me towards his car.

THE DOCTOR WAS RUNNING LATE. I perched by a window, grateful for the fresh air. We chatted quietly as we waited for my name to be called.

Finally my name came over the Tannoy and slid across a screen at the front of the room. I stood too quickly; stars burst into my vision. I wobbled. Sam launched himself from his seat. Supporting my arm, he insisted on walking me to the exam room. Once I was safely seated in the spongy chair, he turned to leave, but I grabbed his hand.

"Stay." I nodded, insistent. He had been so wonderful – our relationship progressing so perfectly – that I didn't want to shut him out of anything. For the first time in so long, I didn't feel alone. I hoped he would open up to me more, too. He'd shut me down on certain subjects enough times that I learned quickly which were off-limits.

His eyes met mine, and he dropped into the chair next to me. As I explained my symptoms to the weary-eyed doctor, Sam placed his hand over mine. The doctor typed as I spoke, nodding with an occasional "uh-huh" to encourage me on. And then we sat in silence, waiting for his diagnosis. He turned to look at me.

"Periods regular?"

My face flushed – his question had caught me off guard – and I nodded.

"So you haven't missed one recently? There isn't a chance that you could be pregnant?" he asked, glancing at Sam, who had gone rigid in the chair beside me.

"Erm ... I ..." I swallowed hard. My mind had gone blank. I couldn't recall when my last period was or when it was due. I'd been so caught up with Sam, not paying attention to much else.

"I'm on the pill," I blurted, hoping to redirect the conversation. He frowned, then clicked his mouse a couple more times. Sam's fingers dug painfully into my hand.

"I'd like you to do a pregnancy test, just to rule it out. I don't want to prescribe you anything until we know for certain." The doctor's eyes shone with kind warmth. Sam withdrew his hand sharply, as if suddenly remembering it was there, as I made to stand.

A couple of minutes later, I returned bearing half a plastic cup of pee. My skin tingled with embarrassment. I'd rather not have Sam witnessing this, but there was nothing to be done about it at this point. I wondered if they'd spoken while

I was out. The doctor took the cup from me, then retrieved a small strip of paper from a packet, dipping it into the still warm liquid. We waited in silence once again. Finally, he held the strip up against the packet, and his eyes flicked from one to the other.

"Ah." He cleared his throat. "It appears congratulations may be in order. You are indeed pregnant, Tessa." He held up the test as if it were a prize, smiling at me over the rims of his glasses.

My mouth dropped open. I waited for him to burst out laughing, tell me that he was kidding. But of course, he didn't. He glanced between Sam and me, reminding me that Sam was sitting right beside me.

I tore my eyes away from the test strip and turned to look at Sam. His face was a mirror of my own, pale with shock. The doctor was speaking again. Something about midwives, information leaflets, and further appointments, but I couldn't take it in. I thanked him, scraping my chair back as I stood too quickly to leave. He assured me that someone would be in contact with regard to my next appointments.

I wanted to say something to Sam but had no idea what.

Should I apologise?

Nothing seemed appropriate, so I stayed silent as we walked back to his car. This time, he didn't open the car door for me. On the drive back to my apartment block, we exchanged hardly a word, with only the radio presenter to cut through the silent tension. When he pulled up outside my building, neither of us moved.

"I have to get back to work." Sam's voice was low, void of emotion.

"Of course." I nodded, grabbing for the door handle. "Thank you for taking me."

The exchange was so alien – I'd become accustomed to our blissful serenity. Before he had time to respond, I bolted

from his car and across the road to the door of my building. I
didn't want him to witness my tears.

THE AFTERNOON PASSED IN A DAZE. I was terrified and felt so
alone. Without Sam, I really had no one. I couldn't face the
awkward conversation it would mean having with my father
– both of us acutely aware that it should be Mum I was
confiding in. My parents lived too far away to be of much
help. I couldn't imagine giving up the buzz of the city for the
tiny town I'd grown up in. Not that it mattered, anyway, since
Mum was suffering with dementia, Dad spending most of his
time caring for her.

Sam was clearly in complete shock and – I had to face it –
not exactly pleased. I couldn't blame him. We hadn't known
each other long. We'd never even discussed our relationship
in the long term, let alone children.

My stomach rolled again, but this time it felt different.
Once past the initial shock, I couldn't deny that, actually, I
was excited. If I had no family close by, perhaps here was an
opportunity to build one of my own. From the look on Sam's
face, I could be doing it alone – that I had to face – but I
would be doing it. Of that I had no doubt.

DARKNESS WAS JUST CREEPING across the room when the
doorbell rang, and I started at the sound.

I considered ignoring it, having just settled down with a
book. But then it buzzed again, longer and more insistent. I
dragged myself from the sofa and shuffled over to lift the
handset.

"Hello?" I huffed.

"Tessa, it's me. Please don't hang the phone up. Please, please let me up. I desperately need to talk to you."

His pleading tone panicked me. I pressed the door release with no hesitation whatsoever. He appeared at my unlatched door in seconds, panting slightly, holding the biggest arrangement of flowers that I'd ever seen in one hand and something that I couldn't make out in the other. He was talking before he had even made it through the door. I shoved it closed behind him.

"Tessa, I'm so, so sorry for how I behaved this afternoon. There's no excuse whatsoever for me being an utter arsehole, but I can only tell you that I was ... a little shocked to say the least."

"It's okay ..." I started, but he held up a hand.

"No. It isn't." He shook his head. A muscle flexed in his jaw. "I was a dick, and I can't apologise enough. But I've had some time to think and ..." I saw him gulp, felt the panic rising.

"I think I'm really excited about this ... Is that okay? If you think I'll be good enough, and if you want to, I really want us to have this baby ... together."

He studied my face. My heart swelled at the apprehension on his face.

"Yes," I squawked. "Yes, yes! That is *so* okay!" I blabbered. "I'm excited too! I want us to be a family."

Tears were streaming down my face. Through the blur, I saw that Sam's eyes were full, too.

We clung to each other, crying and laughing, Sam still clutching the huge bunch of flowers. As he pulled away, Sam reached down and took something out of his bag: the tiniest baby grow.

TWO DAYS later the sickness eased, and I was feeling almost back to myself – apart from the constant smug grin plastered onto my face. I hadn't decided how I was going to tell my boss – I'd stuck to the sickness being a nasty bug for the time being. We were likely going to have to face judgement, having been together such a short time. But nothing could dull the sheen of pure joy that sparkled on my skin. It felt right. My intuition told me this was where I should be, that I belonged. I was holding off telling my parents. I wanted to introduce them to Sam first, let them see how wonderful he was. He shut me down every time I mentioned telling his mum and stepdad, so I pushed that aside, too, not wanting to open us up to any negativity. The judgement we might face for now was from friends, but I'd been investing all of my time into Sam and was lacking any serious friends to judge.

One night after work I was wandering around the supermarket, trying to decide what I fancied cooking for Sam and me, when suddenly I thought I felt dampness in my underwear, like I'd wet myself. Humiliated, I dashed to the loo, leaving my basket and its contents abandoned outside the toilets.

As I pulled down my trousers and underwear, a smear of blood ran down my leg.

22

SAM

PRESENT DAY

I couldn't tear my eyes away from her face. My body had frozen. Her eyes remained fixed on the road ahead, her lips pursed.

"Well, hello to you too," she huffed sarcastically. "Not quite the greeting I was hoping for, Sam, especially after saving you from that circus back there." She sniffed and glanced in my direction.

Her voice flooded my head with memories, melting away the years. I rubbed my scars and blinked hard but still couldn't take my eyes off her face. She hadn't changed much. Of course, she looked older, the lines around her eyes giving her away. But other than that, she was just as I remembered her.

"I know. I'm sorry, Claire, but it was a bit of a shock. You're the last person I was expecting to see. I do appreciate you saving my arse though."

She raised her eyebrows and glanced sideways at me.

"What *are* you doing here though?" I couldn't refrain from asking.

"I came to see you." She muttered the words without

looking at me, keeping her eyes firmly fixed ahead. "I wasn't expecting quite that much of a mess, but I did think you may need some support. You're still my brother, Sam, like it or not."

"How did you find out?" The words were barely a whisper.

"Which part? The fact that you had a wife and child or that ... something had happened to them?" She threw me a look, something sparking in her eyes. It was my turn to keep my eyes fixed forward. Guilt washed over me, and heat rose to my face. I was glad not to have to meet her eye.

Claire and I had been close growing up. I was so young when we lost our father, but I did have some clear memories of him. I knew he and my mother loved us. My mother did not cope at all well being left as a single parent; she quickly remarried. I didn't blame her for it, apart from the fact Frank was an arsehole of a man.

Claire, almost ten years my senior, became more of a mother to me than our own. She brimmed with the confidence that I severely lacked, and I leaned heavily on her.

Our mother and stepfather had stuck around, if not fully present, until I reached sixteen. They considered me old enough to make it on my own then, told me they planned to move abroad, use Dad's life insurance money to travel around and enjoy the time they had left, as Frank put it. As if we'd stolen a huge chunk of it. I wasn't sad to see them go, just concerned about what it meant for me, where I would end up.

Claire, by then married and with her first baby already, took me in.

I lived with Claire and Martin for just under three years. Mum came back regularly enough at first, but the visits trailed off. We hardly heard from her outside of hastily written Christmas cards containing small wads of guilt cash. I had always been grateful to Claire for taking me in, giving that lost teenager a place to call home.

She remained my rock over the years after I went off to uni, then got my first job and a place of my own. I often spent time with her boys, Tommy and Lucas. I loved being an uncle.

And then I met Lindy.

23

TESSA

FOUR YEARS PREVIOUS

I didn't leave my apartment for almost a week after the horrific incident in the supermarket. I called the doctor's from the cubicle, begging for his help. His words were kind but his meaning clear. There was nothing he could do.

Sam was wonderful. He held me as I sobbed, sobs that I felt would never cease. He brought food when he finished work – insisted that I eat. It seemed pointless now that it was only my body to care for. And it had failed me.

On the sixth day, he had a different air about him. Something had shifted; perhaps he'd just gotten sick of my wallowing. I was in my standard new position, watching reruns of some TV show, lounging on my sofa. I think it'd probably moulded to my body by that point. If I ever moved, I'm sure there would have been a Tessa-shaped void.

He appeared and stood in the middle of the room, a presence, blocking my view of the TV. I craned my neck, trying to see past him.

"Tessa, you need to get up and get dressed." His voice was

kind but firm – I'd never heard him use a tone like that. I allowed my eyes to meet his for the first time in days. He looked so handsome, dressed in a dark coloured T-shirt that fit the curves of his arms and chest. My eyes trailed over his scars, and my body betrayed me with a longing to reach out and touch him, to see his lopsided smile. I could suddenly smell him, too – his light, crisp scent – like I was waking from a deep sleep to a fresh world again. It hurt like hell, and I reverted to my stubborn determination to punish myself.

"No, I don't," I spat back at him. Who was he to tell me what to do? I stared into his eyes, defiant, spiralling into self-sabotage.

"Yes, you do." His tone remained calm and steady. "I've booked us a table at the Italian place that we love. I thought maybe we could go and see a film afterwards, too, if you wanted to."

I gawped at him. What on earth was he thinking?

"You think some fancy dinner and a film are going to fix this?" I could hear my voice was dangerously low, filled with venom.

"I don't think anything is going to magically fix this, Tessa, but we need to start somewhere. We can't hide away in here forever and—"

I cut him off. "So we just go out for dinner?" The calm in his voice had only added fuel to the flames of rage inside me. "See a film and pretend this never happened?" My voice, having started out a hiss, had risen to hysterical shouting. "You might not give a *shit* about what happened, but I do! In fact, you're probably relieved, aren't you? Lucky escape, I guess!"

"Don't you dare." His low voice stunned me into silence, how it sizzled with his own fury. "Don't you *dare* accuse me of not caring."

I stopped, staring at him.

"You may think you're the only one affected by this, but that was my baby too. I wanted it as much as you did. You know nothing about ... Don't you try telling me ..."

As quickly as my anger had enveloped me, it vanished. My heart broke watching his tears spill over. All of the fight had left him, leaving him broken. In that moment, I loved that man. I loved him more than I had ever loved anyone or anything.

I sprang from the sofa, wrapping my arms around his neck and holding him. He dissolved into me, and we fell to the floor in a heap, still clinging to each other, and sobbed together until we had nothing left. We lay on our backs on the floor, letting the silence wash over us, heal us, as we clung to one another's hands.

I have no idea how long we lay together. Eventually Sam broke the silence.

"Shall I call the restaurant? We may still be able to get a table if you fancy going." His voice cracked with nerves as he broached the subject again. I sucked in a deep breath, rubbed my sore eyes, and decided it was time to be a grown-up.

"Yeah, do that. I'll jump in the shower while you ring."

Sam turned onto his side and leaned on his elbow. His eyes moved over my face as a watery, lopsided smile played on his lips.

"I love you," he whispered as he stroked my face.

A lightness came over me – along with a rush of something that, for the first time in days, didn't resemble despair or sadness.

"I love you too." I held his gaze, overwhelmed by how much meaning my words held.

We went to the Italian place together that night, shakily rebuilding ourselves and our relationship, united by our grief.

I forget exactly how long it was until reality hit once

again, shattering the fragile film of happiness. It was then that I learned just how bad Sam's parasomnias could get.

24

SAM

PRESENT DAY

C laire drove us out of the city, eventually pulling into the car park of a secluded bistro pub.

"What are we doing here?" I demanded, my eyebrows knitting together in confusion.

"You haven't eaten, have you?"

I opened my mouth, ready to protest, but Claire held up a hand. "Don't bother to argue, Sam. You look as though you haven't eaten in days. What use will you be to that little girl of yours when we get her back if you keel over from starving yourself?"

My eyes dropped away at the mention of Cora, a stark reminder that the years had not in fact melted away and that I was still, very much, living in my current nightmare. I swallowed past the huge lump in my throat. Unable to form words, I gave a single, sharp nod.

The place was dreary and looked like it was last decorated the decade I was born. I wondered if it was intentional on Claire's part – only three of the many other tables were inhabited. We made our way towards the back, beyond the reach of daylight, where only the old bulbs cast a dull yellow glow over threadbare furniture. We slipped into a booth. Claire thrust a menu under my nose.

When Claire asked a few minutes later what I wanted, I realised I'd been scanning the menu without taking in a single thing.

"If you don't pick something, I'll just order for you." She shrugged, deadpan.

I decided on a burger and fries, which Claire headed towards the bar to order. I stared at her retreating back as she walked away. My mind couldn't process the events of the previous couple of days, none of it having truly sunk in, and I sat dazed under the dull glow. A few minutes later, Claire slid into the booth opposite me, having brought drinks for us both. We sipped in silence for a few minutes, neither of us sure what to say to the other. When I couldn't bear it any longer, I broached what felt like a relatively safe subject.

"How are Martin and the boys?"

She studied my face for a few seconds before she replied.

"Good. Tommy and Lucas are growing up really fast. They're so big now – men really, even in their mid teens." She sighed, her focus somewhere in the distance. "You could have been to see them, Sam. They didn't understand why you just disappeared like you did. They deserved better."

I dropped my head to look down at the stained wooden tabletop, grappling with the shame.

"I know." It was no more than a mumble. I couldn't think of what more I could say to her, words dancing out of my reach.

"Why didn't you contact me? If you'd have told me that you two had split ... I would have loved to meet Tessa, been around when Cora arrived." Sadness tinged her words and washed over her face; the guilt rooted more deeply in my heart. Knowing she was right made being called out on it harder to swallow.

"Maybe I was just worried that you might disapprove of Tessa too. Maybe I didn't want your judgement this time," I snapped back. Her face slackened with shock before darkening, all traces of sadness replaced by anger. I instantly regretted my bitter words.

"That's totally unfair, Sam!" Claire hissed back at me, narrowing her eyes. "It wasn't *me* who caused the problem. I was only ever trying to look out for you." Tears brimmed in her eyes, and I was left, once again, feeling like the worst human on the earth. I breathed out a huge sigh, rubbing my face and wondering how much more of a mess I could possibly make of my life.

"I know. I'm sorry. I didn't mean that. I'm just ... everything's an utter mess, Claire."

She hesitated for a second before fixing her eyes back on me.

"Sam, I know this is a stupid question given the circumstances, but – are you okay?" She glanced away from me, and I got her meaning. My heart gave a heavy thump. I knew my daughter was alive, and that was all that I had the strength to focus on. If I allowed my thoughts to move to Tessa, to the reality of what had actually happened, I feared I would never be able to get myself up again, let alone push through to continue my relentless search. Claire's concern was that I was in some sort of denial. Maybe I was, but I had to keep going, whatever that meant.

A young waitress appeared at our table, carrying plates filled with food, and I was thankful for the distraction, uncertain as to how to respond to my sister. The waitress stole a few quick glances at my face as she placed the plates in front of us. We thanked her, and my stomach growled loudly; suddenly I was aware that I was ravenous.

"People are already starting to recognise my face, Claire," I whispered, tipping my head towards the retreating waitress, who was still glancing backwards at me as she walked away. My leg bounced under the table, and my stomach took a tumble.

Claire shook her head, picking up her fork. "You're being paranoid."

I glanced after the girl before focusing on the food in front of me. After smothering my chips in salt and vinegar, I shovelled them into my mouth as quickly as I could swallow. For such a dive, the food was quite good. I lifted my head to swig my drink and noticed Claire's attention was focused on her phone screen. She was frowning. The creases around her eyes seemed to have deepened, her fork abandoned on her plate.

"What is it?" I asked, my own fork suspended in mid-air.

"I've had a message from Martin." She glanced up at me. "There's stuff hitting the news."

I retrieved my own phone from my pocket, but it remained blank when I tried to wake it. My battery had died, having not been charged since ... A surge of frustration engulfed me, followed by a desperate desire to give up. I chucked my phone onto the table and fixed my eyes on Claire, waiting for her to say something more.

Her eyes flicked around, studying the screen. She visibly paled. Her eyes darted up to meet mine, her eyebrows knitted. "You're not going to like this, Sam."

25

TESSA

FOUR YEARS PREVIOUS

Sam and I slowly came to terms with our loss. I still regularly found myself feeling hollow and empty, like I'd failed somehow. I should have been able to protect our child from harm. Sam stayed at my apartment so regularly after the loss of our baby that we were practically living together. We barely noticed the transition as he moved the last of his things. I witnessed his nights of restlessness. Tossing and turning, thrashing around, sometimes going as far as yelling out in his sleep. I was mostly sympathetic towards him when it happened and tried not to let it bother me too much. It seemed a small price to pay for such a perfect man.

We'd been together for such a short amount of time, but it felt like forever, our experiences having knitted us together so tightly.

One night, a few weeks after the miscarriage, I came home from work as usual and busied myself making our evening meal. Sam seemed off; he was jittery, his movements uncharacteristically clumsy.

We sat down to eat. He picked up his knife and fork but within seconds dropped them down again with a clatter. "Tessa, there's something I need to talk to you about." He looked so flustered that panic prickled, setting me on edge. I felt breathless, and my appetite crumbled. I pushed my plate away and stared up at him, desperate to hear what he had to say whilst never wanting him to speak the words.

"Okay," I squeaked. "What is it?"

"The thing is, Tess ... well, I've been thinking, and I ... I don't know how exactly to ... but I ..." He sighed. "God, I've made a great job of this." He sucked in a breath and focused his attention back on me.

"Look, Tess, I know this might seem crazy because we've only been together such a short time and everything, but I feel like we have something amazing, and after everything that we've been through since we met, I just know so clearly what I want. I love you, and I ... well, I ..." He trailed off; his stream of jumbled words dried up. His eyes darted around as his hand disappeared under the table.

I didn't see it coming at all when his hand reappeared, clutching a small velvet box. I gaped at him as he cracked open the tiny box.

A silver ring with a small but perfectly cut diamond winked out at me. The light caught it with a twinkle, tiny rainbows dancing out from it, mimicking my excitement. I froze, the air electric as Sam stared at me, waiting for my reaction. I guessed it was only a few seconds that passed, but it felt like an age.

"Please say something." Sam blinked rapidly, colour filling his cheeks. "If you don't like the ring, we can change it ... or have I just totally misread things? Is it too soon? It's too soon, isn't it?" His rambling snapped me back from my stunned silence.

"Yes, yes, of course my answer's yes. I just can't believe ... I love it. I love you!" I scraped my chair back from the table, reaching him in a few short strides and collapsing into his arms. He held me to him, our food totally forgotten.

"I want you to be my wife, Tessa." Sam pulled back from me; his face was filled with more conviction – more confidence – than I had ever seen. He held my face in his hands. "And when you're ready, I want us to try again to start our own family."

I couldn't speak, lost for words to fit the moment, the best moment of my entire life. I was the happiest I had ever been.

LATER THAT NIGHT, I was startled awake, unsure what had disturbed me.

My body felt heavy with the pull of sleep. My eyes were still sealed shut, but when I heard the noise again, I realised what had woken me and wrenched them open. Not that it made much difference in the blackness of my bedroom. I could just about make out the familiar shapes of my furniture. I heard the sound again, something like a low growl, coming from the living area. My heart hammered. Had someone broken in? I shot bolt upright, fully awake and alert to every tiny noise.

I turned to shake Sam awake, needing him to tell me what to do about the intruder, comforted at the thought of him there. The bed beside me was empty. I breathed a sigh of relief as my heart returned to a normal rhythm. I usually slept so lightly; I couldn't believe he had managed to get out of bed and into the kitchen without me hearing him.

I lay back down, smiling to myself, waiting to tell Sam how foolish I'd just been, believing him to be an intruder. I stretched out an arm into the space where Sam should be and was surprised to find the sheets cool. Too tired to feel concerned, I allowed myself to sink back into my pillows just as a thundering crash broke the silence. I jumped so hard I cricked my neck.

"Shit," I hissed, trying to slow my ragged breathing whilst rubbing at the burning sensation in my neck.

I swung my legs out from the warmth of my bed, and my bare feet met the freezing cold wooden flooring. I decided at that moment that wherever I lived from then on, I wanted a plush, thick carpet in my bedroom. I shivered as I heaved myself out of bed and folded my arms across my chest, trying to hold on to some warmth. I shuffled into the open-plan living and kitchen area. The space was illuminated by the streetlamp located directly outside, its bright head level with – and seeming to peep straight into – my window.

I could make out Sam's outline in the kitchen.

Chunks of glass covered the floor, glimmering in the light. They looked like lumps of ice. Or diamonds, I thought to myself, twisting the ring that still felt out of place on my finger. I picked my way across the floor towards him on the balls of my feet, my teeth chattering with the cold. The clearing up could wait until morning; I just wanted to be back in the warmth of my bed with Sam wrapped around me.

"Hey?" I whispered into the darkness. "Are you okay?"

He whipped around so quickly he startled me. I took a stumbling step backwards. As I dropped my weight onto my back foot, glass sank into the fleshy pad of my foot.

I let out a yelp and snatched my foot up from the floor.

Sam was still facing me. In the dim light, his eyes appeared black. He stared straight in my direction, but it was like he didn't see me at all, like he was staring straight through me.

"Sam?" I whispered, heart hammering. He held his stare, fixed.

"Why would you do that to me?" He growled the words through his teeth in a voice that I didn't recognise.

I flinched. "Do what, Sam? Are you okay?" I was beginning to feel afraid, the goose bumps on my skin no longer from the cold. It seemed ridiculous. It was still Sam in front of me, but I couldn't see his handsome features or bring myself to look at his eyes.

I limped forward again, picking my way through the glass, and placed my hand on the cool skin of his arm. It was as if I'd shot an electric current through him.

"GET AWAY!" He screamed the words as his arm flew upwards and made contact with my chin, snapping my jaw shut and slamming my teeth together. I stumbled backwards and lost my balance, landing with a dull thud.

I was too stunned to feel anything at first. I watched him cross the room in a few long strides, glass crunching under his feet, his eyes fixed ahead. He disappeared back into the darkness of our bedroom.

I stayed there on the floor, listening for any tiny sound. I heard nothing, so eventually, numb from the cold, I dragged myself upwards and hobbled to the sofa.

I pulled a throw around my shoulders and began to sob, digging the diamond of my new ring into the pad of my thumb.

I didn't know what hurt most, my bleeding foot, bruised jaw, or the fact that I was too afraid to go back into my own bedroom, where I was pretty sure my fiancé was now sleeping peacefully.

26

SAM

PRESENT DAY

Woman murdered, baby missing, violent husband released
without charge

I reread the terrible headline three, four times, heat spreading upwards from my neck. Tiny droplets formed along my upper lip. A numbness set in, detaching me from my reality, as if I were reading someone else's horror story. Would I be pointing the finger at the "violent husband"? I wondered, absent-minded, if the tabloid actually paid someone to come up with a headline that shockingly bad. I continued to skim the page, Claire's phone clutched tightly in my clammy, trembling hand. I hadn't realised before then that I was shaking.

"Wife found dead" ... *"Baby daughter missing"* ... *"No other suspects or persons of interest"* ... *"allegedly trashed a hotel room"* ... *"No arrest so far due to a lack of evidence"*

I only read the parts that stood out. My stomach lurched at the emphasis on the words "so far" talking of my arrest, my recent meal sitting heavily. The article was poorly written enough that I held a shred of hope people wouldn't be reading such trash. The number next to the word "comments" dashed such hope.

I scrolled down, unable to tear my eyes away, knowing I should stop myself. I didn't need to know what strangers thought of me.

Of course it's the husband, who else could it have been?

It's always someone who knew the victim!

I hope they lock him up for life when they prove it was him, a monster like that should not be walking our streets!

I can't believe they let him go, goodness only knows what he's done with that poor baby.

RIP to the poor woman, I hope that creature rots in hell for what he's done to them.

It's pretty obvious that he must have killed his baby too, where else could she be? He's probably hiding her to protect himself.

The comments went on and on, more of the same, laying the blame firmly with me, wishing the worst on me. I couldn't blame them – in their position, I would've probably thought the same. Who was I kidding? I couldn't even be certain if I was innocent myself. I deserved everything I got, but the worst had already happened.

My eyes were drawn to a link for another article – I tapped on it and watched a story load – about my jumping into the car with a "mystery woman". There were the photos from earlier in the day. I did a double take at the sight of myself, barely recognisable. I looked like a deer in the headlights as I leapt into Claire's car. I didn't bother reading the comments for that one. Aside from anything else, the insinuation of what I was doing with Claire made my skin crawl, and I felt nauseous given the knowledge that she was, in fact, my sister.

I finally managed to pull myself out of the rabbit hole of articles and comments and stared blankly at Claire for a few seconds. I couldn't sacrifice space in my mind to what the press or public thought of me. I needed to find my daughter, and I needed to know if it was down to me that she was missing in the first place. I watched her swallow hard as she picked at her nails, obviously unsure of what to say to me.

"I need to charge my phone," I stated, emotionless. "The battery's dead, and if the police find anything, that's the only number they have to contact me on." Pain knifed me as I recalled giving the officers Mike's address and phone number, listing it as the place I'd intended to stay. Anxious not to burden Claire with anything further, I'd avoided mentioning our feud.

She studied my face, concern passing over her own. She blinked and gave a sharp nod.

"I have a charger in the car. Let's go."

WE REACHED the safety of the car, where Claire dug out the charger. As I plugged it in, my stomach lurched again at the thought of switching it back on.

Neither of us said anything more as we drove back towards the city. I held down the power button on my phone and waited for the screen to light up.

Within a few seconds, I was staring down at a photo of my beautiful wife cradling our child, sitting on a picnic blanket in our local park. Tessa beamed up at the camera. A pang of regret shook me, that I hadn't made the time for more of those family days. I'd made her laugh – I couldn't even remember what I'd said – and I'd snapped the picture at the perfect moment, catching her shimmering, natural beauty. My breath caught at the sight of them. I had just been reminded – without ever really forgetting – that they were no longer there. The phone buzzed numerous times in my hand. Something had taken over me, the pain seeming physical, and suddenly all of the air had left my body.

I was gasping, panic filling my burning lungs instead of much-needed oxygen. My chest contracted, and my vision blurred. Claire darted glances at me, trying to keep an eye on me while keeping her focus on the road.

"Sam ...? Sam, what's happened? Are you okay? Breathe, Sam, deep breaths. I'm going to pull over as soon as I can find somewhere."

Concern drenched her words, but they were muffled, coming in and out as though my head were dipping under-water as she spoke. My lungs ached from the lack of air; pins and needles prickled at my fingers. The question passed through my mind: would it really be the worst thing if I didn't make it?

Cora's face popped into my mind, as clear as if she were in my arms, and I forced myself to suck in whatever air I could get. Claire veered the car into a small layby, slamming us to a stop. Lights peppered my vision. I tried to blink them away. She threw off her seatbelt and bolted out of the car, appearing at my door in milliseconds. She wrenched it open and knelt at my side.

"Sam, look at me. You're having a panic attack. You need to take deep breaths – in and out – count with me and try to focus your mind on breathing ... nothing but breathing ... That's it, keep breathing, nice and slow ... one ... two ..."

My panic subsided slightly – I was not, at least, having a

heart attack. Time moved in a strange way around us, and I lost all track of how long it took me to catch my breath again. I nodded at Claire, signalling that I was okay, as my aching lungs reinflated.

Relief passed over her face. She worked as a health care assistant at her local surgery, but emergency care was probably a little beyond her. The realisation struck me that I didn't actually know if that was what she currently did, so much time having passed. I felt the hot sting of tears, and I spluttered slightly.

"I'm so sorry, Claire." I sobbed then, for all that I had missed, all that I had lost, and all that I could never get back. My sister held me, assuring me it was okay, over and over.

When I was finally spent, I sat back in the car seat and closed my raw eyes. The photograph of Tessa and Cora filled my mind again, burned into my memory.

Something snapped within me, and my eyes flew open.

Claire was sat on the tarmac in the layby, leaning back on her hands and gazing into the distance. Her head whipped around as my sudden movement caught her eye.

"Claire, I know what I have to do."

27

TESSA

THREE YEARS PREVIOUS

"So, the good news is, everything looks perfectly normal."

The fertility doctor beamed at me, expecting me to be delighted. I felt far from delighted. It had been over a year since we'd lost our baby, and we had been actively trying to get pregnant since. I just couldn't understand it. How it had happened so easily the first time, even despite contraception. Now we were doing all the right things at the right times, yet nothing was happening.

We hadn't confided our problems to anyone. At least I didn't think Sam had told Mike. I had no one I felt close enough to that I could unburden myself; I just blinked back tears each time I congratulated a colleague or acquaintance on an upcoming arrival. I'd scour social media, bitter with jealously at each scan photo and smiling announcement, questioning if they were more deserving than me. The not-so-subtle questions had begun to slip into conversation with work friends. Now I was married, wasn't it time to think of starting a family? After all, my biological clock *was* ticking. I'd brushed them off, feigning disinterest and making jokes about being too busy with the new house and being newly wed. Sam had worked his way up within his company and was now a high-ranking accountant in their financial department. His increase in pay had meant we could afford to take on the mortgage. My low-paid admin job for the council topped us up just enough that we could cover everything. It was a dead-end job that I'd been in for far too many years, but my focus was not on my career. My desperation to start a family outweighed any other ambition.

I had secretly held out hope that after all of the poking and prodding by the fertility specialists, the endless examinations and tests would show up something nice and simple that was wrong. Potentially caused by the miscarriage. They would fix it, and hey presto, I would be pregnant. So the news that everything looked fine left me feeling unjustifiably devastated. I swallowed down my shame. How many women would kill for the news I'd just received?

I let out a deep sigh. "Okay. So, what next? I start the medication anyway, right?" I tried to keep the desperation from my voice.

"Yes, we can start you on a drug to see if we can help things along. This *is* good news though, Mrs Fulford. Try to relax now. There's no reason why this shouldn't happen for you." The doctor smiled again.

A swell of irritation coursed through me. Such ridiculous cliches never failed to infuriate me. *"Relax and it'll happen!"* I'd have to bite my tongue, literally, to hold back the venom burning to drip from my lips. *Of course, because it's that easy! Why hadn't I thought of that!*

I buried my frustration, reminding myself that it wasn't the doctor's fault. She was, in fact, trying to help. I took a deep breath and released my clenched fists, suddenly aware of my nails biting into my flesh.

"Thank you, Doctor Wheeler." I offered a tight smile.

"You're very welcome, Mrs Fulford. I'll write your prescription out for you." She had already turned back to her computer.

It still felt alien hearing my married name. *Mrs Fulford.* A smile played on my lips as I fiddled with the bands on my ring finger, enjoying the soft noise they made as they chinked together.

I'D LEFT the appointment a horrible mash of emotion. I knew I should be thankful, relieved even, but a sad emptiness consumed me. I tapped out a message to Sam to let him know just how "fine" everything was. He'd offered to accompany me to the appointment, but I had declined. He'd already taken enough time out of work, and a part of me was afraid of him hearing what they had to say.

My unjustified resentment towards the world – and everyone in it – made me itch to do something reckless. I'd made no plans for the afternoon, uncertain of what the outcome of the appointment would be, and lurched unsteadily between a compulsion to mope – allowing myself to wallow in it all and sob the afternoon away – and an impulse to get dressed up, slather on a mask of make-up, and hit the town, enjoying my unwanted freedom. I shoved the front door open, slamming it back against the wall, and hurled my keys onto the table. The warmth of our beautiful new home – usually bringing me such joy – did nothing to lift my mood. I paced for a few minutes before stomping my way through to the kitchen and retrieving a dusty bottle of wine from the back of a cupboard. I poured a large glass, hesitating before topping it up further and gulping back a mouthful. As I flopped onto my sofa, my fingers twitched with the temptation to dial Bella's number, aware she would remind me of all the reasons to be glad I wasn't pregnant. I could suggest we make an afternoon of it, hit a cocktail bar or two.

The cold clutch of loneliness beckoned me, dragging me back to that same afternoon when we'd been properly introduced. I winced thinking about it. I took another slug of wine and closed my eyes as the liquid caressed me, wrapping me in its soothing embrace, and allowed myself to drift back into the memory of my first real encounter with Bella.

I'd watched the delivery van pull onto my road that morning. It felt like forever ago but was only around a year. Having been off work for a couple of days by then, with what turned out to be tonsillitis and not early signs of pregnancy as I'd hoped, I'd felt stir-crazy. I still cringed when I had to phone in sick, afraid my boss would make assumptions about an upcoming pregnancy announcement. My mind was numb with boredom, nothing to fill the hours but concern about being too ill to utilize my fertile window. "Please be my laptop," I mumbled to myself, sighing heavily as I craned my neck to watch where the van was headed. I had agreed to continue some of my workload from home, on the understanding that I would rest as much as needed. I was desperate for the distraction.

I cursed under my breath as he pulled up at the bottom of Bella's drive and stumbled out of his van. He ambled up to her front porch with a pronounced limp and rang the bell. He shifted his weight from one foot to the other. I found myself wondering – almost delirious with the tedium of solitude – if he needed to pee.

After his second attempt, still having had no reply, he turned and shuffled back towards his van, muttering to himself. Moving to the passenger door, he retrieved another parcel, throwing Bella's back onto the front seat. After checking the details, he glanced around at the houses before fixing his gaze onto mine and moving stiffly in my direction. I made a snap decision, chewing my nails with nerves. When he made it to the door, I opened it at the first chime of the bell.

"'Ere you are, love," he rasped in his gravelly smoker's voice, thrusting the parcel towards me.

"Thanks," I croaked, my voice not sounding so different to his, with my horribly inflamed tonsils.

Clearing my throat as best I could manage, I made to step back. But before letting him get too far down the path – making out as if it was an afterthought – I called after him, voice hoarse with my burning throat. "Did I see you have a parcel for the lady at number seven?" I tried to sound casual, to remind myself that I wasn't a thief. This was just my best opportunity. "I could take it for her if you like? Save you coming back?"

He turned and eyed me; my cheeks flamed with unfounded guilt.

"Needs signin' for," he grunted. My stomach turned, and I wished he would clear his throat.

My face reddened further. I nodded enthusiastically. "Of course, absolutely!" I gushed, feeling as though I had been caught out. "I just thought ..."

"S'long as you're happy t' do that, I can shove a card frew, tell 'er to collect it from 'ere."

"Oh ... great. I can pop it over to her later when she gets back." I nodded with far too much enthusiasm, perplexed by my desperation that this stranger believe she was already my friend. I tried to lean against the door frame in a laid-back stance but ended up bumping my elbow and head simultaneously instead.

He eyed me again, one brow lightly raised and a tiny smile of amusement playing on his lips. He turned his back, hobbling towards his van and yanking open the side door. He reached inside, then retraced his steps, this time with Bella's parcel in his nicotine-stained fingers.

I signed for it quickly, trying not to recoil as his fingers – with their collection of unidentifiable filth caught under the nails – brushed my own. He turned away, seemingly unfazed, and I wheezed my thanks at his retreating back. The mix of the cold and the pungent scent of him had not done my swollen throat any favours.

I passed the rest of the day attempting to get into the work I needed to catch up on. Edgy and restless, I found myself scrolling social media, checking for announcements and seeking excitement through anyone else's life. I conjured up scenarios where the people behind those tiny profile pictures flocked to my door with soup and flowers. I felt the shame prickle at the realisation, once again, that I had no one I could call on – not a single real friend. A surge of motivation spurred me on; I continually popped to the window to watch for Bella's return. When her car finally pulled onto the driveway, I paced, not wanting to seem like I'd been waiting at the window watching for her – which, of course, I had.

I tousled my hair in the hallway mirror and gave myself a critical look up and down. Considering I felt like death, I didn't look *too* horrendous. With a small shrug, I made my way outside. Outside her front door, I sucked in a deep breath, steeling myself before pressing the bell and waiting, stomach in knots. What would I say? I should have thought that through before rushing over in my determination not to chicken out. It was too late now. Bella pulled back the door, a cloud of light, floral perfume and freshness enveloping me. I blushed furiously.

"Hi, I'm Tessa ... from number six ..." I sputtered, pointing back towards my house unnecessarily and fighting the urge to cough. "I took in a parcel for you earlier today. Just thought

I'd pop it over." I held up the prized parcel – as if to prove it really existed – and attempted an awkward smile.

Bella's eyes flicked between me and the parcel, as if considering something, before locking them back on mine.

Another wave of embarrassment washed over me, imagining myself through Bella's beautiful eyes. With my mousy, style-less hair hanging in messy strands and, thanks to my tonsillitis, pale complexion and sunken eyes, I must have been quite a sight. I'd always considered myself relatively attractive, but standing in front of Bella at that moment, I'd never felt less so. Finally, she broke the oppressive silence.

"Thank you." Her smooth, even tone was as beautifully intoxicating as her scent, but I sensed her impatience. I shrank a little further into myself, wondering what I'd been thinking. Why would someone like Bella want to be friends with me?

Dizziness crashed over me. I tried to regain my composure, reaching out a hand to steady myself against the door frame.

She tilted her head, narrowing her eyes warily. "Are you alright?"

Her voice rang with the slightest note of something resembling concern, and she dipped one perfect eyebrow. A strange look took hold of her features as she glanced at my hand gripping her door frame; she flinched and took a tiny step back.

"Yeah." I bobbed my head like some sort of nodding dog, praying for the dizzy spell to pass. "I look and sound much worse than I am." I waved a hand, voice cracking as my vision blurred.

"Oh Christ," Bella muttered, taking hold of my arm as I tried to hold the parcel while keeping my balance. "You'll have to come and sit down a minute!" In my semi-conscious state, I wondered if it was concern behind her clipped tone and the odd look that clouded her perfect features.

It wasn't at all how I had pictured it. I had envisioned myself being so charismatic, so confident, that Bella would find herself begging to become my friend. But me almost fainting *had* broken the ice and – somehow – resulted in her helping me home. I'd made her a promise that as soon as I was up to it, and didn't have to be carried home, I'd take her for a coffee as a thank you.

Unsurprisingly, after my embarrassing episode on her doorstep, Bella hadn't seemed hugely keen to meet with me. Eventually she relented, though, and allowed me to entice her out to the coffee shop on the corner. This time, with me managing not to practically pass out on her, we'd seemed to hit it off, forming an unlikely but comfortable patter of conversation. Bella had casually made the decision for me as to whether we had a "second date" with the cool remark: "Coffee's on me next time."

My phone buzzed in my hand, and I snapped my eyes open, expecting to see Bella's name. We rarely went more than a couple of hours without exchanging texts by then. Sam's light-hearted reply to my earlier message was a stark reminder.

> That's great news sweetheart! Let's make sure that we "celebrate" properly tonight! ;0)

I threw my phone onto the sofa and reached for my wine, wishing that I could share in his joy. I understood what "cele-bration" insinuated, but trying tonight was pointless. Sam had gone for tests previous to mine and had been given the all clear, too. I'd been so anxious in the months awaiting my appointment that I'd ordered every type of ovulation test I could find. I needed to know if my body was working. I never told Sam that I was doing the tests, worried that my overeagerness might scare him – or piss him off. I didn't want to make the whole process into some clinical chore.

The first month, when the three different ovulation tests showed lines and smiley faces, I was filled with a euphoric joy, almost as though I were holding a positive pregnancy test. It just had to mean it would happen that month.

I ensured I set everything up so our timing was perfect. I convinced myself that I had all sorts of symptoms that I'd never had before. I was sure I felt queasy, that my breasts were slightly swollen. I needed to pee more. It must mean something.

So when my period arrived, like clockwork, I had to face not only the crushing disappointment but also that I had been an utter fool. I'd imagined up a baby that had caused all of my so-called "symptoms".

I'd been assuring Sam that this month I'd be having to test and so burned with mortification when I had to take the walk of shame back to the bedroom.

Sam held me and kissed my hair.

"There's always next month. Stay positive, sweetheart."

28

SAM
PRESENT DAY

Claire gripped the steering wheel and blew out a long breath, screwing her eyes closed.

"Haven't you always said no type of therapy would help?" She wagged her head with the slow effort to absorb what I was proposing.

"It won't. Not to *cure* me, anyway. But that's not what we're talking about here. I just need someone to get inside my mind." I dropped my head into my hands and kneaded my eyes, overwhelmed by the weight of what I was considering – all too aware of the implications it could carry, considering what I knew.

She bobbed her head and lifted one shoulder. "I guess it makes sense. This way you can clear everything up, focus on what actually happened to Cora."

I gazed out of my window, unsure of how to respond.

"I remember when it all started." Claire's voice was soft and distant. "The parasomnias, I mean. It used to really freak me out seeing you like that. Your eyes always looked so weird." She huffed out a humourless laugh. "It was so strange, knowing you had no memories the next morning of whatever you'd done. I always wondered what it was that was playing out for you in those nightmares."

Silence hung between us, both swept up into our memories of a childhood trauma experienced so differently.

"Sometimes even now, when I'm woken up during the night by a noise, for a second or two – before I'm properly conscious – I'll think it's you breaking something or falling again." Her fears for me obscured her features like a mask. Once again, my heart ached for this woman, who, like a mother, displayed such unconditional love for me even after my selfish abandonment of her.

A few more beats passed before either of us dared to move. I remembered my phone clutched in my hand. The charger was making it warm, and that, along with the mixture of emotions, left them clammy.

"I should ..." I held up my phone and waved it around. Claire gave a weak smile and a single nod, turning to gaze out of her own window.

My stomach rolled. I was more prepared to see the faces on my screen this time, but my heart ached at the sight of my beautiful girls.

There were a number of messages and several voicemails. I swallowed hard, wincing at the sight of Tessa's father's name, the number of missed calls from him having now reached double figures. There were text messages from him, too, a sign of desperation. Tessa had tried to get him into exchanging texts, but he'd always brushed her off, asking what was wrong with good old conversation.

Unable to face his messages, I turned my attention to the voicemail notifications from unknown numbers. The first was from an old friend, one I hadn't spoken to in years, rambling on, offering his sympathy. I deleted the message before listening to the whole thing. I had no time for small talk and niceties.

The second was from a journalist. I had no idea how he'd managed to get hold of my number. His smarmy voice oozed sympathy for my "situation". He gushed on about how I should have the opportunity to tell my side of the story – and that was where I cut him off, deleting that message, too. I wasn't so stupid or self-absorbed to think that he cared about my "side of things" – only the scoop he was after.

The third message began to play. DI Garcia's voice filled my ear, sounding tinny through the phone, as he needlessly identified himself – I feared that voice would be burned into my memory for the rest of my life. A look of grave dismay came over Claire at my audible reaction to it, so I switched it to loudspeaker.

"Police." I mouthed the word, and her eyes widened. Garcia continued, his voice now dominating the car.

"I'm just phoning to inform you that the forensics team have completed the search of your house. You can collect your keys whenever suits you. Unfortunately, as of yet we don't have any further news on your daughter but have no reason to believe that she came to any harm within your home. If you remember anything else, it would be most appreciated if you could let us know. In the meantime, we'll continue to work around the clock to find her – and whoever is responsible for this."

With that, the line went dead, and the automated recording chimed in to offer options for what to do with the message. I hung up, a lump forming in my throat at the news on Cora. She was alive. I just knew it – felt it. On the surface, the message was no more than the officer updating me on the investigation, assuring me that they were doing all that they could. I could read between the lines, though, and knew exactly what he was insinuating.

"Doesn't sound like the friendliest of chaps." Claire's head was cocked, studying my reaction with a frown.

"No, well, I guess it doesn't matter as long as he gets to the bottom of this shit heap." I sighed. I was holding back, for some reason, on explaining his assumption of my guilt. But by the sceptical look on her face, she knew.

I skimmed the other messages that had come in through various apps, ignoring Keith's. Most were from acquaintances, people whom I was "friends" with on social media. I deleted most without reading them. Those people were parasites, desperate for a shred of gossip to make their own mundane lives more exciting. A few were words of genuine concern and support from true friends, and I made a mental note to reply to those if and when I ever had the headspace.

The last one was a text message from my boss. I opened it with trembling fingers.

> Hi Sam, I was so sorry to hear about all that you are going through. Obviously, we will not be expecting you at work any time soon. I'll sign you off on compassionate leave, so please, take all the time you need. Take care of yourself.

I wondered, briefly, if they *were* being compassionate, or if it was best for the firm that I wasn't there. It was just another thought I had no capacity to process, so I filed it away with the others, grateful, I decided, to be free of the demands of work for the time being.

Claire was drumming her fingers on the steering wheel, her eyes vacant.

"I guess we may as well go and collect my keys, then." My voice was a pitch too high. "I need to find the best hypnotherapist I can for this – to give it the best shot. With that in mind, it's probably best if I inform the police of my plan too, hopefully get them on board. They might even suggest someone they've used before." I attempted to keep my tone light, inject a note of confidence, but could hear the cracks breaking through my facade.

Claire's face set in a steely expression.

"No way, Sam – absolutely not. If you tell them what you are thinking of doing and why, they're going to jump to the conclusion that you're guilty! You just can't." Her nostrils flared, desperation and anger radiating from her.

DI Garcia's message was not so subtle after all, and Claire had easily read between the lines, too.

I considered my reply, aware of how my admission would hit Claire. But she had to understand it, the importance of what had to be done. Skipping around the point wouldn't help. A desperate fear crept over me; my skin felt too tight.

"I know there's a chance they'll think I'm guilty, Claire – I'm pretty sure they already do, at least some of them." Garcia had worn such a cynical expression when he told me how there'd been no sign of a break-in. Remembering that, I tried to swallow, but my mouth had gone completely dry. "But no matter which way I look at it, I just keep coming back to the same conclusions. The truth of the matter is, they think I'm guilty because everything *points* to me being guilty. And the thing is ..." My voice was trembling now. "I think they might be right."

29

TESSA
THIRTEEN MONTHS PREVIOUS

Blood rushed in my ears, and spots appeared at the edges of my vision. My nerves jangled. I reminded myself again to take a breath.

I was being stupid. I knew that. How many times had I been here? I knew the outcome already. So why could I not resist that desperate little prickle of hope? Goose pimples spread over my skin.

I hadn't slept a wink, waiting the entire night for the first ache of cramps to signal the failure of my body, another long month ahead. I didn't know how many more times I could face it, the look of disappointment that would pass over Sam's face, his vain attempt to hide it whilst doing everything to console me. I wanted this for him as much as myself.

The room was in partial darkness, curtains still drawn against the dim light of the morning. Sam was bustling around downstairs, preparing for the working day ahead. He had left the door ajar, and artificial light from downstairs stretched as far as it could reach across the bedroom. I lowered my feet, sinking them into the plush carpet we'd had put in shortly after the move. My mind jumped again to that night back in my flat when I had stepped out onto the cold floor. The incident still haunted me.

The following morning, Sam had been mortified by his actions, desperately apologetic, despite them being out of his control. If I was honest, it had rocked me to my core. More than the bruises, I couldn't shake the image of his fixed black stare, the voice coming from my fiancé that I didn't recognise and never wanted to hear again. I had to take some responsibility, though. I'd handled it badly, trying to wake him, probably aggravating his nightmare further.

Doubts had crept in. Was bringing a baby into the situation wise or fair? But my own selfish longing had overruled. Surely it wasn't always that bad. A one-off extreme case, I assured myself, pushing my concerns to the back of my mind. Fatherhood might be just the thing to free Sam from his condition.

I couldn't give up on my dream of becoming a mother, having come so far. If I couldn't have that dream with Sam, then I might as well give up all hope. I consoled myself with silent reassurances that it would be different once we had a baby – everyone says becoming a parent changes you. That an instinct kicks in. Something, whatever was amiss, would click into place for Sam. It had to.

I shivered and shook out my hand. I wanted a family with Sam. I'd made that decision, and it could well be out of my hands now, anyway. Hope sparked. I would not allow petty qualms to ruin anything for us. I was just overreacting, worrying over nothing.

I weaved towards the bathroom on wobbly legs. I certainly needed to pee. My breathing was coming in short gasps, my heart hammering painfully.

If I was pregnant, I wondered, could being this anxious be harming the baby? Instantly I felt foolish. Why was I even getting my hopes up?

But your period is late, the voice in my head argued.

By one day! I reminded myself. And that could be the medication. My battling thoughts were doing nothing for my nerves.

"Just do the bloody test," I mumbled to myself, shaking my head. Perhaps I could already feel the subtle early cramps, I thought. Was there any point wasting a test? But I couldn't hold out for another day.

I retrieved the pack of pregnancy tests in the bathroom and focused on the instructions, hopping from foot to foot on the cold tile. Not that I needed to read the instructions – I could've probably recited them word for word – it was just I had to be sure I was doing it right, that the outcome, whatever it turned out to be, was undoubtably accurate.

Once I was absolutely sure about it, I ripped open the packet and removed the plastic cap. My heart beat faster, and I felt dizzy with anticipation as I perched on the toilet and slid the test underneath me – worrying, as always, that I was getting it wrong.

It won't matter because it will be negative anyway, I chastised myself.

I replaced the cap and placed it onto the window ledge, forcing myself to look away from it. Dashing back to the bedroom, I grabbed my phone and started the timer. Three minutes to wait.

Too nervous to do anything else, I paced the bedroom floor, watching my feet sink into the carpet and counting seconds in my head. The chill had gone; my entire body felt clammy. My heart fluttered, and my breathing came in short bursts as I willed the minutes to pass. I forced myself back to the bathroom, picking up my toothbrush in trembling fingers.

The phone buzzed and beeped on the toilet cistern where I'd left it. I flinched at the sound, dropping the toothbrush into the sink with a clatter. Now that I could look, I found myself not wanting to. So long as I didn't look, I could cling on to the dream: dancing for joy at the sight of two pink lines. Once I saw the stark space where the second line should be, my dream would crumble for yet another month.

If I didn't look in time, though, the test wouldn't be valid. Even if I thought I saw the second line, I couldn't be sure.

My body felt alien, wobbly and tingly as I peeled my sticky feet from the tiles.

I stopped short before I could see it, already tasting the bitter sharpness of disappointment.

"Please, please!" I whispered, screwing up my eyes, holding back desperate tears.

I took the final step and lifted the test from where it waited with its tiny window, the one that could change my life. No amount of screwing up my eyes would stop the tears. They flowed in streams until the test in front of me was a blur.

30

SAM

PRESENT DAY

We pulled up outside the police station. The journey had been wrapped in nervous silence. I was both terrified for Cora and acutely aware of how all this could go for me.

Where are you, Cora?

My leg bounced. Each time I became conscious of it, I would stop, only to find it had started up again as soon as I forgot.

My mind turned to images of a prison cell. I wasn't built for prison. The possibility had never entered my head. Tessa and I had watched a documentary on life within prisons once, and it had made me feel grubby just watching it. I didn't belong there, wasn't one of them. They were con men, rapists, and murderers.

And what exactly are you, Sam?

My stomach churned around the food I'd consumed earlier. I had almost lost my nerve a number of times. Claire would be only too pleased should I change my mind.

I couldn't let her see my resolve waver. Her conviction of

my innocence would infect my mind. I couldn't afford for that to happen.

"Are you sure about this, Sam? Because it's not too la—"

"Certain," I cut in before she had the opportunity to plant doubts.

"Right." Her face crumpled before she could turn away. I unfastened my seatbelt and vaulted from the car before she could notice the cracks forming in my composure.

I stood by the car door and stretched my limbs, realising that I had been stuck in that box for some time. The irony was not lost on me. My aching body was grateful to regain full circulation.

I kept my back to the station and took in my surroundings. Things I wouldn't normally notice struck me now, a poignant reminder of what had happened, what might be to come. The way the wind caught the leaves on the trees, how they swayed and whispered. The strips of sun bursting through the breaks in the clouds to strike anything in their path. The glisten of the blades of grass. An elderly lady with a slight limp walked her dog, some sort of terrier. I imagined her going home to her husband, having her children and grandchildren come to visit. Sadness swelled. Would I ever see my child again? Would she ever have children of her own?

I hoped that the woman with the dog realised how lucky she was.

"Sam?" Claire interrupted and broke me out of my reverie. I glanced over at her and tried to answer the concern on her face with a reassuring smile.

"Let's go," I announced with much more conviction than I felt, turning towards the station.

WE WAITED at the desk behind a man who was complaining loudly about waiting times for police response. The young officer at the desk gave the same answer repeatedly.

"I understand, sir. We are aware of the response times and are doing all that we can, but we're stretched incredibly thin at the moment. I apologise that we couldn't attend more quickly, but we do have to prioritise."

The young officer didn't appear very sorry. I fought the urge to inform the man that he was now slowing the response times down further.

I was a ball of nervous energy and just needed to get it over with. My patience was wearing thin. At my loud sigh, the man whirled around to face me, an expression of fury contorting his face.

"Problem?" he growled at me through his teeth, eyes narrowed to slits.

"Just the current waiting times," I shot back, mirroring his expression.

"Sam!" Claire hissed my name.

"And just what makes you think that you're more important than anyone else?" Spittle flew, venom like, from his lips.

"Oh, only that my daughter's life could be on the line, but please, you take your time, have your pathetic whinge, make yourself feel validated!"

He glared at me, fury burning in his eyes. The man must have been in his sixties, but he was lean and muscular. He stepped towards me.

"Just who the fuck ... " he snarled, poking me in the chest with his finger.

A red mist descended on me, the emotion of the last couple of days reaching boiling point and bubbling over. I grabbed his jabbing finger and twisted hard.

The man let out an animal-like yelp and pulled his hand

away from me, cradling his injury. He curled his lip as he eyeballed me up and down.

"You're some sort of psycho!" he hissed.

I shrugged, aware that I was goading him but unable to quash my boiling anger.

Claire stepped forward. I noticed for the first time the officer behind the desk watching the scene unfold.

"All right, fellas, let's just both cool it, shall we? I'm sure neither of you want any trouble." He regarded me as if I were a wild animal. My rage frothed, and I silently willed him to push me further.

"Hey! You're the creep who murdered his wife and baby!" The accusation came from a young scruffy-looking woman. Her words hung in the air.

I glanced around, all eyes now fixed on me, none of them friendly. My anger melted into fear, but more for Claire than myself. The silence was thick, heavy.

"Mr Fulford?" The commanding voice echoed around the bare waiting area.

I turned to see DI Garcia holding open a door, his expression unreadable. For the first time, I was relieved to see him.

"I think you should come with me." It wasn't a question.

As I scuttled towards the open door, happy to follow him through it, I heard him mumble under his breath, "Before you cause any more shit."

31

TESSA

THIRTEEN MONTHS PREVIOUS

My mind simply couldn't process what I had seen. I looked again, not sure it was real, that it wasn't some cruel trick of my mind. I swiped at the tears blurring my vision, rubbing my eyes with my pyjama top to stem the flow. Blinking a few times, I held the stick up to the light.

There was no mistaking it. The illustration on the box was clear in my memory. Sure, it was faint, but it was there. That perfect second pink line.

I cradled the test, as precious as if it were my unborn child, and allowed the tears to fall freely, happy to let them flow. Numb and frozen to the spot, I worried that if I moved, I'd wake up to find I'd been dreaming, and it would all come crashing down.

I picked up the box – just to absolutely confirm it – and checked the test against the image on the instructions. I grinned like a fool, did a mad little jig, and punched the air. I had imagined this moment countless times, and here it was, my dream made real.

I ambled down the stairs in a state of disbelief, the test clutched by my side. I checked for the second line again a couple of times on the way.

In the kitchen, Sam was packing his lunch. He turned at the sound of me, and his face crumpled, just for a moment. I stood gawping at him, unable to find words.

"Oh, sweetheart ... it's okay. We won't give up." His words were so soft and kind, I choked again on my attempt to speak.

Sam moved towards me with outstretched arms.

"No." I gulped, the word coming out as a squeak. Sam continued as if I hadn't spoken and wrapped me in an embrace, ready to start his ritual of kind words and comfort at my failure. I pushed back gently from Sam's arms.

"Sam, we don't have to ... I mean ... I'm—"

"I *want* to! We'll keep trying as long as it takes." He stroked my cheek, not understanding my disjointed sputtering.

"No!"

Sam flinched. I was making such a mess, I gave up and just held up the test.

Sam stared at the stick in my hand, then looked back at my face, his knitted eyebrows making creases across his forehead.

"What's that?" he breathed, too afraid to assume.

Emotion was overtaking me again as I watched Sam's eyes. I could only nod, a grin breaking across my face and slowly turning into a strange giggle.

"It's not?" Sam exclaimed, eyes ablaze, flicking between my own and the test clutched tightly in my hand.

I laughed hysterically and thrust the test in the air like a trophy.

THE REST of that morning was a blur. I didn't remember Sam's words, just his yell of delight as he jumped around the kitchen before scooping me up.

We both called in sick to our jobs and spent the day making plans, discussing baby names, and reading up on what I could and couldn't have during pregnancy. Floating on euphoria.

Over the following days, I took a further five tests. I just had to be certain. The lines got darker and darker until I plucked up the courage to take the one that showed it in words. My heart still skipped as the timer flicked on the tiny digital screen. At last, the word "pregnant" appeared. I danced around the room while Sam held the test in his hand and chuckled.

"I think we knew what it would say, sweetheart." He smiled warmly, secretly enjoying the moment as much as I was.

"Yes, but now we have it confirmed in words, Sam, *in words!*"

He chuckled again softly, shaking his head.

AS THE WEEKS passed and the sickness hit, the joy of my pregnancy morphed into something else, something I hadn't been the slightest bit prepared for: fear.

We had waited so long and wanted this baby more than we'd ever wanted anything. Now I was finally pregnant, I had so much more to lose.

I continued to take tests, afraid that if I didn't see the lines, it might not be real anymore. I begged Sam for an early reassurance scan, but he gently refused each time. We would see the baby soon enough at our twelve-week hospital scan, he insisted, and that money could be put to much better use.

Sam knew I was anxious, but he had no idea just how extreme it had become. I considered confiding in Bella, but she didn't seem the right person. We spoke most days via text and met at least weekly for coffee or lunch. I hadn't told her about my pregnancy, expecting her reaction of visible horror before she pulled herself together. On more than one occasion whilst we'd been out together, she'd stunned me with her nasty comments about women who were pregnant or had young children. I had no idea how I'd given her the impression that I felt the same. Perhaps she was picking up on my jealousy and was misreading it.

The time that stuck with me most was during a lunch date we'd had. I'd discovered that morning I'd failed for another month and sat gazing at a young mother. She was fighting with her toddler, trying to hold her down and strap her into a buggy as she bucked and screamed. All the while, she was defending her swollen stomach from kicks and swinging arms. I wondered how far along she was, if her pregnancies had been planned. The woman had met my eye, hair sticking up and cheeks pink, a sheen of sweat shining on her nose and beading on her lip. She offered an apologetic smile. I gave a tiny shake of my head and a sympathetic smile of my own.

"Jesus. It's bad enough that she had one she can't cope with. Why would you be stupid enough to do it again?"

I flinched, shocked at the harsh tone that laced her words. I knew her opinion on having children. She had never shied away from voicing it, and I had never judged her, but her comment seemed unnecessarily cruel and judgemental. Or maybe this time it just felt too close to home. I had assumed her feelings were about having a child of her own, that she might even be a little excited upon news of my pregnancy. I had hoped she might see herself as some sort of aunty figure to the child of her closest friend, but her comments left me feeling shaken.

"All they do is make you fat, tired, and stupid. I mean, they even call it baby brain," she'd scoffed. My eyes widened as I turned my focus back towards her just in time to witness the scowl she'd fixed on the young mother. "Who on earth would ever make the conscious choice to ruin the rest of their lives with *that*?" She'd nodded towards the screaming child, her lip curling and nose wrinkling in clear disgust.

I was almost afraid that if I told her, she'd propose that a miscarriage would be a blessing in disguise, feeling upset with her just at the thought.

Every waking thought was hijacked by the pressure of keeping the tiny little life inside me safe. I'd also begun suffering horrendous, vivid nightmares – a cruel irony, as Sam's seemed to have eased. I felt an unjustified bitterness, as though he'd freed himself of them by transferring them on to me. I'd jolt awake, covered in sweat, and trying to tease out dream from reality. During the nightmares, I would have a terrible miscarriage, or I would go, full of joy, to my scan, only to be told that no baby existed. I was driving myself insane.

I took multiple trips to the toilet, laughing it off with Sam as another pregnancy symptom. We joked about how I should set up camp in the bathroom, what with my sickness and my weak bladder. What I didn't tell him was it was actually to check for any sign of bleeding, the beginning of the end of my perfect dream. I couldn't allow myself to hope that it would work out.

A couple of weeks away from our first scan, I was practically counting down the hours. I snuggled down into our bed as Sam undressed and read out loud from the app I had downloaded about our baby's progress.

"So, it's almost the size of a lime!" beamed Sam as he folded his jeans. "I can't wait to see him or her on the screen."

I focused on the image of the foetus on my phone, my other hand resting on my belly as I tried to imagine that same little creature growing inside me. I said a silent prayer for my baby to keep going, and for the scan to come around quickly.

32

SAM

PRESENT DAY

The office we followed Detective Garcia into was a hive of activity. I glanced around, relieved to not have all eyes lift to stare at me. Those people had seen it all; nothing fazed them anymore.

My rage had fizzled, leaving me shaken and humiliated by the scene in the waiting area. The looks from those strangers would never leave me. There was no doubt as to what those people thought I was. I returned my focus to what needed to be done.

Garcia stopped at a desk and rummaged in a drawer for a few seconds before turning back to me, my keys, bearing a label on them that I didn't recognise, pinched between his thumb and index finger.

"Here you go. We've got loads of calls to go through from the appeal. Nothing to lead us anywhere yet, but someone will call you with an update later on." He thrust the keys in my direction without looking at me. As I took them, he turned away, dismissing me without another word. I could feel Claire's eyes on me, her will that I take the detective's signals and walk away.

Part of me wanted to, desperate to be out of the drab building, to bury my head and try to forget what was happening around me. I could leave it to the police to prove what I had or hadn't done. It was, after all, their job. But this time, I wouldn't run. I tightened my grip on the phone clutched in my hand, conjuring up the image of Tessa and Cora that it would display at the touch of a button, and focused on what needed to be done.

I cleared my throat, ignoring Claire's dagger-pointed stare.

"Erm, DI Garcia, there's something else, actually. Is there somewhere that we could go and, erm, have a chat?"

Irritation prickled at my own words, sounding so blasé. I once again understood his hatred for me. Garcia turned back to face me, making no effort to hide his distaste.

"Is it important, Mr Fulford? Only, this morning you said you had nothing further to add."

"Do you really think he'd be asking to speak with you if it wasn't important?" Claire spoke with a venom I'd never heard. My head whipped around. "That's why we're here, Detective. Believe it or not, *we* actually want Cora home safe more than you do. Are you going to refuse to listen to offered information?" She looked Garcia up and down, her eyes narrowed to slits, as she delivered her last cutting words.

Unease flashed in his eyes, but it was gone in an instant, making me wonder if I'd imagined it. He glared at her, clearly irked by her tone.

"And you are?" he challenged, screwing up his face and mirroring her look up and down.

"Beside the point, really, isn't it?" She cocked her head, keeping her eyes fixed on his. Her motherly instinct towards me had rendered her fearless.

They remained as they were, eyes locked, in silent challenge. I got the feeling I could leave the room and neither one of them would notice. My gaze flicked between them for a second or two before I decided enough was enough and followed Claire's lead.

"So, Detective, can I speak with you, or do you not have time to listen to potentially critical information regarding my family? You did insist I speak with you if I thought of anything."

I made sure to emphasize the words "my family" to remind him of who I was in his investigation, regardless of his feelings towards me.

Garcia tore his eyes away from Claire and regarded me once again, an unreadable expression fixed on his face. His lip twitched as he called back to no one in particular, "I'm conducting an interview in room three, if anyone needs me."

There was no response as he strode out of the room. Claire and I exchanged a look before falling in behind him.

ONCE WE WERE all seated in the interview room, Garcia's eyes bored into me.

There had been no pleasantries, no offers of refreshments this time. He was keen to get rid of me – if only so that he could continue to hunt me down.

Sat opposite him, his full attention on me, I found myself lost for words. Perhaps my grief had driven me to insanity. I was sat in a police station, in front of an officer who despised me, about to propose my guilt for a crime, not having any idea if I was guilty. It was ludicrous. A manic giggle bubbled up inside me, but I stifled it with a strange cough-like choking noise.

"You okay?" Claire whispered. Her worry was palpable, frown lines running so deep I worried they'd be permanent. I nodded and cleared my throat again.

"So, not to hurry you, but would you like to fill me in as to why I'm sitting here with you rather than looking for your daughter?" The detective's taut patience had snapped. Claire fixed him with an icy stare; he ignored her existence entirely.

I took a deep breath and nodded again, keeping my face fixed.

"Detective, please believe me when I tell you there's not a person on this earth who wants to find my daughter more than I do." My voice shook. Garcia shifted, clearly uncomfortable with the show of vulnerability from someone he viewed as a suspect. Claire placed her hand over mine on the table, and Garcia's eyes fixed on them instantly, one eyebrow rising.

"I am willing to do *whatever* it takes to bring her back safely," I continued, the words now flowing more easily.

The detective eyed me with a flicker of interest.

"A thought occurred to me whilst I was going over things with Claire – my sister." I put emphasis on the final word and gestured towards her.

Garcia glanced in Claire's direction, who lifted her head, sticking out her chin defiantly.

"So." I sighed deeply, rubbing my temples and considering how to deliver the next sentence. "I know you think that I did this." I met his eye; he offered no denial. "The problem is that I am terrified that you might actually be right." My voice was calm, but I swallowed hard, the lump in my throat returning along with a huge wave of nausea as my stomach plummeted. *No going back now.*

Garcia's head snapped up, his eyes boring into my own, trying to weigh up exactly what I was saying – if this was a confession. His forehead creased, but he said nothing.

To fill the silence, I did so.

"The truth is, I *don't know* if I am guilty of this or not, but right now, I don't see many other possibilities. I'm deeply ashamed to admit it, but my wife did suffer thanks to me and my sleep condition." I couldn't meet his eye. "I would never have hurt her knowingly. But I do need to know the truth – my daughter is the only thing that matters now. And of course, justice for my wife." I nodded sharply. "The only way I can think of finding out for certain is somehow digging around in my subconscious." I continued, a sense of peace coming over me, "So I'm here to ask for your help."

A puzzled expression passed over the DI's face. "How so?" he questioned, sitting forward and tilting his head slightly.

"I think we need to find the best hypnotherapist that we possibly can, see what they can draw out of me." I met his eye to emphasise how serious I was.

Garcia was watching me with scepticism. A few beats passed.

"I mean, it's a little unorthodox, to say the least." He raised an eyebrow, but I could tell that something in him had thawed slightly.

"I know." I sighed. "But it's the only thing that I can think of trying that might actually work." I shrugged, shaking my head.

He raised both eyebrows and leaned back in his chair, arms folded across his wide chest.

"I suppose it's got to be worth a shot." He shrugged. "We've nothing to lose by trying, I guess."

I nodded, thankful that neither of them were able to read my thoughts, because the words that were going through my brain were not words I was willing to share with anyone.

I may not have much left to lose, but you have no idea just what I'm hiding.

33

TESSA

TEN MONTHS PREVIOUS

I stirred and shifted on the bed, trying to keep my brain switched off. A harsh hiss of a whisper broke the silence around me. My body stiffened – that was what had disturbed my slumber. I was on my side, my body facing Sam, but I was too afraid to move.

"I ... didn't ... do ..." Sam thrashed. His whole body jerked, and his hands slammed, palms up, into the pillow either side of his head. My breathing quickened, and I focused on keeping it even. Maybe if I kept quiet and still enough, Sam's nightmare would end, and I could just go back to sleep.

I counted my breaths, in and out. My heart was slamming against my chest. I wondered if my baby was getting used to the constant chaotic changes in its rhythm.

"You can't do anything," Sam snarled. Goose pimples rose all over my body at his aggressive tone.

That was the part I hated most about Sam's sleep condition: he was unrecognisable, far from the man I knew and loved. I found myself genuinely afraid of the stranger who appeared in my bed during those nights.

I kept deathly still, wondering what I should do, hoping

that it would be over before I had to decide. I squeezed my eyes shut.

"No, you won't ..." The eerie calm that had come over Sam's voice somehow unnerved me even more. I struggled to hold back a gasp. I willed myself to fall back to sleep and only wake when it was all over.

But sleep had escaped me, too far in the distance now for me to catch it up. I was suddenly desperate to be away from the intruder beside me. I attempted rolling over, hoping to creep out of bed without catching Sam's attention. I'd barely made it onto my back before the mattress shifted beneath me. I couldn't breathe, all the air forced out of my body.

I had taken a blow to my stomach, my pregnant stomach. One of my husband's thrashing limbs had struck me. As I choked for air, my hands flew to the tiny swell of my belly. I no longer cared about keeping quiet or still and was certain that it was only the emptiness of my lungs stopping me from screaming.

I wasn't sure if I was just winded, or if a panic attack was taking hold of me, but I continued to suck in as much air as I could, clutching my stomach and silently making promises to my baby that if he or she would just hold on, I would take better care from now on.

Sam had finally gone still beside me, whatever it was that had taken hold of him having played out, leaving the room oddly still around my spinning wheel of panic.

My only fear now for the well-being of my child, I reached for him, making contact with his sleeping form with all of the strength that I could muster.

"Hmmmm." Sam stirred but didn't wake. I threw my arm at him once again, using everything that I had to gasp his name whilst striking out.

"*Sam.*" My voice sounded so strange, like I'd inhaled helium.

Something broke through Sam's subconscious, and his eyes flew open. He sat upright and turned his head towards me in one fluid motion, an equal measure of confusion and panic crossing his face.

All I could do was watch as he slowly took in the scene before him, his eyes meeting mine, panic having prevailed.

"Tess?" he gasped, his eyes locking onto mine. "What's happening? What can I do?"

His eyes darted between my face and my stomach, which I was clutching with both hands. I was still gulping in short bursts of air, my vision swimming, a film of tears over my eyes. I could no longer see Sam, just his blurry outline.

I continued to try to suck in breaths, but the effort was too much. I was hyperventilating, panicking. Sam's muffled voice was moving farther away into the distance.

I allowed the blackness to swallow me until I heard nothing at all.

34

SAM
PRESENT DAY

I trudged into the brightly decorated waiting area. The room was tiny, consisting of only a desk slightly outsized for the space and two leather tub chairs. The plump woman behind the desk lifted her eyes from the screen in front of her and fixed me with a warm smile.

"Can I help you?" She tilted her head. I couldn't tear my eyes from her gleaming white teeth, highlighted further by her rosy cheeks.

"Erm ..." I cleared my throat, wondering once again if I was doing the right thing. I had been expecting more of a doctor's office, but the tiny waiting area with its bright walls looked more like a nursery. Suddenly I was doubtful.

I gave myself a mental kick up the arse, reminding myself why I was there.

"I have an appointment. Mr ..."

"Fulford? Oh yes, you're very lucky Helen agreed to squeeze you in. Her appointments are sought after, you know," she prattled, beaming up at me. I could only manage a nod and something probably close to a grimace in return.

She faltered – a frown flickering across her features –
before her professional mask slid back into place.

"If you'd like to take a seat, sir, Helen will be with you
shortly."

She gave a sharp nod. Her beaming face brought to mind
a Stepford wife, perfectly programmed for her professional
role. My stomach tightened in a pang of grief thinking of my
own perfect wife. I mumbled a half-hearted thanks and
slumped into one of the vacant chairs, dropping my head into
my hands.

Between Garcia and Claire and me, we had researched
and found who we hoped was our best chance for discovering the truth. It had been late evening by the time we
contacted Helen, Garcia managing to track down her
personal contact details and persuade her to see me, even at
such short notice. I was both thankful and racked with
anxiety at the quick turnaround; there was little time to
change my mind. I hadn't returned to my house, too emotion-
ally drained from the day, too unstable to face the home that
was no longer anything more than a building. Claire and I
had gulped down greasy fast food in the car before driving to
a motel and checking into a twin room – although neither of
us got much sleep. I was scared of having a nightmare if I
allowed myself to sleep, the trauma and anxiety making it
more likely. I couldn't afford a repeat of the mortifying scene
from the last hotel; it still made me burn with shame.

My nerves jangled during the wait. Dark clouds of doubt
hung over me, and my knees bounced rapidly. Claire's
concerned face filled my mind, and a wave of guilt washed
over me. She'd offered repeatedly to accompany me to the
appointment, but I couldn't bear to have her there. I had no
idea what the appointment might uncover, which was exactly
why I was sat there scared shitless.

I wondered how the confidentiality worked. Would they

have an obligation to tell the police *anything* that I disclosed? Especially considering the circumstances under which she'd agreed to see me. How would she know if something I recalled was an account of a real event or just something that I'd dreamt up under the spell of a parasomnia?

My blood ran cold, and goose pimples rose on my skin. How many times had Tessa begged me to try this kind of therapy and I'd refused, too afraid of what might have been dredged up and brought to the surface? Now she was gone; there was no marriage left for me to salvage. I made to stand, self-preservation kicking in. I couldn't risk it. Claire might well find out so much more than she'd bargained for. I wasn't sure I could deal with that too without crumbling. She'd turn her back on me. I knew she would. And if we didn't find Cora, she was all I had left.

I started at the call of my name.

I cursed myself for not getting more information before volunteering for this. Of course, I wouldn't have come if I had. By now I had little choice but to go through with it. Besides, I owed it to my daughter. I pushed my own selfish fears aside and turned towards the voice. The woman standing in the doorway was roughly ten years my senior. She was attractive and looked every bit the professional, dressed in a fine trouser suit, light brown hair twisted back in some sort of clip. I couldn't decide whether her professional manner was reassuring or deepened my anxiety.

"Mr Fulford?" she asked again, tilting her head at me, eyes kind but full of questions.

I inhaled deeply and nodded, meeting her eye. "Thank you for agreeing to see me." It was all that I could bring myself to say. The events of the recent days had rendered me incapable of polite small talk.

Her smile widened in slight amusement. "Your friend in

the force didn't exactly give me much option. He can be pretty ... persuasive, can't he?"

DI Garcia had pulled more than a few strings to make the appointment happen quickly. I found his assertiveness arrogant, but Helen seemed amused by it. Perhaps he'd assumed he'd charmed her, gotten into her head, his ego blinding him to the irony of his self-assurance.

"Would you like to come through?" She gestured into a large office area and stepped aside for me to pass her.

To my relief, the room was decorated in a neutral pastel green and cream. There was a well-worn plush sofa and a couple of big leather office chairs.

"Please, go on in." Helen's voice came from behind me. I realised that I had been lingering in the doorway. "Take a seat, and we can get started."

I scanned the room, wondering where to position myself, if there was a seat that was specifically for me.

"Wherever you like." She smiled. "This works best if you're relaxed and as comfortable as possible, so you decide where that's most likely to be for you."

I caught myself wondering if my choice of seat was some sort of test, whether that choice would reflect what kind of person I was or something.

Feeling ridiculous, I moved towards the sofa in a few strides and sank down onto the cushions, leaning into its plump arm for support. I was certain I could have slept had I not been so tense, passed out there and then from exhaustion. My stomach flipped – my knees were bouncing again. Helen glided across the room and settled herself into one of the leather chairs.

"So." She retrieved a notepad and pen from the table next to her, eyes flicking upwards to take in my bouncing knees without comment. "First off, I'm truly sorry for your loss, Sam. Is it okay if I call you Sam during our appointments? I find being as informal as possible often helps us to relax."

My head snapped up. "Appointments? This is just a one-off." My harsh tone was unintended. "I don't plan to make a habit of this."

If she was at all surprised by my outburst, she didn't show it.

"I know why you're here, Sam, and the importance of what you are hoping to find out." I assumed her look was meant to be reassuring. "We'll do everything we possibly can to help you, but the emphasis is on the *we*. If you aren't willing to work with me, this isn't going to be possible, I'm afraid."

Her voice kept steady, betraying no hint of annoyance that I'd pushed my way into her schedule, or that, since arriving, I'd acted an utter arsehole. She studied me for a few seconds.

"Unfortunately, as much as we'd like to, we can't always put a time frame on these sessions. When we're digging for something that the brain has chosen to bury, it can take some time to break through the walls of resistance that it's carefully constructed. Our minds are incredibly complex." Her eyes remained fixed on my face. A flicker of sympathy appeared in them. "I can't imagine how difficult all of this must be for you. If you're willing to put in the effort to work with me, I'll do everything that I possibly can to help you get to the answers you need – if you possess them. Of that, I give you my word."

A severe expression had come over her features, but the sympathy in her eyes remained. I thawed slightly, realising that this woman was offering to do everything she could to help me, when I was nothing more than a stranger to her. Potentially a stranger who had murdered his wife and child – even by his own admission. She owed me nothing whatsoever.

I met her eye and managed a watery smile.

"I don't think we can say fairer than that ... Thank you," I replied weakly, wondering if the sympathy in her eyes would be replaced by disgust once she'd excavated what my mind had suppressed.

35

TESSA

TEN MONTHS PREVIOUS

The claws of fear sank into my heart. On rubbery legs, I stood and turned to look, breath coming in short rasps. My hands trembled as I leaned on the sink. I thanked God that there was nothing untoward, praying again that meant everything would be okay. I flushed and rinsed my hands, the warm water a welcome feeling on my ice-like fingers. A shiver ran over my ill-clad body.

When I opened the door, I was met with the faces of the paramedics. Sam also turned, his face wretched and pale and his hair sticking up at funny angles, looking like a lost little boy in his pyjamas. I couldn't meet his eye.

"No signs of any bleeding," I mumbled. Now the chaos had died down, I felt awkward with the two strange men in my bedroom, while only partially dressed in my own flimsy pyjamas. I crossed my arms tightly over my chest.

"Well, that's a good sign," the older of the two paramedics offered, his soft, kind eyes matching his tone. He looked to be in his mid fifties and was accompanied by a much younger – and very attractive – colleague. Both were tidying up the bits of equipment that they'd used. "These little ones are pretty well protected in there."

I inwardly cringed at what they had witnessed and that their being here had been such a waste of time.

I nodded and attempted a half smile. "Hopefully, yes. I'm so sorry to have wasted your time," I blurted, my cheeks burning.

"Not at all," the paramedic replied, his voice full of sympathy. "Panic attacks are terrifying, and it's always best to be checked over when you pass out. Especially in your condition."

The memory surfaced again. I had been so certain I was dying. I winced with humiliation all over again.

He winked at me. "Give the hospital a call later on. We'll pop the report through for you so hopefully they can bring your scan forward – reassure you a bit."

I avoided meeting his eye, my cheeks still burning as I managed a grateful nod. "Thank you, I'll do that."

They both wished me all the best as they passed carrying their bags of equipment.

Sam cleared his throat. "Thank you very much. I'll show you out." The wobble in his voice betrayed his worry.

As they left, I lowered myself cautiously onto the bed. I rested my forehead against my fingertips, my emotions cresting. I heard the padding of Sam's feet but couldn't bring myself to look at him. I peered through my fingers to observe him shifting his weight from foot to foot. He took a couple of tentative steps towards me and placed his hand on the top of my bare arm, stroking it gently.

Sam withdrew his hand at my slight flinch. I allowed my hands to drop away from my face and took in the sight of my husband. His eyes darted around the room, and his Adam's apple bobbed, his skin pallid. He cleared his throat.

"You surprised me," I lied. I couldn't bear hurting him any further.

"Sorry," he mumbled, rubbing his scars.

I wagged my head, miserable at the fraught silence that hung between us. I wanted to go to him, wrap my arms around his neck, and have him hold me to him. But the echoes of the previous night's horror made it impossible to let down the walls.

"I'm going to watch some TV for a bit, grab a cuppa." I rose from the bed, hesitating as I passed my husband, grasping for a way to close the void yawning between us.

As much as I adored Sam and would have given anything to make our marriage work, I just couldn't shake the image of the unrecognisable monster he became.

I'D BEEN DOZING on the sofa in front of trashy early morning TV for a couple of hours when Sam appeared hovering in the doorway. I felt a stab of sympathy and wished to have his arms around me, comforting me.

"Hey." He forced a smile, then wrung his hands, searching for something else to say. "Have you called the hospital yet?" he asked, his voice apprehensive as he eyed me.

I let out a sigh and ran my hands over my face.

"I tried, but the clinic doesn't start until eight thirty. I'll try to get through as early as possible – hopefully they can squeeze me in somewhere."

He nodded. "If you want to rest for a while, I could always call them?" He rubbed the back of his neck before brushing his fingers over one of his scars. I could see he was desperate to be helpful, to atone for whatever his crime had been.

Sam had woken the previous night to discover me writhing next to him. I had lied to the paramedics about what had actually happened and had no idea what Sam actually knew, either.

I shook my head gently. "Thanks, but I wouldn't be able to sleep. I'm going to head up and take a shower though. I want to be ready if they call me in."

I stood, letting the blanket that I'd bundled myself up in puddle on the floor. Feeling the chill of the room, I wrapped my arms around myself, hoping that Sam might wrap me in his as I passed.

I watched his hand twitch, just the slightest movement, and willed him to take hold of me. I needed him to somehow convince me that things were going to be okay, that there was a way to fix everything.

His hand hovered for a second or two before dropping back against his side, his nerve lost. I averted my eyes and passed by without another word. As I made my way up the stairs, I wondered how it was possible to hold so many contradicting feelings for someone.

Just who exactly am I married to?

A considerate, loving husband by day, a terrifying stranger by night.

36

SAM

PRESENT DAY

I snapped awake and sat bolt upright.

"It's okay, Sam. Take a few deep breaths, no rush."

I had no idea where I was, and the woman's calm voice, that I didn't recognize at all, only deepened my confusion. My eyes widened, and I blinked a few times before my memory returned. The last thing I remembered was Helen's soothing voice competing with the one in my head insisting that I'd made a mistake, that it was never going to work.

I was still in enough of a sleep fog to remember parts of the dream that I'd been having, intruding in snippets. The sinister faces of my nightmares sniggered at me from the shadows just beyond the light of consciousness: predators skulking and taunting in my peripheral vision.

Disorientation mingled with the residual terror. My chest heaved, and my breath caught, wondering what I might have unwittingly revealed.

"What did ..." I sucked for more air before continuing, surprised by my shortness of breath, as though I had just sprinted uphill. "Did you ..." I gulped, my stomach churning. "Did it work?" I tried to bring her face into focus.

She studied me for what could only have been a second or two but felt like an age, her expression unreadable as her eyes flicked across my face, reading something written in my features.

"Are you okay, Sam?" Her voice startled me. I had been swept up in a vision: police bursting into the room, dragging me away while Helen remained sat, the same impassive expression etched onto her face. I rubbed my hand across my face and realised how clammy I was. My underarms felt sticky, and I was suddenly conscious of my body odour. I sucked in a deep breath to steel my determination, then met her eye with what I hoped was calm composure.

"Thank you, yes, I'm fine." The adolescent squeak of my voice was not convincing. I cleared my throat before repeating my earlier question. "Did it work?" I was slightly firmer in asking.

She seemed to be studying me again. Although it was incredibly unnerving, I was determined to hold her gaze.

"Well, that depends exactly what you're referring to." She tilted her head as she spoke in her infuriatingly calm tone. "If you're asking if the hypnosis was a success, then the answer is yes. You did incredibly well for someone so very sceptical."

Heat rose to my face. I searched her expression for a hint of irony, but if it was there, she was too intelligent to show it.

"Right," I urged her on, undeterred. "And did you manage to get anything useful?"

Her eyes filled with sympathy once again, and she slowly shook her head.

"Nothing that'll help with the whereabouts of your daughter, I'm afraid." She leaned forward. "Can I be honest with you, Sam?" Her question caught me off guard, putting me on alert, afraid of what she might say.

Masking my fears, I nodded. "Of course, please." I opened my hands palms up, trying to appear receptive despite what I was actually feeling. She placed her hands on top of the notebook in her lap and regarded me with a drawn expression.

"I think you may have had a very traumatic past, that things have happened to you that you never had a chance to deal with properly." My face flushed again, but I remained silent, allowing her to continue. "I would really like the opportunity to help you deal with it, but I'm not sure that dredging it all back up is the best way to go about it. I think maybe we could use these sessions to help you move forward, to clear and potentially free your mind from the awful torment in a much more positive way."

I wondered what I must have said to her whilst I was out of it, wishing now that I had accepted the offer to have the session recorded. I hadn't wanted that at the time, afraid – stupidly – that it could be used as evidence against me. I lifted my head and stuck out my chin.

"I don't know what you're referring to." The lie came easily, out of habit. "And my only priority is trying to help my daughter and get justice for my wife. I'm not after a bloody therapy session."

I slammed my fist into the sofa cushion, my frustration mostly aimed at myself. My fears had been just. I had given her access to my mind, and she had drawn out secrets I'd worked so hard to keep buried.

Helen silently shifted herself back again in her chair and regarded me with a downcast expression. I took in a deep breath and huffed it out.

"Can we please try again? I want you to take me under again, probe a bit further, and see if you can get something useful this time. It must be there!" My voice was rising again. I clamped my teeth shut, willing myself to get it together, to find some composure.

"I wouldn't be willing to go any further today, I'm afraid." She must've noticed the anger clouding my face, as she held up a hand and continued, "I know how important this is to you, Sam, and of course I see why. We all want your daughter brought home safe and well, but even our short session has taken its toll on you. It'd be incredibly unprofessional of me to push you further than I think is in your best interest, for your own health and well-being. I have a duty of care to you."

She wasn't going to be persuaded. I couldn't afford to burn bridges, but it still took everything I had not to argue the point with her. Although I wasn't sure exactly what she'd found, I was stunned to realise that she had managed to get into my head, to open what I'd kept so tightly closed. Were she no longer willing to help me, would anyone else have the same success? I couldn't be sure.

I squeezed my fists and gritted my teeth, biting back an angry response.

"So, what if I go off, have a break? Can I come back later?" I suggested, attempting to keep the desperation out of my voice.

She shook her head slowly. "No. Not today. I can assure you we wouldn't get anything useful once you're mentally drained to this point. You need some decent rest."

I arched an eyebrow. "My daughter is god knows where, potentially alone – maybe worse – so rest isn't exactly easy to come by right now." My voice dripped with sarcasm. I knew she didn't deserve my petty contempt, but I couldn't stop myself.

"I know." She nodded. "And I really, really wish I could do more to help you, Sam." Her words were so genuine, I felt a stab of guilt.

"Tomorrow, then?" I managed to steady my voice. Getting hysterical wasn't going to help.

I watched her internal battle, her mind wrestling with her options. She heaved a deep sigh and met my eye.

"If you can get here early – before my clinic starts – I'll see you." I lit up, ready to gush my thanks, but she held up her hand once again. "But only if you are in a fit state for the session. It'll be my decision. So if you want it to work, Sam, I strongly advise that you really try to rest."

I decided not to push my luck any further and left her office with a chorus of thanks. I questioned her on payment, but she waved it off, simply stating it had been sorted. I left uncertain as to what that meant, but too weary to attempt to find out.

Once outside, I lifted a hand to shield my pounding eyes from the late-afternoon light. I drove home thinking back on what Helen had said. I wondered – not for the first time – if karma was responsible for the bad things happening to me.

I thought of Claire and her unwavering support. Feeling another stab of guilt, I made a decision. It was about time I repaid her with some honesty. She deserved to hear the truth from me before it came out.

It was the absolute least that I owed her.

37

TESSA

TEN MONTHS PREVIOUS

I clasped the phone to my ear. "Okay, I understand." I sighed. I did not understand, actually, and wanted to scream. "Thank you."

I hung up and met Sam's eye. He stared at me, waiting, having only heard my side of the conversation. I sighed again. "They said they couldn't offer an earlier scan. They're jam-packed and can only accommodate extra scans in an urgent situation."

Sam's brow creased, and he opened his mouth to say something. I cut him off.

"They don't consider me an urgent case because I don't have any pain or bleeding. No sign that anything is wrong." The last words came out with anger. I was glad that was the case, but I was equally desperate to be certain.

Sam opened his mouth, then closed it – probably aware that nothing he could say would be the right thing. My mood had suddenly turned dark, and I couldn't stand to look at him gawping like a fish out of water anymore. I stood, scraping my chair back across the kitchen floor. Sam jumped.

"I'm going for a lie-down," I muttered as I made to leave the room.

I'd gotten as far as the doorway when Sam's quiet voice stopped me.

"What did I do?" His voice rang with trepidation. I didn't answer, keeping my back to him.

"You'll barely let me near you, and I know you lied to the paramedics." His voice was wrenched. Some part of him had to know, I thought, but he needed to hear it out loud, to be sure. I'd told the paramedics I had gotten up in the dark to use the toilet, and somehow knocked my stomach with the door handle. My worry about the baby brought on the panic attack. Sam awoke to find me overcome, so he called for help.

The story of the door sounded far-fetched even to me, but something had stopped me from telling the truth. Embarrassment – fear of them making assumptions about my relationship with my husband, fear that they might think my unborn child was in danger and shouldn't be left with us.

The paramedics thought me neurotic and gently explained that it would be very difficult to hit myself hard enough to hurt the baby.

But I knew the truth. It hadn't been a slight knock; it had been a blow inflicted on me by my husband.

I turned slowly in the kitchen doorway, gradually lifting my eyes to meet my Sam's. They were brimming with anguish, bloodshot against his deathly pale cheeks.

"You're right. I didn't bump into the door, Sam." I delivered the truth with as much empathy as I could, feeling an ache of sorrow for him. It really wasn't his fault.

"You were having one of your nightmares, and you hit out at me in your sleep." I softened my words, hoping to make them less painful. My sympathy surged at his look of horror, rattling me.

"We both know it wasn't your fault. I'm sure the hospital's

right and that everything's absolutely fine." His face remained a mask of agony despite my attempt at a smile.

"You didn't do anything intentionally." I closed my burning eyes for a second. "I'm sorry if it seemed like I blamed you – I was upset. I'm going to rest for a while. I'm exhausted."

He gave a tiny nod, his face unchanged. I turned and left the room, the space between us widening in every sense.

BACK IN OUR BEDROOM, I slipped in and out of a restless sleep. I indulged myself in dream-like visions of holding our baby for the first time, of Sam seeing his or her little face, and watching the pride radiate from the new father. I blocked out all thoughts of the previous night's events; torturing myself wouldn't help.

A soft knock broke into my subconscious. For a second or two I wondered if I had really heard anything or if it'd been part of my dream.

Sam's face appeared around the door, and he blinked in the semi light, waiting for his eyes to adjust. I watched him as he searched out my face. He looked so handsome it made me ache. His eyes met mine, and on seeing that I was awake, he shuffled in.

"Hey, how are you feeling?" His voice was barely more than a whisper, and I was overcome with a desire to be wrapped in his arms.

"Better, I think." I nodded to emphasise the point. Desperate to bridge the gap between us, I threw back the duvet on his side of the bed.

"Do you want to come in?" I kept my eyes soft, a warm smile on my face.

Something lit up within him at the gesture. He moved towards the bed without hesitation.

"Well." He paused, and apprehension flickered across his face again. "I would love to, but actually I came up to tell you that you need to get up and ready to go out." He blinked rapidly, failing to conceal his anxiety.

"Go out?" I mumbled, confused. "Where? I'm sorry, Sam, I'm really not in the mood to go anywhere right now."

He held out his hands – palms down – still looking nervous.

"I hope I've done the right thing," he started, and my stomach flipped. I couldn't begin to imagine anywhere I'd want to go.

"I called the private clinic, you know the one you can pay for the scans ... I had to do a bit of begging and pleading, but given the situation, I convinced them to squeeze us in. They're going to check the baby for us, but we have to be there in" – he glanced at his watch, angled it to get more light onto its face – "an hour and twenty. That's if you want to go ..." He trailed off and watched me for a reaction, unease creeping into his expression.

"Oh ..." His handsome features crumpled into defeat. "I thought it might help – I can ring them back ..." He slumped.

I launched myself onto my knees and threw my arms around him. The idea hadn't even crossed my own anguished, sleep-deprived mind, yet my husband had executed such a beautifully considerate plan. Love surged through me. "Thank you," I gulped, pulling back from him slightly. His face lit up once again, and he pulled me into a strong embrace.

My memory flashed back to the time in my small apartment, after our miscarriage, when Sam had dragged me out for dinner – and out from the hole of despair that I was spiralling into. I thought of the baby growing inside me and how lucky we were that this was happening for us. How much I genuinely did love him despite his flaws.

"We'll get our first glimpse of our baby today," I gasped and gave a watery smile. Sam beamed back at me, nodding with glee.

I pushed aside the sharp jab of fear that damage could already have been done. I was going to enjoy the moment.

"I can't wait!" Sam mumbled into my hair, stroking it.

I screwed my eyes shut and sent off another silent prayer that our baby would be okay – along with our marriage.

38

SAM

PRESENT DAY

T he drive home took forever. I was lost in my thoughts and memories. When I pulled onto my driveway, I realised with a start that I recalled nothing of the journey. I was on edge, worrying about the press that might be lingering around. I couldn't see any and didn't see why they would hide. I reached for my phone, clearing the numerous missed calls from Keith again, and tapped the news app. A huge story had broken, arrests made in connection with child trafficking. That explained the lack of press, but my stomach took a dizzying lurch. My chest heaved as I struggled to be rational. They didn't have Cora, I knew it in my gut.

I cut the engine and remained in my seat, clammy hands gripping the steering wheel. Earlier it had seemed so clear – tell Claire everything and face up to the truths of my past. But now that I was there, I was terrified of the repercussions.

We had agreed to return to the house, having run out of excuses to avoid it. Claire seemed to sense my anguish and suggested she go on ahead whilst I attend the hypnosis appointment, shrugging and claiming not to have anywhere else to go. I knew this was her way of giving me a way out, allowing me to save face. We both knew she planned to use the opportunity to sweep the place and clean up before I returned, but the agreement was unspoken. I added it to my list of reasons why I was so incredibly grateful and indebted to my sister.

I looked up at my house, a place that Tessa and I had worked so hard to make a home. The house was old, full of character, but in need of work. It was beautiful now. We'd thrown ourselves into it, the excitement of getting onto the property ladder a welcome distraction from the family we were missing. Each room had been carefully planned out. I'd complained about the cost of it all, but I had loved seeing Tessa so happy as the shell of a house became our home. Sometimes I thought I could still smell the fresh paint, the new carpets. I'd loved arriving back there, each and every time feeling a sense of pride and warmth at seeing the place. That feeling had only increased in recent months, knowing that not only my beautiful wife, but now my child would be waiting inside for me.

A wave of grief swallowed me, so powerful it took my breath away.

How was I ever going to manage to go on without them?

I'd thought my life had meaning before, but I'd had no idea how fulfilled it could be before Tessa and Cora. The pain of their loss was almost physical. I wondered, if Cora wasn't found, whether my body would just stop functioning, give up and let me die to escape the pain that would otherwise never leave me.

A knock on the window frightened the life out of me, reminding me that I was still sitting in the car.

Claire's panic-stricken face was staring at me through the driver's window. I pushed open the door and wrenched myself out of my seat to match eye level with Claire. We both attempted to speak at the same time.

"Has something happened?"

"Is there any news?"

We searched each other's eyes; the sadness that I saw in hers mirrored my own. I shook my head, and she nodded, staring at the ground.

"Are you okay?" She gestured behind her to the house, perfectly aware of why I had been reluctant to go inside. Taking a shuddering breath, I nodded, keeping my eyes fixed on the house.

She led the way back inside, making me feel like a guest in my own home. Everything felt so familiar yet alien, like I was seeing it out of context. The smell of food filled my nostrils. My stomach gurgled, and my mouth watered. I'd had no idea I was even hungry.

"I hope you don't mind. I thought you'd need something to eat, so I raided the fridge and cupboards and threw something together."

The sight of the set table brought a stark reminder: the many past dinners here with my wife, the future of many more that I'd taken for granted – where Cora would join us, enjoying her first taste of food and eventually sharing tales of her day. I felt the familiar lump form in my throat and struggled not to collapse into a heap.

"It's just pasta, I'm afraid. Nothing exciting. I hope that's okay."

I'd just been staring at the table in silence. Claire shifted, chewing her lip and waiting for me to react.

I swallowed hard. "It's great, Claire. Thank you so much."

Her relief was palpable. I forced a smile and dropped into Tessa's chair at the table, unwilling to see anyone else taking her place, even my sister.

She moved around the kitchen, dishing the pasta up, and placed a generous portion in front of me before sitting down with her own. She pushed the food around her plate and took tiny bites. I swallowed down a couple of forkfuls of my own, knowing from the smell that it should taste delicious, but everything I put in my mouth was like chewing on cardboard.

I went through the motions, chewing and swallowing, until Claire broke the silence.

"How did the session go?" she asked quietly, almost as if she didn't want to. Her hushed tones brought a further reminder that there was no longer a baby in the house to be quiet for.

"It worked, but we didn't get anything useful." My voice was unnaturally loud. Claire cowered.

She cleared her throat and placed her fork onto her plate.

"Well, I guess it's a good start that she managed to ..." She paused. "I don't know what the term for it would be." She shrugged. "But it's good that it seemed to work. Does she think that she'll be able to help?"

I was reluctant to share Helen's advice, her hesitation. I simply shrugged in response.

"She's fairly optimistic about it."

Claire picked up her glass of water and stared down into it, seemingly unsure if she should continue the conversation.

"When will you see her again?" she asked eventually.

"First thing in the morning."

Her head whipped up to look at me. "That soon? Is it okay for you to do it again in such quick succession?"

Having had this argument with Helen already, her question irked me. I glowered at her.

"What would you rather I did? Had a couple of days off? Maybe pop off on a mini break for a few days R 'n' R?"

Claire shrank. I let out a deep breath, regretting my harsh words. I dropped my head into my hands.

"I'm sorry. I'm not trying to question your decision. I'm just concerned for you. You have to look after yourself too." Her voice was soft and heavy. "We'll do whatever it takes to find Cora, Sam, but you don't deserve to be punished!" Her firm words stirred up a whirlwind of anger within me.

"But what if I *do*, Claire? Just what exactly do you know about what I deserve? You reappear in my life after all these years and think you know everything about me when actually you know nothing at all! Maybe I deserve everything I get."

Her jaw went slack, hanging open.

My anger was misdirected, but I couldn't help myself. It roiled within me. I shoved my plate with the back of my hand, and it hit the floor with a satisfying smash. The shattered pieces flew in every direction, and the red pasta sauce splattered on the tiled floor, creating what looked like a crime scene.

Claire let out a yelp and shoved her chair back from the table, staring at the latest mess I had created.

Neither of us moved for a few seconds, unsure what to do or say.

Claire eventually broke the spell, moving towards the cupboard under the sink. She said nothing but began to pull out bottles of spray cleaner and cleaning cloths. She straightened and ran the hot tap, reaching for Tessa's rubber gloves.

"Leave it, Claire." My voice was a low growl.

"It needs sorting." Her own tone was clipped. "It'll stain the ..."

"Jesus, Claire. Please just leave it!" I slammed a fist onto the tabletop, causing everything on it to jump up and rattle.

She turned to face me and met my eye. Every trace of nervousness and sympathy that was present in them earlier was now gone. I recognised the glint of anger shining in them – so similar to my own.

She threw the rubber gloves in my direction with all of her might. They landed on the floor with a strange slapping noise.

"So just what the fuck do you want me to do, Sam?" she bawled at me, her tone shrill. "Because if you cast your mind back a little bit, you might remember that it wasn't *me* who cut you out of my life!" Her eyes blazed, and she flailed her arms around wildly as she shouted, "Yes – I hated that bitch, but I would have never walked away from *you*."

The emphasis on her last word stabbed my heart. She gasped, breathless with anger.

"You never even tried to get back in contact once you had rid of her. Never even gave me the chance to meet Tessa or Cora. Yet here I am, trying my best to put all that aside and support you, when all you can do is throw it back in my face!" She jabbed her finger in my direction, her face screwed up in a grimace.

I knew I should be the one to stop it, to apologise and beg her to forgive me, but I was deeply ashamed of so much that I'd done, and having her there meant I had to face up to so much more.

"I never asked you to come!" I roared back at her. "You just turn up out of the blue and think you can be some sort of hero, just fix everything, even though you know *nothing*!" I spat the venomous words.

"Oh well, poor you! How awful of me to come here and try to help you after you shit all over me in the first place!" Her voice dripped sarcasm. "The martyr act is getting old already, Sam. Why can't you just suck it up and accept that people care?"

"Because I don't fucking deserve it!" I stood up, scraping my own chair back, but Claire didn't move from her spot, holding eye contact.

"So you keep saying." She rolled her eyes at me, voice lowered as if she were bored.

"There are things you don't know, Claire." I sighed, a deep heavy sigh, and dropped back into my chair. I stared at the empty place mat in front of me, unsure of how to continue.

Claire turned to the fridge and retrieved a bottle of wine, then pulled two glasses from the cupboard and set them down on the table.

"Well, in that case, maybe it's about time you told me." It was a statement rather than a request. She unscrewed the lid of the wine bottle, breaking the seal with a satisfying crack, and filled a glass.

39

TESSA

TEN MONTHS PREVIOUS

C old jelly made contact with my exposed stomach. I flinched, and Sam gripped my hand as the sonographer spoke.

"So, when the scan begins, I'll probably be quiet for a short time while I'm working out what's what in there." She gestured towards the tiny swell of my belly with her free hand and offered a reassuring smile. "That isn't anything for you to worry about. I just need to figure out what I'm looking at before I can start to explain and show anything to you. Is that okay?"

I forced a smile in return and nodded, not trusting myself to speak, afraid that my emotions would escape with the words.

Sam's grip tightened on my hand. His palms were slippery with both of our sweat.

I watched the sonographer's face as she moved the small probe over my belly, gulping down nerves, body tense. She pushed harder, and I gritted my teeth, trying not to squirm with the desperate urge to pee.

"Sorry," she offered without looking at me. "I'll be as quick as I can. I know you're dying for the loo."

Her eyes flicked across the screen, constantly moving and taking in what she saw. She *click-clicked* a button, frowning and tilting her head slightly. My stomach plummeted. The fist of my free hand was clenched so tightly my nails bit into the flesh of my palm.

I pictured the scene, her turning to deliver bad news, face full of sympathy. A single tear rolled down my cheek, then another. I didn't dare move, instead allowing them to trickle down my cheeks, soaking into my hair and running into my ears.

The sonographer glanced down at me. Her smooth skin creased with confusion and concern.

"Oh gosh! Are you alright?" she gasped, watching another tear slide down the side of my face. I managed a shaky smile and sniffed.

"Uh-huh, sorry." I sniffed again, the words catching in my throat.

"Oh, no, no! Don't be sorry."

Her assistant, who had helped me fill out the forms and shown us into the room, appeared at the sonographer's side and offered me a box of tissues.

I released my hand from Sam's grip to pull one from the box. "Thank you," I mumbled, rubbing my eyes and nose, thankful that I hadn't bothered to put on mascara.

"You're welcome. It's very common – we're prepared!" She waved the tissue box around and gave me a knowing smile.

The sonographer, her eyes fixed on the screen again, agreed. "It certainly is. Happens more often than not." She glanced up with a warm smile. I was sure they were just being kind but was grateful to them all the same.

"Anyway." The sonographer clicked a couple of buttons, and a big screen on the wall in front of us lit up. I hadn't even noticed it was there, imagining the scan as you see in the films, all crowding around the sonographer's tiny screen. My eyes flicked as I tried to make sense of what I was seeing.

"Mummy and Daddy, I'm *delighted* to be able to introduce you to your beautiful baby." Her beaming tone rang sincere. "Can you see that lovely strong heartbeat?"

My body went so weak with relief and euphoric joy that I was grateful to be lying down; otherwise my legs would have given out from under me. "Is it okay? Is it healthy?" I blabbered, tears flowing again.

"It's still too early to check everything, but from your dates, everything seems to be just perfect." Her eyes sparkled as she reassured us. I squeaked in response, unable to form words.

Her assistant caught my eye and moved around the side of the bed, holding the tissues. She held the box out to my left, and I turned and saw Sam. I hadn't given him a thought while I was caught up in the screen and the sonographer's report. He was trying to blink back eyes full of tears, but a few drops had escaped.

I reached for his hand and squeezed it, giving a little giggle of delight. More tears formed. He gripped my hand and shook his head slowly.

"That's our baby!" His voice was barely audible as his eyes met mine. I beamed and nodded at him, feeling another little giggle rise up.

The scan continued with the sonographer drawing funny lines and circles, pointing out what different bits were and which direction the baby was facing. I watched in amazement, struggling to connect what I was seeing on the screen to what was happening inside me. That it really was our baby we were looking at.

I struggled to take in anything else for the remainder of

the appointment, too giddy to hear anything above the voice in my head repeating – *That's my baby, my healthy baby!*

I wiped the gel from my stomach with a wad of paper towel handed to me by the assistant and straightened out my clothing. We were asked to wait in the reception area whilst they printed our report, plus a couple of photos of the scan. I perched on the sofa in a blissful daze until the assistant appeared again.

"Here you are." She handed over a small pack. "Your report is in there for you to take to your hospital scan. They'll be able to use it to monitor the changes between now and then, make sure everything is going as it should. There's one of our leaflets about the services that we provide, just in case you decide you want another peek at any time." She winked at me. "We do gender scans and three- and four-D a bit further down the line. Your photos are in there too." She glanced over at a nervous-looking couple who were sitting on the opposite side of the room and lowered her voice. "Lisa managed to get some really great ones, so we popped a couple of extra in for you." She lifted her shoulders and wrinkled her nose, then offered her congratulations once again.

I picked up my bag and caught the eye of the woman who was waiting, filling out her forms opposite us. I offered a reassuring smile, wanting to say something, but nothing seemed appropriate. Her eyes flicked down to the pack that I was clutching; a flare of jealousy sparked in them.

Sam reached for my hand. "Ready?"

I turned my gaze from the woman to Sam, who was animated with joy just as I was, and nodded with delight.

With one last round of thanks and congratulations exchanged with the receptionists, we left, a spring in both of our steps.

We pulled out of the car park in a state of excited chatter about our future. I thought back to the woman in the clinic. I wondered how her scan was going. I remembered the look of envy in her eyes and felt a pang of shame – I had enjoyed that moment. I had enjoyed being on the receiving end of the envious looks.

I imagined myself with my growing bump, people stopping me to tell me that I was glowing, sharing experiences and advice. I pictured more envious looks with Sam next to me, full of pride. People would see that we had the perfect life.

When I glanced over at Sam, my heart dropped. The events of the morning – the reality of our situation, why we'd ended up there – smashed into me, and I felt nauseous.

He stole a quick glance at me and rested his hand on my knee.

"Okay?" he questioned, a tiny crease in his brow. I forced a bright smile and placed my hand over his.

"Of course, just a little queasy," I replied, placing my free hand over my stomach, pushing the niggling doubt and worry away.

We had plenty of demons to face, but not at that moment. I wouldn't allow anything to ruin that moment for me. We had overcome so much.

40

SAM

PRESENT DAY

Claire filled both glasses, leaving only a small amount of wine in the bottle. Condensation formed on the outside of the glass, and I watched it with an odd sense of calm whilst Claire screwed the lid back into place.

She took a couple of gulps before fixing her stare on me, hands clasped on the table. I fiddled with the stem of my own glass, clutching it between my fingers and spinning it, allowing it to wobble. For a few moments we remained in silence – apart from my glass quivering on the table as I twiddled it – both of us lost in our own thoughts. There were things I needed to tell her, but I didn't know where to start, how to form the words.

As it turned out, I didn't need to. Claire finally broke the silence.

"Look, Sam. I don't know what it is that's gone on, and why you're so certain that you're to blame. Every marriage has its problems. I haven't come here to judge you – *or* Tessa. You're my brother, and nothing you can say would make me want to lose you again, but if you're not ready to talk to me—"

"I had one of my nightmares that night," I blurted, cutting her off. I couldn't stomach another word of kindness. This rendered her silent; then her face clouded over, brows knitting.

Her face scrunched. "What night?" The realisation then slid over her features, smoothing them out until slack. She laid her palms flat on the table and swallowed hard before she spoke again. "But ... I mean ... that doesn't actually *mean* anything." She tapped the tabletop lightly with her palms.

Her words were feeble. I wasn't sure if she was trying to convince me or herself. I gave her a withering look and rubbed my hand across my face, fingertips lingering on my scars.

"Unfortunately, Claire, we both know that it probably does." I shifted my focus back to my glass of wine and swirled it.

Claire reached for her own glass and swallowed down a couple more mouthfuls. She made to put it down, paused, then kept it clutched in her hand.

I lifted my own glass to my dry lips with a trembling hand. This was only the tip of the iceberg of the secrets I had to share. The sweetness of the wine masked the bitter taste in my mouth. I gulped back more than I should have, hoping it would calm my nerves.

"Do you actually remember anything at all? Of the night or the dream?" Her face remained fixed in a frown.

I took another gulp and shook my head, closing my eyes as I let out a breath.

"Nothing." I felt breathless with nerves, my heart thumping faster. "I didn't remember right away, but now I know I *did* have one that night and that there was no sign of a break-in here." The words were flowing now, and I needed to continue lest I change my mind.

"It wouldn't be the first time that I'd ... *hurt* Tessa during one of my episodes." I couldn't look at her, keeping my eyes fixed on my wine. "There was a time, early on in her pregnancy, that we were afraid I might have hurt the baby during a nightmare." My breath caught on the words, and I burned with shame. "We had to have a private scan to make sure she was okay. So I know for certain that I am capable of hurting them. Both of them. I just *have* to know what happened to Cora. I need to know that she'll be okay to carry on ... even if I can never see her again."

The panic that gripped my heart caught me off guard. I sucked in a couple of sharp breaths, needing to keep it together. There was more to say.

"If we find her, Claire, if she's okay, will you do something for me? I know it's more than I deserve, but you're the only person I can trust now." I looked up at my sister. Her face was still slack, her mouth hanging open, and her skin had a grey tinge.

I let a few seconds pass, allowing her time to process. She remained frozen, so I decided to press on, hoping that the seriousness of my request might snap her back into focus.

"When we find Cora, if she is ... okay ... will you please take her for me, Claire? I know it's a huge ask, but I need her to be with someone I can trust, someone who'll love her and who I know will take as good care of her as she deserves."

Claire's jaw snapped shut, and her eyes glazed over.

"But you're her father, Sam. She should be with you." Her words came out high pitched.

She understood why I was asking but refused to accept what I was saying. I reached over and took her hand.

"And there's nothing I would like more, Claire. But I killed her mother. We'd been arguing. No court is going to accept that it wasn't intentional, that it happened during a *nightmare*. I think we both know I'll be going away for a long time for this." My words rang with quiet sorrow, laced with emotion. Even saying them out loud, I couldn't believe them.

Tears streamed down Claire's cheeks. I was too numb to cry, so I stared back into my wine. It was too much to witness her pain – pain that I had caused.

She sniffed and wiped her eyes with her sleeve.

"You know I would take her – without question, Sam." She gulped. "But I won't have to, I just know it. You didn't do this. I know you didn't; you just aren't capable. You do not have it in you to kill someone. You're my brother; I *know* you!"

She was near hysterical, and I felt a pang of guilt. There was much more. I held another secret – perhaps the worst of them all. The one that I'd been so terrified someone would discover that I'd almost let it destroy my marriage. The one that would change her opinion of me permanently, leave her with no choice but to believe what I was telling her.

"Do you honestly expect me to believe that you murdered your wife, took your daughter somewhere, and what? Just dumped her there? With no memory of any of it whatsoever?" She scoffed, conflicting emotions battling in her eyes.

The small amount of pasta that I had eaten sat heavy in my stomach; I thought I might throw up.

I glanced at the mess spread over the kitchen tile already and hoped that, if I did puke, I would make it to the bathroom. I clasped my wine glass and took another couple of swigs, knowing I shouldn't but needing the alcohol to get out the horrible truth.

"I've left the house before with no knowledge of it," I mumbled. "You know that as well as I do. The number of times I've woken up with mud all up my legs ..."

"That's different." She couldn't meet my eye. "So what if you wandered into the garden a few times as a child. It hardly makes you a murderer."

"The thing is, Claire ..." My heart went up a gear, and my

head swam with the suffocating fear and alcohol on a half-empty stomach. My throat burned, and I swallowed hard, desperate not to be sick, needing to get this done. "There's something else, something—"

A shrill sound cut me off.

"Shit!" Claire swung her gaze all around before managing to locate her handbag hung on the back of the kitchen door. She dug around in it, muttering. The phone stopped ringing just as she retrieved it, swiping at the screen, her face clouding with worry.

It pinged with a notification while she continued to jab at the screen.

"Everything okay?" My chest fluttered.

Her eyes didn't leave the screen as she replied.

"It's Tommy." Her face crumpled. "He's in trouble."

41

TESSA
TEN MONTHS PREVIOUS

The rest of the day passed in a blur. In the evening we decided to order a takeaway as a celebratory treat. We pored over the photos of the scan and tried to work out what we were looking at in each one. We made plans for the nursery and decided that we didn't want to find out the gender – preferring to keep it a surprise for the birth.

We ate our food while discussing baby names, screwing up our faces at some presented by an app we'd downloaded, dissolving into giggles when one of us looked shocked at the other's serious suggestions. A text from Bella cut through my warm mood – I imagined her reaction to my pregnancy news. I wanted desperately to send her photos of the scan, for her to shriek in excitement for me, but I knew that wasn't who Bella was. I closed the message without replying, promising myself I'd speak to her the following day.

After we'd cleared away the empty takeaway containers and tidied the kitchen, we collapsed onto the sofa in front of some trashy sketch show and laughed along.

But as the evening drew to a close, a bubble of panic formed within me.

I felt so protective over my baby. The day's events had made it so much more real – seeing it on that screen, watching the tiny heart patter away, and clutching those precious black-and-white photos. I couldn't risk losing that, regardless of the consequences. I glanced over at Sam, his eyes fixed on the TV screen, an amused expression lighting up his face, mouth turned up slightly at the corners in that beautiful lopsided way. I felt a pang of guilt at the thought – to bring it all up again, to burst the sanctuary of joy we had created that day. None of it was actually his fault. It was difficult to associate the man in front of me, the man whom I loved so much, with that stranger who appeared during the night, who made me feel so afraid in my own bed.

I placed my hand over my stomach and pictured the tiny form growing within. I had no choice. My baby already mattered more to me than I ever could have imagined. I watched Sam for another couple of seconds, considering how to broach the difficult subject. He must've sensed my eyes on him, because – with a start – I realised that he had turned to meet my gaze. I flinched as I pictured those kind eyes turning dark.

"You okay?" He wore a soft expression as he placed his hand over mine.

"Hmm, just a bit tired." I nodded, heat rising to my face as I shifted with the guilt.

"Well, that's because you're busy growing a perfect human." He beamed. "Why don't you go up and get an early night? I'll sort everything out down here and follow you up. We could watch a film in bed if you fancy it? Got to make the most of that kind of thing now." He chuckled, radiating joy.

I felt sick with his eagerness to please. "Erm, actually, I

wanted to talk to you about that." My face flamed as I stumbled over the words.

He cocked his head, waiting for me to continue.

"I think ... well, the thing is ... I mean ... I *know* it isn't your fault." I held my hands up, trying to emphasise the point. I was getting flustered, and my words were tumbling over each other. Sam turned his body to face me and brushed my hair back from my face with his fingertips, the gesture so gentle I doubted myself.

"What is it, Tess? Talk to me." His words were so soft. I fought an urge to just forget it all. "Hey!" He cupped my face in his hand and stroked my cheek with the pad of his thumb. "What is it?"

I sniffed, feeling wretched but knowing I had to face it. It wasn't just going to go away by itself.

"Sam, I'm scared," I managed to squeak out. His brow creased for a second before his face melted into a smile, and he nodded gently.

"The baby's doing great, Tess. We have our twelve-week scan coming up where we'll get to see it again too. Things are good. You don't need to be worried." His voice was so soothing and full of reassurance. If only it really were the baby making me afraid, I could just take his words of comfort and snuggle into his arms, blissfully forgetting everything else. But that wasn't our reality.

"Not about the baby." My tone was flat. Sam's brow creased once again.

"What is it, then?" he asked, moving himself upright, eyes narrowed and focused completely on me.

I chewed my thumbnail, trying to find the words. Everything felt so cruel. I pulled in a deep breath.

"I'm afraid of *you*, Sam." I winced. Unable to meet his eye, I picked at a bobble forming in the fabric of my jumper. "Well, not you, but the you that you become." I risked a flick of my eyes up to meet his but was unable to hold his gaze. I chewed on my bottom lip, trying to form the next sentence. "I know you would never do anything to hurt us, but during your dreams ... things happen. We have the baby to think of now and ... well, we would never forgive ourselves if anything happened." I found myself using *we* in an attempt to soften the blow, to show that we remained a team and I was not laying the blame solely on him.

An awkward silence followed. I wanted to fill it, to relieve the discomfort that I had caused. The TV continued to blare out the gags, the canned laughter bouncing around our living room suddenly feeling horribly inappropriate.

"Okay." Sam's voice was low. He drew out the word like he was still thinking it over. I heard the sound of nails running over his stubble. "So, are you asking me to leave?"

I didn't know what came as more of a shock: his question or the calmness in his voice. My head snapped up to meet his eyes for the first time. Looking into those eyes that I knew so well, I saw a mixture of sadness and understanding, not the panic I imagined must be carved into my own.

"God, no! That's not what I want at all! Do you *want* to leave?" My voice had risen, becoming shrill. Had he been thinking of leaving? The thought hadn't even crossed my mind.

"Of course I don't." His eyes darted down to glance at my belly before locking back on my own. "But if you're afraid of me, Tess – telling me that you feel unsafe with me – I don't honestly know what else to suggest." His eyes were full of anguish and question. I hated that something beyond both of our control was causing so much pain. I wished I had the answers.

"Sam, I love you. I don't want this to come between us. What we have is ..." I threw my arms up, lost for the right words. "And now we're going to have a *child*." I placed both of my hands on my stomach and smiled despite myself. "But until we work something better out, we need to make sure that we keep the baby safe."

He rubbed his face, closed his eyes, and sighed a deep, pained sigh.

"Of course we do. There isn't anything more important to me than you and our baby." He seemed exhausted. "What do you want me to do?" His fingers searched out his scars.

I picked at my jumper again and tried to keep the wobble from my voice as I spoke.

"I think we should have separate rooms – just until we find a more permanent solution," I added quickly.

I didn't miss the forlorn look cross his features, but he hid it quickly and nodded sharply. "Okay," he breathed in a whisper.

"And I would like some way to secure the door of my room – so that I know I'm safe." The look that crossed my husband's face at that moment would stay with me for as long as I lived.

WE DIDN'T DISCUSS it any further. Sam collected a couple of things from our room and en-suite, transferring them word-lessly to the guest room and main bathroom.

I had always liked to keep the spare room made up. I felt it completed the room, having the bed made rather than a bare duvet and pillows strewn around the place. Right now, I wished it weren't so that I could offer to go and do it for him. A small peace offering to show my solidarity, that I didn't blame him.

In a slightly awkward exchange, we found that the chair from the dressing table in the spare room could be used to wedge the door closed. Sam carried it through to our room, refusing to let me lift it, and dropped it to the floor behind the door.

"I can pick up a bolt tomorrow," he uttered. My heart skipped at the suggestion. Somehow his offer to help me secure myself, to lock myself away from him, seemed to make it all the more real – confirming that he believed it necessary.

"Maybe. Let's see how things go." I shrugged, attempting to steady my voice. I kept my eyes averted. I didn't want to let things go so far as having to bolt my door. That felt so much worse than a makeshift chair barricade, for some reason.

I thanked him, and we exchanged an uncomfortable goodnight, neither of us sure exactly how this left things between us.

I didn't sleep well that night, alert to every tiny sound, wondering if Sam was sleeping soundly or missing me beside him. Wondering if he was up wandering, outside the bedroom door.

SAM LEFT for work before I was up the following morning. Groggy and lonely, I fiddled with my phone, considering the idea of calling him, wanting to hear his voice. I decided against it. For the first time ever, I worried it might be uncomfortable to speak over the phone. I flicked back through my texts and found Bella's name. Guilt panged when I remembered her message from the previous day. I fired off a quick text before I had time to change my mind.

> Hi, fancy a coffee later after work? My treat. Xx

As ever, I agonized over the words, not wanting to come across as needy. I wasn't sure why I still felt that way, having formed a solid foundation with Bella now. We spoke almost daily via text, and I felt our friendship was strengthening. I showered and dressed before checking my phone again, relieved to see that I had received a reply.

> Sure, free from 5.30. See you at the usual
> place. Xx

AT FIVE TWENTY, I was perched at a table, watching the door. When Bella breezed in, I smiled despite the familiar stab of jealousy at her perfection. It felt good to have a friend, someone who was there to see me.

We grabbed our coffees and made small talk for a while, chatting about work and other safe subjects. With our easy chatter, some of the tension left my body. The conversation moved to Sam. Bella often asked about him and seemed to observe me closely as I spoke of him, showing a polite interest in a fellow professional. I often thought of how well they'd get on when they finally met and was ashamed to admit my jealousy at the idea. Sam was so easy-going and seemed to get along with anyone. I imagined Bella thought of him as the perfect man – the image I had conjured up for her. Without thinking about it too much, I made the choice to confide in Bella about what had happened between us – partly out of desperation for someone to speak to about my situation, partly in hope that it would strengthen the bond I craved between us.

"So, I'm pregnant," I announced with a shy shrug. As expected, Bella made very little in way of reaction, face paling and tightening slightly, but without a word of congratulations. "Not too far along yet – only around eight weeks – but we had a scan yesterday. We saw the heartbeat." My face flushed with the pleasure of the memory.

"A scan? Already? Isn't it a bit early for that?"

My cheeks darkened. I shifted in my seat.

Stumbling over my words, I explained Sam's nightmares – a toned-down version, anyway – and about our sleeping separately now before blurting out my fear for my marriage. In not saying much at all, I'd shared a great amount more than I'd meant to.

When I dared to glance up at her and took in the horror on her face, I instantly regretted my decision and tried to backtrack.

"I mean, I'm probably making it sound much worse than it is. I'm overtired and hormonal." I gave a little laugh, but it sounded horribly forced.

She regarded me in silence for a short time. I shifted under her scrutinising gaze.

"Do you want my honest advice?" she asked, her tone so sharp and serious my stomach fluttered.

"Sure." I nodded, half-hearted, wishing I had the guts to say no.

"Things will only get worse. They always do. Can you really be sure what a man like that is capable of? And now you have a child to think of. You have no choice; leave the bastard." Her tone was deadpan, so blunt and final, I could only stare at her, reeling from the sting.

42

SAM

PRESENT DAY

"What kind of trouble? Is he okay?" I stood, ready to do whatever she needed.

Claire looked up at me through tired eyes. "Tommy's gotten himself in with a bad crowd. They're encouraging him to dabble in drugs, cause trouble at school, that kind of thing." She winced, and shame flickered in her eyes.

I shrank with regret and dropped back into my seat, unable to reconcile the idea of a "bad crowd" and drugs with Tommy as I'd known him, an innocent, carefree child. I'd missed so much of their lives. I wondered if, had I been around more, I could have helped prevent this. Remembering why my sister was there, I decided they had probably been better off.

"Go, Claire. Be with your family. They need you."

She met my eye; her cheeks flushed. "I *am* with family, and *you* need me – whether you realise that right now or not." She glared at me before allowing her eyes to fall to her phone screen, which had lit up once again.

"Unfortunately, it doesn't seem to make a difference what

we do. We can't get through to him." Her shoulders sagged. "I'll just call Martin back, check he's okay."

I nodded at her retreating back, unsure if she meant Martin or Tommy. I picked up my glass and took a few sips, savouring the cool liquid. I thought back over what I had just told Claire, the look of dismay on her face at the meaning behind my truths.

At the thought of what I had been about to share, I swallowed a bigger gulp from my glass. What she would know by now had her phone not interrupted us – it had all been spilling out. I'd barely scratched the surface. I'd been ready to tell her everything, to unburden myself of every secret.

I couldn't get the expression on her face out of my head. How could I bear to lose anyone else? Claire had only just come back into my life. I knew what would have happened had I told her everything. I was sure of it. How could she ever be near me again if she knew?

Part of me wished her bloody phone had never gone off, that we could be sat there at my kitchen table in the aftermath of my confession. Another part felt nothing but relief that I'd been stopped in time. Why did I want to tell her the truth? For the right reasons? Did I actually believe that she needed to know, or was it more selfish? To unburden myself? I couldn't be sure of an answer; my brain fogged with confusion and alcohol.

Claire's muffled voice moved closer. I couldn't decipher her words, but I could tell from her urgent, hushed tones that it wasn't good. Her footsteps paused in the hall. I stood and moved towards the doorway, keeping hidden behind the wall and straining to catch the end of the conversation. I could just about make it out, filling in the blanks from the other end.

"I know. You said, but as *I* said, I just can't right now, okay?" There was silence for a few seconds before Claire's low voice filled it once again. "And what difference do you think it would make even if I did? Maybe this is what he needs to sort him out."

I felt guilty to be eavesdropping, even worse that I was coming between Claire and her family.

"He is still my brother, Martin. I won't turn my back on him, not now. I'm sorry. I'll be home when I can."

Her shuffling footsteps moved towards me. I made a dash back to the table, avoiding the mess of pasta on the floor and grabbing for my wine glass.

Claire appeared, running her hand through her lank hair, and I suddenly noticed how exhausted she looked. She had both me and her son to thank for that.

She stepped over the pasta and dropped back into the chair opposite me, unscrewing the lid from the wine bottle and topping up her glass, which wasn't yet empty, with the last of the wine.

"I take it things are bad, then?" I asked feebly, watching her pour.

"He was arrested, underage drinking. Some low-class drugs on him." I didn't point out the irony as I watched her drain the bottle. She waved her hand around. "Generally being little shits, I think. Hopefully it'll be the kick up the arse he needs." She kept her eyes focused on her glass. Our roles had seemingly reversed as she swirled the liquid around in it, avoiding looking at me.

"And Martin thinks you should be home with them."

She shrugged. "It wouldn't make a difference either way. He doesn't listen to a bloody word either of us says."

"But maybe he just needs your support?"

She stuck her chin out, fire filling her eyes as she met my gaze. "Well, maybe now he'll know how that feels."

That was her final say. I did not push any further. I wondered if maybe she needed to be here with me as much as I needed her to be.

"Anyway." She heaved a deep sigh. "What was it that you were going to say before?" She held me in an expectant gaze.

Once again, I was drawn to the dark circles under her eyes, the grey creeping into her hair, and the lines etched into her brow, which all seemed to have appeared in recent days. It occurred to me for the first time since everything happened how terrible my own appearance must have become.

I opened my mouth, then closed it again when no words came out. I couldn't do it to her – not then. She already had enough to carry without my selfish need to confess. She watched me closely, waiting.

"Just that we'd been arguing a lot too." I shook my head and rolled my eyes. "I wonder if that's what caused the dream that night."

She pulled a face and shrugged.

"All couples argue, Sam. There's nothing unusual about that." She glanced at her phone, absent-minded, exposing where her thoughts were lingering. "Especially with a new baby," she continued. "The early years are really tough. Until recently, I would have said the toughest." She rolled her eyes and gave a dry humourless laugh before lifting her glass again.

"Yeah, I guess." I nodded, offering a smile of sympathy. Her words stung, leaving my mouth bitter. *Early years.* I'd barely had more than weeks with my daughter. My mind drifted, picturing her perfect face, trying to envisage where she could be.

"What were you fighting about?" Claire sipped her drink.

The question caught me off guard, bringing me back to focus. I thought of Tessa's missing wedding bands with a pang and paused, considering how much to admit.

"She worried about my nightmares, about the ... *effect* that they might have on Cora," I added carefully.

Claire nodded, chewing her lip thoughtfully.

"So what did she want to happen?"

I paused again before answering, "For me to look for some help, see someone about them." I shrugged.

"And were you going to?"

I squirmed. I didn't know how to answer without admitting too much, so I bent the truth. "Yeah, I guess I would've looked into it if I'd gotten the chance." The lie rolled off my tongue.

Claire regarded me with narrowed eyes. She could always sniff out my lies.

Saying nothing more, she reached for her glass and made to stand. She stretched and turned to me. "Would it be okay if I took a bath? I'm knackered and think we could both do with some rest."

"Course, help yourself to a towel out of the airing cupboard. Bathroom is the first door you come to; the guest room is the last door on the left. It's made up, but you might want to put fresh sheets on." I knew that my sister would easily put two and two together and realise that I had been sleeping in that room. I hadn't entered the bedroom since the police had left so actually had no idea what state it was in, but I didn't have the energy to worry about it, knowing Claire could – and would – fend for herself.

"Thanks." She moved to the doorway, glass in hand, making no comment. "Don't worry, I'll manage. Just shout if you need anything. Goodnight, Sam."

"Night," I called after her.

I remained at the table for a long time, dredging through old memories, things I wished I could forget. I remembered the arguments building up with Tessa, becoming more and more vicious as they continued, unresolved each time. Papering over the cracks, trying to make things work regardless.

I could never explain to her why I couldn't get help for my

condition, and it made her justifiably furious. Unable to understand why I wouldn't at least try for the sake of our family. Towards the end, I'm pretty sure she was considering leaving me. After all, she hadn't been wearing her wedding rings. I was certain she'd had them on when we'd gone to bed. What on earth had happened during the night to cause her to remove them?

A jab ran through my body. The little voice in my head taunted me.

That there's your motive, Sam.

43

TESSA
NINE MONTHS PREVIOUS

Bella's words echoed through my mind.

Leave the bastard.

Was I being selfish by staying with Sam? Bringing a child into the situation? *Should* I leave? I knew he would make a great dad, just as he was a great husband.

Most of the time, anyway, the little voice in my head jibed.

We'd been sleeping in separate rooms for the past few days, mine with the door barricaded shut, and hadn't discussed it since. We were polite to the point of awkwardness around each other the rest of the time, neither of us knowing exactly where the sleeping arrangement left our relationship, both of us wanting to make things work but seemingly unable to broach the subject.

The situation was torturous. We had it all. Our relationship was as close to perfect as I thought possible. We had the house, our beautiful baby ... on the surface things couldn't have been better. My heart cracked every time I agonised over this seemingly minor issue. I couldn't think of sacrificing my relationship with the man I loved, taking Cora away from her daddy, all for the sake of something Sam had no control over. Even if I did leave, Sam would have rights to access our child, and unless I was willing to throw him to the wolves, making him out to be an unfit father, it would mean leaving them alone together regularly. Besides, people would think I was crazy to give up on my marriage over such a small problem. But only I knew how that small problem was mushrooming.

Bella and I had been exchanging texts, her checking in with me more regularly. I had appreciated her concern, and ordinarily, I would have been delighted to be forming such a tight bond with a friend, but her messages, the assumptions, made me feel like a victim, a battered wife. I hated it. That wasn't happening. Humiliation burned that I'd made it sound that way. When she texted me a few days later, suggesting meeting for coffee again, I was in two minds. I wanted to see her and could do with a chat, a chance to clear my head and unburden myself, but I didn't want her judgement.

At first, I just typed out a couple of responses before deleting them and throwing my phone aside. It beeped with another message, and I wondered if she'd changed her mind. A message from Sam appeared: he was going to be late home again.

I sighed and sent a message to Bella, agreeing to meet. I didn't fancy sitting home alone all evening. Maybe I could clear things up, explain that I'd exaggerated before.

"So you're still sleeping in separate rooms?" We sipped our drinks at the local coffee shop, where it had become our routine to meet, a place we had both become comfortable. I tried to always arrive first and be the one to buy the coffees. I had asked that Bella only buy me decaf, but I was almost certain she was ordering regular by mistake.

"Well, yes. But it's more about me being comfortable and him not being disturbed by my tossing and turning," I lied, forcing a laugh.

She stared, and I squirmed in my seat, feeling every bit the liar I was.

"Well, you look terrible," she replied bluntly, but her expression was soft. She cocked her head. "*Are* you sleeping at all?"

I ran a hand through my hair. The pregnancy symptoms and lack of sleep hadn't exactly given me the "pregnancy glow" that I'd envisaged.

"Not brilliantly," I admitted. "But that's due to the pregnancy," I added too quickly. "I feel rubbish so much of the time and just can't switch off." I waved a hand around and rolled my eyes, trying to make light of it all. She studied my face again.

"Why don't you take something to help you sleep?" she questioned. "You should be getting your rest before the baby arrives." She glanced down at my stomach. I had the slightest bump forming. That was the first time Bella had acknowledged the baby at all, never even having offered congratulations, seemingly always more concerned by my problems with my husband.

"Oh, no, I couldn't," I replied quickly. "I wouldn't risk taking anything while I'm pregnant." I placed a protective hand on the slight swell of my belly. Her eyes slid down again, but she still said nothing about the baby.

"There are plenty of things that you can take that are perfectly safe." Her words took on an authoritative tone, and I felt ridiculous, blushing slightly. "It'd do you good." She shrugged.

Before the doctors had stepped in, I'd considered asking Bella, with her pharmaceuticals knowledge, about finding a medication to help me conceive. I'd dismissed the thought, though, aware it was too much to ask of someone I was still only getting to know, and I wasn't even sure it would be legal. I didn't want to appear stupid to someone so intelligent, wondering how she didn't view me as inferior already. And I hadn't wanted her to know of my struggles to conceive. I'd been so eager for her friendship. Knowing that part of her appeal was that she felt less of a threat, I hated myself. She lived alone and was single. She wouldn't be another woman to fall pregnant ahead of me, showing off her bump and exchanging knowing glances with everyone but me. Shame burned to acknowledge that even to myself.

I didn't want to admit to her that it wasn't only the pregnancy, that I also didn't want to risk being in a medicated sleep with my husband prowling around our house. Even with the door barricaded, I needed to be alert if ... *If what?* the voice in my head questioned. I pushed it aside and focused back on Bella.

"Oh, right. I hadn't thought about it before. Maybe I'll look into it," I lied.

"I can help. We can make sure that we get you the best thing for your ... situation." Her eyes flicked to my belly again. Her choice of phrase seemed odd, but I was pathetically touched that she cared. I flashed the brightest smile I could muster and nodded. "Thank you! That's so kind." And before I could stop, I found myself adding, "If you're sure it's not too much trouble."

I regretted my stupid acceptance of something I didn't even want. My desperation to please was one of my worst traits. Bella waved a hand, dismissing my false concern.

"Of course it's not. I'd be happy to help!" she gushed. It was the most animated I'd seen her, so eager to please, and I wondered secretly if, in fact, she was as desperate for my friendship as I was for hers.

SAM and I had been skirting around the topic of our sleeping arrangements, even avoiding anything that could slip into the subject. For the first time since meeting him, our conversations felt forced, our time together tainted with undertones of unspoken thoughts. It was as though something rotten had lodged in the core of our relationship and was turning everything black from the inside out.

My thoughts had become consumed too. I should have been daydreaming about impending motherhood, making plans and spending too much money on "must have" gimmicks. But instead, I worried about protecting my child from his or her own father, and how I'd cope as a single parent.

My mind refused to switch off, racing through scenarios all night whilst I imagined hearing Sam's movements outside my bedroom door. I wondered if the chair would hold if Sam tried to force his way in. The sound of his growling voice was so clear in my mind, I didn't know if it was real or not. My heart pounded as I waited for him to crash through the door, unable to envisage him as anything other than the monster I had grown terrified of. I was left disorientated, full of doubt, sheepish even, when greeted each morning by my husband's wonky smile. I could hardly bear the fact that the big strong arms that made me feel so safe were also the source of my biggest fears. The irony would've been comical if it weren't so painful.

We sat down for our usual evening meal. I'd cooked a pie from scratch, knowing it was one of Sam's favourites. We made tense small talk, my stomach clenching at the wedge between us. I would've given anything to get our marriage back on track. I pushed my food around my plate, nibbling at tiny forkfuls while Sam shovelled his down. Eventually he paused and took note of my barely touched portion.

"Hey, are you okay? Feeling queasy again?" He spoke through a mouthful, gesturing to my plate with his fork still clutched in his hand.

I shoved my plate into the middle of the table and looked up at him, angst welling inside me.

"Sam, we need to talk."

A look of fear passed across his features. He eased his fork down, chewing on the last mouthful of food. Swallowing hard, he wiped his mouth with the back of his hand.

"Do we?" A nervous tone had entered his voice. "I thought this arrangement was what you wanted. Oh god, did something happen?" A look of terror flashed in his eyes.

"No, no, everything's fine." I held up my hands in a gesture of reassurance, and he visibly unwound again. A pang of love for him knocked me off balance, leaving me desperate to fix things somehow.

"We can't just carry on like this forever though, Sam – this is supposed to be a marriage. I miss you, and I don't want to have to go to separate rooms at the end of every evening and barricade myself inside. And what about when the baby arrives?" My words tumbled out, nothing like the calm, measured speech I'd been practicing in my head. "I hate the way this is coming between us. I love you. We need to find a permanent solution before it's too late."

He stared down at the scraps of food left on his plate but remained quiet. His expression gave away nothing, the silence deafening. My eyes searched every inch of his face as I tried to read his thoughts, but he gave nothing away. An impassive mask had slipped down to obscure his features. Desperation tugged at me.

"Don't you want to work this out?" My question came out in barely more than a whisper as if I might not want the answer. My hands moved to rest on my stomach as panic swirled. Had Sam decided he'd had enough? I had, after all, forced him to move out of our room, kicking him out of his own bed.

He breathed out a deep sigh and kneaded his forehead with his fingertips, his face seeming to crumple.

"Of course I want to work it out. You and the baby are my entire world. You mean everything to me."

Relief flooded through me, but it was short lived, abruptly replaced with heightened panic as he continued on.

"But I don't know what you expect me to do, Tessa." He dropped his head into his hands. "You knew the situation from the beginning, *knew* I had this problem. I never hid it from you. And I did try to warn you." He shook his head.

A spark of irritation flared within me. His emphasis was clear; I too was responsible.

I narrowed my eyes at him. "Let's be fair here, Sam. I don't think I ever imagined having to lock myself away every night to avoid being assaulted. Warning or not!"

His eyes darkened, and I was instantly filled with regret. I had let the situation spiral, nothing like how I had imagined it. Sam and I rarely argued. Even when we had, it was minor disagreements that fizzled almost as quickly as they arose. I couldn't stand how this was coming between us.

"Oh, well, isn't it incredibly convenient how you can just forget how things started, and place the blame firmly—"

I held up a hand and cut him off. "I'm not." I closed my eyes and took a calming breath. "This isn't about blame or lashing out at one another." I kept my voice even as I could. "In fact, quite the opposite. I'd really like us to be united – a strong partnership – when our child arrives."

His shoulders sagged, and his eyes softened. "That's what I want too. Of course it is. But these nightmares aren't something I have any control over, Tess. Do you honestly think I wouldn't have done something by now if there was some quick fix for it?"

"I'm not suggesting there *is* a quick fix." I clenched my fists, attempting to stay calm. "But surely there are things that are worth a try?"

He seemed to shut instantly at the idea.

"Nothing will help, Tess. Just leave it!"

As hard as I tried to stay calm, another spark of anger flared. Why was he not willing to meet me halfway with this? Surely it was worth a try.

"How the hell am I supposed to leave it, Sam? You think this is *normal*? That we can carry on like this? Are you honestly happy to bring a baby into this mess?"

He stared straight ahead of him, eyes fixed on anything but me. Hopeful that anything I was saying might be getting through to him, I continued, keeping my voice even.

"There are all sorts of therapies you can try these days. Some of them have amazing results for terrible conditions people suffer with, we could ..."

I was looking down, picking at my nails, when he slammed his fist onto the table so hard everything on it clattered. I jumped, tipping my chair slightly and only just keeping my balance, heart hammering.

"I said *no*, Tessa!" His eyes fixed on mine, flashing. The reflections in them made them appear almost black. "No one is going poking around in my head, okay? Now just god damn leave it alone like I fucking asked you to."

With that, he pushed back his chair, thundering out of the kitchen and up the stairs, leaving me clinging on to the seat of my chair, heart still thudding.

Bella's words, mocking and uninvited, rushed back into my mind.

Things will only get worse.

I remained frozen in my chair, unable to bring myself to

move as the shock of what had just happened sank in. Sam had never lost his temper, never lashed out like that. I didn't recognise the man who just did, leaving me shaken and afraid in my own home.

Only I did, didn't I? But usually he was hidden behind a nightmare.

44

SAM

PRESENT DAY

I blinked in the semi-darkness of the living room, taking a second to get my bearings, uncertain whether I'd actually been asleep. Remembering why I was on my sofa, with a stiff neck and throbbing back, I knew further rest was out of the question. I searched out the remote and turned off the TV, then moved about as quietly as I could, aware of the early hour and not wanting to disturb Claire. Mouth dry and stale from the previous evening's wine, I bent and gulped back water directly from the kitchen tap. My head pounded in objection. I'd set the alarm on my phone out of optimism, but, of course, it hadn't been necessary.

Unable to face entering our bedroom – the image of the last time I'd been in there scorched onto my brain – I'd fallen asleep on the sofa. Although I couldn't bring myself to say it out loud, part of me was also afraid to sleep whilst Claire was in the house. Just what I was capable of was now horrifically clear, and I couldn't have lived with myself if I had hurt her too.

I'd dozed all night, jolting awake each time I managed to slip into an unsettled slumber, visions of Tessa, Claire, and

Lindy all merging into one. At one point, I'd sprung up from the sofa, certain I could hear Cora's cries. I strained for any sound, hearing nothing but the hum of the fridge. Adrenaline and despair surged through me in equal measure. I flopped back down and put the TV on, keeping the sound only a notch or two above muted so as not to disturb Claire.

I had to get to Helen's office before her first appointment. I headed upstairs to shower but hovered on the landing outside our bedroom and en-suite. It was stupid, avoiding the room, but I didn't feel strong enough to face it. Deciding to deal with the room later, I grabbed a towel from the airing cupboard and turned into the main bathroom.

When I emerged again onto the landing, feeling now refreshed and marginally more human, I almost collided with Claire. She didn't look as though she'd managed to get much more sleep than I had, her hair dishevelled, the dark circles under her eyes seeming to have deepened overnight.

Her brow knitted, and she patted her hair in an attempt to smooth it down.

"Oh sorry." She yawned, screwing up her face. "For some reason, I assumed you had an en-suite." She shrugged and shook her head. I was grateful that my cheeks were already flushed from the heat of the shower, hiding the blush creeping over them. I'd assumed she would stay asleep long enough for me to shower and leave the house.

"Erm, yeah. We do," I mumbled, avoiding her eye, wiping away the water dripping down my face.

"Oh. Is there a problem with ..." She froze, then her eyes widened, and her hand flew to her mouth.

"Oh God, Sam, I didn't think." She slapped herself on the side of the head with the flat of her hand with a wince. "Where did you sleep?" Her cheeks were burning now, and I wondered if she was also struggling with the wine's after-effects.

I scratched the back of my neck with my free hand, my other fist clenching my towel.

"I didn't really feel sleepy, so I just watched some TV on the sofa." I shrugged.

She sighed and glanced towards my closed bedroom door.

"Do you want me to get you anything?" Her eyes clouded, and her voice came out thick.

I cleared my throat. "I think I can grab everything I need from the clean washing downstairs. But thanks."

She gave a single nod.

"Okay, let me jump in the shower, and I'll be ready."

My own brow creased. "Ready for what?"

"To come to your session with you," she replied flatly. I was preparing my words of protest when she held up her hands. "I'm coming, Sam, and that's final. I understand if you don't want me in the room, but I can hang around in the waiting area. I'm here to support you, so that is what I am going to do. I want to be there for you, just in case you ... remember anything."

Her meaning hung between us.

DUE TO THE EARLY HOUR, Helen's receptionist had not yet arrived. Claire remained alone in the waiting area, as promised, while Helen took me back to her office. I made up an excuse about fearing Claire would be a distraction. Perhaps she knew it was down to my fear of what she might hear. I just didn't want her to find out that way.

We took the same seats as the previous day. Helen retrieved her notepad.

"So, you don't look like you got too much rest." She tilted her head, a smile playing on her lips.

I shrugged. "Some," I lied. "Sleep is pretty evasive right now. No prizes for guessing why."

She nodded and tapped her pad with her pen. "I'm assuming nothing more has come to you since our last session?"

"Nothing." I sighed, shaking my head.

She sat up straight. "Okay, well, let's not waste any time, then."

THE SHOCK in coming to was less severe the second time around; I figured out where I was and what was happening much more quickly. Panting, the rush of blood pumping around my body the same as after one of my nightmares, I was desperate to know.

"Anything?" I gasped out, my stare fixed on Helen. She shook her head. The disappointment crushed me. She allowed me a few moments to catch my breath and pull myself together before she spoke again.

"Are you feeling okay?" She studied me, her eyes clouding.

"Fine, thank you." I reached for the glass of water on the table next to the sofa and took small sips, the cool water refreshing on my scratchy throat.

"So, what next?" I croaked.

"Sam, I can only share with you what I see, what *you* share." She placed her notepad and pen to one side and linked her fingers, leaning forward. "I'm really not sure you know anything about what happened to your wife and child." Her eyes remained fixed on mine as she spoke, her tone sombre.

"You have a lot locked up in that mind of yours. You talked a lot of your father and of someone called ..." She leaned towards her pad and lifted the pen out of the way. "Lindy?" Her name was a punch to the gut. I felt my colour drain, certain that I visibly paled.

She paused, watching me carefully.

"It seems that traumatic experiences from your past are what your mind is drawn into during these sessions, blocking everything else. You haven't mentioned Tessa or Cora at all."

Reeling from her words, I sipped my water again and cleared my throat to buy myself a little time.

"It doesn't mean I didn't do anything, though, right? I could just have buried it deeper, blocked it out somehow?"

She lifted her eyes and twisted her mouth.

"It is possible, yes." She nodded. "But if that is the case, Sam, it could take us a long time to excavate that. We'd have to work through what we have, and your brain clearly doesn't want to remember it." She shook her head again, her gentle words ringing with kindness.

As though someone were standing on my chest, I gasped – I wasn't going to find my little girl this way. I had pinned everything on this. Panic rose, as did the nausea.

"I feel sick," I muttered, covering my mouth.

She pointed to a tiny door in the corner of the room behind me.

I launched myself from the sofa and into the tiny cubicle. I heaved a few times, producing bile and the previous night's wine. My throat stung, and I felt wetness on my cheeks. The thought of never seeing Cora again, never even knowing what happened to her, made my head spin, and I retched again.

I splashed some cool water on my face and rinsed my sour mouth under the tap as best I could in the tiny basin, avoiding my reflection in the mirror.

When I stepped back into Helen's room, she looked up from the notepad that she was scribbling away in. I wondered if she was writing about me.

"Are you okay? Would you like me to fetch your sister?" she asked, forehead creasing.

"No, no, I'm okay now," I lied. She looked unconvinced but didn't push it further.

"Sam, I'm honestly not sure that this is going to get you the answers you need. Plus, it's taking a heck of a toll on your body. You need to stop punishing yourself. I *really* want to help you, but I am just not sure that I can." Her face was open and her words earnest, my disappointment reflected in her eyes.

"I understand." I nodded, any fight I had left drained from my body. I crossed to the sofa and retrieved my jumper. As I made to move away, curiosity got the better of me, and I turned back to Helen.

"Just out of interest ..." I tilted my head and rubbed another crick in my neck, then brushed my scars. "What *did* I share with you today?"

45

TESSA
NINE MONTHS PREVIOUS

Sam didn't reappear for an hour or so after our fight. Only the occasional sound of his moving around upstairs reminded me of his presence.

By that time, I'd distracted myself by searching out old crochet patterns, deciding I would make something for the baby. I hadn't felt the pull of my old hobby for a long time. Making things just to pass the time had lost its shine when I feared I'd never get to make what I really wanted to.

Whilst rustling through a cupboard, I stumbled across old photos of my parents, smiling to find my father's old maps tucked up at the back. He'd been a collector of anything and everything. Junk, mostly. When Mum's deteriorating health forced them to downsize, he'd been left with little choice but to declutter. He'd given me the maps, along with some photographs. I wasn't sure if it was a meaningful gesture or if he just couldn't bear to see them disposed of, but I treasured them, pulling them out frequently to finger the crinkled paper and think of the places I'd see in the future. I spent hours imagining the hands those maps had passed through before my own, remembering the plans Dad and I had made, hoping against hope I'd have the chance to do the same with my own child one day. They offered freedom when I felt trapped, just as my dad had told me they would. When my child was old enough, I'd take him or her anywhere they wanted to visit – I'd live out Dad's dreams.

Having lost the desire to do anything, I moved to the sofa, curled my legs beneath me, and pulled the throw around my shoulders. The future suddenly seemed so uncertain; I felt cold and shaky from Sam's outburst. I'd never seen him behave like that before – at least not while he was conscious.

Light footsteps sounded on the stairs. "Hey, fancy a drink?" he called as he passed the door to the living room and headed for the kitchen.

His ordinary suggestion only provoked me. How could he expect to carry on as normal, pretend nothing had happened, after how we'd left things? I remained silent, lost for a response.

"Tessa?" His head appeared around the doorway, eyes meeting mine. His facial expression shifted from questioning to shock in a millisecond. I could only imagine what a fright I looked, with my tear-stained cheeks and red-rimmed eyes.

The rest of his body appeared in the room, and his brow creased.

"Are you alright?" he asked stupidly, taking in the full picture of me.

I glared at him, tightening my face. "Are you seriously asking me that question, Sam? Have you just wiped everything that happened earlier from your mind?"

He genuinely looked taken aback, and I wondered if I'd dreamt the whole thing myself – his condition catching.

"I didn't know it'd upset you." His face was a picture of innocence. "It was a silly disagreement, that's all."

He crossed the room to perch next to me on the sofa and

placed his hand over mine. "I'm sorry you're upset, Tess." He brushed my hair back from my face. My anger softened.

Was I overreacting? No doubt I was hormonal, crying over every advert on TV with a child or animal in it. But I *had* felt shaken by his behaviour.

"You scared me, Sam, reacting like that. I was only trying to ..."

"I know. I'm sorry." He wiped the pad of his thumb over a tear running down my cheek. "I shouldn't have gotten so wound up. It's just – I've tried *everything* before; nothing works. It's frustrating as hell. I would give anything to change, Tess."

He fixed his eyes on our hands, his still placed over mine.

"Also, it brought back bad memories of my mother. She was always on at me to do something about it, telling me I was broken, needed help. It took me back, and I snapped at you for it, but I shouldn't have. I was wrong, and I am truly sorry." He looked into my eyes, and my body softened.

I'd met his mother only once. She'd seemed meek, and I couldn't conjure an image of her saying such awful things to her child, but he had no reason to be dishonest. I knew the strain his relationship with his mother caused him. He rarely spoke of his parents. I did know that after his father died, things were difficult and only became worse when his mother remarried.

I turned my hand over and linked my fingers through his.

Bella and I had continued to text, me avoiding any mention of Sam, her subtly asking how things were "at home".

I kept my replies upbeat and positive, making regular mention of how excited I was about the baby. Bella took little notice of the pregnancy, skipping over the topic in her replies. Her feelings about it clearly hadn't altered.

I hoped that would change when she met the baby. The thought made me smile.

My phone screen lit up with a new message. I glanced to see Bella's name.

> Coffee today? I have the tablets for you, thought you could use them asap. Xx

Unease returned – I didn't want the tablets but felt obliged to have them. I could always just thank her, bring them home, and not actually take them – but I was a terrible liar. She would see right through me.

The situation couldn't be avoided, so I replied by accepting her invitation for coffee but not mentioning the pills. Sam was getting ready to leave for the gym. The company would be nice, I convinced myself.

Bella had never invited me to her house. I'd only been inside that one time, when I'd collapsed on her. Once again, I suggested that she could come to mine for coffee that day, but she declined as always, telling me it was her shout and she'd see me at the usual place. I did sometimes wonder if she wasn't fully opening up to me, if there was a reason she felt uncomfortable with people in her house, if there was something she was worried about. In a strange resemblance to my husband, Bella wasn't comfortable discussing her family, shutting down and changing the subject if it ever arose. She needed to be in control. I was curious about her past, but as with Sam, I never pushed. My friend deserved my patience and understanding; she would open up to me when she was good and ready.

We'd only been sat down for a few minutes, pleasantries barely exchanged, when she produced the pills from her handbag.

"So, you obviously shouldn't take these *every* night," she explained, pushing the bottle towards me. "But they'll help you catch up when you need them." With a bright smile, she nudged the bottle towards me again. I forced a tight smile and retrieved the small bottle, squirming – I had no intention whatsoever of taking them.

"Oh, thanks," I managed, trying to seem normal but seemingly forgetting how.

"No problem." She nodded, oblivious to my guilt. "I double-checked – they won't do any harm to ... you know." She gestured toward my swollen midriff.

"The baby," I retorted, feeling a flicker of annoyance.

She raised an eyebrow slightly before her face snapped back into her perfect, wide smile. "Uh-huh." She nodded, narrowing her eyes with her grin.

I felt a pang of guilt at my snappiness. From there, I attempted to keep an easy conversation flowing, asking about her work and social life. She seemed distant, so – to my shame – I returned to the subject of the pills.

"Thanks so much for the tablets," I gushed. "I really owe you one."

She visibly brightened, her focus back on me.

"No problem, you're welcome. I was happy to do *something* to help." She beamed. "How are ... things? And Sam?"

A knot formed in my stomach. I was hoping to steer away from this topic, saving myself from any further untruths.

"Yeah, good. Better actually, thanks," I lied, stumbling over my words.

Her eyes narrowed again. "Are you still sleeping separately?"

I was slightly taken aback at the bluntness of her question.

"Well ... sort of ... we ..." My phone pinged and vibrated on the table. Grateful for the interruption, I grabbed for it, throwing Bella an apologetic look while willing my cheeks to stop burning.

"Sam?" Bella challenged. I might have detected a hint of sarcasm in her tone.

"Yep." I smiled brightly, lifting my shoulders. "He's just finishing up at the gym and wanted to know if I fancied meeting up in town."

She raised her eyebrows but said nothing.

As I was tapping out a reply, I found myself opening my camera app. I didn't know what came over me. I supposed I'd always felt so inadequate, having no real friends. I wanted Sam to see that Bella really existed.

Extending my arm as far as I could manage, I grinned up at our image on the screen. "Say cheese!" I snapped a couple of shots before noticing Bella's look of utter horror.

"What the *fuck* are you doing?" she hissed at me, fury twisting her every feature. I froze, so totally gobsmacked by her reaction I was unable to reply. "You can't just take photos of someone without their knowledge or consent," she scolded me.

I sat rigid and struggled to string a sentence together. "I'm sorry, I didn't mean to ... I was only going to send it to Sam as a bit of fun. I didn't think you'd mind." My face burned.

"Well, that's awfully presumptuous of you," she bit back. "And I *do* mind. So I'd appreciate it if you would delete it right away." Her tone was icy. Tears pricked at the corners of my eyes. I tapped the screen with trembling fingers, deleting the image while she watched over my shoulder to ensure that it was gone.

Once it was done, I dropped my phone into my bag, its presence making me feel horribly awkward. I peered up at Bella, unsure of what to expect. She lifted her coffee cup to her lips and sipped from it.

"Thanks." She smiled, having visibly relaxed. "Sorry to be

a bore. I'm *really* camera shy and absolutely despise photos of myself." She gave a tinkle of a laugh. "You know how it is." She shrugged.

I forced a smile and nodded. "No problem," I spluttered, still not fully trusting myself not to burst into tears. It was though it never happened, as if I'd imagined the whole thing. For the second time in a matter of days, I wondered if my hormones were making me crazy. First Sam, now Bella. Was I reading too much into things? Being completely oversensitive about nothing? What other explanation was there? It had to be me. I gave myself a mental shake and fixed a smile back onto my face as Bella jokingly moaned about her irritating co-workers.

In bed that night, the events in the coffee shop flooded back to mind. I reached for my phone and tapped, opening my gallery.

The image of me, all smiles, and Bella, looking horrified, filled the screen. I'd snapped more than one photo, a usual habit, to compare and keep the best shot. She had only watched me delete the last one.

At the time, I'd been so irked by her reaction I'd seriously considered cooling our relationship. Now, humiliation throbbed as the realisation dawned on me. I thought about Bella's reaction to the photograph, and to my problems with Sam. The countless times I'd gazed over at her house and never seen anyone come or go, no friends or family visiting. It was so rare I even saw Bella outside her house, I assumed she used the back entrance, at the bottom of the opposite gardens. She'd always seemed so independent, but on occasion so reserved, cold – as if she was reluctant to be around anyone but me. Her move here had been so sudden, and she never spoke of her life before. She'd been so insistent – forceful even – when I'd spoken of the issues in my relationship. For the first time, I realised what had been niggling at me, something sparking in my mind, a piece finally slotting into place. She was running. An abusive partner of her own lodged in her past.

My heart broke for her, for what she must have suffered through. It was no wonder she had reacted that way to my admission about Sam. Guilt and shame gnawed at me, thinking what my overblown dramatics must have dredged up for her. My finger hovered over the delete button, but at the last second, I changed my mind and saved it into a separate folder, obeying some instinct urging me to keep hold of it.

Despite the obvious explanation, I couldn't shake the feeling that I was missing something.

46

SAM

PRESENT DAY

I left Helen's clinic in a daze. I was terribly relieved that Claire had insisted on driving us even against my protest. I wasn't sure I'd remember how to drive. She kept asking me if I was okay, her concern palpable in her constant glances.

After another journey that I could barely recall, Claire insisted that I relax on the sofa while she made us some drinks. I barely noticed her until she placed a steaming mug on the coffee table in front of me with a small clunk. I started and blinked at her a couple of times before she came into clear focus. She dropped into the armchair, her hands wrapped around her own mug, and sank back into the embrace of the seat.

"Want to talk about it?" she asked gently. My behaviour must have seemed strange. I'd barely uttered a word since leaving the clinic.

"Talk about what?" I asked; we both knew what she was referring to.

She gave a small shrug. "Whatever happened in there that freaked you out so much. You look as though you've seen a ghost." The cliché had barely left her mouth before her cheeks flushed, and she slapped herself on the forehead. "Shit – I'm so sorry! I didn't think."

I shook my head. "It's fine." I forced a smile.

"What happened?" she pressed, cheeks still slightly pink. "Did you get something?"

I heaved in a deep breath and raised my eyes to the ceiling.

"Nothing of any relevance to Tessa or Cora." I sighed. "She believes I either really *don't* know anything, or that I've buried it too deep for us to retrieve in a few short sessions. DI Garcia's going to love that." I rubbed hard at my eyes before dragging my fingertips over my scars.

Her expression was unreadable as she gave a tiny nod. "So, what did happen?"

"I mentioned Dad – and Lindy." I didn't look at her as I said the name, but in my peripheral vision, I saw her draw back. My fingers moved faster.

"*Lindy?*" Her face clouded over, her voice full of loathing confusion. "What about her?" She screwed up her nose, and her top lip curled as she asked. She made no mention of our dad.

"We didn't discuss it too much." I shrugged. "It's irrelevant, really, just bad memories that are floating around, I guess." I gestured towards my head.

She pursed her lips. "They must be pretty bad for you to hold them alongside what happened to Dad." She raised an eyebrow.

"Well, things didn't exactly end on the best of terms," I admitted.

"There's a surprise." Claire's voice dripped with sarcasm. I shot her a look.

"Sorry." She held up her hands. "I just mean—"

"I know what you mean," I snapped, cutting her off. I didn't need a lecture on my ex.

She nodded and pressed her lips together into a thin line. The silence hung between us for a few beats, and I became lost in my own thoughts and unwelcome memories. Her voice snapped me back to the present.

"Can I ask about what happened?" Her eyes narrowed. It was my turn to look confused, a knot of panic forming in my chest. "With you and *her*," she confirmed, her lip curling.

My shoulders relaxed at what she was actually asking. For the first time in years, I allowed my mind to tumble back in time.

LINDY and I had first met in an overcrowded bar. As an unattractive teenager – with a smattering of horrid facial scars that mingled with endless spots and relentlessly greasy hair – I'd never had much luck when it came to girls. I still thought of myself as that gawky teenage boy, but as Claire often liked to remind me, I'd grown into my looks. Not long out of uni, it still took me by surprise when girls threw me appreciative looks or flirty glances, and I would often look around, wondering who they might be looking at. I'd lose my nerve when anyone tried to get close, lack of experience and an abundance of issues leaving me without much in the way of self-confidence.

Something about Lindy piqued my interest though. She was different, slightly older, with an air of confidence about her that turned heads, not conventionally beautiful – more striking in her appearance. But more than anything, she showed no interest in anyone around her, like she was the only person in the room.

Through mutual friends, we'd ended up forming a small,

boisterous crowd. I found myself drawn to her despite her showing no interest in me. Perhaps that was why.

She crossed the crowded bar with ease, slipping through groups of people, men turning to watch her and eager to allow her through. Despite the volume of people waiting for orders to be taken, waving clutched money, she immediately drew the attention of the barman and within seconds was leaning in to shout in his ear.

I felt a pang of envy watching her getting so close to him, his hand resting on her arm, their exchanging of smiles as they shouted back and forth to confirm her request. When she returned with the drinks, I attempted to catch her eye. Eventually, having almost given up, I skulked off to the loo. When I returned, the girls in the chairs next to hers had vacated, having moved off to the makeshift dance floor to drunkenly sway to the jukebox.

The empty seats were closer than my own, so I slipped into the one next to her and reached across for my drink, knocking hers over in the process. She jumped back from the table. Liquid had already dribbled off the table and soaked her skirt.

The guy on her other side, whom she'd been talking to, shouted something at me and attempted to clean her up with a wad of tissues offered by another of the girls.

A chorus of shouts came from the other side of the table.

"*Wayyyy.*" "*Smooth, mate!*" "*Good one!*" "*Strip it off, then!*"

She turned and regarded me coolly for a few seconds before she spoke, face set in a serious expression.

"Well, aren't you going to offer me your trousers?"

47

LINDY

SIX YEARS PREVIOUS

I hadn't been interested when I'd first seen Sam. Of course, it hadn't been the best start when he spilled my drink on me, but that wasn't the problem.

He was one of those guys who was irritatingly good looking. A perfectly symmetrical face and a pearly white smile. I wrote him off as pompous and arrogant, barely casting a glance in his direction for most of the evening as he failed to notice the silly girls swooning over him.

His type seemed to have the opposite effect on me. I'd had my share of men, some pathetically weak, but there was nothing that I wanted less than a domineering man who thought he had the right to control me. I was the one in control of my life, and I intended on keeping it that way. But Sam was different, seemingly unaware that he was blessed with good looks. His mannerisms were awkward, and once I was closer, I noticed a smattering of scars on his otherwise perfect skin as well as a smile that was slightly crooked, giving him an endearing goofy look.

I'd wandered into that bar completely alone after an awful day at work, inserted myself into their crowd, camouflaging myself among them. Everyone assumed I was someone else's friend.

We ended up chatting until last orders, him seeming delighted that I was laughing with him, blissfully unaware that, as it happened, it was mostly *at* him. But there was something about him that did intrigue me – the almost brash exterior, so transparent to me. I saw so much hidden behind those eyes and in his self-conscious motion as he rubbed his face. He was completely different to the person I'd expected, anxious and mouldable. Exactly what I'd been searching for. And so I drunkenly – so I made it seem – agreed to pass over my phone number before hailing a taxi and heading home alone. It was important that he thought he'd initiated things.

Over time, our relationship developed. Sam chased me for a "real date" and, although I would never admit it, I'd revelled in the attention. We came to joke that I wore the trousers in our relationship. His expression was so panicked when he'd knocked that drink over the night we met, I couldn't resist the temptation to play with him a little.

He'd called my bluff, though. When he unbuttoned his jeans, whoops and cheers erupted from our crowd of friends, drawing the attention of everyone around us. I'd acted my part, relenting, begging him to stop his terrible Full Monty-style dance and laughing until tears streamed down my face and blurred my vision. The laughter had been genuine, and I'd enjoyed the easy company. I'd kept my eyes on him for the rest of the evening, touching his arm and flashing him dazzling smiles.

Looking back, I couldn't pinpoint exactly when we became more than friends, but just as planned, Sam moved into my apartment, and things were going well. Only on occasion did I lose my temper. I wasn't an unreasonable person and – as I'd had to remind him from time to time – I had allowed him to move into *my* home. He needed to respect that.

Sam had lost his father when he was young, which of course had a huge impact on his life. His mother had remarried and moved away, which only left his interfering, overprotective sister to deal with.

He had been so excited, insisting that we should meet and that we would adore each other. His forcing the matter only became a source of irritation to me. Admittedly I made excuses as to why I couldn't make it each time he set something up. Perhaps I stood them up once or twice.

When we did finally meet, I knew instantly that I had been right to avoid her. She flapped around Sam like a mother hen, jumping to see to his every whim. It made my stomach turn, acid sour in my mouth.

I couldn't bring myself to look at him by the time we left, any feelings towards him diminished by the sight of his sister's undignified pandering. His begging, on the way home, for me to tell him what he'd done wrong only added to my disgust.

When I finally relented, he had looked so confused – actually trying to argue that he couldn't understand the problem. Of course, his being so deliberately obtuse had flared my temper. I was only human. I'd made it abundantly clear at that point that if he was going to behave in such a manner and continue to humiliate us both, he should just pack his things and go back to his perfect sister.

He'd seen sense then and apologised, which I was gracious enough to accept after such a performance. He explained to his sister that she needed to curb her pathetic behaviour, and we tried a couple more times to meet, but each time resulted in another fight. I could see that she was purposely trying to rile me, and I wouldn't stand for coming second to anyone. He didn't need her. He was with me now;

we didn't need anyone else. After an explosive row, with his continuing to be unreasonable, even after I'd explained to him – *so clearly* – why he needed to stop seeing his sister, I had grabbed the thing closest to hand, a cut-glass vase, to throw in my frustration.

My intention had never been to actually hit him. The few shards that caught him were an accident. It was me who suffered the loss of my vase, but I let it go once he had cleared up the mess and admitted his responsibility in driving me to it.

We agreed soon after that: Claire was the problem, the one causing the horrific rows between us. Things would be perfect between us if it weren't for her. I acknowledged it was a shame he would miss out on spending time with his nephews – but I should be enough for him. Was it really so unreasonable of me, not wanting such a dreadful presence casting a shadow on our otherwise perfect relationship?

Claire, being the odious creature that she was, couldn't respect Sam's decision. She insisted on pushing the matter, trying to force her way back into his life and come between us. I pointed this out to him, of course, that she was proving my point. I had been right about her – she never wanted us to work, disapproving of me right from the start.

I couldn't let her mess with his head, worm her way in and plant her poison, so I was left with no choice but to intervene. I was smart about it – doing things in such a way she could never *prove* I was behind it – but I made sure she knew.

When she tried to place the blame on me, it only pushed Sam and me closer. I sobbed on his shoulder, railing against such horrendous accusations, distraught that she had always "had it in" for me. He lapped it up and cut her out completely – just like that. It was easier than I'd expected.

It was for the best. I only *ever* did what was best for him.

48

SAM
PRESENT DAY

I shivered at the uninvited memories trickling into my consciousness. The familiar sensation took over my body, like fire and ice running over me simultaneously. I'd been blindsided by Lindy. The memory of it crippled me with shame. The more Claire had tried to expose her, the further tangled I had become in her web of manipulation.

I had fallen, hard and fast, for her, believed that I was totally in love. Believed I had called the shots. I think, in reality, it was actually more infatuation – the slightly older woman, and my first real girlfriend. The woman who'd shown no interest in me becoming, for that reason, the only thing I was interested in. Of course I was ashamed to admit it, but it was what I believed to be true once I eventually saw things more clearly.

It hadn't started out that way. The early days had seemed perfect. I couldn't believe a woman like her would choose to be with me. It felt like I was walking on air. I followed her around like a little lost puppy, more than happy to do whatever she wanted. At her beck and call so long as I continued to be included. Mike would roll his eyes, a huge grin plastered over his face, when I'd cancel our plans, making my pathetic excuses. We spent less and less time together, Lindy preferring it to be just the two of us, but Mike didn't mind too much. He'd had his fair share of girlfriends filling his time but seemed completely smitten since meeting Lauren.

We never really discussed our living arrangements. I'd been in a flat share with friends I'd met through student accommodation. Lindy would *never* have slummed it in a place like that, needless to say. She lived alone in a small but impeccably kept apartment. I stayed with her more and more regularly until, eventually, I'd moved in with her.

I'd been so excited about introducing her to Claire. Naively, I had truly believed that they would adore one another, become firm friends who would laugh fondly together about me. The two women who meant most to me in the world.

I could not have been more wrong.

From the moment they met, I could sense the tension – a cool atmosphere that never shifted. They were painfully polite to one another but seemed to be sizing each other up rather than developing a relationship.

I never understood Lindy's instant, furious dislike of my sister – but being the coward I was, I accepted she was right and allowed the blame to fall on myself and Claire.

We fell into a pattern. Lindy would stop speaking to me without explanation. It was out of the question to ask; she would just snarl at me that I should know. I would try desperately to work out where I had gone wrong that time, and to fix it, only ever seeming to aggravate her further.

I was so afraid that she would leave me, realise that she could do better. I did everything I could to keep her happy, following what I believed to be "the rules" down to the letter, but somehow I always got it horribly wrong.

Her temper never failed to shock me. So many times, I

thought for sure I had seen her anger maxed out, only for it to be exceeded the next time. Of course I considered leaving on a couple of occasions – a near miss with a glass vase being one – but she'd explain so convincingly why she had been so mad, why her reaction was absolutely justifiable, that anyone would have done the same – and I would be flummoxed. Her perfect logic left me unable to string a sentence together. I would find myself agreeing that, in her shoes – if she were acting as I had – I would've lost my temper too. I believed that I was the problem, that the relationship would be normal were it not for me being impossible to live with. Lindy swore no one had ever caused her to react like she did, reinforcing my belief that all of my relationships would be like this until I learned better. Each time, I would find myself begging her forgiveness, clearing up the mess that I had *forced* her to create. And then things would be so good again for a while. Those good times kept me there, showed what it could be like if I could just get everything right. I was in so deep by then.

Deep down, I knew it was wrong to cut Claire out of my life. I'd already gradually alienated myself from most of my friends, ignoring their messages, declining invitations. I couldn't even remember when I'd last seen Mike. It was just easier that way. Lindy hated me going out without her, and it always resulted in a fight. So, I just … stopped.

My head was such a mess by that point – my own thoughts continuously overruled by Lindy on such a regular basis – I seemed to have lost any ability to disagree with her or form an opinion of my own. On the occasions that I felt ready to challenge her, she would seem to know exactly how to scramble my mind, responding with such valid certainty, or breaking down, seemingly devastated that I could think such things. My own mind atrophied, my thoughts defaulting to how Lindy would think or feel, always trying to get one step ahead. Always failing.

Still, I should never have allowed her to come between Claire and me. I bitterly regretted that and wasn't sure I'd ever truly forgive myself for it.

"You know I didn't make those things up, right?" Claire's voice broke me from my reverie. "I know it makes no difference now, but honestly, Sam, she did do everything I said."

I nodded slowly. I think I'd always known but was just too weak, too worn down and pathetic by then, to challenge her over it. So, for self-preservation, I accepted her story and turned my back on Claire.

"Yeah," I whispered. "I know. I realise now how messed up she really was." I gave an apologetic shrug.

Claire screwed up her nose. "Worse than messed up, I'd say. Who posts shit through someone's letter box?"

I cringed at the reminder.

"And what she painted on my front door was ..."

"I know, I know, Claire, and I am *so* sorry I didn't do something about it then, but trust me – I suffered for it."

She looked down at the floor, rubbing one foot over the other.

"Yeah ... sorry. She was certainly a piece of work."

My eyebrows shot up in agreement.

"She made me believe no one else would ever want me." I spoke the words for the first time, never having spoken of it before. "She'd call me broken and damaged, remind me how my own mother didn't care enough to stick around, how fucked up it was that I had the parasomnias – laughing when I tried to leave, asking who else would ever be stupid enough to put up with me and my *issues*." I glanced up at Claire, whose eyes brimmed with tears.

"I'm so sorry, Sam. I should've done more – shouldn't have let her scare me off so easily. It was just ... well ... I had the boys ... she was ..." She shook her head, searching for the words, her face frozen with horror. "I was afraid," she admitted. "I – I—"

"I know," I cut in. "You are not the one who owes an explanation here, Claire."

"But ..." The tears were falling down her cheeks, dripping onto her dark jeans, disappearing into the fabric. I held up a hand to stop her.

"No! It's on me." I nodded to reassure her. She wiped her cheeks and just barely met my eye.

"How did you get out in the end?" She sniffed, gulping back the emotions. "I can't imagine she just ... waved you off as you left?"

I gave a humourless laugh. "No, not exactly." I rolled my eyes, almost able to feel the fear all over again.

"She decided she wanted a baby."

Claire's head snapped up, her mouth slightly open, eyes wide. I sighed and nodded, my own eyes wandering to a photograph of Cora hanging on the wall.

"Of course, I was never consulted about the idea. I only found out after she'd been off the pill for just under a year. She was furious that it hadn't happened and blamed me. Something else that must've been wrong with me." I rolled my eyes again. Claire stayed silent, waiting for me to continue.

"I met a girl. She was on my course and started working at the same bar as I did. I tried to avoid her to begin with, but we got on well. I liked her – just as a friend, you know."

Claire nodded and silently held her gaze.

"I have no idea how Lindy found out that we were friends, but she hit the roof. She accused me of sleeping with her, said that's why she hadn't fallen pregnant. She trashed the few possessions that I owned and cut up half of my clothes. I tried to stop her and almost ended up on the sharp end of the scissors myself."

Claire shook her head, her disgust visible on her face.

"Even that probably wouldn't have been enough to make me leave her," I admitted, shocked by my own honesty. "But the girl suddenly dropped off the planet. She left the course, stopped turning up for her shifts at the bar. I asked around some mutual friends, but no one knew anything. It was just too much of a coincidence."

Claire let out a breath and sat back in her chair. "What did she do?" she asked, closing her eyes in preparation. I watched her gulp.

"Truth be told, I'm not certain," I answered, shaking my head. "I couldn't contact her, so in the end, I just asked Lindy outright."

I swallowed hard, remembering the look on her face as clear as if she were sitting in front of me.

"She looked right at me, all mock innocence, and asked why I was so bothered about her. She laughed and said she didn't know why my *mistress* had dumped me and run off. Probably because she'd realised I was such a freak. But what really bothered me was what I heard her mutter as she was walking away from me."

WE SAT in silence for a few minutes, both lost in our own thoughts, unsure of what to say next.

"Tessa fell pregnant once before. Not long after we first met."

I didn't know where the admission had come from. Claire turned her focus on me, lines creasing her face.

"I totally freaked out when we found out, thought she'd done it on purpose to trap me, even compared her to Lindy in my mind, thinking I'd been duped again. I panicked, considered running off." My fingers searched out my scars again. I didn't look at Claire. I wasn't sure why I was telling her every-thing now.

"I came to my senses though. Tessa was nothing like Lindy. No one is." I fought the urge to shudder. "I was delighted, actually, once I'd gotten over the initial shock. The pregnancy didn't last long though. Tessa had a miscarriage." I heard Claire's sharp intake of breath.

"I blame myself for that – always will. I wished the baby away when we first found out. What kind of father does that?"

"Oh, Sam."

I shook my head as I stood and retrieved my mug. The liquid had turned tepid. I excused myself, explaining the need for some time alone and saving her unwarranted sympathies.

Exhausted now with the emotion of it all, I decided it was about time I faced my bedroom. I dragged myself up the stairs and paused outside the door. The room that once represented safety and comfort was now just a stark reminder of all that I'd lost.

My heart fluttered at the familiar swish of the door as it rubbed over the thick carpet.

I didn't know what I was expecting to see, but everything appeared strangely normal. Some things had been shifted around slightly – the bed stripped of all the bedding, taken as evidence – but mostly, it would've been hard to tell that anything had happened there. My eyes were drawn to Cora's empty cot, and my stomach plummeted. Being up there, in that room, I could almost have convinced myself that my family were downstairs, waiting for me. But that cot, I would never forget the terror of finding it empty.

I touched some of Tessa's things, breathed in the scent of her from a discarded T-shirt, and found myself staring at her hairbrush, strands of her hair still tangled in it.

"What did I do, Tess?" I moaned, the pain raw and fresh.

I collapsed back onto the bed and buried my face in the mattress, breathing in the smell of her and allowing the agony of the past couple of days to wash over me, the tears to fall freely. Once I was spent, eyes stinging from the tears, I lifted myself onto my elbows. Something on the bedside table caught my eye.

Tessa's phone. The police had already searched it for anything of relevance and returned it with her personal items, her wedding and engagement bands still not having turned up.

For a second, I dismissed the idea. We'd always valued one another's privacy and trusted each other completely. But an overwhelming desire to see her and Cora, looking happy and carefree, spurred me on.

I pushed the button, prepared to unlock the phone – we'd always known each other's passcodes, having nothing to hide. Well, not on my phone, anyway. When the screen lit, I remembered the police had deactivated her passcode during their searches. A warning flashed that the battery was low. The charger was plugged into the wall, so I slotted the free end into the phone. It bleeped as it sucked in the charge. New notifications flashed, but I had no interest in snooping through her messages or social media.

I opened her photo gallery, losing myself in happy memories – trawling through hundreds of photos and videos of my wife and child. Hearing her ripped at my heart, but the sound was so beautifully normal, I couldn't refrain from playing them over and over.

Finally, when my eyes ached too much to continue looking, I sat up, leaning to replace the phone on the bedside table. But something in the gallery caught my eye, and I drew it back.

I tapped the screen a couple of times and dropped the

phone with a yelp as if it had burnt me. I couldn't make sense of what I had just seen, certain I must be mistaken. Yet the image was burned into my brain.

"*Claire!*" I screamed, my voice shrill. "Claire, you have to get up here right now – you *need* to see this."

49

LINDY

SIX YEARS PREVIOUS

Our bond was only made stronger when I discovered Sam's little problem. We'd been together a few months when it first happened. I had awoken in the night to sounds of a male voice.

I didn't recognise it as Sam's to begin with. He'd sounded so different – brimming with panic and fear. Sat bolt upright in my bed, he stared straight ahead of him, eyes wide and fixed. To be truthful, it unnerved me that first time. Wrenching my head around to see the point his eyes were locked to, I expected to see something horrific, an intruder, at least. But I saw nothing.

I called his name, expecting him to turn to me – to answer. When he didn't, my frustration simmered, thinking he was being deliberately obtuse. It took me a few seconds in my sleepy haze to realise what was happening. He was still asleep.

The parasomnias – as I'd later learned they were called – seemed to occur more regularly after that, growing in intensity. Sam's doctor's explanation was that they often became more common and severe during times of stress. We couldn't

understand why that would be. Sam had nothing to be
stressed about – he was a carefree student leeching off me. So
we dismissed that as a potential cause. The doctor had been
right in part though: they *did* continue to happen more regularly and did seem to increase in severity. He'd become
agitated – sometimes even violent.

Of course, in my line of work, I could have looked further
into drugs to ease things. Drugs that weren't available for an
NHS doctor to prescribe. But his condition only offered
another reason for no one else to want him. I learned to avoid
his swipes, well, unless of course I needed a little leverage –
something to use against him. The odd bruise to threaten
him with if he couldn't keep himself in line, a horror story to
tell him if I needed to induce a little guilt. Once or twice, I'd
even given myself a knock or two, encouraged the bruises to
shine when I'd needed them to. I adapted quickly, finding
ways to use his condition to my advantage. I'd always been
resourceful, able to turn things in my favour. I'd had no
choice but to learn that particular skill with the type of
parents I'd been lumbered with. I assured him that there was
nothing that could help with a condition as severe and
dangerous as his.

I'd made it clear that if Sam were *ever* to betray me, I
would have no choice but to expose the truth, to show myself
for the battered girlfriend, suffering on the wrong end of his
violent outbursts for too long. It would only be fair to pre-
warn any future conquests of his, to ensure they didn't suffer
the same fate. I'd remind him how lucky he was that I put up
with his issues, how he'd initiated the relationship, aware of
who he really was, and entrapped me. He'd never find
anyone else willing to accept his countless flaws.

Things were ticking along perfectly. Sam managed to
avoid doing anything stupid most of the time, with only the
occasional need for me to straighten things out – remind him

of the rules and consequences. In fact, things were so good, I decided it was time for us to become a proper family.

I'd wanted a baby for as long as I could remember. My father had brought me home a doll around the time of my fourth birthday – she had one eye missing, and some of her hair had been pulled out, but I adored her. She had no clothes, so I would make her blankets and makeshift outfits from anything I could find, wrapping her gently and rocking her to sleep. Until I awoke one morning to find her gone. I searched frantically for her while my mother watched on, an amused expression twisting her face, until she finally told me she'd disposed of my beloved Sadie, having decided I was too old for dolls. I was seven.

There was a small group of women who worked as assistants in the office where I was based. They were all below me in the ranking, of course, but still managed to make me feel excluded from their trivial conversations and inside jokes whenever I entered the place.

I found myself oddly drawn to them but couldn't understand why. I *hated* them, knew that they weren't good enough to be part of my life. They were no more than assistants. It came as a shock when I realised that two out of the four were sporting perfectly neat little baby bumps. Debra and Lucy cooed over them, a shameful display of fuss, while Gemma and Becky lapped up all the attention, acting as though they were the first women on the planet to achieve such a simple thing as pregnancy. I cringed and seethed, in equal measure, at the entire performance every time. I was left with little choice but to report them to their management – anonymously, of course.

But that seed they'd planted in my head had sprouted into a vine that twisted itself around my brain, slithering through every crack and crevice until it had taken full possession. I deserved a child of my own, someone who would love me unconditionally and be mine, who would never leave. My child would choose to stay because I would be the best mother possible, offering them everything that I never had, showing everyone what it meant to be the best kind of mother. If those silly little office tarts deserved it, there was no question that I did. The decision made, I threw out the half-popped packet of pills that I had always been so meticulous in taking, along with the untouched packets I had for the future months. They were no longer required.

I'd been so excited that first month, feeling righteous in my lone mission, bringing an oblivious Sam along for the ride but knowing that it was what I needed. I was certain it would happen instantly – after all, how often do you hear of bimbos falling pregnant after a one-night stand? When my period arrived, I was disappointed, for sure, but undeterred, googling and planning to ensure that my timings were right the following month. I just needed to put in the effort, now I was more educated on the subject, to ensure it happened this time.

When it didn't, my anger and frustration grew – especially towards Sam. There was no question that it was down to him. Here I was putting in the work for the pair of us while he was swanning around without a care.

I watched him – noticed a lightness in his step – and my suspicions grew. When I followed him, my suspicions were confirmed. I saw him with *her,* watched them laugh together, saw her touch his arm. *She* was the reason for the failed attempts. The blood roared in my ears. How *dare he* do it to me? I was no one's fool.

She had to be dealt with, shown the error of her ways. No self-respecting woman takes advantage of another woman's property. So, as any scorned partner with an ounce of dignity would, I tracked her movements, watching her whilst I sipped coffee in a booth, and used the time that she was on shift to find out a little information on her. Then I followed her home.

We arrived at a scruffy building. She fished around in her bag for her keys, locating them and singling out the correct one. I took quick, light steps up behind her until I was close enough to smell her shampoo mingled with the stale beer on her clothes. I lunged and grabbed a fistful of her hair at the root, held it tight in my grip and yanked as hard as I could. She let out a loud yelp and stumbled backwards, flailing her arms to keep her balance and attempt to get free. I pressed the blade of the small pocketknife that I carried in my bag – for personal protection usually – against the taut flesh of her neck.

I pushed her forwards so that she was against the wall and pinned her there with the weight of my own body. She went limp, her feeble whimpering noises riling me further.

"Now," I hissed in her ear, keeping my voice low and casting my gaze around. I didn't want to draw any attention. "I really *am* a reasonable person, but if you will behave like a dirty little slut with another woman's man, you have to accept the consequences." My voice was low and steady.

"I don't know …" she squeaked.

"Ah, ah! I'm speaking," I interrupted. "We both know there really isn't anything here for you. A course that you could continue anywhere, a crappy dead-end bar job. I think it'd be best all round if you decided to take a transfer. Head off somewhere you can be closer to family. After all" – I glanced around us again and lowered my voice another notch – "having a sister with *such* a young baby, you must want to be closer to … you know … make sure nothing *unfortunate* was to happen to them."

I pulled a little tighter on her hair. A gasp escaped from her. Satisfied, I let out a little snigger. Then in one swift movement, I removed the blade from her neck and shoved her head forward with the hand clutching her hair. The dull thud and snick of her face against the brickwork only added to my satisfaction.

A few days later, when Sam asked me about her, I denied all knowledge while trying to suppress the hint of amusement in my voice and the smile twitching at my lips. I convinced him that I knew nothing about what had happened to his little bitch, but I was rash and couldn't stop myself from having a little whispered gloat as I walked away. I guessed I wanted him to know what he was responsible for. I can't recall the exact words, something along the lines of *the slut won't mess with someone else's property again, that's for sure.*

I could only assume that Sam heard those words, and that's why he tried to run from me.

50

LINDY

SIX YEARS PREVIOUS

W hen I arrived home the next day to find Sam missing, I couldn't make sense of it at first. He knew not to go out without telling me where he was going. I'd told him to quit his job at the bar; he didn't need any more opportunity to mess around on me. If he couldn't be faithful when given freedom, I'd have to tighten the leash. No new notifications appeared when I checked my phone. Something must've happened, I figured. But when I checked his cupboard, his few possessions were missing. Certain that it couldn't be, I called him continuously, sending messages ranging from furious to concerned in tone, all the while assuring myself there was some reason he'd moved his things – and it had better be good.

It would all be straightened out, and Sam would learn that this *performance* had not been acceptable. I'd heard of tracking apps that could be put on a person's phone. That would be more appropriate, I decided. Then I could just check in on him anytime without having to call. He knew to inform me of exactly what he was doing – no excuses. He would have to make it right.

When my calls and texts remained unanswered a few hours on, I saw the undeniable truth. The ungrateful bastard *had* left. Fleeced me, taken advantage of my kindness, when he was nothing more than a pitiful student. It was me who'd scooped him out from the dregs of society. I raged, throwing and knocking over anything in my path. My fury grew – he was making me do this. I tried to track him down, of course. First I returned to where his mistress had been living but was unsurprised – and satisfied – to find it vacant. Next was his sister's crap-heap of a house, where I watched and waited. I wasn't stupid enough to go knocking on the door. I would hardly be welcome, after all. But I hung around outside for an entire evening and again the following day.

He wasn't there.

My god, Sam would suffer when I got him home. Some serious lessons would have to be learned. I was livid.

It took me over a week to track him down, hiding out in some dive of a bedsit on the rough side of town. I didn't know how he'd managed to get the money together, even for a hell-hole like that. I'd monitored everything he was earning, allowing him a small portion of it once he'd paid his share of the bills. I was justifiably furious with him but smart enough to know that it would have to be dealt with later.

I waited for the right opportunity – when he arrived home after a late evening shift at his new bar job. I was sporting a lovely black eye in preparation. He'd thought he'd been so clever, but I was so much smarter, always one step ahead of him. I padded up behind him as he was sliding his key in the lock. Noting the similarities with my encounter with his mistress, my lips twitched with a tiny smile. As he moved to push the door closed behind him, I wedged my foot into the gap and leaned my body forward. "Hello, Sam."

His face paled, and his jaw dropped; it was almost

comical to watch. I raised an eyebrow with a small smirk. "Oh, you weren't expecting me?" I feigned hurt and surprise.

His face hardened, sparking irritation. I thought we had passed this stage.

"What do you want, Lindy?" His voice was cold, emotionless. He didn't get to treat me that way.

"You need to come home now, Sam. Stop these pathetic games. I'll let it go if you come and apologise, but nothing like this is *ever* to happen again."

He shook his head, giving a little laugh.

"I'm not going anywhere with you, or near you ever again," he snarled. "I'm only sorry it took me so long to see you for what you are."

My body shook, and my vision blurred. I stuttered, struggling to get the words out.

"What I am?" I seethed. "What about what *you* are, Sam? We both know who has the issues here." I gestured at my black eye. "You *will* come home with me right now, or I'll make sure everyone knows what you're capable of," I hissed.

"Do it, then." He looked me up and down with such cold distaste, it took my breath away. "I'll never go near you again. I'd rather go to prison. It wouldn't exactly be an adjustment for me." He sneered, but his words were infuriatingly calm.

I screamed with frustration and swung my arm, bringing it down onto his face. He managed to soften the blow with his own raised arm but still took a whack.

We both froze, waiting for the other to make the next move, a mark already beginning to appear on his cheek. A low voice broke the thick silence. We both swivelled towards it.

"What the hell's going on?"

I stared at the stranger, swallowing the frenzy of rage fizzling under the surface, clenching my teeth.

"Nothing at all. My partner and I were just about to go home, right, Sam?"

I flashed him my brightest smile, but his face didn't alter. His eyes flicked to Sam and then back to meet my own. He lifted an eyebrow.

"And you always feel the need to give him a wallop to get him to do that, do you?" he asked, deadpan.

Heat rose to my cheeks, my mind racing, trying to think up a plausible explanation. Before I could respond, the stranger turned his focus back to Sam.

"This the psycho you were telling us about?"

My breath caught in my throat, and my guts clenched. I didn't think it was possible for me to be more furious until I heard Sam reply.

"Yeah – sure is." He threw me a look, and my insides constricted. "But no need to worry, she was just about to *fuck off*, right, Lindy?" He narrowed his eyes at me before breaking into a false smile.

"Oh good." My head flicked back around to the stranger, who continued, "But if you do have any more trouble with her, just say the word, and I'll get that cop mate of mine to do what we talked about. He owes me a favour anyway. Would be no skin off his nose to plant enough gear to get her out of your hair for a long time, mate. Better all round to have bitches like that off the streets." He winked at Sam and stood aside, gesturing for me to pass him by. It was the first time they had acknowledged that I was still there.

My panicked brain fired, searching for solutions to this unthinkable scenario. I sizzled with wrath, but I had to play this right, already having been wrong-footed by someone so inferior. "But, Sam, I'm pregnant!" I wailed out the lie.

His face flickered, emotions crossing it in quick succession. A humourless laugh filled the thick silence. We both turned.

"Oldest trick in the book, that one," the stranger barked out. "How stupid do you think he is? Please. Do come back when you've got some proof."

"If you let me leave, you will *never* see your child, Sam," I hissed.

Something skittered across his face, and then it reset, full of defiance.

For the first time in my life that I could recall, I was dumbfounded and – although I would never admit it – slightly unnerved. Sam's face had broken into a sickly smile. He knew I was out of moves. I jutted my chin and walked past the stranger, scowling at him.

"You take care now," he called after me. "And watch out for those cupboard doors." He gestured towards his eye. I gritted my teeth, blood rushing.

I continued to watch Sam for a while after that, but – for now at least – he was untouchable. I couldn't go to prison. I stored away my bitterness towards him, biding my time. Somehow, he would pay, I vowed.

That was until I met Paul.

MY DESIRE for a child of my own had become all consuming, which was why I'd allowed Sam to slip through my fingers like that. He'd seemed so perfect, so malleable. I'd really believed he'd bestow me with the child I'd planned for when we met. I decided to put things with Sam on the back burner for a while, consoling myself with reassurances that his time would come. The best hunters anticipate their prey stumbling into their trap; I would never give chase.

Everywhere I looked, loathsome women dragged gaggles of offspring behind them. To anyone taking notice, there were unfit mothers everywhere. So busy updating social media with their pathetic posts, boasting about how wonderful little Freddie was, they didn't see the neglected child standing right in front of them. Countless times, when watching as a mother was called to by a lonely child, desperate to have her attention, only to be waved away, ignored while her face was buried in a phone screen, I fought an internal battle. I seethed, the temptation clawing at me to carry those children away and then watch as the mothers finally searched in vain.

I wanted my own parents to witness my success from the sidelines: I had the career, the money, the beautiful home. All I needed now to complete the picture was the perfect family. I had considered their punishment too, conjuring visions of their house burning to the ground with them inside. I imagined messing with the brakes on my father's old beat-up car. I could easily make it seem like some kind of horrible accident. But I wanted them to see me thrive first, triumphant in all I achieved while they barely scraped by. I'd never allow them into my life, but I would show that hideous excuse of a woman what a real mother should look like, how I could still be everything she never was or could hope to be. They'd watch on, their lives fading as mine blossomed.

My yearning for a child weighed so heavily that, when an opportunity arose, I didn't hesitate. Having got it so wrong with Sam, I wasn't going to make the same mistake again. This time I searched for an older, more mature participant. Paul and I met in that same bar I passed on my way home. My period was imminent. After a tough day at work, I'd found myself back sitting in that dingy light, watching everyone moving around me. He'd offered to buy me a drink, and we ended the night in my bed. I'd never have considered a relationship with a man so much older than me before. We dated for a short time. It slipped my mind to tell Paul that I was no longer taking my contraceptives. That my periods still arrived like clockwork eclipsed all other concerns. Before I knew it, Paul had not only moved into my apartment but, somehow, was taking charge.

It was careless of me – letting him get too close, take too much control – but he had a purpose. Caught up as I was in my determination to become a mother, I failed to notice the subtle shifts in our relationship.

It was like I'd woken up one day and found myself living in a different life. He controlled everything, from our finances to my routines. I no longer cared, telling myself it would all be fixed once I had what I needed. I was crumbling under the weight of my desperate need for a child. Nothing else mattered or compared.

It didn't take long for Paul to decide he was ready for a family. He made it clear – the time had come for me to stay at home and provide children. Sixteen years my senior, he'd had his years of playing the field, and he didn't want me out "flaunting" any longer. He wanted sons, strapping boys to take care of him in his retirement years, to run his business and keep him financially secure when he was no longer able. I gladly obliged. He'd collected contraceptive pills for me the entirety of our relationship, unaware I'd been flushing them away. It was none of my concern what he wanted or why. With his blessing, I purchased every type of ovulation kit that I could find. We tried for six months before Paul decided enough was enough. He wasn't willing to waste any more time.

He'd been reluctant to go to a doctor, certain there couldn't be anything wrong. Still, he was keen to use his finances to hurry things along. After hours of trawling the internet, we decided a fertility clinic was our best starting point. They waved away our concerns, assuring us that six months was nothing, that we should just give it more time. Of course, I could never admit the truth that it had been much longer.

To my relief, Paul was as dismissive as I was of the doctor's advice, especially as they gently dropped in mentions of supplements he could take, due to his age. We opted for private treatment right away.

I'd lost track of how much time passed. Our relationship had never had the strength to weather such a storm. The days of mutual silence were as bad as the turbulent arguments, which quickly became violent. I relished the pain of his fists, happy for my failing body to be punished. I'm not sure even now why I suggested we visit the cottage. We were both so far beyond wanting to fix things, but I couldn't stand the idea of him leaving, his smug expression as he found a replacement and knocked her up right away. I had no plan, but I would never again allow a man the pleasure of humiliating me.

He seemed unaware of the relevance of the time of the month as we packed the car and made the drive.

Upon our arrival, Paul had cracked open the bottle of wine and poured us both a glass without hesitation. He offered mine without making eye contact, as if already aware of my failure. I'd stared at him as a heat clawed the back of my neck, the loathing causing my vision to swim.

I lashed out. The back of my arm sent the glass flying from his grip. In that moment, as we watched the glass splinter and the red liquid spread across the floor, I felt returned to myself. Paul, without reaction, turned his back to walk away. Seeing that liquid, littered with sparkling shards, and the back of his retreating head, something snapped. I lunged for the fire companion set. Dashing after him with an animalistic roar, I felt lighter than I had in ages. The weight of the instrument clutched in my clammy palm made contact with a satisfying thwack.

I'd washed the blood and coal dust from my hands, then

hummed to myself as I'd mopped the floors clean. I glowed. It was as though I had been unconscious, allowing another person to take over my life in the way I'd sworn to myself I never would. He might have wormed his way in for a while, but I had been the one to escape, to elude even one more suffocating day waking up to him. I felt rejuvenated and liberated – that he didn't get to just walk away and that the morning would not bring yet another row.

He never had been a morning person.

It was absolutely by chance that I found Sam again a few months later. I'd called into a supermarket on the way home from work late one evening and spotted him at the other end of an aisle. He'd filled out and matured, but I would've recognised him anywhere.

I dumped my basket, filled with ready meals for one, and stalked him around the shop, captivated. My adrenalin surged thinking of the inevitability of the encounter.

He left on foot, groceries in bags. Deserting my car, I followed him back to his infuriatingly beautiful home. I watched from across the street, looking in through the window, as an average-looking woman greeted him, both of their smug faces disgustingly content. Deeply buried resentment resurfaced in a dizzying rush along with a flash of fury. He'd left me and chosen *her*?

Why should he get to live happily in a posh house, with some average little tart, while I was left to suffer alone? After what he'd put me through? Sam owed me. He might well have slipped through my fingers once, but I wouldn't allow that to happen again. Not when he was responsible for so much going wrong in my life. I'd taken back control now, learned from my mistakes. It was time he made things right.

I turned away from his window, already a plan forming in my mind.

I'd hide in plain sight, remain just in the stage wings of his life whilst I gathered what information I needed. How to hit him where it would hurt the most. Then I'd watch him try crawling back to me. After that night, Lindy would no longer exist. At the thought, a genuine smile lit up my face for the first time in longer than I could remember. A new image, a new name.

I let it roll off my tongue, testing out the shape of it, enjoying the feeling on my lips. I repeated it over and over in my head, the name thrillingly exotic to me.

Bella.

51

SAM

PRESENT DAY

Tessa's phone lay a few inches away on the bed. I'd yelped as I'd thrown it and watched it bounce away. I stared down at it for a few seconds before I could bring myself to touch it again, reaching out with caution, as if it were something venomous.

Claire's footsteps pounded up the stairs at full tilt. She burst into the room, eyes swirling.

"What? What the hell is it? Are you okay?" she panted, chest heaving as her eyes moved over my face, searching, trying to grasp what was happening.

"It's ... There's ... She's ..." My brain seemed to have lost contact with my mouth, too much rushing through my head for me to process.

"Sam, you're scaring me." Claire rushed towards me and perched on the end of my bed, placing her hand over mine. "What *is* it?"

Still unable to find the words, I swiped the screen to unlock the phone. It opened to the photo again. Shockwaves hit my body at the sight of it, my breathing turning ragged. I turned the screen towards Claire.

She held a hand against her chest, closing her eyes for a second and blowing out breath. "I thought it was Cora." She took a second to compose herself. I offered no form of apology, knowing that she would understand my reaction when she saw it for herself.

Her forehead wrinkled, eyebrows scrunched so low I wondered if she could still see it properly.

"What am I looking at?" she asked, studying the photo and shaking her head. "That's Tessa in front, right? I recognise her from your photos." Her hand still pressed against her chest.

She glanced up at me for confirmation, eyes meeting mine.

"Yes," I managed to squeak before nodding back towards the phone. Her eyes returned to the screen, moving around to study the photo.

"Who's the woman she's with?" Her eyebrows knitted again as she squinted to see the image more clearly. "She looks totally pissed off about some ..."

Her eyebrows jumped almost to her hairline, and she sucked in a breath with such force it would have been comical sounding in a different circumstance.

"Holy fuck!" She sprang backwards off the bed and backed into the wall behind her, recoiling the same way I had. Her bulging eyes flicked between the abandoned phone and my bewildered gaze as we mirrored each other's horror.

"Is ... is that ...?" she stammered.

I hadn't recognised her myself, to begin with. Her appearance was totally different. But once I'd seen it, there was no mistaking her.

"Yeah," I huffed. "It is. What the fuck was Tessa doing with Lindy?"

Claire puffed out her cheeks and blew out her breath. "Nothing good. We can be certain of that much." She scowled. "We need to take this to the police, Sam." She jabbed a finger at the phone.

I considered her suggestion, rubbing my temples and screwing up my face. My skin still tingled. Lindy sitting next to Tessa – my Tessa – with that look on her face. I hadn't had time to process what it meant, but my throat burned with acid at the sight of that woman next to my wife.

"It doesn't actually prove anything," I muttered, shaking my head. Did it?

"Oh, please tell me you aren't going to try to defend her?" She spat the words with a grimace.

"Of course I'm not," I snapped back. "But we both know what the police think of me. Do you honestly believe they're going to be all that interested in this?" I waved the phone around. "A single photo that shows ... what? Tessa sat drinking coffee of her own free will. I mean, she's even the one taking the photo."

A short silence passed between us.

"Do you think Tessa knew who she was?" Claire asked, a perplexed expression tugging at her cheeks.

I shook my head. "I never told her anything about my relationship with Lindy."

Claire shot me an exasperated look.

"I was ashamed, Claire. What kind of man lets a woman do that to him? I wanted to put it all behind me," I snapped.

She lifted her eyes to the ceiling, sucking in a breath.

"This ends here, Sam." Her voice was firm, full of conviction. "That *woman* has gotten away with enough. We're taking this to the police."

GARCIA STUDIED the photo again before fixing me with an impassive look.

"So what is it you're getting at exactly?" He placed the phone onto the table between us and met my eye. "You believe the woman in this photograph is potentially your ex-girlfriend?" He raised a dark eyebrow, disinterest radiating from him.

"No, we don't *believe* it is," Claire cut in. "It *is* her.'

Garcia flicked a glance in her direction, barely able to conceal an eye roll. He returned his focus to me as if Claire hadn't spoken.

"And if – just for argument's sake – we did agree that it is your ex, Mr Fulford, your wife hardly appears to be under duress. It is, in fact, quite clearly your ex who seems distressed, if her expression is anything to go by." Garcia leaned back in his chair, linking his hands behind his neck.

I tapped my fingers against the tabletop, my frustrations growing.

"Do you have any reason to believe that they didn't just ... happen to meet by chance?" He jutted his hands into the air. "Did Tessa ever mention to you that she was having a problem with your ex? That she was bothering her? Perhaps Tessa was the one to reach out." His tone was mocking, patronising, full of false concern. The implications in his last sentence weren't lost on me.

Claire scoffed beside me. "This isn't some bizarre coincidence." She threw up her own hands and waved them around. "You don't know Lindy. Tessa is dead and that ... that *woman* ..."

"Claire!" I shot her a warning look, irritation rising. She'd insisted on us coming here and was now making us look irrational, hysterical even.

"What? Murdered her?" Garcia goaded. He pulled a face as if considering the idea. "But explain to me, why? Why would she turn up after not seeing or speaking to you for so many years, completely out of the blue, and murder your wife?" He gave us a questioning look. "Seems a bit of a stretch, don't you think?"

He turned back to me. "So, am I safe to assume it wasn't an amicable split?"

Claire made a snorting noise. I gritted my teeth and ignored her.

"That's one way to put it." I grimaced. "Lindy was ... Well, she was a very difficult person to live with." I tapped my fingers on the table again.

"Huh, well, that's an understatement," Claire muttered. We both ignored her.

"Go on," Garcia ordered.

I blew out a breath. "I didn't realise at the time – not until I got out, anyway – but I guess she was what you would call ... abusive." I shrugged.

"How so?" Garcia raised an eyebrow.

"She was incredibly controlling, manipulative. And on the odd occasion ..." I paused, clearing my throat as the humiliation crept in. "Violent," I added quickly.

Garcia's face remained impassive, but I didn't miss the flicker of interest cross his face. "Right. And how did the relationship end?"

"Is that relevant?" Claire chimed in.

"Yes." He didn't even glance at her as he answered, deadpan.

"I left," I offered simply. "She took things too far, and something finally clicked, I guess."

His eyes narrowed. "How did she take things too far?"

I let out a sigh and attempted again to explain the very little that I knew about my friend's vanishing act.

"I guess I saw things differently when I witnessed her do it to someone else," I admitted, giving a small shrug. "I'm not sure I ever would've left her if that hadn't happened."

He looked thoughtful before asking, "She never came after you? When you left her, I mean?"

"Erm ... she tried." I squirmed, wondering how much to tell him.

He arched an eyebrow in question.

"I threatened to go to the police. I had a friend who witnessed her violence, said we'd give statements to say as much if she didn't back off." The half-truth slipped from my lips.

I wasn't sure if I was being paranoid, but Garcia looked doubtful.

"And that was it? She just ... left you alone?" he pushed, making it sound as unbelievable as it was. I gave a tiny shrug of one shoulder.

"She might've had more than we know about to hide," Claire added forcefully. I'd been so wrapped up in my own thoughts, I'd almost forgotten she was there. I nearly flinched at the irony of her words. The only noise was the low hum of the recording device.

"I have to ask though," he continued "If she was as bad as you say, wouldn't you want to see her punished? Why *didn't* you report her?"

I considered the question for a few seconds before I answered, making the choice to be honest.

"Fear. Of not being believed. Of how much worse things would get if I wasn't. Why would she have left me alone if she thought no one believed me? And doubt. Wondering if things were actually as bad as I thought. If Lindy was right when she said it was me who caused her to get so mad. What she'd say about me. But mostly, more than anything, humiliation. How could I tell people that I let her treat me like that? That I wasn't man enough to stand up to my girlfriend? Put yourself in my shoes. Would *you* have reported it?"

For the first time since meeting him, I witnessed a look of understanding cross the DI's face.

"Honestly?" he answered quietly. "I really couldn't say." He nodded towards the tape recorder in an exaggerated gesture that I couldn't miss, leaving a long pause before adding, "It's not about what I would do." The true meaning behind his words was not lost on me. I nodded my gratitude.

Garcia assured us before we left that he would follow up as much as he could. He was quick to add that, without good cause to consider Lindy a suspect, he would be limited. One innocuous photograph wasn't evidence of much. I offered my apologies again for the fruitless hypnotherapy sessions, but, as before, he gave no reaction.

For the first time since my living nightmare began, I felt a flicker of hope – I might not be responsible for the death of my wife. Something had shifted in Garcia too. It was subtle enough that an onlooker could easily have missed it, but he seemed to have softened, if only slightly. I couldn't imagine ever considering him an ally, but he certainly felt less of an enemy.

But the alternative reality to my guilt made every tiny hair on my body stand on end. A cold sweat broke out all over my skin, any trace of hope draining from me. My head swam with the vision of Lindy and Tessa together, and my stomach clenched. I had to ask myself – would it be better if I *was* guilty.

52

LINDY

TWO YEARS PREVIOUS

I had always hated my given name. I'd often wondered over the years how my mother and father had looked at me as a newborn and thought, *Yes, our tiny new baby looks like a Belinda.*

Not that my father would have had any say, of course.

It was probably my mother's way of punishing me for being born. Perhaps the breakdown of our relationship had been made inevitable by their saddling me with such a name.

It was at secondary school that someone – one of the girls in the more popular crowd – had first called me Lindy. I'd never thought to shorten my name, but I liked the way it sounded. Of course, once one of *those* girls had given you a nickname, it was no longer up to you. I was only too grateful for something I didn't mind; plenty of others had come off a lot worse. Lindy sounded fun and intelligent, and as expected, it stuck, with even the teachers addressing me by my new name.

My mother, unsurprisingly, was the only one who refused to accept it. I reminded her numerous times that I preferred Lindy, to which she would always give a little snigger, curling her lip before continuing to call me Belinda as if she hadn't heard me. The domineering character that she was, my requests also fell on deaf ears with my snivelling milksop of a father.

I wasn't sure which of the two of them I detested most.

As soon as I reached sixteen, I left. The two of them deserved each other, and I no longer cared how she punished him for my actions. I knew I'd let them off too easily. I had bigger concerns, though. I swore to myself that, when the time came, they would suffer for how they'd treated me. I was resolute in my decision to make it alone; I would never be reliant on another person again.

I knew she wouldn't hunt me down, never caring that much whether I was even alive. I'd been in the way for so long, I had no doubt she was glad to see the back of me. Her punishments and beatings would all be heaped on my father now. I relished the thought that at least one of them was suffering.

I had to do some things that I wasn't particularly proud of to achieve my independence, but to avoid crawling back to my parents, there was nothing I wouldn't have done. Selling my body was preferable to seeing the smug look on my mother's face at my failure, or the relief on my father's at sharing the burden of her once again. Of course, I wasn't the "stand on a street corner" type; I had standards. Seducing a college professor or lecturer was all too easy, as was learning the names of their wives and their home addresses. As I got better at detecting a man of money, my pay cheques increased. It was a means to an end.

I'd never spoken to Paul about my parents; he accepted my dismissive comments about the distance and us all being so busy whenever the subject arose. I never asked about his family either, equally disinterested in any other part of his personal life. When we received our test results back from the private fertility clinic, I was so certain that he would be the problem – after all, age wasn't on his side. It had clearly been Sam's fault that it hadn't happened for us – how could it have when he was too busy running around with other women the entire time? It stood to reason that if there was a problem, it must lie with Paul. They offered to speak with us individually, but we agreed to find out together, both so certain that the other was responsible.

I'll never forget the sinking horror I felt in the moment they laid the blame with me, confirmed that I was damaged, unable to do what every woman should be able to. The mixture of fury and pain that I felt was breathtaking. My fingers twitched at Paul's small nod of acknowledgement – as if he knew as much – desire to inflict pain onto him gripping me.

The smug little cow in that clinic had the audacity to tell me my infertility had likely been caused by an STD that had gone untreated too long.

Well, it was clear that if anyone was at fault for that, it was my parents. I would never have had to do the things I had done if they'd been the kind of parents they should have been, the parents that I'd deserved.

Or perhaps Sam was to blame? After all, I had no idea just how many women that lecherous rat had had on the go whilst I had trusted him so blindly, sitting home waiting for him.

I seethed at the injustice. Because of *their* selfishness, *their* shortcomings, *I* was the one who was being punished in the cruellest possible way. I vowed to myself in that moment, I would not be the only one to suffer.

Paul and I barely discussed it. What was there to say?

I felt his looks of disgust though, knew that he felt justi-fied in his judgement, in his placing of the blame firmly with me. Looking back, I suppose I can see now: that was the moment my resentment towards him really took root.

WHEN I SAW Sam again in that supermarket, it was like fate. I was certain now that I deserved some form of closure.

That man did not just get to run off and live happily with someone else after what he'd put me through. My fury at seeing his perfect home with another woman knocked me sideways. It took me right back to those days when I'd found out he was being unfaithful. I'd lost *everything* because of him. How could I just let it go?

Of course, I had to be smart about it. The idea of the police sniffing around unnerved me more than ever. If I charged in guns blazing, it could backfire. I couldn't show my hand too quickly.

The thought of my transformation appealed to me for more than one reason. I wasn't the Lindy he'd known anymore; I was so much more now. It felt strangely exciting. The idea of infiltrating Sam's life without his knowledge – like I was taking back the last bit of control. But everything was dependent on him not discovering me until I was ready. I couldn't be caught off guard by him again. It wasn't the first time I had disguised myself, but this time was different. This time Lindy had to be completely erased – no traces to be seen even to those who got up close.

I returned to the supermarket in high spirits and went back inside. My mood lightened further when I discovered my basket still sitting where I had discarded it in my haste to follow Sam.

"Oh, I was just about to sort that lot out. I thought it'd been dumped."

I turned to see a young girl with a nose ring and a tattoo

disappearing into the sleeve of her uniform. Normally, I wouldn't have given her the time of day, but nothing could dampen my mood, so I awarded her a bright smile.

"Oh, no, I just left my purse at home." I held it up and gave it a little wiggle. "Got it now though." I grinned like a loon.

She gave a wary smile in return and trotted off. I snarled at her retreating back – I should have just told her to piss off.

Undeterred from my mission, I pondered over hair dye colours for a while before adding a box to my basket along with a bottle of Prosecco. I had reason to celebrate.

I collected my car and returned home, so pumped with adrenaline that I wondered if I'd ever sleep again. I popped the cork of the Prosecco bottle and poured a large glass. Then, after reading the instructions carefully, I applied the hair colour. Whilst it was processing, I brought up a playlist on my phone and set to work shopping for the other things I needed.

I hummed along to the music and nodded, the bubbles lifting my mood further, like a giddy schoolgirl with my first taste of alcohol.

I rinsed the dye out of my hair and roughly dried it off before turning to observe myself in the mirror. The change was undeniably a bit of a shock. It would take a little getting used to, but the more I turned my head, viewing it from as many angles as the position of the mirror would allow, the more it seemed to shimmer. I'd been worried that the dark shade would wash me out, but it seemed to have had the opposite effect. My eyes stood out, my skin radiant. I sighed to myself, irked that it had taken me so long to realise who I was supposed to be, that I'd waited so long to shed that old skin. But it would be worth the wait. With another swish of my hair, I turned and changed into pyjamas before settling down with my glass.

I tried to watch a film, but my mind was elsewhere, totally preoccupied by how I would make it all work, what exactly I would do. An idea struck, and my stomach flipped. I lunged for my phone and rapidly typed the road name into Google. The map popped up, asking me if I wanted directions. I clicked the small photo in the corner of the screen, changing it to street view. I realised with a crush of disappointment that I couldn't move the map along far enough to see Sam's house. But then the ping of a notification drew my attention, lifting my mood once again.

A smile crept over my face as I opened the notification and read more. If I'd been the type to believe in signs, here one was, staring me straight in the face.

"Coming, ready or not." I giggled out loud.

53

SAM

PRESENT DAY

I stared down at the phone as it vibrated in my hand, the screen flashing with an unknown number. I had no desire to answer. My every expectation was that it would be another journalist having tracked down my number, fishing for a story.

Just as it was about to cut to the answerphone, an image of Cora held in some stranger's arms, waiting for me, filled my mind, and I jabbed at the green blob to accept the call, hope rising.

"Hello?" I wandered into my kitchen, already beginning to pace, searching out things to fiddle with.

"Mr Fulford, there are some things that we should ... that I need to ... discuss with you. I think it would be best to speak face to face. Are you home right now?"

The urgency in his voice threw me, my exhausted brain taking a few seconds to process his words and place the voice.

"Detective Garcia?" I asked stupidly, unable to make my brain function well enough to say anything more. I hadn't been expecting to hear from him so soon, having spoken with him just the previous afternoon. He hadn't even taken me seriously, as far as I knew. He had more likely been humouring me, I had decided. I'd have to chase him up, push for him to investigate further.

"Yes, it's me. Did you hear what I said? I'm on my way over to your place now. Are you home?"

That was why he sounded different. My mind drifted with the thought. I was on his speakerphone.

"*Sam!*"

His raised voice finally penetrated my fog, snapping me out of my dumbfounded state.

"Yes, yes, I'm here," I replied, giving my head a shake to straighten my thoughts. "What is it? What've you found? Is it Cora?" I was fully alert now, breathless as fear gripped my chest. Was he coming to deliver bad news about my daughter? My head pounded.

"No, nothing on Cora yet, I'm afraid." He sounded genuinely sorry. "But there is something I think could be important that I need to discuss with you urgently. I would really rather not do it over the phone."

He arrived in under fifteen minutes, but it felt much longer as I paced the hallway, waiting for him. Claire perched on the bottom step, watching me pace with an anxious look carved deep into her features.

I'd filled her in on what little information I had, her look crestfallen on learning they weren't yet any closer to finding Cora.

Garcia took a seat, declining Claire's curt offer of coffee. We settled down opposite him. He threw a glance in her direction.

"Are you happy to discuss this in front of your sister, Mr Fulford?" he questioned, his tone grave.

I didn't hesitate. "Of course." I nodded, wondering what the hell he was about to say. I couldn't think of a reason he would rush over here unless it involved arresting me. As of yet, I hadn't found myself in cuffs.

Claire placed a hand on my trembling forearm – I must have looked as forlorn as I felt. My eyes teared in a wave of gratitude. I fought to suppress them.

Garcia fixed me with a hard stare. My heart thumped. He ran his tongue over his lips before he started. The suspense was driving me crazy, a medley of scenarios playing out behind my eyes.

He drew in a breath. "So, after our meeting yesterday, as promised, I did a little digging around." His eyes were fixed on mine, his brow furrowed. "I wanted to bring you up to speed because ... well, it could be nothing, but I did find some information that could, potentially, be relevant." He gripped his chin in his hand, rubbing his stubble.

Claire went rigid, her grip tightening on my arm. My stomach took a dizzying lurch.

"What information? What have you found?" She breathed the questions.

His eyes moved across to consider her, but this time he didn't appear irked by her interruption. He sucked another deep breath, running his tongue over his teeth. "Mr Fulford, you said that you hadn't seen your ex-girlfriend Lindy or been in contact with her in a long while. Is that correct?"

My brow knitted. In all my thoughts of Cora, hearing Lindy's name had caught me off guard. "Yes, that's right," I confirmed, voice thick. I realised I was rubbing my scars.

"How long do you think it was since you last saw her?" he pushed on.

I raised my eyebrows, attempting to recall details I'd purposely blocked out. "God. Years ... it must be around six now. Why? What is going on?" I demanded, my initial fear quickly turning into frustration. I was getting more questions than answers.

He held up his hands in a gesture of surrender and nodded.

"I'm not sure how it all fits yet, but I'll get to the point. He took a deep breath. Within the space of six months, Lindy's parents both died, and her partner was reported missing. Not by her, I might add." An unreadable expression crossed his face.

"What are you telling us?" Claire's tone was sharp. She turned to look at me, meeting my eye for a second before turning back to Garcia.

He continued as if Claire hadn't spoken. "Shortly after these events, it seems she decided to move."

"And?" I questioned, irritation rising once again that he was here to discuss Lindy and not my daughter.

"*And* the address that she moved to, Mr Fulford, is number seven Victoria Road."

Claire turned to me once again with a puzzled look just as I was grasping his meaning.

"She's been living across the street?" I whispered. Goose pimples broke out across my skin.

Garcia didn't respond, simply dipping his eyes.

"*What?*" Claire shrieked as she registered my words. "Victoria Road is *your* road? *This street? She is living here?*" Her head swivelled between Garcia and me, her shrill voice assaulting my pounding head and causing me to flinch.

"That's the thing," Garcia went on. We both returned our focus to him. "We believe she was, yes. But we couldn't get an answer from her. She'd started calling herself Bella, and on checking with the landlord, it seems that she may have done a flit. She never gave notice and has left a substantial number of possessions behind, but it appears that she's moved out."

"When?" Claire gasped, voicing the question that I was unable to.

"We can't be certain." Garcia avoided my eye. "But it looks to be very recent."

All of the air had left my body. My fingers tingled, and my limbs didn't feel as though they belonged to me. I was aware that Garcia was speaking again, but the sound was muffled, as though I were submerged underwater.

"Sam?" Claire's hand was on my arm again, her voice gentle. I looked at her face but struggled to keep my focus. "The officer is asking if you have any idea where she may have gone."

I attempted to pull myself together, aware that if my fears were to be confirmed, Cora needed me more than ever.

If she's even still alive! the cruel voice in my head taunted. I pushed it away and focused. The realisation slammed into me. I locked eyes with Garcia, feeling the last of my colour drain.

"Tessa had a friend called Bella. They were really close, but I never met her. She lived across the street. Bella and Lindy are ..."

I gulped back the tide of nausea, unable to finish my question. Garcia nodded gently, and my hand flew to my mouth.

"Do you have any idea where she might have gone? Anywhere she used to go to stay?" He repeated his question with all the patience he possessed.

Still processing the latest horror, I willed my brain to think straight. "She didn't get on with her parents, but maybe she could have gone to them?" My voice sounded odd as I trawled back through memories that I'd worked so hard to suppress, searching for any tiny clue.

Garcia cleared his throat. "As I mentioned earlier, her parents passed away a while ago now." He didn't meet my eye. I couldn't help but think there was something he wasn't telling me.

"Her parents' house was badly damaged and still sits in disrepair, so we know she isn't there," he confirmed.

I felt both sets of eyes on me, waiting for me to give them something more, something that might help, but I had nothing.

"I don't know." I shook my head. Anger and disappointment flared in equal measure. I felt so useless. "She never had any friends, as such, no other family that I knew of ..." I trailed off, not sure what else I could add.

Garcia nodded and made to stand, placing a notepad that I hadn't even noticed before into his breast pocket. "We're going to continue to search for her. I'll keep you updated with anything we find." His tone was sincere. I dragged myself to my feet, my exhausted body protesting.

"I'll see myself out," he added, eyeing my shaking legs. "Take it easy, Sam."

My head snapped up. "Wait!" I called after him. He came to a halt.

"You said both her parents died. Why is that relevant?"

He chewed his lip, pausing before answering.

"It may not be. But they died in ... strange circumstances," he conceded. "Arson. The person responsible was never found."

My breath caught. "And you said her partner went missing?" His words were only just dawning on my overwrought brain, connections firing.

"He did," Garcia admitted before adding quietly, "Still is."

I heard Claire's sharp intake of breath beside me.

"After going through so much, it's fair to say we are *concerned* for her mental well-being," Garcia concluded.

Silence hung between me and Claire as he left, neither of us brave enough to voice what we were both thinking.

That monster had taken my baby.

54

LINDY

TWO YEARS PREVIOUS

"You're absolutely certain you don't wish to view the property first?"

The estate agent's affected posh accent grated on me.

"Absolutely certain," I replied, mocking her snooty inflection.

Although I felt no obligation to explain myself to such a small person, I just as much didn't want to stir any curiosity by seeming odd, so I gritted my teeth, bit back my irritation, and forced myself to continue.

"I've had a good look at the photos online. It's more about the location for me. I have family and friends living close by. Plus, it's convenient for work."

"And you say it's just yourself? You are aware that it's a three bed?"

Anger flared again. Who the hell was she to dictate how much space I needed? Nosey bitch! I swallowed the bitter taste, glad it was a phone conversation and that she couldn't see my grimace.

"Yes, I'm aware," I replied curtly, attempting to rein in the sarcasm. "But, *like I said,* I have family close; my nieces and nephews will need space to stay."

"Well, okay." She dragged out the words as if still sceptical. "I suppose it never hurts to have the extra space anyway. You never know what might happen. I'd only been with my partner eighteen months when our *little surprise* came along!" She gave a little tinkle of a laugh.

My blood ran cold, and I couldn't keep the ice from my voice as I replied to this stupid, ignorant woman. It was all I could do not to scream at her.

"That's quite an assumption," I hissed. "Not everyone *wants* the tie of children holding them back. Some of us have bigger plans and no room for surprises – or *mistakes.* Now are you going to speak with the landlord, or would you rather transfer me to your manager?"

IT TOOK A FEW FRUSTRATING WEEKS, but after paying out an eye-watering amount on the checks and deposit, and a full month's rent up front, I finally had the keys to number seven.

I brought the bare minimum of my possessions – not that I had too much. I was far from sentimental. As luck would have it, all of the houses had access via the back. Gates at the ends of the gardens, giving access to attached garages, led into grassy alleyways, where neighbourhood kids liked to play. This arrangement allowed me to come and go sight unseen. Still, I moved the few boxes late in the evening, long after the neighbours' curtains were drawn. I'd order new furniture.

As different as I looked, I still couldn't risk bumping into Sam. In all likelihood, he'd still recognise me, even with my shiny, almost black hair and ice blue eyes, thanks to my new contact lenses. Those had become a permanent part of my routine along with the heavy makeup that I now wore, giving my skin a dewy glow. It still caught me off guard, seeing the stranger reflected back in the mirror, but I was impressed by what I saw.

The effect I was having on the male population was also hard to miss. I had never before made much of an effort with my looks, as I wasn't looking for a man to "complete me". Noticing the heads turn to watch me pass, though, was undeniably pleasant. It offered a sense of power and control, my body might have been broken, but they still lusted after it, the damage invisible to them.

With the risk of the move falling through having lifted, I was where I needed to be, and I had business to attend to.

Positioning myself in front of a plain wall, facing into the full-length mirror, I stripped down to my underwear. It took me a while to get the hang of how to stand, the angle of the camera right, but once I did, I click clicked away, taking photo after photo. I unhooked my bra and snapped a few more, ensuring I avoided getting my face in them but that my long glossy hair fell into some of the shots.

Once done, I slipped into a fitted dress, wrote the note, and addressed the envelope, giving it a spritz of perfume, then left the house. I detoured to the local pharmacy, which advertised photo printing. Heading straight to the machines, I plugged in my phone. I remained standing, positioning my body so as to keep the screen hidden from view.

With the prints paid for, I slotted them into the envelope and smiled to myself as I started on the short walk to the car showroom.

It hadn't taken much tracking down on social media to find out everything I needed to know. This wasn't my first trip there. I clutched the envelope under my jacket, ready to slip it into his bag – which I knew he kept under his desk – at my first opportunity.

I breezed through the doors, all smiles and hair flicks. The salesmen fell over themselves to get to me, but I knew exactly who I was there to see.

"Hi, what can I do for you?" an overweight balding guy with coffee breath and yellowing teeth asked, eyes roaming all over my body.

I fixed a bright smile in place. "Oh, it's Steve I'm here to see, please. He's been ... *helping me* with something." I gave a sly giggle and tossed my hair again.

"I'm sure he has." The salesman raised an eyebrow. "Come on through."

LATER THAT EVENING I stood across the street, observing her through the living room window. I couldn't resist watching my handiwork unfold. Steve had returned home a short time before – time to put my plan into motion. Using the fake profile that I'd made, I typed out a private message and pinged it to her. I watched as she read the words. Even from out there in the dark, I could watch her face fall. She looked around her before ducking into the hallway, returning a few moments later with my envelope. I'd sealed it before tearing it back open myself. It had to look like he'd already seen it. My breathing quickened as she peered inside and retrieved the contents. Her world crumbled, along with her face, as she read my note, telling Steve how much I missed him when he was with her and that I was *so* looking forward to the next time. Then she saw the lipstick marks that I'd smudged onto the envelope. The photos cascaded from her hands as she slid down the wall, ashen faced. I grinned, turning and walking away, having seen all I needed to.

That petty estate agent bitch would think twice before gloating about her perfect little family again.

I HADN'T DECIDED how I was going to deal with Sam yet. For the time being I would just observe, learn a bit about who he'd become, what mattered most in his life. I needed to be well informed, prepared, if I was going to hit him where it really hurt. And he deserved that – to learn how it felt to *really* hurt.

The house had been a total stroke of luck, popping up on my map search like that. It had seemed impossible to ignore, like I had been meant to find it.

The landlord had been only too happy for me to take it, delighted at getting the hefty rent paid by a single person rather than a family – children who would leave sticky finger-prints on paintwork, drawings on walls. Despite the chunk of my bank balance that it was eating up, I did like it there. The house was light, spacious, and airy – the type of place I'd imagined raising my own family. I was struck by the irony – Sam would have been there with *me* if he hadn't betrayed me so badly. Who would have ever thought we'd end up neighbours?

My temper flared at the memories. Why things had worked out the way they had. His reckless behaviour and blatant disregard for my feelings. The repercussions of his selfish actions. He simply *had* to learn.

Over the following weeks, I watched his comings and goings. I passed his latest conquest on the street a few times. I could sense her desire to start up a conversation, but I had no interest in her. Sam didn't *love* her; he wasn't capable. He only knew how to *use* people. So I brushed her off each time. I had bigger fish to fry.

But then, in another twist of fate, she arrived on my doorstep one evening with a parcel clutched in her clammy hand, addressed to me. If she hadn't caught me so off guard, turning up unannounced like that, I would have found it amusing how she delivered the replenishments of my daily disguise.

She looked like death warmed up. I held back a smile, briefly picturing her dropping down dead on my front porch. But that would've messed up my plans. Sam would've been bound to uncover my identity.

I said as little as possible as she blabbered on, hoping to get rid of her as quickly as possible, but then she stumbled, as if she was going to collapse, and as she gripped onto my doorframe, I saw them.

The diamonds on the engagement ring caught the light as she reached out, the wedding band sealing the fact that the marriage had already gone ahead. I was glad of all the makeup I now wore, hiding the draining colour of my face. I felt dizzy, as though I might collapse myself. He'd *married* her? How could that be?

The rest of her chance visit was a blur. I'd been blindsided, having taken my eye off the ball for too long with Sam. I had no option but to take her inside; it would've seemed too odd not to. I managed to pull myself together enough to engage in small talk, relieved she wasn't well enough to notice my agitated state. As I helped her home, she insisted on buying me coffee as a thank you. I was reluctant, still reeling and furious. I never wanted to see the woman again. In the end I agreed, just to get rid of her, knowing I'd blow her off.

But once she was gone and I was able to regain myself, the memory of the exquisite rings shining on her finger brought with it new ideas. Perhaps a coffee with Tessa Fulford wouldn't be such a bad idea.

In fact, perhaps it could be the perfect opportunity.

55

SAM

PRESENT DAY

I felt stale, my body ravaged from lack of sleep and spikes of adrenaline.

I swallowed down some toast – each bite feeling lodged in my throat – while Claire watched on, ensuring I ate.

I would have been deeply grateful to my sister for being there – for her unwavering belief in me – but I was starting to feel suffocated.

I found it hard to believe just how much had happened in the space of a few days. I was more exhausted than I'd known possible. Every muscle in my body ached, pleading with me to stop. My brain was shutting down, and I was struggling to piece things together, to differentiate between what was real and what my incapacitated mind was inventing. I wasn't even sure if I was actually awake.

A glimmer of hope surfaced – that it was all just one of my dreadful vivid dreams. The pain was far too real, though.

"Are you okay?" Claire's voice brought me back to consciousness. I stared at her, trying to figure out what she'd asked.

"Sorry, I know that's a stupid question," she continued, wincing.

"I don't ... I can't ..." My words were slurred, and I tried to remember if I'd had a drink.

"I think you might be in shock," Claire replied calmly. "And exhausted. Let's take you upstairs for some rest, shall we?"

Her voice swam in and out as she spoke. I was vaguely aware of her half helping, half dragging me up the stairs before the softness of the pillow dragged me under.

I AWOKE FROM A DEEP, dreamless sleep, feeling groggy. A stab of agony hit before I could remember why. A distant noise sounded continuously. I couldn't place it at first and willed it to stop – until I realised what it was.

I scrabbled around for my phone, desperate to find it before the call was missed. I couldn't find it. Panic surged. What if it was Garcia with news of Cora?

Ignoring the throbbing of my head, I sprang from the bed and darted across the landing and down the stairs. Claire appeared in the doorway to the kitchen, my phone pressed against her ear. I gripped the newel post as I waited for the spinning in my head to stop.

"Yes, thank you for the update." She held up a hand to stop my interruption. "Absolutely, I'll tell him now. Thank you." She moved the phone from her ear and disconnected the call.

"Who was that? What's going on? How long have I been asleep?" I fired the questions at her in a rush.

"A few hours. Come and sit down, Sam." Claire turned back for the kitchen, but I reached for her, grabbing her arm and spinning her back around.

"No!" I was aware I was yelling but didn't attempt to stop. "Just tell me what you know."

She nodded and held up the phone. "That was DI Garcia. I was just about to come wake you. They've found that Lindy's partner owned a property, a small apartment. They're on the way there now to check it, see if that's where she is."

I took a couple of deep breaths to steady my surging emotions – desperation for them to find her mixed with fear of the outcome if they did. What if she *didn't* have Cora? Where would that leave us? But if she did, what might that monster have done to my beautiful baby?

I shut out the thought, not able to bear it.

"Where? Where are they going?" I barked, already heading towards the front door.

"They wouldn't tell me." Her voice was low. I spun around to glare at her.

"What do you mean they wouldn't tell you? Why didn't you *make* them? That's my daughter they're looking for!" I was aware I was being unfair, directing my anger at Claire, but she was the only target I had.

"I did try, Sam. I begged them to tell me, but they wouldn't budge. Just said they'd inform us of any development right away. They have local officers on the way there right now. They'll be there before we could even get on the road."

I ran my hands through my hair and paced the hallway once again.

"So what am I supposed to do?" I bellowed back. She was by my side a moment later, wrapping me in her embrace.

"Oh Sam, I can't even begin to imagine ... but we just have to hold on. It won't be much longer." The wobble in her voice only shook me more.

I didn't know how long we stood there, clinging to one

another, but eventually, the shrill ring of the phone broke the spell, and we jumped apart.

Claire still gripped the phone in her hand and stared at it for a second before looking up at me. I lunged and grabbed if from her, almost knocking her off her feet. I swiped desperately at the screen to make sure we didn't miss it. As I was about to place it to my ear, I registered the look on Claire's face and jabbed at the loudspeaker.

"Yes, hello? Do you have her?" My words tumbled out in a rush.

"Mr Fulford?" DI Garcia's tinny voice filled the room, and Claire's fearful eyes locked on mine.

"Yes, I'm here. Do you have my daughter?" I was shouting again, the strain of awaiting his answer almost unbearable.

"We checked the property belonging to Mr Francis. I'm afraid there was no sign of either of them. It doesn't look like anyone has been there in a long time. We're double-checking with the neighbours to be certain, but ... I'm really sorry, Sam."

I let out a breath, fighting the urge to howl or lash out, my shaking legs barely supporting my weight.

"Mr Fulford? Did you hear what I said?"

Claire blinked her unfocused eyes and reached for the phone, gently prising it from my tight grip, and placed her free hand onto my shoulder.

"Yes, we heard. Thank you." Her voice shook, and she swallowed hard.

"I'm so sorry." Garcia's voice was too loud. I rubbed my face. "We will keep looking and let you know if anything comes up."

Claire thanked him again before cutting the call.

"I'm so sorry, Sam." She placed her hand on my face, cupping my cheek. I placed my own hand over hers, gave a watery smile and a tiny nod.

"Don't give up on her, okay? There's still hope." I didn't miss the doubt clouding her eyes.

"I know," I lied and gripped her hand. I heaved a deep sigh. "I need to take a shower," I whispered, pointing towards the phone still clutched in Claire's hand.

"I should take that though, just in case."

She looked down at it as if she had forgotten she was holding it.

"Yeah, of course." She nodded vigorously, holding it out to me.

HOT JETS of water ran over my goose-pimply skin. My brain was working better with the couple of hours' sleep I had managed, but even with the heat of the shower turning my skin a deep shade of pink, I couldn't get warm. My body shivered, the clack of my teeth echoing against the tile. I wondered if I would ever feel warm again.

A flash of memory came like a lightning bolt – as quick as it was there, it was gone again. I chased after it, like the last flickers of a dream when you first wake. I retraced my train of thought.

My body, the cold ... The memory danced just below my consciousness before it crashed to the surface.

"Holy fuck!"

I rushed to get out of the shower. Feet slipping in my haste, I almost pitched onto my face. I grabbed my towel and reached for clothes with the other hand while attempting to dry myself.

"Please, God, let me be right," I prayed, shameless.

56

LINDY

TEN MONTHS PREVIOUS

I kept to our agreement and met with Tessa for coffee a week or so after she appeared on my doorstep. She was every bit the dull, desperate housewife that I'd expected her to be. I was disappointed in Sam for settling.

The way she babbled on, making tedious small talk, reminded me why I neither wanted nor needed friends. Who could possibly enjoy that? I nodded in all the right places and feigned interest, amusing myself by making up the answers to her questions on the spot.

My intention had never been to befriend his little wife – way too risky – but once we were there, I couldn't help wondering if I could make it work. She was only too happy to fill me in on all the details of her life. Granted, I hadn't managed to get much out of her about Sam, but I knew the best way to hunt was to lie in wait. It'd come if I was patient enough.

My patience was well rewarded.

Once we'd met a handful of times, I'd become restless, coming to doubt the success of my plan. I needed to step it up a gear.

Tessa texted, asking if we could meet that evening. I mulled it over for a short time, contemplating making an excuse, before deciding to give it one more shot with her. If I got nowhere again, I'd just have to go after Sam directly. I was losing patience.

We met as usual, but something piqued my notice when she arrived. There was something different about her. She had a different air when she dropped down opposite me. I fought to hide my curiosity. She attempted to chat, but the conversation was strained – forced even. After a tedious half hour, it spilled out of her, turning everything on its head.

Her announcement left me almost too enraged to find words. Heat spread over my body as I hid my trembling hands under the table.

She's pregnant, she's pregnant, she's pregnant.

With great difficulty, I managed to store that first revelation away in my mind. If I allowed it to take hold, I'd throttle her, finding satisfaction in the smugness draining out of her eyes. But I was saved from myself by what she told me next. It was as though she'd sliced me apart and saved my life in the space of a few seconds. The two things that she had just shared, juxtaposed, made a tussle of my emotions. I focused on what needed to be done, willing myself to hold it together.

I was aware that my face was giving away my battle for composure, so I did the only thing that I could think of at that moment. I stared at her full in the face, giving in and allowing the horror to break out on my own. I waited for her to finish before meeting her eye and finding my voice for the first time since she began.

"Things will only get worse. They always do. Can you really be sure what a man like that is capable of? And now you have a child to think of. You have no choice. Leave the bastard."

It wasn't my finest moment, and certainly not how I would have planned to deal with it – not if I had known she was about to divulge the problems in her marriage. But I had to do something to conceal my loss of composure.

I didn't know why I felt so shocked. I had worked hard on her, though, continuously dripping in remarks about how disgusting pregnancy was, the horrendous sacrifices that came with having children. I thought I'd done enough to sway her simple mind, but I'd underestimated her. Perhaps part of me had hoped Sam would also suffer the inability to have children. After all, this was partly his fault.

The clash of emotions was fierce. I even considered walking away, leaving him to his happy little life, now that there was to be a child involved.

But why should he get to walk away from all of it like nothing ever happened? He'd lied, cheated, deceived me. He'd betrayed me so badly, he deserved to pay, impending fatherhood or not. In fact, probably more so.

I stared down at the small ring of keys pressed against my palm. I'd been gripping them so tightly they had punctured my skin, a tiny dome of blood appearing – a grim reminder of all of the pain I'd suffered from the selfish actions of others.

Tessa, dabbing at her eyes, had let on about her plans to go to the post office after our date – probably hoping for an offer to keep her company. As she'd crossed the small cafe to use the facilities before we left, my eyes fell on her handbag hung on the back of her chair. Taking a quick glance around me to ensure no one was looking, I'd grabbed for it and dug around, quickly withdrawing her keys and slipping them into my own bag.

"HOW MANY COPIES?" the guy behind the counter asked me.

"Just one of each, please," I replied, flashing him a bright smile.

He winked at me and turned to his machine, where he got to work. The smell of hot metal filled my nose. I rolled my eyes at his back and tapped my fingers on the counter, eager to get going.

The machine stopped its piercing squeal, and the man turned back to me, palming the three shiny new keys.

From there I took a detour back to the coffee shop. I ordered a drink and perched at the same table as before. When I felt enough time had passed, I pulled Tessa's keys from my bag and made my way to the counter. I hovered at the end.

"Sorry to bother you."

The young girl behind the counter fixed me with a hard stare, obviously expecting a complaint or request of some sort.

"It's just, I found these keys on the floor over there." I pointed towards my table. "They must've dropped out of someone's bag." I gave a small shrug and plastered on a helpful smile.

"Oh." She held out her hand, disinterested but relieved. "Thanks." She nodded and slid them underneath the till.

"No problem at all," I muttered as I walked away.

———

I'D HAD enough time to process Tessa's pregnancy announcement, but I couldn't bring myself to think about it too much. Every time I pictured her with her expanding stomach, it was like a punch to my own. I hated her and alleviated my fury by conjuring up images of telling her exactly what I thought of her, of wrapping my fingers around her neck. I never mentioned the baby while we were together, making the point that the idea of children repulsed me, enjoying the way she squirmed at my obvious disgust.

Taking her keys had been an impulse. I had no plan but liked the idea of having access to the home that should've belonged to me. That bitch was already carrying the baby that should, by rights, have been mine. Access to the home that they'd stolen from me was the least I was owed.

I'd only been in a few times, when I knew they were both out. Being "friends" with Tessa did have its advantages. I enjoyed touching Sam's things, examining his life, regaining my control over him. I wondered if he knew I'd been there, felt the connection too. I liked to move things around a little, just to play with them, imagine them becoming annoyed with one another for leaving things in the wrong places.

When I was in that house, I could pretend Tessa didn't exist, block her out, imagine it was me living there with Sam, pregnant with his child. I would finger the soft baby clothing that hung in preparation, sit rocking the Moses basket on its stand. But I couldn't keep Tessa away. She always returned, with her ever-expanding, perfect baby bump.

The unjustness of the situation gnawed at me. A bitterness rose on my tongue, and my heart raced every time I saw her. But it had become an addiction. I was too involved, watching the baby grow, just out of reach, knowing it should be mine. Like a scab, I knew I should leave it alone, but I just couldn't stop picking at it.

The more I witnessed, the more convinced I became that Tessa wasn't worthy of being blessed with a child. She would make a lousy mother.

I did all I could to widen the cracks between her and Sam, to worm my way in between them as she spewed their troubles at me, but her shutters had come down. I'd pushed her too hard.

I knew enough though, and she was transparent. I knew

things hadn't improved, as she tried to make out. I could see it etched into her face. She was afraid of him, afraid for that unborn child, yet she chose to bury her head because she was selfish. Just like my mother had been. Sam would treat them badly – of course he would – and she would stand by and watch like the pathetic coward she was.

How could I stand by and allow that?

Something had to be done. My child deserved more than that. My child would never know that kind of pain, whatever the consequences.

57

SAM

PRESENT DAY

I hammered down the stairs two at a time and spun into the living room. I reached the cupboard at the back of the room and swung open the door, throwing handfuls of things out of it and onto the floor.

"What *are* you doing?" Claire's voice came from behind me, but I didn't have time to stop.

"Looking for something."

"Yes, well, I could have guessed that much. What is it that you're looking for? And can you not do it without causing such a mess?" I heard her move closer and gather up the debris I'd strewn about.

"Maps," I replied simply.

"Maps?" she questioned, deadpan. She might have thought I'd finally lost it completely.

"Yes, Claire, maps! Like drawings of towns and roads and stuff," I huffed.

"Yes, thank you, Sam. I'm aware of what a map is." She mirrored my tone, ruffling papers as she collected them up behind me. "I just can't grasp why on earth you would be looking for one, especially right now. Haven't you heard of a sat nav?"

"I can't use a sat nav. I don't know where I'm going yet." Finally, I spotted the maps behind Tessa's photographs and buried under a pile of old takeaway leaflets. I grabbed for them, bundling them up in my arms. Stepping over the mess I'd created, I carried them through to the kitchen table.

Claire appeared beside me and watched as I flicked through them.

"Okay, you've lost me completely. Excuse the pun." She shrugged one shoulder and rolled her eyes. "What's going on?"

"I don't have time to explain everything. I can do that later. But there's a chance I might know where Lindy's gone." I didn't look up from the map I was busy spreading over the table, but I sensed her start at my revelation.

"What? How? Where?" Her questions came in a rush. "I don't understand. If you think you know something, then you need to call the police," she insisted.

I ignored her and continued searching, uncertain of what I was looking for, hoping against hope I would know it when I saw it.

"When we were together, Lindy told me about something that happened to her as a child. It was whilst she was staying at a cottage owned by her family. I don't remember the name of the exact place, but I'm pretty certain that it was in Cornwall. I thought if I looked at the map, it might jog my memory. She could be there." I lifted my eyes to meet Claire's, just for a second, before I dropped them again and continued desperately scanning the map.

Hers were filled with uncertainty. "So call the police, Sam. Have them help search. If there's a chance that you could be right, then we need to find her."

"Like they involved me in searching her boyfriend's place? I'm not getting the police involved, not yet," I insisted. "I have nothing solid to give them. And besides, there's a good chance that they don't even own it anymore. Or that I'm wrong. I need them to keep searching for her too. I can take this part."

Her brow creased, eyes clouding with doubt. "Sam, I really think ..."

"I'm not asking, Claire. If you don't want to be involved, that's fine, but this is *my* daughter, and this *is* how I am doing it." I paused, collecting myself before I went on. "I know her, Claire. If there's any hope of getting Cora back, I honestly think my best chance is if I can speak to her rather than if a ram raid of police officers comes barrelling in. I *have* to try." My rational mind shrieked, perfectly aware of how out of my depth I might be getting, begging me not to go it alone. But I couldn't share the truth with Claire. I couldn't let the police be the ones to challenge Lindy – not when I knew what she held over me. I'd be sacrificing myself.

Claire studied my face for a few seconds, clearly doubting my decision, but gave a small nod before joining me, leaning over the map.

"Who even owns maps anymore, anyway?" she asked, screwing up her nose. "You could've just checked on a map online, you know. Are you a complete technophobe?" It was her attempt at lightening the mood, to dissipate the tension that had drawn between us.

"They belonged to Tessa's dad. He collected them." I shrugged. "He gave them to her when her mum got ill, and she could never bring herself to part with them, knowing how her dad loved them."

"Oh." Her cheeks flushed. "Sorry. I didn't know."

I shook my head and waved it away, dismissing her

apology and ignoring the sensation of my stomach dropping. I had lost count of the times Tessa's dad had tried to contact me over the last few days. I'd continuously rejected all of his calls, unable to face him. I had only met her parents once or twice, but I knew her mother was incapacitated, her father her sole carer. They wouldn't be able to travel to London, so if I didn't take the calls, I didn't have to explain anything. I swallowed down my shame.

"Can I do something to help?" Claire hovered over my shoulder. I didn't lift my eyes from the map of Cornwall I'd dug out; flicking them, I studied it, looking for anything that might spark recognition. It occurred to me just how far away Cornwall was.

"You could drive while I keep looking?" I suggested without looking up.

"Drive where?" Her tone was apprehensive.

"I know it was Cornwall." I frowned, frustrated that I couldn't retrieve any more information. "Lindy only ever mentioned the place once or twice by name, but I *know* she told me it was in Cornwall, so we should go in that direction, get a head start."

Claire regarded me as if I were crazy.

"I can't sit around here doing nothing anymore, Claire! I have to try. This is something I can actually do." I released a heavy sigh, and her eyes softened.

"Let's go, then." She raised her eyebrows and lifted her hands in surrender. "But grab some snacks, will you? It's quite a trip you're planning."

An hour and a half's drive later, I'd searched the map until I felt travel sick. My eyes ached from scanning each and every town and village name. Remembering nothing else about the place Lindy had told me about, I had to accept defeat for the moment and take a break.

Claire reached her hand into the open packet of crisps,

shovelling a cluster of them into her mouth. My own stomach growled, but I couldn't bring myself to eat, nauseous from the mixture of lingering travel sickness and apprehension.

"What was it that you remembered?" she asked between crunches, spraying a tiny piece of crisp onto the dashboard. I stared at it, trying to figure out her question.

"You said that you'd remembered something Lindy had told you – that's what made you think of this place. I'm just curious, what was it?"

Understanding dawned. I'd never explained any more to Claire after searching the maps like a madman.

The memory of the raw pain on Lindy's face as she'd recalled the incident still took me aback. It was rare that she showed any emotion besides anger, seeing others as a sign of weakness.

On that particular evening, she'd come home in a foul mood. I didn't recall what had upset her, or if I ever even found out. She'd poured herself a large glass of wine – another rarity for her – then slowly made her way through the whole bottle without offering me so much as a drop – not that I would've accepted. It would have been the wrong thing, somehow.

By some miracle, I'd managed to make it through the evening without upsetting her further, telling myself she might appreciate the space but in truth giving her a wide berth out of self-preservation.

She'd taken herself to the tiny balcony off the living room, where she drained the bottle. Eventually, knowing that there was no way I could go off to bed without ensuring I first had her permission, I tiptoed across the room and opened the balcony door as quietly as physically possible, sick with trepidation.

She didn't move, remaining totally still as I eased outside, goose pimples rising all over my body. I wasn't certain if they were from the cold or the rising anxiety.

I paused, lingering next to her, unsure of what to say, anticipating the backlash if it happened to be the wrong thing.

"What d'you want, Sam?" Her emotionless slur startled me. My legs wobbled.

"I ... I just came to check if there is anything you need. Can I bring you anything? You must be frozen."

Her head spun, eyes boring into me, slightly out of focus. I waited for the torrent of abuse.

"Ha! This isn't *cold*. If you think this is cold, you need to grow a pair," she slurred, scowling at me. "*I* know how *cold* feels." She jabbed at her chest with a finger.

I lowered myself into the chair beside her and placed my hand over her icy fingers. She didn't attempt to pull away. Instead, her features softened.

"What kind of parent *does* that to a child?"

I stared at her, hoping that the question was rhetorical, trying desperately to think up a reasonable answer, just in case it wasn't.

"She made me run. I was *six years old*."

I had no idea what she was talking about but tightened my grip on her fingers in a show of support.

"I knew that day was too good to be true," she continued, oblivious to me. "I couldn't believe my luck when she said we could go to the beach. It was one of those beautiful, bright spring days, you know? When from inside it looks like it should be hot enough to bathe, but actually it's still so cold."

I didn't dare interrupt her flow. She'd never opened up about any part of her past. I held completely still.

"I'd been playing by the shallows, having one of the best days of my life. I don't even think I knew about tides. I was only six. A huge wave came from nowhere. It knocked me off my feet and rolled me around. I thought I was going to drown." She paused, taking a deep breath. "I wasn't afraid of drowning though." She wagged her head gently. "I was afraid of how she was going to punish me if I didn't."

I waited, allowing her a moment.

"When she saw me coming up that beach, I'll never forget the look of fury in her eyes. Oh, she pretended for the onlookers that she was all concerned, ushering me up off the beach towards the car. But I knew, I *knew* the shit I was in, even then."

My heart broke for that terrified six-year-old her.

"When we got back to the car and I went to climb in, she slapped my face so hard. God, if my skin hadn't already been stinging enough from that bitter wind. She refused to let me get in, told me it was my own stupid fault and that I'd ruined the day for us all. She told me to make my own way back to that horrid damp cottage, that I wouldn't be soaking and ruining her car seats too. I wasn't even sure of the way. I considered running away, but where would I go? My mother had always made it clear that no one would want me; even my own parents didn't." She sniffed out a laugh but didn't look at me.

"My father climbed into the passenger seat without a word. He never even tried. I got lost twice. Took me forty minutes to get back. I only made it because I could see the castle. I've never felt cold like that in my life. Honestly, I thought I might die. I wouldn't have cared if I had. She made me strip to my underwear outside the front door when I got back, wouldn't allow me to shower or dress for hours. And of course, I took a beating for it too. That was standard practice." She gave a humourless snort.

"I was ill for a week afterwards. My *mother* said I ruined the entire trip. God, I hated that shithole of a cottage almost as much as I hated the pair of them." Her face hardened, the brief show of emotion having passed.

As if she had just awoken from a trance, she blinked, turned, and fixed me with a cold stare, pulling her hand out from mine.

58

LINDY

THREE MONTHS PREVIOUS

The further the pregnancy progressed, the more certain I became. That woman was neither fit nor deserving of becoming a mother.

Perhaps it *was* fate that had pushed me that way, knowing that Sam's child needed me. I'd never believed in that kind of rubbish before – always a firm believer of making your own luck – but it seemed impossible to ignore.

I was even beginning to wonder about Sam. If he realised what a huge mistake he'd made, realised that his child deserved better than the woman he'd been deluded enough to impregnate. Could there still be a chance for us?

One morning, as I sat watching Sam leave for work, irritated by the sight of Tessa waving him off, a thought struck like a bash in the head. Had Sam only been with this woman in order to provide me with what I deserved? Had he planned to bring our child to me as soon as her usefulness had expired?

Had he known that I was there all along? Had I been missing his signals? As he lowered himself into the car, Sam's eyes lifted for the briefest of moments, seeming to lock onto mine. If I'd needed any further convincing, that had done it. It was so clear to me now: Sam *knew* I should be the mother of his child. He was working to gain my forgiveness, making up to me for all he had done. He had been waiting for me to come back for him.

It was agonising watching her carry my child. It took every ounce of self-restraint to keep my emotions in check, having to hide my true feelings with the mask of disinterest. I'd watch on in disgust as she selfishly indulged in cakes and caffeinated drinks without a second thought about what was best for the baby. She couldn't do a single bit of research into what she *should* be giving her unborn child. She was a failure already, and the baby hadn't even arrived yet.

There was no question that I would have to step in and be a mother to the child. It was just a matter of logistics. I needed to ensure suspicion never fell on me, that there'd be no cause to so much as look in my direction.

So I decided Bella had to move away. Australia seemed like a bit of a cliché, but Tessa was deluded enough to believe anything I told her. It had to be somewhere far so that she didn't try to continue with our friendship or make plans to come and visit. I needed to vanish from her life without drawing attention and know that, even if she ever found an ounce of intelligence and put it all together, my trail would be cold, sending her off in the wrong direction entirely. So the announcement was made.

I found it hard to contain my amusement at her crestfallen expression. The light mood didn't last long, though. I had to endure her gushing about the baby, pretending that she cared and stroking her swollen belly. I despised her; she was mocking me.

I faced an internal battle for the rest of the pregnancy, half of me desperate to avoid her, to make up an excuse every time she suggested meeting and avoid suffering her company and her pathetic gloating. But without seeing her, I also missed out on watching my child grow. I knew I was a glutton for punishment, but seeing that bump made me shiver with excitement for what was to come.

And then she arrived.

The anticipation of meeting her made me breathless. The wait for Sam to leave for work seemed to go on forever. I knew I had to be smart. I had to play the game a little longer. I couldn't just bulldoze straight in – he wouldn't be expecting me yet, and I didn't want to spook him. Our reunion would be special when the time came. We both knew we had to bide our time.

Eventually, my waiting paid off.

I couldn't have been more thrilled to see the uncanny resemblance to her daddy. We would laugh about it with strangers in time, Sam and I, about how unfortunate it was that she was all him, how we hoped she would grow to look like me. They would nod along, admiring her mother's perfect swish of hair and piercing eyes.

I suppressed a smile at the thought of it all. For the first time in as long as I could remember, I was excited about the future. Sam, me, and our little girl. We were finally going to be the perfect family.

THE WAITING BECAME HARDER as the weeks dragged on. The physical pain of seeing my baby with that woman was eased only by the knowledge that she would eventually be where she belonged. It was only a matter of time. Tessa had everything that should've been mine: the husband, the home, and now my child. But it would come right.

Witnessing her feeding the child from her breast was almost too much. My fingers twitched with the temptation to reach over and tear her away as I imagined winding Tessa's lank hair between my fingers and yanking it out by the roots. My nails bit into my palms, and I clenched my teeth. She had no right to behave like that.

The state of her house was appalling. I could barely contain my horror at the wreck of her kitchen during one visit, disgusted that she could be so bone idle. I'd had no option but to clean up; my baby couldn't be living in such a health hazard.

Despite how careful I was being, I came close to being discovered that day in the coffee shop. Tessa had just left her with me. I would never leave her with *anyone* once she was mine. She didn't care about her like I would. I checked to make sure that Tessa wasn't watching us. I knew it was risky, but I just couldn't help myself. I'd been so restrained.

I cooed at her, whispering, reassuring her of how much better our lives together would be once it was just us. She stared back at me through her daddy's eyes, and I knew she understood. But then I caught Tessa watching, a smile playing on her lips, and vowed to never slip up like that again. I wouldn't risk so much as another glance at Cora until she was safe with me.

I had intended to hold off a little longer, wait until my plan was watertight, but then came the final straw.

Her brazen attitude as she recounted her irresponsible behaviour floored me. My temper flared, threatening to explode, as she giggled about it – drinking wine with Sam and his friends. How *wonderful Lauren* had assured her that it would be fine. Lauren was only lucky that I didn't have the time to deal with her. I had bigger fish to fry. I had to save my daughter from this heinous woman before it was too late.

The matter was settled. I had to act. And quickly.

59

SAM

PRESENT DAY

Sympathy flickered across Claire's face as I explained Lindy's childhood. But her face hardened again quickly as she remembered who that innocent child became.

"There's no denying that's a terrible thing for anyone to suffer through, especially a child." She screwed up her face, emphasising her disgust. "But that does *not* excuse the things she's done." Her face flushed. "She probably only told you to send you on a guilt trip, to keep you trapped in her web. That's if it even really happened. Who knows with her!"

Her assumption – that I was too naive to know when I was being lied to – irritated me.

"No, Claire," I bit back, "you weren't there. I'd never seen her get emotional like that before. It happened, and it happened at this cottage." The force of my anger bewildered me at first, until it suddenly occurred to me where it was rooted. If Lindy's story really was made up, just another fiction to sucker me in further, we were currently on a fool's errand, no closer at all to finding out if she had my daughter.

Claire's jaw tensed, and a tiny muscle twitched in her

cheek. She must've just come to the same thought. "Yeah, of course. You're absolutely right." She gave her head a dismissive shake. "You knew her better than anyone," she said with a firm nod. "You would have known if she was deceiving you."

We continued our journey in silence, each caught up in our own thoughts. I lost all track of time as I fell back into unpleasant memories and ran through a string of scenarios for the outcome of this trip.

I was truly torn. If my daughter was actually in the hands of this woman, that would prove my innocence. But I was also fast coming to grips with what Lindy was capable of and just how unstable she might be.

The ringing of my phone shattered the car's silence, startling us both out of our solitary daze. I scrambled to wiggle it free from my pocket, cursing when it jammed against the seat belt. Claire threw nervous glances in my direction, silently pleading with me to answer it in time. With a final yank, I retrieved it and swiped the screen without hesitating to even check the caller ID.

"Hello?" My voice rang with urgency, my adrenaline already pumping.

"Sam, it's Detective Garcia."

My pulse raced at the sound of his voice.

"What is it?" I snapped, desperate to know and terrified to hear in equal measure.

"I'm afraid I don't have anything too concrete just yet," he admitted. My heart plummeted. "But we do have a potential lead that we're following up. I wanted to bring you up to speed and check if you might be able to shed any light on it for us."

"Oh?" My throat was dry. I wondered if he would've bothered to "bring me up to speed" had he not needed my help.

"We've been having another look into the case of Lindy's missing partner since discovering his apartment. We weren't sure what we were looking for, but we found that he owned a car. We believe Ms Draper did have her driving licence, yes?"

"She could drive, yes," I confirmed. "But you aren't calling just to ask me that, I'm assuming?"

Claire tossed me another glance.

"No." He cleared his throat. "We ran a trace on the car through the missing persons team, just on the off chance. We weren't actually expecting to get anything, but we got a hit. A couple, actually."

I shook my head, not following.

"What does that mean? A hit?"

"What I mean is the car was registered to a missing person. Although it was still at his address when he went missing, the team put a trace on it so that it'd be flagged up if it was picked up anywhere," he explained. "The car was picked up on the motorway," he continued, impatience creeping into his own voice, "which we can only assume means one of three things. One – Mr Francis is no longer missing and has retrieved his car. Two – it's been stolen, which *is* possible, as neither Mr Francis nor Ms Draper are around to report it."

"And three?" I snapped.

"Three is that Ms Draper has taken the car herself."

It took me a second to connect the dots.

"Where was she going?" I asked, breathless again.

Claire's head whipped around, and I feared she'd lost all focus on the road.

"Well," Garcia replied with a begrudging sigh, "that's where you come in. We were hoping that you might be able to tell us."

"How the hell would I know?" I snapped back.

"I'm not saying that you necessarily would." The frustration in Garcia's tone matched my own. "But I figured it had to be worth asking," he continued. "Do you have any idea why she might have been headed down south?"

I froze, almost losing my grip on the phone.

The DI didn't miss my hesitation. "Sam?" he prompted, voice low.

I gave myself a mental shake. "Erm ... no. Sorry. I've no idea," I lied. There was silence from his end.

"You're certain about that?"

"Nope. Like I said, not a clue. I'm sorry."

His doubt was almost audible in his silence, but he didn't push any further. "Okay. If you're certain. If you do think of anything at all, please give me a call right away. Any time. It could be crucial to us tracking her down. And finding Cora."

"I understand," I replied, desperate to get him off the phone. "Thanks for the call."

We assured each other we'd stay in touch and exchanged a brief goodbye before hanging up.

The second the call ended, Claire fired me a look. "Please tell me you did not just do something as stupid as to lie to the police. Sam?"

"Okay. I didn't do something as stupid as lie to the police."

"For fuck's sake, Sam." She slammed her hand against the steering wheel, and I jumped, the outburst being so out of character. "It's one thing not to inform them of something you aren't certain of yourself," she continued, her voice rising with her frustration, "but it's quite another to outright lie when they're asking you for information. It's like ... obstruction or something! You could get into serious trouble."

I understood her anger, but I was undeterred. I couldn't let them get to her first.

"How would they even know that I knew anything?" I steadied my voice. "To be honest, right now, I actually *don't* know much more than they do."

She rolled her eyes, then glared again.

"Look, Claire, just give me a little time to think, okay? I just want to decide on the best way to keep Cora safe – if she has her. You said it yourself, I knew Lindy better than anyone. I'm the best person to handle this."

I watched her turmoil, torn between the legal "right thing" and her loyalty to me.

"As soon as we know anything useful for sure, I'll call and tell them. I promise," I insisted. "I'm doing this for Cora," I added quietly.

Her face softened as I expected, and she heaved a deep sigh.

"She's your daughter, Sam. You have to do what you believe is best." She sounded exasperated. "But don't let it be said that I didn't warn you. I might be going along with it for your sake, but that doesn't mean I like it. If everything the police found out is to be believed, it appears she's one very dangerous woman and most likely increasingly unstable. I certainly don't want to find out just what she's capable of if push comes to shove."

60

LINDY

TWO WEEKS PREVIOUS

Time was so of the essence, I could almost hear the clock ticking. I was afraid for my child, left with someone so incapable. My insides burned at the recklessness of her actions.

Who knew what she'd do next? If she could gloat about getting drunk whilst responsible for a baby, what else was she capable of? It was obvious the woman was unhinged. Bringing my plans forward presented some risks, of course – I'd planned on taking more time to get things finely tuned – but there was no choice but to take them. For Cora's sake.

The name stuck in my throat – something else that would change as soon as she was where she belonged. For the sake of the bond I knew we could have, I couldn't have her thinking I'd ever curse her with a name like that. I knew the damage such a thing could cause. Of course, they'd both have new names once we were all reunited. It would be best that Sam's identity be changed too, for his own safety. We didn't want anyone coming after us. We could choose a new surname together now that we were to shed our past. That would be one of the first things we'd do.

To gain control of my rage, I clung to these thoughts and to how soon my daughter and I would be together. I took a deep breath, gritted my teeth, and tapped out a message to Tessa.

> Hey, I wanted you to know, work have come up against some problems and need me to start in the new office sooner than they had planned. It's pretty crazy but they are offering me a massive bonus if I agree to be out there by the middle of the week, so it looks as though I'm off! B x

I should probably have gushed about our friendship and how I'd miss her, but after how she had behaved, I just couldn't bring myself to. It was all I could do not to rush round and snatch my child away from her.

My phone pinged, and I reached for it, narrowing my eyes and reading her message in a mocking tone in my head.

> Noooooo! How can they do that? It's so soon! I can't believe you won't be here, what will I do without you? We'll have to make sure that we get to say a proper goodbye and I know Sam would love to meet you. Let's arrange an evening for you to come to us. I can cook something as you'll be so busy packing. We'll miss you so much. I can't believe it. Xx

The crying-face emojis she'd added made me want to vomit. How could a grown woman be so pathetic? I reread the part about Sam wanting to meet me and wondered if it was a message from him. Could this be his way of letting me know that he was ready? That he understood why I had to step it up? We both knew I couldn't accept the invitation; it was too risky for us to be together in front of Tessa. A bond like ours was difficult to disguise, even for someone as naïve as her.

I paced while thinking of a reply that wouldn't tip her off to my true feelings.

> I know, all very sad but they need me there! It was always the plan, now just a little sooner than expected.

I drummed my fingers on the table. If I turned down her invite too quickly, she'd push or, worse still, drag Sam over to me, making for an impossible situation for us both. I needed to get it right.

> Dinner sounds perfect! I would love to meet the infamous Sam too. I'm sure we'll get along great. XX

I wondered if Sam would read my message. He'd know, of course, that I had no intention of going, but he'd get the meaning. Things were in motion; we would soon reunite.

I HAD to push our dinner plans as far back as I could manage by claiming a busy schedule with work and packing. I waited until after lunch to press send on the message I'd written far ahead of time:

> So sorry, going to have to take a rain check on this evening. The shipping company have screwed up majorly with my stuff and I have to drive to collect the boxes to get them onto the flight in time. I hope you haven't gone to too much trouble. B x

It gave me a bit of satisfaction, picturing her disappointment, imagining that she had gone to plenty of trouble. Her reply came as a sickly-sweet plea that I not worry, offering to do anything she could to help. Anger swelled, and I let out a roar as I threw my phone across the room. I wanted to rile her up. I wanted her frustration, distress even, not her offer of help. The woman was insufferable.

We messaged back and forth, me assuring her that I'd make time to say goodbye, knowing that whether or not I stuck to that would depend on my self-restraint. I'd have to weigh up my desperation to see my daughter against my ability not to leave with her there and then.

In the meantime, I drove to a shopping centre a few towns over. I couldn't risk being seen by anyone who might remember me. I took my time fingering the precious fabrics of the little dresses and lacy socks before I turned to the boys' section. The time for more enjoyable shopping would come later.

I selected a number of outfits – dungarees and soft all-in-one suits in pale blue shades – and turned to the nappies. The options overwhelmed me.

None of the packs were labelled by the child's age in months as I'd expected. They were all by weight. Having never even held her, I was clueless. I settled on a size and a brand, certain it couldn't be that important.

I was relieved to find the milk powder easier to decipher and scooped a couple of tubs into my trolley.

I considered going to the self-serve till, but the security tags on the clothing would be an issue, so I opted for a manned checkout. The woman serving smiled down at my purchases as she scanned and removed tags, then glanced at my midriff. "For your little one, are they?" she asked, holding up one of the tiny sets.

The question would have irked me, normally – a total stranger thinking she had the right to ask – but that day was different. That day I *was* buying for my child.

"Yep." I nodded enthusiastically. "That's right, my little boy. He's home with his daddy right now."

Her smile widened. "Enjoy him while he's so small. They grow so fast." She let out a sigh, her eyes becoming distant.

My smile was genuine as I replied, "Oh, I fully intend to."

I DECIDED to indulge in a flying visit, that it was best all round. That way, I could check in on my daughter before leaving her for a few days and avoid raising Tessa's suspicions. I watched to make certain Sam had left for the day before agreeing to pop over. That morning, I'd packed the few things I had for my daughter so as to remind myself why I needed to keep my head and follow the plan. One misstep could destroy everything I had worked so hard to put into place.

I gritted my teeth throughout the entire sorry performance, stealing glances at Cora to keep my focus, entertaining a fantasy where Tessa was hired help in *my* home with *my* child. Not that I'd ever require help.

I cringed inwardly at Tessa's emotional display. How truly weak and pathetic this woman was. I watched her fuss over my child, fire coursing through my veins at her blatant show. My anger seethed at her gloating, and I mentally counted off the days to keep from throttling her.

I risked another glance at Cora – the child who had eluded me until then – and breathed deeply to keep my calm.

Just as I was making to leave, Tessa announced her need to use the loo. She called over her shoulder as she left the room for me to watch Cora while she was gone. As if she cared.

I didn't waste a second. As soon as she was out of sight, I moved over Cora's basket and scooped her up, cradling her close. I whispered, telling her how Mummy had to go and get everything ready for her, but that I'd be back just as soon as I could. I promised I would keep her safe and that we would be together again very soon. I planted soft kisses on her perfect skin, breathing in her beautiful scent. As she gazed up at me through her daddy's eyes, I knew without a shadow of a doubt I was doing what had to be done, what was best for her. Hearing the pad of footsteps, I eased her back into her basket and moved back to my seat, where I made as if I'd been completely engrossed in my phone the whole time.

LESS THAN AN HOUR LATER, I was putting the last of the bags into the car. Using Paul's car was far from ideal. I had, of course, been hoping to have something in place when the time came, but bringing my plans forward left me with little choice. That I'd gotten something useful out of my relationship with him was a comfort, and at least the vehicle wasn't registered under my name. The police had never looked too hard for him. The officer who'd questioned me easily swallowed my account of Paul's affairs and how handy he was with his fists. Manipulating a man to believe what I wanted him to came easily; a few flutters of my eyelashes and some crocodile tears had him falling over himself to comfort me. Paul had been written off as not worth searching for.

I smirked at the irony when it occurred to me – they might even pin this on him. I slid into the driver's seat of his car and stared at the house across the street for a moment before starting the engine.

"Mummy will be back for you *very* soon, baby," I vowed as I pulled away.

61

SAM

PRESENT DAY

Claire and I barely exchanged a word for the rest of the journey. I understood her misgivings but lacked the energy to convince her further.

As signs welcomed us to the South, Claire's voice finally broke the silence.

"Where are we going, Sam? I don't know about you, but I am exhausted."

I glanced over at her and felt a tug of guilt. She looked washed out. I'd barely given her well-being a thought, being so caught up. I winced at my own selfishness. Reaching for my phone, I tapped the screen to pull up the map.

"According to this, there's a travel lodge a few miles away. Are you happy to crash there for the night if I get the directions?" The darkness was drawing in, and I needed some time to think, decide where we were going. I promised myself it would only be for a few hours.

She glanced over at me, her face weary.

"I'd be happy to crash anywhere right now, to be honest." A tiny smile played on her lips. "Are you sure you can manage with that sat nav? Do you need me to pull over and show you how to use something that isn't a paper map, mister technophobe?"

I threw her a withering look before breaking into a smile, grateful to her for cutting the tension.

We grabbed some fast food and then checked in, carrying what little we had with us up the stairs. Claire glanced at my hands, noticing that I was still clutching the map.

"You need to get some rest, Sam," she insisted. "You'll do better if you take a break."

"I know. I will," I assured her. "I just need it to hand in case I remember anything more."

She regarded me with soft eyes and placed her hand on the top of my arm.

"I'm right next door if you need anything. Or if you do think of anything," she added. "But please do rest, okay?"

I nodded, and we exchanged a brief goodnight, parting ways into our adjacent rooms.

I showered and lay back on the bed, unable to switch off. I flicked through television channels but couldn't find anything that held my attention. I must've dozed for a while because the next time I glanced at the clock, it was four thirty. Knowing that I'd had as much rest as I was going to manage, I showered again, dressed, and pulled out the map.

I used the tiny kettle to make myself a strong coffee, using two of the sachets provided and plenty of sugar. Spreading the map out on the bed, I studied it once again. I stared at it until my eyes blurred and my coffee stood cold. A light tap on my door caused me to start.

Claire stood on the other side. She looked brighter, but the dark circles under her eyes gave her away. Her hair was still damp.

"Hey." Her voice was a raised whisper. "I heard you moving about so thought I'd come over." I stood aside to let her into my room.

"Did I disturb you?" I asked, pushing the door closed behind her.

"No." She shook her head. "I didn't sleep much either. Anyway, what's the plan?" She gestured toward the map still spread out on my bed. I let out a deep sigh, a feeling of hopelessness sinking through me.

"To be honest, I don't have one." I shrugged, dropping my eyes to the floor. "I really hoped that by coming here, looking at the map, something would trigger a memory and, somehow, I'd just know where to go. You know? But ..." In the cold light of day, my plan was ridiculous. I felt foolish for having dragged Claire along without any idea of what I was doing. Claire moved over to look at the map.

"Nothing sounds familiar, then?" she questioned gently.

"Nothing," I confirmed. "I keep thinking maybe something does, but then I read another name and wonder if that one does too. It was so rare that she spoke of her past. She kept a couple of photos of her and her parents buried in some of her stuff. She didn't know I knew about them. That was the only thing she ever really shared. It's useless." I paused, feeling my face flush. "Claire, I'm sorry for bringing you here like this. You were right. I should've just spoken to the police yesterday. Let's get out of here. Once we've had some breakfast, I'll call Detective Garcia, tell him I've remembered the cottage."

She moved towards me and wrapped me in a warm embrace.

"Don't apologise to me, Sam." Her voice was muffled, her face against my shoulder. Her damp hair smelled of fruit shampoo, reminding me of Tessa. I took a sharp breath in against the raw pain.

She gripped me tighter. "I'm the one who should be sorry. I have no right to push you into anything. We'll do what you think is best, okay?"

She stepped back but kept her hands gripped on the tops of my arms. "But the one thing that I refuse to do" – she shook my arms gently – "is give up. And neither will you. Now let's grab something to eat. It'll help us think."

She released my arms and ushered me towards the door. I pulled her back and wrapped her in my arms once again, so grateful to my sister, who owed me nothing.

———

MY HUNGER surprised me when we reached the lobby and the smell of food filled my nostrils. Claire must've felt the same – we quickly suggested in unison that we eat there. We both managed to eat more than we had the entire time we'd been together. Between the rest and food, I could actually think straight. I pulled myself together, feeling pathetic for my display of self-pity upstairs.

Claire took a sip of her coffee to wash down the last of her food.

"So if you're not sure where we're going, we could just head further down?" she suggested. "Or if you really *do* want to speak to Garcia, we could see if they've managed to pinpoint an area where she may be?" Her lip still curled slightly at the mention of his name.

"Not that he would tell *us*, of course." I shrugged, rolling my eyes. "But at the moment, this is a wild goose chase. We may as well be looking for a needle in a haystack," I conceded.

Claire nodded slowly, continuing to savour her coffee. We finished up and headed to the front desk to return our key cards. The couple in front of us at the desk were taking an age to pay their bill, arguing over every part of it after insisting on having the entire thing itemised. The receptionist working the desk threw us apologetic looks and reached to press a buzzer behind her, hoping to summon backup. I offered her a look that I hoped portrayed understanding.

Claire folded her arms and huffed, rolling her eyes at me.

"Take the bags out to the car if you like. I'll follow if I *ever* reach the desk," I offered.

"I could use the fresh air, if you don't mind," she agreed. She took my small bag and moved past the complaining couple towards the doors, throwing them daggers.

As she passed, my attention rested on the rack of leaflets that was common in hotels of that kind. Sadness surged, causing my breath to catch. I would never get to take my little family to visit those types of places. I fought the urge to knock down the rack. Then my eyes fixed onto one particular leaflet. Something clicked; a spark went off in my brain.

I searched for Claire, but she was already halfway across the car park outside.

With a burst of adrenaline, I thrust the key cards onto the desk, grabbed the leaflet, and pushed my way out of the front doors, feeling all eyes on me as the receptionist called after me. I didn't stop.

62

LINDY

ONE WEEK PREVIOUS

The wait was the hardest part. I filled my time as best I could, cleaning and preparing the cottage. I was just ready to have her home with me, where I knew she belonged. She was in my thoughts every waking moment. I imagined us cuddled up together on the sofa, spending long lazy days on countryside walks. The moment she and I would be reunited with her daddy.

It was going to be perfect.

I worried about her, of course, remorseful for leaving her with someone so unstable. But it had to be done. It'd be for the best in the long run, a means to an end. I yearned to go back for her, to feel the weight of her in my arms once again, but I had to bide my time. Tessa had to believe that I was on the other side of the world before I could make a move. I couldn't risk drawing any suspicion.

I enjoyed the irony. The loathing I'd always harboured for that cottage. The pleasure my mother took in dragging me there. I wasn't sure she liked it any more than I did, really. But the joy that she took in watching me suffer made it worth it for her – cutting us off from everyone and everything. Now it was to become my sanctuary. Our sanctuary. I laughed out loud. That would have really pissed my mother off, the fact that this place ended up being my saving grace.

It would be perfect – a quiet location, away from nosey neighbours or suspicious acquaintances. A fresh start for us both.

I wondered how long it would take Sam to join us. I couldn't leave him any details about where we were going; any hint was too much of a risk. But he'd find us, I just knew it. I typed out another message to Tessa. It was all about keeping the enemy close.

I HAD PUT the first steps of my plan into action the previous day. I'd googled the time and weather in Australia, then called Tessa to let her know that I was settling in just fine. I edged the conversation towards how she was coping and heard the crack in her voice as she assured me all was well. I'd laid it on good and thick, assuring her that she sounded exhausted and really deserved a break. Then I moved to the true purpose of the call.

"You got the last pot of sleeping pills I dropped in for you, right?" I asked casually.

"Oh yeah, thanks for that." She sounded edgy again.

"And you said that they're working well for you still?" I questioned, needing to be certain.

"Yep. Perfectly, thanks. Not that I take them all of the time, obviously."

I bit down hard on my lip to stop myself spurting back at her about it – suddenly acting as if she cared. Steadying myself, I continued to gently encourage her.

"Tomorrow's Friday for you guys, right?" I played dumb.

"Sure is. Thank God for the weekend! Sam can take a shift

or two then." She huffed out a laugh. I smiled to myself – this couldn't be playing out any better.

"You really need a proper night's sleep, Tessa. Why don't you pop a couple of those pills tomorrow night and let Sam take the night shift for a change? It'll make you feel like a new woman to get a full night's rest," I urged her.

A few tense seconds passed before she responded, "Yeah, maybe I will." I closed my eyes in relief.

We continued our conversation. I didn't even mind how mindless it was, too distracted by revelling in my own genius to care about anything she prattled on about. Eventually, I faked a loud yawn.

"Well, I'd best get on. Loads of unpacking still to do," I groaned. "I'll call again soon," I lied. "Oh, and Tessa – promise me that you'll take those pills and get some proper sleep tomorrow night. Otherwise" – I delivered my parting blow – "you're going to be in no fit state to look after that baby."

This time, there was no pause.

"Yeah, you're right. I will. In fact, I'm looking forward to it already." She laughed – her irritating little laugh – and I grimaced.

Not half as much as I am, I thought as we said our good-byes and hung up.

I spent the rest of the day in high spirits, humming as I chose the outfit to bring her home in. I always dreamed of choosing the "coming home" outfit for my most precious bundle.

Things were working out just as planned. With Tessa out of the way, the rest would come off perfectly.

Luckily for me, Sam slept the sleep of the dead. That was the reason the parasomnias could take such hold. Once he was out, he was dead to the world regardless of what was happening around him.

Knowing that Tessa would place the blame with Sam when Cora was discovered gone, driving in the final wedge – that was just icing on the cake. Guilt would consume her, and everyone would shame the drugged-up mother, just as she deserved.

I'd thought of every detail.

63

SAM
PRESENT DAY

I caught up to Claire just as she reached the car, grabbing her by the shoulder and spinning her around to face me. She lifted a hand and swiped at me. I ducked just in time.

"Jesus, Sam, what the hell are you doing? I thought someone was attacking me."

"Sorry ... but there's no time; we have to go! Look!" I panted as I waved the leaflet under her nose. Her brow creased as she glared at me. She snatched the leaflet from me and held it still, studying it while her face creased even further.

"You want to visit an ancient castle?" She shook her head, rolling her eyes and curling her lip. "Once again, Sam, you've lost me."

She sounded outdone with me, but I was wired with adrenaline. I grabbed the bags from her and launched them onto the back seat.

"Get in. I'll drive." I was already reaching for the handle to the driver's door. "I'll explain on the way."

She was still clutching the leaflet for Tintagel when I

finished my explanation. I noticed with a flicker of annoyance that her face hadn't altered.

"Sam, there's more than one castle in Cornwall." Her voice was gentle, but she looked at me as if I'd completely lost it. "No doubt it narrows things down if you're sure about this, but we still can't be certain this is the one. Or how close she would be even if it is."

I plucked the leaflet from her hand, waving it in front of her.

"This is the one, Claire. I *know* it." My voice was raised in frustration and desperation to be right.

"The photo she had of her as a child was in front of this exact castle, Claire. It's almost exactly the same photo as this one. She told me they walked past that castle all the time whenever they stayed at the cottage. She was a six-year-old girl. All she dreamed of back then was being a princess. But her mother would never take her in, told her the likes of her could never be a princess; she wouldn't waste her money on such nonsense. If they walked by, Claire, the cottage has to be close to the castle."

That part of the story had slipped from my exhausted mind until the leaflet photo brought it crashing back. My adrenalin pumped as I repeated what I'd already told her. She widened her eyes and drew in a deep breath.

"Well, it's the best that we've to go on at the moment." She shrugged. "We'll do whatever we can."

Claire dozed in the passenger seat as I drove the rest of the way, wishing the road stretching out ahead would melt away faster. Some instinct told me I was getting closer to my baby with every mile that passed. I prayed I was right and not just losing my mind completely.

WE'D SPENT the entire day working through crowds, endlessly showing the photograph of Lindy along with one of Cora, which Claire had crudely cropped in place of Tessa. We were met only with shaking heads and odd looks from strangers as they walked by. I guessed it wasn't the norm for a couple to be out searching for a woman and a child. I wondered if anyone would tell us even if they had seen them.

I gazed over to Claire still brandishing her phone in anyone's face she could get close enough to. People were avoiding her, giving her a wide berth. My heart ached at what she was doing for me.

She looked as defeated as I felt.

I crossed the street and placed my hand on her shoulder. "I think we've done enough for one day." I sighed. "Let's go and find somewhere to get some rest."

Her face fell.

"I'm okay to carry on for a while longer, if it's what you want?" she offered, her voice full of compassion. But her eyes gave away her fatigue.

"No. We both need to recharge," I insisted, offering a weak smile.

WE FOUND a bed and breakfast and paid the extra for an evening meal.

We barely uttered a word whilst we ate, the combination of tiredness and raw disappointment rendering us both speechless. I'd known it was a long shot but still hoped that, by some miracle, I'd just know where to find her.

I felt foolish for believing that instinct, rather than desperation, had led me there. We drifted up to our rooms and paused to say goodnight outside of Claire's. A feeling of *déjà vu* set in.

"I think we both know we're wasting our time here," I conceded, rubbing my eyes with the heels of my hands. "Let's get some rest tonight and head home tomorrow. I'll pass it on to the police to deal with." I could hear the weariness in my own voice.

Claire chewed her lip before meeting my eye.

"No, not just yet." She shook her head. "We're both tired and deflated, but we've only tried for one day. She wasn't likely to fall into our laps in the first hour, was she? Let's get some rest and regroup in the morning. Maybe we start knocking on doors or something. A local might have information if we mention the family." She paused and watched my face cloud with doubt, strength too sapped tonight to be optimistic.

"Sam, you brought us here for a reason. Some part of you knows something. If she's here, we'll find her." She kissed my cheek before stepping into her room and closing the door softly behind her.

I wished I shared her confidence.

I SUFFERED another night of broken sleep, keeping the television on for company. I couldn't bear the silence reminding me of my family's absence.

The tap on my door at six thirty caught me by surprise. I opened it a crack and took in Claire's face before letting it swing open.

"You're not dressed?" she asked dumbly.

"Well observed," I replied dryly as I dropped back onto the bed.

"Well, move it," she instructed, gesturing towards the bathroom. "Breakfast starts at seven; then we make a start. We can catch people on the way to work."

I huffed and covered my face with my hands. "There isn't any point, Claire. She could be anywhere." I sulked, filled with self-pity.

"So that's it? You're just going to give up, laze around here feeling sorry for yourself?" She spat the words at me. "The point is, your daughter is out there, and we need to do everything we physically can to find her and bring her home. Not just give up on her because we had one hard day." Her voice shook with frustration.

"And what if I'm wrong and she isn't even close, Claire? Then what?" I matched her tone.

"Then we look somewhere else until we don't have anywhere left to look! I will not just give up on her. Family don't just walk away. She needs us."

We both fell silent as the meaning of her words hung between us.

I stood, keeping my eyes fixed on her for a few seconds. Her cheeks were aflame.

"Give me ten minutes to get showered," I muttered as I moved towards the bathroom, consumed by shame.

WE'D BEEN at it most of the day, Claire knocking on every door she could find while I continued the previous day's futile approach.

I was pretty sure my blisters were developing blisters as I hobbled towards Claire. "I'm going to run over to the supermarket and grab some plasters." I gestured towards my feet. "Shall I grab us some drinks and lunch?"

She sighed, all of her morning's enthusiasm having evaporated.

"Yeah, that'd be great. I'll grab that bench." She pointed across to a vacant seat, and we separated.

I limped my way inside and began to collect what I needed. Sandwiches and drinks wedged under my arm, I moved along the bottom of each aisle, trying to locate the plasters. As I peered around the shelves of the next lane, I froze, unable to move or breathe. I stared, transfixed, blinking to clear my sleep-deprived mind – certain I had to be hallucinating.

When she didn't disappear, I dropped the sandwiches onto the nearest shelf and reached for my phone, heart hammering.

I glanced down at the screen as quickly as I could, not wanting to take my eyes off her. Claire answered on the second ring.

"I don't mind what you get for me. I'll eat anything."

"Claire," I hissed into the phone, blood pounding in my ears. "Claire, get the car now. She's in the fucking supermarket!" I hoped she could understand my breathless attempt at speaking.

"Who?" she replied dumbly before gasping out loud. I heard shuffling as she began to move.

"What do you need the car for?" She sounded almost hysterical. "Just get over to her and keep her there. I'll call the police!"

"No, Claire. Please just get the car like I asked," I begged her. "She doesn't have Cora with her."

"Oh." I could feel her defeat through the phone. "I still don't get why you want the car, though? If she doesn't have Cora, why can't you just confront her?" she questioned.

I couldn't tear my eyes away from what she held in her hand.

"She's buying nappies," I breathed.

64

LINDY

ONE WEEK PREVIOUS

I was a ball of nervous energy, unable to keep still. I fired off a text to Tessa, reminding her of her promise. When I received one back, confirming her plan for a nice early night, I felt reassured. I'd made a promise to myself that I wouldn't set off until nine, but I kept checking the clock, wondering if it would hurt to go a little sooner. I'd had Cora's bag packed and ready for hours. I checked through the items, as I'd done a dozen times already, confirming that I had everything I might need. Eventually, the clock dragged its hand to eight fifty, and I made a grab for my keys – I'd waited long enough.

The journey passed in a blur. I drove non-stop, not daring to take any breaks at the risk of being seen. Eventually, I pulled up a street over from the house. I reached for their keys and stepped out of the car into the darkness, stretching my aching limbs.

I slipped through the garden of my own house and let myself in through the back, reminding myself not to touch the lights. I sat for around an hour, observing their house, until I was certain that no one was up. There was always the risk that Cora would wake, of course, but with Tessa on the pills and Sam sleeping as he did, I had to trust that it would work.

I let myself out of the front door and took purposeful strides across the street, making as little noise as I could manage, and slinked through the side gate and into their garden.

I padded up to the back door, clutching the key, and slid it into the lock. I sent up a silent prayer of thanks that I'd thought ahead. On my final visit, I'd been sure to warn Tessa about houses in the area being broken into, thieves breaking windows to get to keys left in doors.

I couldn't be certain she would listen, but it was worth trying. Otherwise, I would've just had to risk the front door.

I stepped inside the kitchen and pushed the door closed behind me, focusing on keeping my breathing steady. As I turned back to the room, my stomach plummeted. My jaw dropped, and I stopped breathing.

Sam.

He was standing directly across the kitchen, staring straight at me.

I gasped, mind racing, trying to think of a plausible explanation for being there – uncertain how he would react to me appearing in his kitchen in the middle of the night.

"Sam." My voice was barely a whisper, breathless with nerves.

"No, you don't." His voice was loud and echoed around the kitchen, bouncing off the tiled walls.

I froze, keeping my voice steady, knowing that there must be a way through this for us both. I reminded myself that it was me he really wanted; this was *our* plan.

"Sam, I know ..."

"I won't let you." He sneered, and it dawned on me. He was sleeping, having one of his dreams. He had no idea I was there.

I let out my breath and steadied myself, gripping on the edge of the work surface.

I sucked back a few long, ragged breaths before my heart slowed. A grin spread across my face. With Tessa having taken the sleeping tablets, and Sam not even in the room, this would be easier than I'd dared to hope. Keeping my eyes on Sam, I crossed the room in long strides while he argued with an invisible tormentor. Having witnessed my share of Sam's nightmares and heard the things he'd unwittingly admitted to during them, I had a fair idea what he was seeing behind those black eyes.

I moved swiftly through the house, unable to resist a quick stop-off into the living room to take care of that wedding photo I so despised. I knew it was a risk, that I needed to be on the road as quickly as possible, but the slow tearing of that thick paper – it was the satisfaction I needed. I crept up the stairs and along the hall until I was standing outside the master bedroom, the layout a mirror image of my own house across the street. I paused, listening for any signs of movement. Hearing nothing, I eased the door open, wincing at the whooshing noise it made as it ran over the carpet.

I paused again, but still there was no sound.

I allowed my eyes to adjust to the blackness of the room. Slowly, shapes came in to focus. Cora's crib and Tessa's sleeping form in their bed. I felt a surge of hatred towards her and wished I could be there to witness her anguish when she discovered Cora was gone.

Consoling my hatred with thoughts of my daughter, I crept towards her crib, leaning in to scoop her up. I slid my arms underneath her as gently as I could manage, moving as quickly as I dared, unable to breathe.

As I lifted her, she let out a little squawk, and I froze again, cradling her close, praying she wouldn't wake.

The room fell silent once again, and I began to move away – my daughter safely against my chest – when a rustling sound stopped me in my tracks.

"What the hell are you doing?"

―――――――

I THUNDERED down the stairs and out into the crisp night air, no sign of Sam as I raced through the kitchen. Cora was stirring in my arms. I needed to get her to the car before she properly woke.

All thoughts of discretion forgotten, I raced to the car, fumbling with the key fob and wrenching the back door open. I placed Cora carefully in the basket that I had wedged in the foot well behind the driver's seat and slammed the door as her whimpering kicked up a notch.

I couldn't allow myself to overthink what had just happened, needing to keep my cool, focus on what still needed to be done. I would find a way past it. I had dealt with situations like this before. No one would be looking for me; there was nothing to link me to any of it. But perhaps an anonymous tip-off to the police to make sure they were aware of Sam's little problem wouldn't hurt. It would buy me time, provide extra insurance – they wouldn't come looking my way so long as they were busy focusing on his every move. Sam would talk his way out of it, anyway.

I pulled away, confident in my decision, and drove a few miles to a secluded spot among abandoned warehouses. Cora's wails were growing in volume as the darkness swallowed the car. Her squeals were piercing by the time I killed the engine and moved into the back seat to get to her.

I opened the bottle of premixed milk with trembling fingers and offered it to her. She squirmed in my arms, thrusting her head from one side to the other, refusing to take it. I gave up trying after a few minutes, flustered and sweating, with her only seeming to become angrier, her little face turning red in the dull light of the streetlamp.

I changed her into the blue all-in-one suit that I'd bought, deciding that the nappy could wait. She struggled and kicked so that I had to force her legs in. If I was pulled over, I needed them to believe I was with my son – they wouldn't be looking for a boy.

Eventually, with her changed, I retrieved the seat from the boot of the car and slotted it onto the base I'd installed earlier. I offered the bottle to the screaming infant once again. To my relief, she guzzled down the liquid this time. I caught sight of the diamond ring and wedding band that finally sat where they belonged. They were a little loose, but that could easily be fixed. I closed my eyes, sucking in air and resting my head back against the seat.

My mind slipped back to the events in the bedroom, Tessa's doubtful looks in the dim light as I tried to explain why I was there. I knew she didn't believe me when I told her that Sam had called, asking me to come over and help, her coolly reminding me that I was supposed to be on the other side of the world – and had never met her husband. I forced a laugh and reeled off a story about there being a mix-up, how I had been forced to return for a short period.

Her eyes had bored into mine, not believing a single word.

Why couldn't she have just taken the fucking pills?

I remembered the coldness in her voice as she spoke the words.

"Put my baby down."

Something had snapped in that moment, hearing her refer to Cora as *her* baby. Realising she hadn't stuck to her part in my plans. She had *everything* and expected me to be happy with nothing. She couldn't even get that right. Fury burned.

"No," I'd snarled back.

She glanced at the empty space in the bed beside her. Then her eyes travelled to the door behind me. She spoke quietly. "Why don't you just put Cora down? We can talk about everything. I've worked it all out. I know what's going on. I know who you are ... Lindy."

Something bubbled up within me. I threw back my head and let out a hyena-like laugh.

"Sam!" She yelled his name so loud it startled me.

Blinded by rage, I dropped Cora onto the end of the bed and lunged at Tessa. She had to shut up. Who was she to call me by that name? That wasn't who I was. Lindy had died along with the others.

It wasn't the first time that red mist had descended on me, but I was no better equipped to control it. I hadn't even considered how it was that she knew.

I straddled her, pushing her backwards, and heard the thud as her head made contact with the side of Cora's crib.

Weak from sleep and dazed by the blow to the head, she fell backwards onto her pillow, eyes rolling back in her head. Still burning with the rage that had been mounting for months, I grabbed the pillow from Sam's side of the bed. I let out a shriek of fury as I pushed it down onto her face, catching sight of the fear that flashed in her eyes as it closed in.

I pushed down onto it with all of my might, using my body weight to hold her down as she thrashed around, attempting to shout from underneath it. Her fight just seemed to fuel my anger, and I bore down harder, forcing the pillow downwards calmly until, eventually, she went limp.

I was roused from my trance only by the small sound of Cora's whimpering.

65

SAM

PRESENT DAY

I slid along the ends of the aisles, unable to tear my eyes away from her, terrified that if I did, I might lose her forever. She moved quickly around the store, scooping things into her basket without much thought.

Once she had marched for the checkout and was scanning her items, I slipped out the sliding doors, ensuring that I kept out of her line of sight.

I spotted Claire's car parked close by. She was peering over the top of the steering wheel and raised her head when she saw me.

I slid into the passenger side. Claire and I exchanged a glance, eyes a reflection of each other's emotions. Fear, apprehension, hope, and desperation hung in the silence, neither of us sure of what to say. My breathing was heavy as the weight of the moment bore down on us.

"I can't be certain she's even in a car – but we need to be ready to follow if she is," I explained unnecessarily – anything to fill the tense silence.

Claire nodded and swallowed hard. "How do you intend to play it?" she questioned.

"I really don't know yet," I admitted, suddenly aware that I had never actually believed we might find her.

She appeared a few minutes later – a shopping bag in each hand – and made off on foot towards the footpath.

I turned to Claire, who was pale, her face drawn. "Looks like we're walking." I paused. "Move the car back. I'll follow her and call you with where we are." I didn't want to admit that I'd rather go it alone – or why.

Claire studied me.

"Then you can bring the car to us. We might need it," I pushed.

She regarded me again before giving a single nod. I made to get out, but she placed a hand on my arm.

"Sam, please be careful. Don't forget who it is you're dealing with here," she warned, eyes brimming with fear.

———

I FOLLOWED FROM A SAFE DISTANCE, struggling to match her quick pace with the blisters throbbing on the backs of my heels.

Eventually, she turned into a secluded driveway that could've been mistaken for a small lane. I held back before going after her.

I padded along to the end, and a small, run-down cottage came into sight. It was strange to see in the flesh the very place she'd spoken of.

I reached for my phone to make the call to Claire and give her the directions. The tiny cross in the corner of the screen informed me that I had no signal. I cursed under my breath. I had to let her know I was okay before she had the entire area swarming with police.

I retraced my steps to the road and along it for a few minutes, continuously checking for signal and hobbling, the blisters making me wince with every step. Finally, the signal bar flashed, and two small bars appeared. I sagged with relief.

I placed the call, explaining as quickly and in as much detail as I could where we were and how to get there. She promised to hold off calling the police until she had my say-so. We agreed she would drive to the lane, coming down the driveway on foot so as not to alert Lindy to her presence.

I jogged as quickly as I could manage back to the cottage.

I froze as I rounded the corner and spotted Lindy coming out of the door, a bundle in her arms.

Cora.

I held my breath as she darted off along the path in the opposite direction, weak with relief that she hadn't glanced my way – there was nowhere I could've hidden. I realised it was a small coastal path running away from the cottage. I wanted desperately to charge after her and snatch my baby, but I couldn't move fast enough to catch her before she saw me, and I didn't want her running off. I wouldn't stand a chance.

Adrenalin pumped through me. I followed behind for a few minutes until she came to a stop. She shuffled towards the cliff edge in a small cut-out area that looked directly down onto the beach below. My heart was in my mouth as I moved closer. She was clutching Cora to her chest. The wind from the sea made it impossible for me to tell if she was making any noise.

Unable to wait any longer to see my baby's face, to know for the first time in days that felt like years if she was safe, I approached Lindy slowly from behind.

"Lindy?" I called softly, not wanting to startle her.

She didn't react. My voice carried off on the wind.

I tried again, a fraction louder. "Lindy?"

This time she whipped around to face me, eyes wild.

"Sam? No, Sam, it's me. It's Bella." She stared at me as if I were an illusion before her face broke into a wide smile. I was taken aback, having been so uncertain as to what her reaction would be. No part of me had been prepared for any of that.

"Sam! You *found* us. Oh, I just knew you would! We did it, Sam!"

Her use of the word "us" made every hair on my body stand on end. I glanced down at the bundle that she was holding and back at her face. She followed my gaze.

"Can I see her? I need to see her, Lindy. I need to know that she's okay." I spoke slowly, with a calmness I didn't feel.

She gazed down at the bundle in her arms again before clutching it tighter to her.

"It's Bella." She glowered through gritted teeth, her voice almost a growl. "And why would she not be okay?" she challenged, eyes hardening. "I'm her mother, Sam. Why would you ask me that?"

My breathing sped up. I struggled not to recoil at her words, the shock reverberating around my head. I swallowed hard, panicked that I was losing control of the situation, out of my depth now I could see the extent of her delusions.

"Of course she is." I forced a smile. "I'm just desperate to see her. I've missed her terribly."

She eyed me for a few seconds as she teetered on the edge of the clifftop.

"And me? Have you not missed *me*?" she challenged, her features hardening.

I couldn't stop the look of horror from registering in my eyes. I blinked it away, but it was too late. She'd seen it.

Her face twisted into an ugly snarl. I'd lost her.

"You couldn't give a shit about me, could you?" She screamed the accusation. "You never treated me any better than my mother did. Here I was, thinking we finally had the family that we deserved – and all this time you were stringing me along again, weren't you?"

I held up my hands in surrender.

"Of course I care about you," I lied, trying to block out the sound of the blood pounding in my ears. "It's just all been a bit of a shock, that's all."

She eyed me again. "Do you love me, Paul?"

Paul. She'd called me Paul. My stomach lurched as the reality of how unhinged she had become hit me. She lifted one hand to push back her hair from her face; the light glinted off Tessa's engagement ring.

I hesitated, distracted by the sight of my wife's ring on her finger, panicking about just what I was dealing with. I faced an internal battle. "Of course," I mumbled quietly, glancing down at Cora again, wishing I could see her face.

She threw back her head and laughed. "Oh, you always were *such* a terrible liar, Sam. The things I know. I could tear you apart. Even after all of this, it's still all about *her,* isn't it? That pathetic excuse of a woman. Cora's better off without her and you know it." Her lip curled into a snarl, and I lost all composure.

"Her name was Tessa! She was a beautiful woman and a wonderful mother. A million times the woman you could ever hope to be. Now give me my daughter."

The words had spilled out before I could stop them. Her eyes narrowed before a sickening grin spread across her lips.

"You've hurt me one too many times, Paul," she hissed. "Now it's your turn to understand what pain and loss *really* feels like."

In one swift movement, she turned and released her arms, flinging Cora over the edge of the clifftop.

My whole world slowed. A primal roar came from within as I lunged towards her and snatched blindly for the material. My fingers grasped at thin air, a second too late.

I met her eyes as a look of pure satisfaction filled them. A blind rage came down over me like I'd only ever felt once before. A red mist. I couldn't think straight for the loathing and grief that overcame me. I stared into her face and screamed as I lunged towards her, shoving her backwards with every bit of my strength, liberating myself from her shackles once and for all.

Time stood still as her face went slack with shock. She wobbled as she tried and failed to regain her balance. I stared deep into her eyes as I watched hers fill with fear, and then she was gone.

I didn't move for a few seconds, rooted to the spot, overcome with shock and grief.

Only when I heard shouts from behind me did I scramble towards the edge, peering down at her twisted form on the sand below.

66

TESSA
ONE WEEK PREVIOUS

I gripped the bottle of tablets in my hand, staring at the unfathomable list of ingredients. My face still burned when I thought of the phone conversation with Bella, having promised her I'd take them that night. Something had been niggling at me for a while. Ever since the awful incident with the photograph, I guessed. I just couldn't make it add up in my mind. I couldn't believe Bella could possibly be camera shy. She was striking with her beauty and radiated a confidence most women could only dream of. It didn't fit.

I wondered again if she'd suffered some form of abuse from a partner she was now hiding from. Was that why she'd moved here, been so reluctant to allow anyone close? Why she'd had to run to Australia? If that was even where she'd really gone. But she could have confided in me, as I had her. If she'd just asked me not to share the photograph, I never would have.

Curiosity got the better of me, and I reached for my phone, opening up a search engine. I tapped in a search for local pharmaceutical companies, unsure if Bella had ever actually mentioned the specific company she worked for.

A few came up, none that rang any bells or listed an obvious local address. I twisted my mouth in frustration. I dropped Bella's name into the search bar, hoping she might pop up. Nothing did. I glanced down at Cora sleeping on my chest. She was huffing out gentle snores. The corners of my mouth lifted at the sound as I contemplated what to try next.

I clicked on the link for the first company on the search. They had a few of the management listed, but Bella's name didn't appear.

I went back and clicked on the second link. This time, the site had photos of all of their employees, listed in order of rank. I flicked through the first few, stopping with a gasp when I came to a photograph of a woman.

The resemblance to Bella had me squinting at the screen. The woman's hair was lighter, a mousy brown, and her eyes were dark, not the piercing blue of Bella's. She wore no makeup, and her skin was pale, nothing like the radiant glow Bella possessed. But her face shape was striking, the confidence unmistakable, present even from within the photo. She held the same air that Bella did as well as the exact killer cheekbones.

The woman in the photograph was named as Lindy. Lindy Draper. I studied the picture until it started to blur before my eyes.

Sam's key in the lock caused me to start, closing the website and flinging my phone away as if it had burned me. I shoved the bottle of pills between the sofa cushions. Guilt gnawed – I'd been snooping on my friend. I wouldn't breathe a word to anyone. If Bella was hiding, perhaps from a previous abuser, I certainly wouldn't be the one to give her away. She deserved her privacy. The last thing I wanted to do was put anyone at risk.

SAM and I finished up our evening meal, and I watched on as he bounced Cora, who beamed at him in delight. I finished the washing-up and dried off my hands, smiling at the sight of the pair of them. Sam was a good man. He adored Cora and always put her first. I was so lucky to have a man like him rather than the deadbeat fathers I'd heard so many women complaining about. My love for him entwined me as the memories of our life together danced through my mind. Sam was everything to me. He'd been there when no one else was, supported me through my darkest times. I couldn't ever imagine my life without him.

He looked up at me and tilted his head, concern now clouding his smile.

"Is everything alright, Tess?"

I blinked him back into focus. "Hmm?"

"You seem ... distant. Is something bothering you?"

I shook my head and attempted a weak smile. "No, I'm fine. Just tired."

He studied my face, unconvinced.

"I'm sorry, Sam, it's not you. I'm concerned about a friend. I think she may have been in some sort of trouble, maybe been abused by an ex-partner. I think she's still running from him. I'm worried about her, hoping she can be safe and free now."

I expected to see relief flood his features.

"A *friend*?" His eyes narrowed and darkened, creases appearing all over his face as he scowled.

"Yes ..." I frowned, unnerved by his response. Why did he look suddenly angry? "It must've been awful for her. I can't imagine being on the run like that. It just got to me."

Sam continued to study me, an unreadable expression on his face.

"Maybe you should sleep in our room tonight," I offered with a confidence I didn't feel. Apprehension snaked its way through my body. Something had caused me to feel a horrid sense of anxiety, and although I couldn't put my finger on why, I couldn't face the idea of sleeping alone.

Sam arched an eyebrow. "I thought you were afraid. What's changed?"

I sighed and rubbed my temples, desperate to clear the air. We were both tired, and I had no idea why he seemed to be pitching for a fight. "I don't know. We can't carry on like this forever though, can we? Maybe things have changed. I haven't heard you up in the night recently."

This was true. Things *had* been moving around in the house without explanation, though, and Sam swore blind it wasn't him. He'd even accused me and my exhausted state a few times before laughing that someone must be sneaking into our house.

I'd been expecting him to be pleased, to be desperate to return to our bed. As he eyed me, I couldn't make sense of his reaction. I'd never thought of him questioning me, having to justify myself.

67

SAM

PRESENT DAY

I stared at the blank wall, shifting in the hard plastic chair as I tried unsuccessfully to regain the feeling in my numb legs. My back throbbed, and my head still pounded as I thought back on the events of the previous few days.

As I'd stared over the edge of that clifftop, the thing that caught my eye hadn't been the body sprawled out on the sand – it'd been the bundle that Lindy had dropped seconds before. It'd caught in the brambles of the bushes below, the fabric billowing in the wind, but there was no sign of Cora.

I'd frantically scanned the ledges of the cliffs but couldn't locate her tiny form anywhere.

Claire had appeared beside me to stare down onto the sand below, a gasp escaping her. She'd dialled 999, breathlessly explaining and begging for help.

We'd made our way back to the cottage to wait for them, Claire having to physically drag me away screaming from my final search for Cora. As we got closer to the dwelling, the tiniest sound had caused us both to stop short. A baby's cry.

I'd forgotten all of the pain in that moment and smashed into that cottage as if my own life depended on it.

There, wrapped in blankets, in a basket on the floor, was Cora. Sleepy and dazed, but undoubtedly alive. I sobbed, cradling her to me, rocking her against my chest.

Claire had hung back, hovering in the doorway, tears streaming down her own face, until I gestured for her to join us. She ran over, throwing her arms around us both, and we sobbed together until the police arrived. They took us straight off in an ambulance, checking Cora from head to toe. She was a little dehydrated and had on a very soiled nappy that was a couple of sizes too big, but otherwise seemed unharmed.

I had assumed that Lindy was carrying Cora when I'd seen her clutching her coat in a bundle to her chest. I was still uncertain as to whether she had known I was following her and wanted to fool me, or whether she'd just played along with my assumption. She certainly wouldn't have wanted me to know Cora was safe in the cottage before she could get to her.

I stayed up all night watching Cora's tiny chest rise and fall, there to comfort her when she stirred. The shock was still cushioning us from reality, but I knew my grief for my beautiful wife was hot on my heels now, making its way to the surface as the adrenalin of the past days finally diminished.

Detective Garcia tapped the door, entering Cora's small hospital room and smiling down at her.

"Could we have a quick word?" He gestured to the hallway.

"How's she doing?" He nodded towards Cora's room. Claire appeared in the hallway, clutching two paper cups of steaming liquid.

"The drugs Lindy gave her are almost out of her system. They say they won't cause any lasting damage, as it was only sedatives." I glanced at my sleeping child, and my face glowed. "They hope she can come home tomorrow."

He nodded again, returning my smile before his face turned harder.

"I just wanted to fill you in on everything that we have ... before the press get hold of anything." He spoke solemnly. "The body of a man was found a short while back, washed up a few beaches over from the one where Lindy fell. At the time he wasn't identified. His DNA wasn't in the system, and he'd been in the water too long to be recognisable. Also, erm ..." He paused, lowering his voice further. "His teeth had been removed. We're now pretty certain it's her partner, Paul. He had a significant head wound ... it'd been inflicted before he was put into the water and was his cause of death." He paused again, taking a breath. "We're working on the case of her parents' murders. We have nothing directly to link her to them yet, but we aren't giving up."

I blew out a breath and nodded.

"As you know, we believe Lindy was struggling to cope with taking care of Cora. With her mental state and Cora being so distressed, we think things went downhill for her very quickly, hence Cora ending up drugged and underfed." He gestured to her through the window. "We know she was leaving her in the cottage, going out without her ... we guess to manage her temper."

I gulped, glancing at my baby and thinking of what could've been if I hadn't gotten there when I did.

"We'll have to take official statements from you both over the next few days, but I was hoping to confirm some details in the meantime. You say you saw her jump. Is that correct, Claire?"

I turned to look at Claire, who wouldn't meet my eye.

"Yes, that's right." She nodded, keeping her face expressionless. "Just after she'd flung the coat over." She shrugged. "Then she just ... jumped."

I thought I saw a flicker of doubt cross his features but dismissed it. It no longer mattered. As he questioned Claire a little further, I wondered if I'd ever be able to be up front with her about my past. Cora and I were set to move in with her for a while, and I was going to put our house on the market. I knew she'd be expecting me to start therapy, but I also knew that still wasn't possible.

I wished I could share with them the fact that Lindy had often talked of burning her parents' house down with them inside, along with the many other threats, but that would have led to questions about why I'd never mentioned anything before.

You see, the thing is, Lindy knew. She knew what I'd done, thanks to my sleep talking. We held each other's secrets in a silent pact.

ALL THOSE YEARS AGO, I'd been in the car with my father. He'd informed me so casually of his plans to leave my mother – to leave us all. I begged that he take me along, and he laughed, actually laughed in my face. I didn't fit with the plans he had for him and his mistress. That red mist had descended on me. Still only a child, I'd lashed out, punching and slapping at him as he drove. He'd tried to fight me off, to hold me back, but my anger had overtaken everything. I'd grabbed the wheel, yanking on it and causing the car to crash.

I've never forgotten the feeling – when the car broke through the barriers at the side of the road, colliding with that tree. It felt like I was watching it happen to someone else, like a scene from a film, slowed down, preparing you for the impact. I'd had so much time to think. The noise had been deafening, screeching tyres giving way to shattering glass and crunching metal, like a tin can being crushed underfoot. I'd thought I'd felt raindrops hitting the bare flesh on my face and neck. I only realised afterwards that it was, in fact, shards of glass and debris. I remembered everything going quiet then, eerily so. Just the slightest ticking of the cooling engine letting me know I was still alive, along with the pounding ache that engulfed my entire body.

But what stuck with me more than anything was the smell. Rubber mingled with blood and heat. It seemed to cling to the inside of my nostrils for weeks, all I could breathe and taste. I'd still smell that sickening scent every time I thought about it.

My father had been killed instantly. *I* had killed him. That had been that beginning of the parasomnias, my punishment for murdering my father. I never spoke of the events of that day to anyone, ever. Everyone assumed he'd swerved to avoid something, that my issues were due to what I'd witnessed, as a victim of the accident myself, of course.

My mother never mentioned his plans to leave us, and to this day I was still none the wiser whether she actually knew. I wondered if she knew what *I* did, and that was why she left us too.

The realisation had hit me after I had pushed Lindy – I had never felt remorse for what I had done to my father. I could have told Claire the truth. After all, I had only been a child. I was certain no one would blame me. But my fear was that she would know, she would be able to sense that I didn't regret my actions, just as I didn't regret watching Lindy fall backwards over the edge of the cliff.

I blinked, remembering where I was, at the sound of my name being called. My fingers caressed the scars on my face – a permanent reminder of what I'd done.

I'd been so relieved to discover the truth of Lindy's

actions. That she'd become so delusional, she truly believed she *was* Bella, and that Lindy had never existed. My own secret dark delusions ran through me like poison, festering under the surface.

I'd been so afraid of what I might have done. Shortly after the hypnotherapy, I did remember the nightmare I'd been seized by that night. I remembered the faces of Claire, Tessa, my mother and father, and Lindy, all merging into one, jeering, laughing at the fact they would all leave me. My feelings and my nightmares seemed to be slipping into one another. Desperation clawed at me constantly, during both sleep and waking. Whatever it took, I needed to make them stay ...

"Sam?" I focused on Claire, her eyes full of concern as she studied me.

"Sorry." I shook my head and focused my attention back on Garcia. "What was that?"

"There was just one more thing that we thought you should know," he repeated, looking incredibly uncomfortable.

I lifted my eyebrows, waiting to hear what he had to say.

As he spoke, I felt a pressure building, as though I were too deep under water. I caught only parts of what he was telling us as the earth shifted underneath me.

"Alive ... off the beach ... on life support ... stable ... expected she'll make it ..."

I turned to look at Claire, whose face had drained of colour. My head spun, and I wondered if I might pass out.

Claire swallowed hard before she spoke. "Lindy? She's alive?" she whispered.

Garcia, wearing a grim expression, slowly nodded.

EPILOGUE

ONE WEEK PREVIOUS

I awoke to the sound of the whooshing noise our bedroom door made as it moved against the carpet. I froze, not sure if I was more afraid of Sam coming or going. The coolness he'd addressed me with earlier that evening had never really subsided, and we had gone to bed with an icy atmosphere between us, unexplained. From the tension in my shoulders, I was clearly no more relaxed than I would have been sleeping alone. Why had I let him back into our room? I'd put our daughter at risk. I'd ask him – no, I'd tell him – he had to move back until we found a better solution.

The footsteps padding across our bedroom were unfamiliar, too light to be those of my husband. I blinked, frozen with fear, and squinted into the darkness. The possibility was inconceivable, that yet another stranger could have appeared during the night.

I watched as a slim figure crept towards our bed, pausing at the bottom before moving around towards Cora's crib. I stifled a gasp.

It had to be a dream. She'd been on my mind, concern

and doubts about her twisting through my thoughts. I blinked hard and tried to focus. She moved almost silently as she reached Cora's crib beside me, leaning in close and slipping her arms so gently underneath my baby. I'd sat bolt upright, staring straight into her face. She flinched at my sudden movement. I could barely make her out in the darkness, but I was almost certain I saw her skin pale. Something about her eyes looked different, but there was no mistaking her now.

"Bella? What are you doing? Why are you here?"

I'd never seen her look so flustered, her usual perfectly calm demeanour shot, as he eyes darted between me and the bedroom door.

"Oh, Tessa? Well, it's a bit of a strange story, really. Sam called me and ..."

"Why aren't you in Australia?"

Her skittish behaviour set me more on edge. I glanced down at Cora, who remained asleep, cradled in her arms.

"There was a mix-up." She barked a laugh, but it sounded odd. "I had to come back for a while."

"And since when were you able to get home from the other side of the world in a few short hours? We were only messaging this afternoon."

She said nothing. Her eyes flew around the room like those of a wild animal, and I could hear her rapid breathing.

"And why would my husband call a woman he's never met? A woman who's meant to be in Australia?"

A jolt of fear shot through me when I realised that Sam was not next to me in our bed. What the hell was going on?

Something had snapped then, confusion turning to fear and defence.

The sound of my own cold, hard voice convinced me that I was absolutely not dreaming.

"Put my baby down."

Her eyes turned hard. A coldness swept over my body, the blackness of her eyes so like Sam's when he became the stranger.

"No." The coldness of her voice chilled me. Did she suffer the same condition as Sam? Her behaviour was almost identical.

I'd never felt such fear, seeing her so unhinged, with my baby clutched to her body.

I sucked in a breath.

"Why don't you just put Cora down? We can talk about everything. I've worked it all out. I know what's going on. I know who you are ... Lindy." I spoke softly, attempting to give over an air of sympathy and conceal my growing fear.

My skin prickled, and terror gripped every part of my body as her eyes blazed. She threw back her head and let out a screeching cackle. This was not the Bella I knew.

"SAM." I'd screamed his name. I had no idea where my husband was, but getting Cora away from the stranger in our room was my only thought.

She flinched, and I remembered what I'd found out earlier that day, her abusive past. Then I softened. It was my closest friend who stood before me. There had to be an explanation. There always was with Sam.

I froze up as she moved so swiftly, barely registering what was happening. I briefly wondered if she was possessed. She released Cora onto the end of the bed, and just as I made to reach for her, thinking Bella had come to her senses, she lunged at me. She was on me before I'd realised what was happening, her hands gripping my neck. My head collided with the side of Cora's crib as she shoved me backwards. It made a sickening noise, and the room seemed to lurch underneath me.

As I struggled to maintain consciousness, my head flopped back onto my pillow.

Bella was on top of me now, her eyes so dark, her face a picture of calm. I no longer recognised her at all. She threw her body towards Sam's side of the bed, and for a second, relief flooded me. I thought she was going to run.

The full weight of her winded me as she lunged back on top of me, pinning me against the mattress. I didn't even see the pillow coming until it covered my face. My lungs and every muscle burned, screaming for air.

I fought as hard as I could, still dazed from the blow to my head, but it only served to use up more of my depleting oxygen. My thoughts came faster and slower all at the same time as the pillow crushed harder onto my windpipe. I thought I heard the sounds of Cora whimpering just before the blackness closed in, and I prayed Sam would help her. But I couldn't be sure the sounds were real.

I HAD no recollection of whether it was seconds, minutes, or hours that passed as the pillow deprived me of air. I broke in and out of consciousness, trying to decipher where I was, suddenly assaulted by the memory of Bella in my room, Sam not in our bed, and Cora.

Oh god, Cora!

The pillow still covered my face, but the pressure seemed to have been released. I felt the weight of someone shift on the mattress beside me and prayed I'd see Sam lowering himself back into bed, Cora safely nestled in his cradling arms, the whole thing having been a terrible dream. It gave me a whole new appreciation for what Sam went through.

My ring finger throbbed. I touched my thumb to it and realised my rings had been removed. I scrambled to push off the pillow, attempting to lift my throbbing head.

But as I pulled myself up and saw who was sitting next to me on the bed, I realised that this wasn't a nightmare at all. This was very, very real. My body turned cold.

Just before the pillow was forced down onto my face again, a pair of dark eyes met mine in the darkness.

THANK YOU FOR READING

Did you enjoy reading *The Sleepwalker*? Please consider leaving a review on Amazon. Your review will help other readers to discover the novel.

ABOUT THE AUTHOR

After spending her working life searching unsuccessfully for a fulfilling career, Laura George found her passion for writing psychological thrillers whilst on maternity leave with her first child. She took a leap of faith and didn't return to work, instead running with her dream of continuing to write.

Now a mum of two, she lives with her children, husband and springer spaniel, Dougie, on the beautiful Devonshire coastline. In the little spare time she gets, she loves nothing more than writing twisty thriller novels for the reader to untangle.

She spends most of her days with her children, in soft plays, on the beach or jumping in puddles, grateful that no one can see inside the corners of her mind as she conjures up the next dark character and plots their fate.

Printed in Great Britain
by Amazon

19457170R00253